Debbie De Louise

Between
A Rock
and
a Hard Place

Publisher's Note:

This is a work of fiction. All names, characters, places, and events are the work of the author's imagination.

Any resemblance to real persons, places, or events is coincidental.

Solstice Publishing - www.solsticepublishing.com

Between a Rock and a Hard Place
A Cobble Cove Mystery
By
Debbie De Louise

Dedication

For my daughter, Holly, who is turning into a beautiful young woman; my mother, Florence, who I am blessed to still have in my life as she approaches her 90th birthday; and my husband, Anthony, who I take for granted but love very much.

Prologue

There has to be payback. Pay out would be even better. Moving to Cobble Cove was the first step. Now we just need to wait. An opportunity will present itself. The holidays are coming, and people have other things on their minds like shopping and parties. They don't know what it's like to suffer. I have to find a way to teach them. Fate will soon make that possible. It has already brought me an assistant.

I feel it on the cold wind that braces this town threatening snow. I hear it in the whispers floating through the streets masked by Christmas carols. I see it in the mirror that reflects my face with its false, charming smile. The time has come. I'm ready.

Chapter One

Alicia McKinney sat behind the reference desk at the Cobble Cove Library trying to keep her eyes open. It had been another long night up with the twins. John had helped, but he was having his own problems right now trying to overcome a writer's block. Their publisher was demanding a draft of their next mystery, and neither of them had the energy to string a complete sentence together let alone write a whole new book. Alicia acknowledged that parenthood was harder than expected, but she wouldn't want it any other way. Her son and daughter arrived a year and a half after the tragedy that perversely brought a school, additional shops, and new people to the small, upstate New York town.

The library director walked through the glass doors. She brushed snow off her imitation fur coat and tossed back her red hair to expel a few flakes. Stomping her knee-length, high-heel boots on the holiday mat by the entrance, she said, "It's snowing out, Alicia. What are you doing here? Where's Jean?"

"Hi, Sheila. Jean called in sick with a stomach virus. I hear it's going around. She may have caught it from her son. A few of the kids have been absent at school." Jean Maxwell, a single mom, was a part-time librarian they'd hired while Alicia was out on maternity leave. Her eight-year-old son, Jeremy, attended the Fairmont Elementary School that had opened a year ago next to the library.

"Sorry to hear that. Is Donald sick, too?" Sheila approached the desk.

"He's helping Laura fill the stacks with the new children's books we just received."

"Bonnie can do that when she gets in, but I can take your place now if you want to leave." Bonnie was a part-time clerk, also new to the library. The full-time clerk, Vera, had that Monday off for working the previous Saturday.

"I'm fine, Sheila. I really am." Alicia stifled a yawn, invalidating her reply.

Sheila walked behind the desk. "I'm your boss, Alicia, and I'm asking you to go. I wish Mac was around more these days. He's so busy selling real estate that he's hardly here."

"I'm glad he's doing well." Alicia also missed her father-in-law. She often checked for him in the reading room, hoping to catch him eating his favorite PB&J sandwich with their library cat, Sneaky, at his feet begging for scraps.

Alicia was tempted to take Sheila's offer. She felt like she could just lie down on the soft mattress of her and John's king-sized feather bed. But, as she was about to head out from behind the desk, Ed the Postmaster appeared with an armload of boxes and a mail sack full of letters.

"Good day, ladies. I have some packages for you."

"Where's Phil?" Sheila asked referring to the town's new mailman.

"He's back at the P. O. I decided to take his route today and let him have a hand at the mail sorting. I think I got the better deal." Ed winked. "Lots of mail coming through the boxes with the holidays approaching especially with all the new folks in town." He placed the three boxes he was holding on the reference desk.

"These two are for you, Alicia." Ed pushed a medium-sized box and a very small one in her direction. "By the way, how are the babies? Still keeping you and John up all night?" He grinned. "That's one thing that doesn't make me regret my bachelorhood."

"They're fine," Alicia said. "At least they're on the same feeding schedules, although now they're both teething." She had recently made the change from breast to bottle feeding and she and John were also starting the twins on baby food.

Ed nodded. "The other package is for you, Sheila. Have a good day, ladies. This sack is heavy, and I have a dozen more stops before I head back and lend Phil a hand with the mountain of mail he's sorting."

Sheila took her package. It was longer than both of Alicia's and looked like it might be a clothing box.

"Thanks, Ed. You have a good day, too. Is it still snowing out?"

"Just flurrying, but that could change. The weather stations aren't talking a storm, though."

Alicia recalled the unseasonable snowstorm that hit Cobble Cove when she first came there in search of her husband's family; but, instead found a terrible truth. She shuddered involuntarily.

"Cold?" Sheila asked. "I can turn up the thermostat if you'd like or ask Walter when he arrives." Walter was the custodian they'd hired to supplement the cleaning woman who came on Thursdays. He usually worked the afternoon and evening shifts now that the library was open longer hours.

"No, I was just thinking about the past."

Sheila smiled. "That can be dangerous. Look, I'm here, and Bonnie should be coming soon. Why don't you go home to John and the kids and catch up on some rest? I'll give you a hand with the packages if you want. I can get Don or Laura to watch the desk while we go. It's very quiet right now. I think most of the patrons are Christmas shopping at Cobble Corner."

"I can manage with the packages, thanks. I haven't even thought about what to get John or anyone else." She picked up the two boxes wondering who had sent them. They weren't heavy.

"You've been a busy mother. I know what that's like, and I only had one kid." She came behind the desk.

"Looks like this one came from your sister-in-law." She read the tag on her own package.

Pamela was generous to the town, always making it a point to send expensive gifts to John, Alicia, and many of the other Cobble Cove residents during the holidays.

"This one must be from Pamela, too," Alicia said reading the gold-foiled address label on her small package. The other looks like it's from Gilly." She recognized the quick scrawl that read, "A. Nostran," and her friend's address on Long Island.

"Why don't we open them?" Sheila suggested. "Then you'll have less to carry. Besides, I'm curious to see what John's sister has given us this year." Her green cat eyes lit up in anticipation.

"You can go first."

Sheila used her long red nails to loosen the tape around the box. She tore open the strip across it and pulled out another box. This one was gift wrapped in red velvet paper.

"Oh, my! This wrapping alone probably cost a small fortune. I hate to rip it."

"I'll get scissors," Alicia offered. She went to the circulation desk and removed a pair of scissors from one of the drawers under the cash register.

"Thanks," Sheila said taking the scissors by the handles and gently cutting the wrapping so that it could be used again. She kept the gold bow intact.

"How lovely," she exclaimed removing a lemon-colored cashmere sweater. "How did Pamela guess that yellow is my favorite color, even though I hardly have any of it in my wardrobe?" She ran her fingers over the fabric. "This is so soft. Feel it, Alicia."

Alicia touched the sweater. It was just as soft as the baby blankets Pamela had sent Carol and Johnny when they were born. Pamela had only visited Cobble Cove once, but she'd been to Sheila's house and seen the yellow-accented rooms and must've surmised Sheila's predilection to the sunny color.

"Now for yours. Open them, Alicia." Sheila placed the sweater back in its box, covered with the still intact gift wrap.

"I'll open Gilly's first. It's the larger one."

"Good things come in small packages, but it's best you save Pamela's for last."

Gilly's box also had a gift-wrapped package within it. Unlike the sweater wrapping, Alicia thought the thin Santa Claus paper was purchased in the grocery store while Gilly rushed to buy food for her three hungry boys. It was especially hard being a divorced mother during the holidays, and Alicia was touched that Gilly would take the time to wrap and send her a gift. She picked up the scissors Sheila had left on the desk. Before cutting open the package, she noted the tag was addressed to Miss Carol Abigail McKinney and Mr. John McKinney, III. The gift was for the twins; two holiday onesies for six-month olds. Alicia knew the red one with reindeers would look pretty on Carol, while the green with snowmen would be perfect for Johnny.

"Adorable," Sheila exclaimed as Alicia held them up.

Alicia placed them back in the box. One final package stood on the desk. It was envelope sized. Pamela's fancy handwriting graced the tag addressed to Mr. and Mrs. John McKinney, c/o Cobble Cove Library, One Bookshelf Lane, Cobble Cove, New York. Why hadn't Pamela sent it to her house?

"Hurry up, Alicia. I can't wait to see what Pamela sent you."

Alicia didn't need the scissors to open the flap of the box. Inside, also wrapped in the same velvety material as Sheila's package, was a small, thin box. It was tied loosely with a golden bow.

Just as Alicia was about to untie it, with Sheila peering over her shoulder, the library doors opened again, and John came through them.

"Caught you ladies fooling around on the job," he grinned, showing his dimple. Although he looked just as handsome as ever, there were bags under his eyes, and the additional gray hairs now shot through his dark waves.

"Where are the babies?" Alicia asked, suddenly remembering he was watching them while she worked because the babysitter had a doctor's appointment.

"Don't worry, sweetheart. Dad is with them. He hasn't had much of a chance to see them lately. When he came by, I figured I'd come get you and maybe we could spend a few minutes together."

Alicia was glad to hear that Mac was with his grandkids, but she worried that his memory issues might be a problem if they left him alone with them too long.

"I was actually just leaving. Sheila thinks I'm too tired to work today and was sending me home."

John smiled, and his dimple deepened. "Observant lady. That's why she's the boss." He walked over to her and glanced at the wrapped package in her hand. "What's that? Looks like something Pamela would send."

"Yes. It's addressed to us. I was about to open it. Gilly sent us the cutest outfits for Carol and Johnny."

"Well, if Pamela's package has my name on it, too, we should open it together."

"You do the rest of the honors then. I've already opened the other box."

"I'll leave you two alone to look at your gift," Sheila said, "I'm going to check on Donald and Laura to see what they're up to in the Children's Room."

As Sheila slipped away, John took the box.

"Before I open it, I think you owe me a kiss, Mrs. McKinney."

She loved the way he said her name after a year and a half of marriage and how his blue eyes twinkled when he looked at her.

"And why is that, Mr. McKinney?"

"I'll show you." He placed Pamela's gift back on the desk. "Come here."

Alicia accompanied him to the library's glass entry doors.

"Look up."

Alicia followed his gaze to where a mistletoe hung from the ceiling. She'd forgotten that Sheila had Walter hang it there the first day of December.

Before she could say anything, John's arms were around her, and his lips were pressed warm and tender against hers. The kiss grew longer and deeper, and she suddenly forgot she was in the library's entrance.

"Go find a room, you two."

Alicia jumped from John's arms to see Donald standing by one of the automated catalogs.

"I think we'll do just that," John said, his voice husky.

"Don't forget your package," Donald said taking Pamela's gift off the reference desk and handing it to Alicia.

"Thanks, Donald." The tall, blonde man in his late thirties, who reminded Alicia slightly of her dead husband Peter, had been hired as a full-time reference librarian at the same time they'd hired Jean the previous year. He'd moved to Cobble Cove with his partner, Roger, one of the teachers at the new elementary school.

"Sheila gave me strict instructions to man the desk while you take the rest of the day off."

"I see. Well, I don't want you to get in trouble." Alicia smiled.

She took John's arm as she clutched the velvety box and Gilly's gift in her other. "Let's make our escape while we can, dear."

They walked outside into the chilly late morning. The snow seemed to have stopped, but she could still feel it in the air.

"So, where would you like to go, ma'am? The day is young, and we are child free."

"Oh, John. We really shouldn't leave Mac alone too long with the babies."

"I know, but maybe Kim will be back from her doctor's appointment."

Alicia raised her eyebrows. "Wishful thinking. You know how long doctors keep you waiting. I hope she's okay. I hear there's a bug going around the school. That's why Jean was out today."

"I think she was only having a checkup."

"Even so."

"Well, what if we go to Casey's for an early lunch or just coffee? I could definitely use that." He brushed his hand over his eyes.

"We're both like the walking dead." She laughed.

"Now I know what my parents went through, but we have twins."

"Lucky us. I mean that." Alicia remembered holding the babies for the first time, exhausted from her long labor but feeling such joy as John stood next to her as they gazed down at their little miracles, the babies neither of them thought they would ever have.

Alicia matched John's long strides as they walked the familiar path down Bookshelf Lane toward Casey's Restaurant. She recalled when she first came to town the diner was the only food establishment in the area. A few other restaurants were now open, but Casey had redesigned the diner and even hired a chef from the Culinary Institute and a waitress, Gloria Langley, who was Walter, the library custodian's, wife. The bulb in the name banner that was once unlit now shined brightly against the gray December sky.

When they walked in, Casey hailed them. "Hey, there. It's the McKinneys. Long time, no see." He was standing behind the bar, his favorite sports show playing on the widescreen TV above it. "How is parenting going?"

John laughed. "It's a tough job, but someone's got to do it."

"You guys look a bit rough around the edges. I have some drinks that might help. Have a seat, and Gloria will be with you. She's in the back talking to Harold."

Alicia glanced around the diner, so different from how it was when she'd first visited it two years ago while she was staying at the inn for what she thought would only be a weekend. The bar was decked with strands of red, green and silver tinsel. Glittering balls in the same colors hung over the dining area tables. An artificial tree with ornaments stood by the entrance. The back wall had been torn down and replaced with a party room that was already booked for every weekend in December. Although it wasn't yet lunchtime, a few diners sat at tables with white cloths and gold and silver candle holders that would be lit around dusk.

"We're hanging in there," Alicia told Casey. "How's business here? You've done a great job with your holiday decorations."

"Things are going great. Since Harold came, people are flocking here for dinner. The lunch crowd has grown, too. I can't take all the credit for the decorations. Edith and Rose put them up."

The ladies who were known as "the cousins" to all the town's residents and also served on the church and Christmas committees enjoyed making things festive in Cobble Cove. This year they were going all out, as it was the first year the annual town Christmas Fair was being reinstated. Last year's holiday season was too busy with all the construction of the new homes and businesses, as well as the public school. This year it was finally time to bring back the annual holiday tradition, and the excitement was growing.

Gloria came from the back room, pencil and pad in hand, her waitress' white apron stretched over her tall, lean body. At 5'10, she was only an inch shorter than John and two inches shorter than her 6-foot husband.

"John, Alicia. Come sit down, and I'll take your orders when you're ready. We still have some breakfast items if you're interested." She handed them both a menu from her apron pocket. Casey no longer kept them on the table, and he'd replaced the blackboard at the bar with a marquee of flashing specials. He was striving to add class to the diner to keep up with the competition of some of the new restaurants, especially the Italian place that opened in Cobble Corner six months ago, right around the time the twins were born. As Alicia sat and took the menu, she placed the packages next to her on the table.

Gloria eyed the boxes, zooming in on the small velvety wrapped one. "Looks like you've gotten some early Christmas presents."

"Gilly sent some cute onesies for the babies, but the other is from Pamela for me and John."

Gloria's gray eyebrows rose. "Ah, no wonder it's wrapped in velvet. Why haven't you opened it?"

"She was waiting for me," John said reaching across and taking the box. "We figured it would be nice to open it together."

"I have to give both of you credit, you have a lot of patience. I wouldn't be able to control my curiosity."

John had taken a knife from the table and was cutting through the velvet paper as he slipped off the gold ribbon. "Might as well do it now."

He paused as he lifted the lid to the box underneath the paper. "Well, I'll be. Pamela's really outdone herself this time."

Alicia tried to see what John held, and Gloria moved closer to get a better view herself. Lying in John's hands were two tickets, a computer printout, some gift cards, and a folded letter.

"These are tickets to the Radio City Music Hall holiday show at Rockefeller center in New York City," John said. "Also what looks like hotel reservations in, get this, a honeymoon suite."

A grin spread across his face as he passed the letter to his wife. "This is too much. Here, read it."

Alicia recognized Pamela's swirling handwriting. She read it aloud:

Dear Brother and Sister-in-law, I would like to spend the holidays in Cobble Cove this year visiting my niece and nephew. Caroline and Cynthia are both away in Europe, and I'm a bit bored staying on Long Island by myself. A thought occurred to me that you two have not had a decent honeymoon. The Mohonk Mountain House is lovely, but there's nothing like taking a horse drawn carriage ride through Central Park, attending a theater show, browsing through museums, ice skating at Rockefeller Center, and enjoying the sights and sounds of the city in December.

I have reserved a honeymoon suite for you at one of my favorite places to stay, The Park Lane Hotel, for a week starting this Saturday. It's my Christmas gift to both of you. While you are away, it will be my pleasure to acquaint your darling babies with their aunt.

I will call you before the end of the week to confirm our plans. Hugs and kisses to all, Pamela.

"Wow!" Gloria exclaimed. "How awesome is that?"

"It's great," Alicia said taking the box back as John closed it up with the contents inside. "But we can't possibly accept."

"What?" John looked puzzled. "Why not? We certainly can use a vacation, Ali, and maybe the change of scene will help loosen up my writer's block."

"I know it sounds wonderful, but the babies are so young."

John laughed. "Ali, my sister raised two girls. She certainly knows how to handle babies."

"John's right," Gloria said. "There's nothing to worry about. I'd jump at the opportunity if I were you."

"Okay, we'll discuss it." Alicia picked up her menu. "For now, can you just please get me two eggs over easy with whole wheat toast and a coffee?"

Gloria jotted Alicia's order on her pad. "What would you like, John?"

"To go to New York," he said." I haven't been back in years. I'd love to drop in on Columbia and see the old campus."

He regarded Alicia who sat with the menu covering her face. "I'll have the same as Ali," he told Gloria as he handed her back his menu.

After the waitress left their table, John pulled the menu down, so he could see Alicia's eyes. They were red rimmed and tearful.

"Oh, Ali. Please don't do this. We both need a rest. You know we do. You don't feel at ease leaving the kids long with my father, but he's the only blood relative in town. Pamela will spoil them rotten with gold-lined diapers and silver teething rings."

That at least brought a smile to her face.

"I know you're right, John, but I can't imagine leaving them for a whole week. You know how fanatic I've been about listening for the baby monitor, and I even have trouble going to work at the library unless I know you're home writing or trying to write. They're still so tiny, so helpless."

John reached over and took her hand.

"Honey, we need time to ourselves. It will be good for all of us. Pamela seems to want to make up for lost time with me and Dad and now our children. You can write instructions for her if it makes you happy, and she can contact either of us on our cell phones. The city is not that far away, but far enough away."

He watched the changing expressions on her face as it wavered close to acceptance and then he made his final plea. "If you agree, I promise we'll make a stop at the New York Public Library." He grinned.

Alicia sniffled, a sob mixed with a laugh. "Sometimes I think I'm still suffering from postpartum depression. I guess it's the lack of sleep."

"Just think of the luxurious honeymoon bed waiting for us at Park Lane."

Alicia put down her menu.

"Mr. McKinney, I do believe you should've continued those law courses. You've missed your calling."

"Nope." John gripped her hand tighter. Alicia could feel his warmth penetrating its coldness.

"My calling, Ali, is to be your husband and the father of your babies."

They jumped when Gloria cleared her throat to announce her presence, so absorbed in one another that they hadn't heard her arrive with their food plates.

Alicia moved the gift boxes as Gloria served them.

"So, have you guys decided if you're going?"

"Yes," Alicia said. "New York City, here we come."

Chapter Two

When they'd finished their eggs and coffee and said goodbye to Gloria and Casey, John and Alicia walked back out into the chilly air. John held the gift boxes.

"Do you want to go straight home?"

"I think that's best, John. Your dad's been with the babies over an hour."

John smiled. "You are such an overprotective mom. Dad is fine with them, but I guess we should relieve him. It's too bad Dora is so busy now at the inn. Even with Edith and Rose working there, she barely has time to watch the twins as we'd originally planned. The place is booked solid for the next couple of months. It's amazing how much business a little news can drum up, especially when it involves murder."

They walked down the hill toward their house on "Stone Throw Road," so named according to John because it was a stone's throw from everything in town.

"It's been two years, John. I think the headlines have worn off already. Now people come because Cobble Cove has so much more to offer, and the Christmas Fair is also a big draw."

"Right. I have to make sure to assign the preview to Andy and Kim."

"Do you miss the paper?"

"I'm still involved, but with the twins and our mystery series, I'm thankful I can delegate some work to journalism majors breaking into the field. It's great that they can earn credit from the state university for interning at the *Courier*."

***

As they walked up the path to their house, Alicia couldn't help but feel the flood of joy she always did returning home. She treasured this new place she shared with John that blocked out the memories of her old life. They'd made many changes to Mac's house when he'd moved into his cottage. Although the house was now larger to accommodate the nursery and two additional rooms the twins would move into when they were older, it was still cozy.

Through the thin curtains, Alicia could see Mac sitting in one of the rockers in the living room with a baby on his knee. Someone else was there next to him cradling the other twin, but she couldn't quite make out who it was from where she stood.

"John, who's that with Mac?"

"Looks like Betty." Betty was the homebound who came out of her self-imposed isolation to attend Alicia's baby shower last spring and had volunteered for the new library board. She'd won the September election for Board president by a landslide.

"Should we just go in or knock to let them know we're here?"

John answered Alicia's question by tapping on the door with the bronze door knocker engraved "McKinney" that Pamela had given them as a housewarming present when they'd officially moved in. A holiday wreath with berries and pine cones hung around it.

Alicia watched as Mac handed Johnny in his blue onesie to Betty, rose with the help of his cane, and ambled to the door to open it.

"Figured it was you, son. Hi, Alicia."

"Thanks for taking the babies," John said. "Ali and I managed to have a late breakfast together at Casey's."

"Glad I could help. I hope you don't mind that I invited Betty over to keep me company."

"Of course not," Alicia said.

John hung his coat on the rack by the door and helped Alicia off with hers. He put the gifts down on the table by the entrance.

"What do you have there?" Mac inquired. "More gifts for the babies?"

"Gilly sent Carol and Johnny holiday onesies," Alicia replied stepping into the living room behind John. "The other gift is for us."

She avoided revealing what it was for fear Mac might be offended that Pamela would be babysitting while they were away, but she knew he'd find out sooner or later. She gave John a warning look not to say anything. By now, he could read her signals and responded by changing the subject.

"Have the twins been good?"

"Slept most of the time. I've gotta say that Little Mac is the splitting image of you as a baby, John." Mac grinned. Little Mac was the nickname he liked to call Johnny.

"Hi, there," Betty said from the rocker next to the fireplace, already lit on this cold December day.

Tiny stockings embroidered with the babies' names hung from the mantel ready for Santa and the twins' first Christmas. Alicia had ordered them custom made from the town's new baby store. The green one, Johnny's, had a snowman on it. Carol's red stocking featured an angel.

"Nice to see you, Betty," Alicia said taking the shut-eyed baby girl from her. She looked down at her daughter's pink cheeks and couldn't help but be amazed at her beauty. She had a fuzz of light hair on her head, slightly more than she'd had at birth. The sweet scent of her, a mix of baby powder and infant magic, overwhelmed Alicia. She hugged

Carol to her chest, suddenly worried she would start suckling, and felt her breasts engorge with milk at just the nearness of the child.

"Has she had her bottle yet?"

"Yes, just a little while ago," Betty said standing up with Johnny in her arms." Both of them finished their formula and had some baby food."

"Here, let me take my son," John said holding out his arms. Alicia watched as Betty gently handed Johnny over to his father and took the cane that was propped behind the rocker, so she could walk over to Mac.

"I think we should put them in their cribs," John said. "They're out like rocks. What did you two do to them? I'd like the secret at two in the morning."

Mac laughed. "Betty sang them a lullaby. She has a great voice. Did you know she was in the church choir as a young girl?"

"She should sing at the Cobble Cove Church," Alicia suggested.

"I'm too shy for that, but I'll come by anytime you need and serenade the twins."

"Is that a promise?" John asked." Even at 2 a. m.?"

Betty smiled, and her new dental work that replaced all her once rotten teeth took years off her 80-year old face. "I don't sleep too well, so that shouldn't be a problem."

"Well, we will keep that in mind," Alicia said, "And thank both of you for watching them today, but I agree with John that they need to go lay in their cribs now."

"Then we'll be off," Mac said. "I'm taking Betty to a movie later. It's my reward for her changing diapers." His grin widened.

"You don't do litter boxes anymore either, Dad. They have Walter do that job at the library now. I never knew that was part of a custodian's duties, but I think Sheila added it to have someone to clean up after Sneaky."

Alicia recalled first meeting the Siamese library cat. He used to spend his time in the cat bed near the local history section. He now resided upstairs in his private abode accessible by cat door through the staff lounge. Mac had moved the cat's bed there, along with the scratching post he'd built to stop Sneaky from tearing apart boxes. Alicia missed seeing the cat in the main library, but he often came to the Children's Room when Laura did story times. The kids loved having him visit there, and Laura, who had several of her own cats at home, always gave him some treats or a bit of catnip.

"Oh, before I leave, John, I forgot to tell you the news," Mac said." You might want to scoop it in the *Courier* in January."

John took his eyes away from his son to look at his father. "Don't tell me. Marge Simper fell again," he joked. Although the content of the paper that now came out weekly instead of monthly had improved, there still wasn't a great deal of newsworthy headlines.

"Nope, but we have an applicant for sheriff if we open that new sheriff's office the town has been meeting about."

Alicia was curious. "If I follow you, Mac, I guess it's someone we know."

"Indeed." Mac's grin widened and his dimple with it. "It's no other than Ron Ramsay."

"Oh, my God," Alicia exclaimed. "I thought he retired." Ron Ramsay was one of the detectives who'd handled the arson investigation when Alicia's Long Island house was destroyed by fire. He was an overweight, unhygienic, rude man who she and John were basing their Groucho Mark's fictional detective series on.

"Well, he's back, Alicia," Mac explained. "He's made Cobble Cove his retirement home. He and I had a long talk when I sold him the house on Crooked Pebble Path. He's turned over a new leaf. He said he took my advice about meditating, and his blood pressure and weight are down.

He said he'd always dreamed of being a small town cop. We don't have much crime here, but it would be nice to have someone with his experience."

"I don't know," John said. "It's very difficult for people to change. Faraday had a lot of faith in Ramsay's work despite apologizing at times for his partner's behavior. To me, he was pretty incompetent."

Betty spoke then. "I would give him a chance, John. People do change. I'm an example of that. You don't know what may have caused all that anger inside him. I think folks would feel safer having a sheriff in town."

John nodded. "True, Betty. The next town hall meeting is Friday. I'll be sure to recommend him when I attend. I'd like to see him before then, though."

"I can arrange that," Mac said. "Maybe the three of us can have lunch at Casey's on Wednesday."

"Kim doesn't have classes until late that day, so she should be available to babysit," Alicia added.

"Great," Mac said. "Betty and I will be on our way then. If you need us any time during the week to watch Little Mac or Carol, let us know."

Hearing the name his grandfather preferred to call him, Johnny woke up and began to cry. His sister then opened her brown eyes and joined him in the chorus.

"Thanks, Dad," John said. "Just when we were hoping they'd continue sleeping."

"Sorry, John." Mac turned to Betty. "I guess that's our cue to go."

John and Alicia watched as the two seniors left the house ambling companionably on their canes.

"Maybe we can still get them back to sleep," Alicia said." Let's take them to their cribs."

Upstairs in the nursery, Alicia lay Carol in her crib while John placed Johnny in the one next to it. The babies quieted down as they heard the tinkle of their mobiles and snuggled into the thick, soft white sheets Pamela had bought them and the warm baby blankets Edith had crocheted. Carol's mobile featured ballerina's in pink tutus that whirled around when the string was pulled. Johnny's featured blue rockets and space ships. The twins also had a musical toy that hung inside their cribs that changed scenes and played lullabies to help put them to sleep.

The walls were patterned in pink and blue paper with cherubic angels, clouds, and harps. Two bookshelves overflowed with picture books, some purchased and some checked out from the library's Children's Department.

Alicia had decorated the room herself, buying many of the items from Cobble Corner's baby store. John had hung the wallpaper. The rocker by the window was the one Mac built and gifted to Alicia before she went into early labor and delivered the twins a few weeks before their due date. Carol had weighed six pounds and Johnny six and a half. They hadn't been considered premature because most twins naturally arrive a bit early.

"Looks like they're settling down," John said.

Alicia couldn't keep her gaze from her beautiful babies. Watching them sleep always tugged at her heart.

"Hey, momma, want to steal a few minutes next door?" John asked with a light in his eyes. Their bedroom was next to the nursery, which made it convenient for early morning feedings, but it also created some tension when Alicia was constantly on guard listening for the beeping of the baby monitor.

"I'm sorry, John, I'm really tired. I think Sheila was right that I needed to take some time off today."

John didn't look surprised or upset. "I was just suggesting we lay down together. I'm beat myself. I really think this trip will do both of us good."

"You're probably right, although I'm still hesitant."

"It'll be fine, honey, but I understand your worry. I don't like leaving them either, but they'll be in good hands, and it'll be great for Pamela to spend time with her nephew and niece." John came over and put his arms around Alicia. Planting a quick kiss on her lips, he said, "Come with me."

***

John and Alicia's bedroom had been modelled after the creamy whites of Pamela's. It was smaller, and there wasn't a divan, but Alicia had tried to match the same color scheme and tone. It was an oasis of softness and comfort. Even the lighting was subdued.

They didn't bother to change completely, although John took off his shirt and tossed it over the bed post. Alicia slipped out of her shoes. Then they got into their respective sides of the bed. Alicia was closest to the nightstand that contained the monitoring device for the babies. She realized that, at six months, the twins were at less of a risk for SIDS, but she couldn't bear taking any chances so was vigilant about responding to the often false alarms.

Alicia melted onto the cushiony mattress, wrapping herself in the luxuriously soft blankets and sheets, another gift from Pamela who promptly ordered identical bedding for Alicia once she heard how she planned to replicate her bedroom in Brookville.

John sighed and put his arm around Alicia. "I love this bed, but I love you more in it with me. It seems all we do lately is sleep on it."

Alicia knew that their love life had suffered with the intensity of tending to twins, but there were still the small signs, the tender things that bonded them – the quick kisses in the morning, the holding hands across the kitchen table, and the teasing pats on the backside that John gave with a grin. They were still newlyweds after a year and a half, and the gift of a honeymoon suite for a week in New York City would give them time to reignite the spark that still lit between them.

"Are you feeling any less tired, Mrs. McKinney?"

"Actually, I've gotten a bit of energy back, yes. What about you, Mr. McKinney?"

John's reply was muffled as he rolled onto her. She yelped in mock dismay.

Just when things were starting to get romantic, a sound broke them apart. At first, Alicia thought it was the baby monitor, but then realized it was the phone.

"Don't answer it," John said. "It's probably a sales call."

Alicia paused. "It might wake the babies." She rolled over to pick it up. The phone was next to the monitor.

"Hello."

"Alicia, Mary Beth here. Is John home? Can I speak with him, please?"

John didn't look pleased as she handed him the phone and said, "It's Mary Beth. She wants to talk with you."

Mary Beth Simmons was John and Alicia's editor with Prime Crime Press, the publisher of their Groucho Marks series. She was a tall, thin, harried Type A personality who always wanted everything yesterday.

"Hey, Mary Beth," John said. "How are you?" Alicia could imagine the editor apologizing for disturbing them, but she was usually so focused on her own needs that maybe she wouldn't even notice that she'd called at an inopportune time.

Alicia watched John listen to Mary Beth's reply. She could hear her speaking, not the words, but the pace. It was fast with a maximum of words. As much as she advised them to be concise in their writing, Mary Beth was the opposite in her speech, using five words for every one needed.

John rolled his eyes as he listened to the chatter. When there was finally a break, he said, "Yes. I see."

The chatter began again. John held the phone away from him, and Alicia suppressed a laugh.

After a few minutes when Mary Beth probably figured out he wasn't listening, there was a pause and John quickly said, "Thank you, Mary Beth. We will. Have a good day."

He passed the phone back to Alicia, so she could hang it up.

"She's pushing for the first chapter again, isn't she?"

"Yep, but she'll just have to wait. I can't write on demand."

"John, I can do it. We can't stall forever."

"Ali, I won't ask you to do that. It's bad enough you practically wrote the last three chapters of the last book. This is my problem, and I have to find a way of dealing with it."

He ran his fingers through his hair. "I really believe the trip will help me. It will help you, too. We'll be refreshed. I'll make sure we don't have a phone in our room, and we'll silence our cells." He grinned.

"John, we'll need to be in touch in case something happens to the babies."

"Alicia, please." He pushed himself off the bed. "The mood is gone. I might as well do something productive. Maybe I'll head over to the newspaper and check on Andy or visit Casey and get drunk at his bar." He smiled. Alicia knew John wasn't a drinker.

"I wish I could help you, honey," she said. "And I'm sorry we didn't get to, you know."

"I'm sorry, too, but we'll have a week to make up for it." He tilted her chin up with his hand and looked into her eyes. "I love you, Ali. Becoming a dad was a lot more stressful than I'd anticipated, but those babies are the world to me, as are you." He kissed her lightly on the lips. "Would you like me to call dad back, and we can go out together?"

"No, I'm sure Kim should be back from the doctor soon, John, and I'd rather spend a little time with the twins myself."

"Sure thing, momma, but call me if you need anything. When Kim gets here, you might want to go out – get your hair done by Wilma or do some Christmas shopping. Irene has lots of nice things. You could even just walk around the Green. It's not too cold out today, and Edith and Rose have done a great job decorating Cobble Corner for the holidays."

"I might just do that, John. Thanks!"

***

After John left, Alicia got out of bed. She was disappointed he hadn't stayed, but she realized he'd been upset by Mary Beth's call. John was the type of man who needed to prove his worth. They had some savings including Pamela's generous wedding gift, but they had two babies now and John still didn't have a full-time job. While their first book, published in September, had earned some royalties, they had to meet deadlines to keep the series going and their readers satisfied.

Walking back into the nursery, she saw the babies stirring in their cribs. They were quiet, but their eyes were open. Johnny had the same shade as his father and, although most babies were born with blue eyes, she had a feeling his would remain. Carol, on the other hand, seemed to have inherited her brown eyes. Both babies were fair. Johnny also had straight dark hair like John, while Carol's ash blonde color was similar to her Aunt Pamela's and older cousins Caroline and Cynthia.

Alicia picked both babies up, one at a time, and marveled at how big they were growing. They would be walking soon and saying their first words. And one day, not so far in the future, they'd be attending their first day of classes at the new Fairmont Elementary School along with Jean's son Jeremy who would likely be in his last year then. Time would pass quickly, but she wanted to hold on to this moment. Staring into their pink, chubby faces. Listening to their baby giggles as she played peek-a-boo with them. Feeling their warm soft baby bodies up against her chest.

***

After Alicia had spent time with her children and checked to make sure their diapers were dry, she lay them both back down in their cribs with their teething rings, Johnny next to his teddy bear and Carol with her tiny hand around her doll. She was about to switch off the nursery light and head downstairs when she heard the door open. She thought John might be back, but then she heard high heels walking toward the stairs, and Kim called up to her.

"Alicia, are you home? I just got back from the doctor."

"I'm here. Come on up, Kim. I was just putting the babies to sleep."

The babysitter appeared at the nursery door. She was dressed in tight-fitting jeans, a pale fuzzy blue sweater that accented her light blue eyes. Her brown hair was tied back in a ponytail.

"Sorry that took so long," she said not even out of breath having run up the stairs. Alicia envied the girl's twenty-year old body.

"Not to worry. I know how long doctors take. Sheila sent me home because she thinks I need more rest, but I feel fine. John was around earlier, but he's gone to do some chores. Since you're here, maybe I'll take him up on his suggestion to go Christmas shopping or do something in town."

Kim smiled. "Of course. You deserve to have time to yourself. I can watch the twins until four and then I have to get ready for my evening class."

"I should be back way before then. How are your classes going this semester?"

Kim walked over to the cribs and looked down at the babies who were starting to fall asleep. In a low voice, she replied. "They're good. Lots of work, but I enjoy it."

"How much longer do you have before you earn your degree?"

Kim was by Carol's crib, and she smiled as the baby opened her eyes and regarded her with a gurgle. She reached down and tickled her.

"So sweet. Your babies are adorable, Alicia. One day, I hope to have cuties like these. But I want to start my career first. If I can afford the classes next year, I'll be able to finish the following spring."

Alicia knew college costs were high. "Are you taking out any loans?" When Alicia studied at Long Island University, she'd earned some scholarships but she'd also borrowed money in her last year at library school. Luckily, she was able to pay off her loan shortly after she married her first husband.

"I'm not sure that's a wise thing to do," Kim said walking over to Johnny and watching as he followed his sister in waking up.

"I hate to have to pay back all that money with interest. I know I won't earn much in the field I'm entering, especially in the beginning, and I can't expect my parents to help much since I have three sisters and a brother at home."

Alicia knew that both Kim and John's other assistant, Andy, were from lower middle-class families. Kim came from a large family compared to today's households and, although Andy only had a younger brother, his dad had died in a car accident a few years ago. His mother was struggling to make ends meet. She felt for the young people who were just starting out and was glad that John was paying them for their work on the paper and that she could offer Kim additional money for babysitting.

Remembering her upcoming trip, Alicia worried about how she'd break the news to Kim that she wouldn't be needed the next week. She might ask Pamela to let the girl watch the babies on occasion. Mac would be around also, but she would rather pay the college student and not have to be concerned with Mac leaving the oven on or the toaster plugged. Although his dementia hadn't progressed much in the last year, she couldn't take any chances. It was true that even Pamela or Kim could forget something, and chances were Betty would accompany Mac when he babysat. It seemed the two unlikely seniors were starting to hit it off.

Alicia turned back to Kim, keeping quiet about her weekend plans for the time being. "I know it's hard, Kim. College was costly when I attended, but tuition has skyrocketed since then."

"That's true, Alicia, but I'd rather not talk about it anymore. It just gets me depressed."

"I understand. I'll be going then. I shouldn't be gone long. You have my cell number and John's if there are any problems."

"Stop worrying. Everything will be fine. Enjoy your shopping trip. I was at the gift shop the other day, and Irene has some awesome stuff out for the holidays. I had to stop myself from buying it all up."

Alicia hoped to purchase a small gift for both Kim and Andy as a thank you for their help on the paper and with the babies.

"Is there anything special you were looking for?" she asked trying not to give away the reason for her question.

"Not particularly, although I saw some really cool silver and gold sun and moon earrings in the shop. They could be worn in both my piercings." Kim had a second ear piercing. Although extra piercings weren't for Alicia, she considered ear ones more attractive and definitely less painful than the tongue and navel piercings some young adults sported these days. She made a mental note to look for those earrings as a possible Christmas present for Kim.

"I still haven't gotten anything for John. He's not easy to buy for."

"Maybe he'd like one of those insulated soup mugs. He can use them for coffee and hot chocolate, too."

Alicia hadn't thought of that. "That might make a nice gift. He doesn't have one, but I'd like to get him something more personal. I'm sure I'll find something. See you later, Kim, and thanks for minding my kids."

Kim smiled showing teeth that probably should've been braced several years ago. Her overbite was noticeable but didn't detract from her looks. She sat rocking Johnny, shaking his blue rattle that she'd taken from the shelf where Alicia kept the baby pictures, other keepsakes, and small toys. Alicia knew she would give Carol a turn on her lap afterwards or maybe coddle them both if she could handle the armful. As nervous a mother as she was, she felt confident leaving the babies with Kim who had watched them since they were born.

"Goodbye, sweeties," Alicia said placing a tender kiss on Johnny's cheek and leaning down in Carol's crib and doing the same. "Bye, Kim."

Kim waved with her empty hand and then went back to cooing at Johnny as Alicia left the room.

***

Alicia had to admit as much as she loved the twins, it was great to have some time to herself. Out in the cool, fresh air, she breathed deeply as she walked the familiar path to Cobble Corner. The shops had been renamed during the town's renovation. Previously the area that housed the stores had been known as Cobble Cove Square. She remembered John taking her this way when he gave her a tour two years ago. When she'd asked why he didn't use his pickup truck so often, he said it was because all places in Cobble Cove were just "a stone's throw away." While that was not literally true, most things were within walking distance. She still occasionally used her car. It now sported two baby seats to match the ones John had added to his truck. But while the weather permitted, she preferred to walk. When the twins were with her, Alicia brought them along in their sunny yellow stroller that Dora had given her. The exercise did her good, and she was already back to her pre-pregnancy weight.

As she headed downhill toward the square, she felt somewhat sad seeing all the bare trees and the non-flowing fountain. In other seasons, beautiful flowers bordered the paths and birds, squirrels, and butterflies weaved through the bushes.

When she approached the gazebo in the center, she saw that it was adorned with fresh holiday garland. Baskets of poinsettias were strung around it, and a gold chair with red cushions stood in front. Strings of lights circled all the trees, and the largest evergreen boasted a golden star atop its highest branch.

She would love to see this lit up at night with John, and the twins would be awed by it. Surely, Edith and Rose had played a part in the decorations, and Sheila had likely assisted. It wasn't Rockefeller Plaza, but Cobble Corner had a charming aura all its own, and she was glad that she and John would be back by the week of the Christmas Fair. This would be her first one, and she pictured John, dressed as Santa, sitting on the large chair in front of the Gazebo with the children taking turns on his lap. She knew he'd missed playing that important role in the festivities the last two years, and was looking forward to volunteering this year with all the new kids in town and those from nearby areas who visited at Christmastime for this special event.

The shop windows, too, were decorated. The bakery featured a display of fruitcakes and holiday pies. Duncan the grocer had placed holiday platters of cold cuts, fruit and vegetable trays, and a fully stuffed turkey in his window. The other shops featured their wares festooned with Christmas bells, balls, and wreaths.

Behind the glass of the gift shop window, Alicia spied a variety of items for men, women, and children with holiday wrapped boxes next to them and tags without prices that read, "For Mom," "For Dad," "For a Friend," "For a neighbor," etc. Irene had done a great job promoting her products for the holidays. Alicia walked to the wreathed door and turned the knob to the sound of a bell jingling. Soft holiday music played through the store as she entered. Irene stood behind the counter wrapping a small box for a customer. Alicia recognized the tall, gray-haired woman as the school nurse who'd started working at Fairmont Elementary in the fall. Both ladies smiled when they saw Alicia enter.

"Hi, Alicia. Good to see you. How are the babies? Have they given you some time off to shop?" Irene asked.

Alicia smiled. "Kim is with them, so I thought I'd do some shopping. It's been a while."

"Glad you could make it. Please browse while I finish this for Leslie. She dropped in on a break and has to get back to her office soon."

"Of course," Alicia replied. "Take your time. I'm just browsing."

Alicia walked around the shop that was crammed with all types of merchandise. The jewelry was set up toward the front on a counter with a mirror. Alicia caught her reflection in the glass – her brown eyes, John often referred to their color as chocolate, also sported large bags under them similar to her husband's. She hardly had any time to apply makeup these days and only used foundation and lipstick sparingly. Her hair needed a more thorough brushing. Its chestnut waves were scraggly. It could also use another cut by Wilma. Maybe she could fit a hairdressing appointment in today as John suggested. She looked like a harried housewife, and she guessed that's what she was. She was reminded of Gilly and her three sons and how her friend always seemed to be rushing. She remembered that she had to call her to thank her for the babies' cute Christmas outfits.

The items on the jewelry display glinted in the light from the nearby window. Irene had placed them well. Earrings hung on a clear earring rack while necklaces were looped around a mannequin's chest. The mannequin was only a black plastic display head wearing a variety of hats also for sale. Next to the head were two separate black-fingered hands holding rings of all types. Scarves were draped across the gift shop's counter along with pins and broaches nestled in black jewelry cases. Alicia searched among the items trying to find the earrings Kim mentioned. She could hear Irene and Leslie chatting from the checkout area.

"I think your daughter will love that purse. You might want to check the baby store across the way for something for your granddaughter, too."

"Thanks, Irene. I don't have time right now, but maybe another day. I have to get back in case one of the kids falls in gym or throws up on his desk."

Irene chuckled." Let's hope they all stay well today."

"Been lucky so far, but that stomach virus is still going around, and flu season is also underway. I wish a doctor other than Dr. Clark would open an office here because people keep calling me at home asking for advice."

Hearing Leslie mention the town vet, Alicia recalled that Sneaky was due for his annual checkup. Laura was supposed to be taking him on Wednesday. She considered reminding her when she went back to work tomorrow.

"That can be tough," Irene commiserated with the nurse. "At least we're finally getting a sheriff."

"Is that so?" Leslie sounded surprised.

"I hear it's that Long Island detective who retired after
. . ." Irene paused probably realizing that Alicia was within
hearing range. She lowered her voice. "I don't know if
you're aware of what happened here two years ago, but he
was involved in a local case. Seems he retired and decided
to move to Cobble Cove. Not that we have much crime, but
you never know. I think people will feel safer with a sheriff
in town."

Alicia was having trouble locating the earrings Kim
mentioned. She walked back to the checkout counter to ask
Irene for help.

As Leslie gathered up her package and started to leave,
she nodded to Alicia. "Have a good day, Alicia. If the twins
are still having teething problems, you might try one of
those gel rings you freeze. They get hard and the twins can
bite down on them. The cold also soothes their gums."

"Thanks, Leslie. They're doing much better now."
Alicia had asked the school nurse a few questions about the
babies when she'd visited the library a few weeks ago to
check out some books. Leslie, a retired pediatrician who
moved to Cobble Cove with her husband, Bill, was partial
to murder mysteries, and she'd read John and Alicia's book
that was on the local author table Sheila recently set up.

As Leslie left, Irene asked, "Is there something I can
help you find, Alicia? I saw you looking through the
jewelry. Those are our custom pieces. The higher end ones
are here." She indicated the glass case to the side of the
checkout desk.

Alicia saw the moon and star earrings hanging on the
top level.

"My babysitter was here the other day, and she was
interested in those moon and star earrings."

Irene smiled. "She has good taste. I'll show them to
you."

Taking a small, gold key from inside her drawer, Irene opened the cabinet and removed the earrings. She slid them toward Alicia.

Up close, the gold moon glittered along with the silver stars. They hung from French wires and would show up even if Kim wore her hair loose.

"How much?"

"They usually sell for $150. They're genuine sterling. The sun isn't real gold, but it's a nice set. I can lower the price to $95 for you, but no lower than that. It would make a great gift."

Alicia hesitated. Should she spend that much? Even though they were doing well, John had stopped accepting the monetary gifts Pamela sent to them on random occasions. He'd told her they could handle things on their own at this point, but neither of them was so sure about that. They had agreed to cut expenses now that the babies had arrived.

She debated about buying the earrings. They already paid Kim more than most babysitters earned per hour. But she knew the girl would not be able to afford the earrings on her own, and it was Christmas.

Alicia took out her wallet and withdrew her credit card. She'd recently had it changed with her new last name, but she and John shared a credit card that they put family charges on. This was the one she paid for herself.

"Thank you. I'll gift wrap it for free." Irene slipped the earrings off the display and placed them in a small, velvet-lined box. Then she showed a few different wrapping papers to Alicia and asked her to choose. Alicia settled on the plain gold paper, and Irene added a small red bow to it.

"She'll love this. You have one lucky babysitter." As she handed Alicia the package, the gold cross she often wore swayed across her turtleneck sweater. While most Cobble Cove residents attended the non-denominational local church, Irene and her daughter travelled to the Catholic Church in Carlsville each Sunday.

"Thanks, Irene." Alicia took the gift, still feeling a bit doubtful. "I have to go. I don't want to leave Kim with the babies too long." Actually, Alicia was afraid she'd spend more money if she continued to look around.

"Have a good day, hon, and please give the twins a kiss for me." Irene smiled.

Alicia put the small gift in her purse and exited the shop. As she did so, she noticed a few cigarette butts by the door. She didn't believe they'd been there earlier. Then a shadow crossed her path. She blinked, and it was gone. It might've just been the glare of the sun after being inside the shop, but she looked in the direction from where she thought it came by an empty building that had yet to be rented. A dark-haired man in a long trench coat stood there smoking. She didn't recognize him, but she had yet to meet many of the new town residents. Passing him by with a smile that wasn't returned, she avoided the baby store across the way, even though she'd anticipated buying her children an early Christmas present. She also abandoned her plans for having her hair done. Instead, she turned towards John's newspaper office and thought she might drop in to see him before going home.

As she approached the brick building, she ran into Andy who was leaving. The tall young man with the thin moustache smiled at her. "Hey, Mrs. McKinney. How are you?"

No matter that she'd asked him to call her by her first name, he still used her married one. "Hi, Andy. I'm fine. I was just dropping in to see John. Is he around?"

"No. He was here earlier. I think he went to Casey's or maybe to see his dad. We're just about putting this week's issue to bed. It's a little late, but he wanted to be sure we covered all the details about the Christmas Fair, and we just got them from Edith."

"I see." Alicia had a sudden idea. It was impulsive, and maybe she should've considered it longer, but she blurted out, "Andy, have you gotten a present for Kim yet?" Andy and Kim were not only co-workers at the paper but also dating steadily.

"No. I don't know what to get her, and I'm a little short on cash lately. I'd like to buy her something nice, but Mom put me on a strict budget for the holidays. She told me she doesn't even want anything from me this year."

Alicia opened her purse. "I just bought this at the gift shop. Kim hinted that she really liked it, but couldn't afford it. Why don't you give it to her? It's a nice gift from a boyfriend, and I can get her something smaller."

"Mrs. McKinney, I really can't do that." Although his words denied it, Alicia could tell he was interested in the offer.

"Please take it. You guys have been so helpful to me and John. Consider it a gift to both of you."

Andy accepted the wrapped box and placed it in his pants pocket. "You really are too kind. Thank you so much. This will blow the socks off Kim."

Alicia laughed. "I've never seen her wear socks. She's mostly in sandals or boots."

Andy looked puzzled a moment, and then he caught the joke. "Good one, Mrs. McKinney." His smile spread to his freckled cheeks. "Thanks again. I have to get to class, but I'll keep the gift in my car and then surprise Kim when we exchange presents."

"Enjoy." Alicia watched the lanky young man walk toward the parking lot. She felt as if she'd done a good deed, even though she was a little worried what John would say when she told him.

Chapter Three

Alicia walked home feeling less confident about her decision to give Andy the earrings she bought. It was bad enough she'd spent more money than she'd intended on the babysitter's gift, but she'd convinced Andy to be deceptive to his girlfriend. Alicia berated herself for putting him in that position. She knew all too well how important trust was between couples. Once, her lack of faith in John had nearly destroyed their relationship.

Approaching her house, Alicia realized she had to tell Kim what she'd done and why. She didn't get the opportunity, though, because John opened the door as soon as he saw her climb the steps.

"Shhh," he said, a finger pressed to his lips. "The babies are sleeping. Kim fed and changed them and then put them down for their nap. I paid her for her time and told her she could leave early and do some studying at the college library before her test today."

"That was nice of you." Alicia walked into the house. John helped her with her coat, slipping it over the coat rack in the entry hall.

"How was your shopping? I don't see any packages, and it doesn't look like you've been to Wilma's."

Alicia couldn't meet his eyes. She shrugged, walked to the rocker by the fireplace, and sat in it.

"I just strolled around the Green. All the shops are decorated, and I noticed the Santa chair is already by the gazebo. I'd love to go there one night with you and the babies. It must be so pretty lit up."

"We'll do it. Things will be even more festive when we return from the City."

"We really should start telling people. We have to make plans."

John took a seat in the other rocker.

"I told Kim. I said that Pamela would probably call her to fill in part of the time, and you know my sister will pay her well."

Alicia gazed into the fire. Her mind was still on the earrings and how she would explain what she'd done.

"Is something wrong, Ali? Are you still uncomfortable about leaving Carol and Johnny?"

"That's not it, John." She turned and looked into his deep blue eyes that always seemed to ignite something in her that was even stronger than the flames in their fireplace.

"Can you tell me about it, Mrs. McKinney?"

Alicia had never been good at lying, and John was adept at reading her.

"It's about Kim and Andy."

"A nice young couple. Are they having problems?"

Alicia fingered her wedding band.

"I wanted to buy Kim a nice Christmas gift to thank her for all she's done for us, and she mentioned she really liked a pair of earrings at Irene's shop but couldn't afford them. I went there today and bought them."

John nodded. "How expensive were they?"

"That's not the point." Alicia looked back toward the fire. "When I left Irene's shop, I ran into Andy. I gave them to him to give to Kim because he was feeling bad he couldn't buy her anything nice this year."

"You gave them to Andy to give Kim as a Christmas present?" John didn't sound mad, but Alicia started to feel defensive.

"I only wanted to help him out. I feel bad that his dad is gone, and his mother is just making ends meet to support Andy and his brother."

"Alicia, I'm not saying you did the wrong thing."

"Yes, but what if Kim finds out? If she goes back to the gift shop wearing the earrings, Irene may tell her I purchased them. Kim might break up with Andy and quit working at the newspaper and stop babysitting for us."

John smiled. "Oh, honey, you do get dramatic sometimes. I doubt that will happen, and I have an easy solution."

"What's that?" Alicia couldn't believe John was taking this so well and even had an idea that might fix things.

"This is what I'll do. I'll have a man-to-man talk with Andy at the newspaper office when Kim isn't around. I'll explain that I know you gave him the earrings. Then I'll have him do some extra jobs to earn back their cost."

It sounded simple to Alicia and a good plan, but there was still the possibility that Kim would find out Andy hadn't originally bought the earrings. Before she could mention that, John continued.

"You can go back to the gift shop before we leave on our trip and tell Irene exactly what you told me and what I'm doing about it. I'm sure she'll keep quiet; and, by the time Andy gives Kim the gift, he will already have paid for it."

Alicia was overcome with relief. "I think that will work, John. What type of jobs are you thinking of for Andy?"

"I could ask him to do some extra work at the paper or help out with chores for us here. Maybe, when we're away, he could paint and set up your office."

While Alicia and John usually conferred on their books together in bed in between waking up to deal with the babies and any romantic encounters they could fit in, Alicia had requested her own office with a desk for household and writing files, as well as shelves for her books. That had been a gift John wanted to give her for Christmas, but he didn't seem to find the time to work on it.

"That would be wonderful."

"What's even better," John added, "is it would allow Andy more time to spend with Kim if I arrange for her to help with the project. She'll be paid, of course, and it'll make up for the lost money that Pamela's watching the twins would've caused her."

Alicia stood up and came over to John's rocker. "Now I know why I married you, Mr. McKinney."

John opened his arms, and she sat on his lap. "This may be good practice for when you're Santa at the Christmas Fair."

"Ho, Ho, Ho, and what would you like for Christmas, Mrs. Klaus?"

"I already have everything I need."

Alicia placed her lips on his. As their kiss deepened, the babies, as if on cue, began to cry.

"Geez," John exclaimed as Alicia hurried off his lap to tend to the twins. "The weekend can't come soon enough."

***

After they'd quieted down the babies, John told Alicia he wanted to try to do some writing. She was a little disappointed because she thought he might want to pick up where they'd left off by the fire.

"Why don't you call Gilly while I'm working?" John suggested. "I know you wanted to thank her for the baby outfits."

Alicia caught the hint he wanted to be alone. The way they usually worked on their books, each one wrote a separate chapter. Since she'd started the last book and actually ended up finishing the final chapters when he got stuck, it was his turn to start the new one. They'd already flushed out an outline and character chart, but John hadn't gotten past the first paragraph of the second Groucho Marks' mystery.

While John went into the bedroom and turned on the laptop he kept by his side of the bed, Alicia checked the babies one last time. Then, before heading downstairs to the room they were currently using as a study and would be transformed into her office library, she looked in on John. He sat in bed with the computer on his lap staring at the blank screen. He didn't notice her standing there, so she quietly tiptoed down the hall.

**

Alicia sat at the worn desk that John promised to replace with a new one large enough to hold a desktop computer. There was only a phone on the desk. The rest of the room was bare. Alicia gazed around the dimly lit room. They had to change the lighting, too. She picked up the phone and dialed the familiar number of her friend. The phone rang a few times before Gilly answered in her normal, breathless voice.

"Hello. If this is an advertiser, I don't have time."

"Gilly, it's me."

"Sorry, Alicia. I get so many of those darn sales calls even though I've tried taking myself off all their lists. How are you, honey? Did you get the gift I sent?"

"I did. That's why I'm calling. The outfits are adorable, and they're the perfect size. I'm glad you bought them big. The babies are growing so quickly."

"Hold on, sweetie." It sounded as if Gilly put down the phone. Then Alicia heard, in the background: "Danny, what are you up to now? Please leave Ruby alone."

Alicia imagined Gilly's son was bothering their beagle. Her friend came back on the line. "You know I can't leave those kids for two minutes without them getting up to something. You'll see." She laughed.

"I see already. Every time John and I have a moment alone, Carol and Johnny start crying."

"That's only the beginning. You guys really need to take a vacation and have someone watch the babies for a while."

Was Gilly a mind reader? "Actually, Pamela just arranged for us to spend some time in the city while she watches Carol and Johnny. It was her Christmas gift to us."

"Nice. Maybe you can stop off here one day. I haven't seen you since May."

"That's an idea. I'll check with John about that. I'm sure we can fit it in. We'll be away all next week. I was a little hesitant to leave the twins at their age."

"Nonsense. You two need to rekindle your passion."

"Oh, Gilly!"

"I have another gift for you when you stop by. I was saving it for closer to the holiday, but you might to use it in New York. It's a naughty nighty, so you can play with Santa."

Alicia laughed. Same old Gilly and her lurid imagination spurred by all the bodice ripper romances she read.

"You are too much, Gilly; but, yes, I'll be sure to make it a point to come by either before or after our trip." Alicia also wanted to get Gilly and her sons presents. Bringing them in person would be ideal.

"You should come visit here in the spring. I know it's hard to get away with the boys, but you need a vacation yourself." Since her divorce seven years ago, the only travel Gilly had managed was to come to Alicia's wedding and her baby shower. She hadn't even seen the babies after they were born except for their photos.

"I know I should do that." Gilly sounded wistful. "Maybe during Easter vacation or spring recess. I want to see the twins before they're all grown up."

"They're growing fast." Alicia paused, hearing a loud sound from upstairs. It was like a heavy thump, as if something had fallen. "Gilly, I have to run. I heard something upstairs. I'll call you before we leave for the trip." She hung up quickly after Gilly said goodbye.

Rushing up the stairs, Alicia was afraid one or both of the babies had fallen out of their cribs, despite the fact the guard rails were high. They already knew how to roll over and were even starting to climb a bit. She hoped John had already gone into the nursery to check and called out to him. There was no reply.

When she got to the nursery, she was relieved to see the twins still sleeping soundly. Everything in the room seemed to be in place, so what had caused the noise? She was surprised it hadn't woken the twins because she'd heard it from downstairs. The thought came to her that it was possible the loud thumps had come from the bedroom instead of the nursery.

Leaving the babies sleeping, she went next door. As she stood in the bedroom doorway, her heart lurched. The laptop was lying on the floor along with their first Groucho Marks' book upturned, pages spread, as though it had been thrown against the wall. John was on the bed with his head in his hands sobbing silently.

Alicia approached her husband and sat next to him putting her arms around him. She didn't need to say anything. John leaned against her, his head by her chest.

"Oh, Ali. I can't do it anymore. I don't even think our trip will help. I'm sorry. I have to call Mary Beth and tell her the series is over."

"No, John. Let's wait. Please." She stroked his fine hair, very similar to Johnny's except his had a few strands of gray. She empathized with his feelings of frustration, but she recalled the agreement they'd made when they'd begun writing together.

"John, there's no reason for the series to end. I know you want to hold up your part of the work, but we promised each other when we started that if something prevented one of us from writing, the other would pick up the slack.

We're a team, and we support one another. If it was me who had writer's block, I would allow you to take over. I wouldn't be thrilled about it, but I would let you."

He sighed. "I know you're right, Ali. It's selfish of me. I'm just letting my pride get in the way. I'm sorry."

"No need to apologize." She smiled. "Don't give up now. Let's take this trip you think will do us good and see what happens afterwards." She put her hand over his. "Just remember we're in this together no matter what."

Chapter Four

John seemed back to his old self the next morning as they sat at the breakfast table with the twins beside them in their high chairs. They had talked over things, and John promised Alicia he wouldn't close the door on the series yet. It wasn't just his writer's block. The stress of the last couple of months as a new father, the sleepless nights, and his concerns with his lack of a career and their financial situation had caught up with him. Without any advice from Alicia, he suggested he might go back to seeing Dr. Gross, the psychiatrist he'd seen after his wife's death. Before he made any appointments, he wanted to see how he felt after their trip to New York.

Since Alicia was no longer nursing and the twins had begun eating some solid food, Alicia and John had created a morning feeding ritual. The high chairs were placed on opposite ends of the table next to each parent. Alicia fed Carol, while John fed Johnny. Both babies were good, if messy eaters. Alicia had a stack of bibs thanks to Dora who'd presented them to her at Thanksgiving the previous month when they ate at the inn. It was their custom to go there every year. Christmas was at home with John helping Alicia cook their holiday meal and Mac bringing fresh rolls and spreads made with his cinnamon, cranberry, and orange preserves and spices. Fido followed at his heels hoping to snag some leftovers. Sheila dropped by unless she was headed to California to visit her daughter and grandchildren. She'd bring a dessert from Claire's bakery.

Since the library was closed for Christmas Eve and Christmas Day, Alicia brought Sneaky home to stay in Mac's old room, transferring his litter box and food bowls there until the library reopened. This year, Laura had offered to take Sneaky, but she was worried he might not get along with her own two cats. The cat had stayed with John and Alicia over Thanksgiving and enjoyed the cut-up turkey "goody" bag Dora handed to Alicia on her way home.

"Look at this kid eat," John said interrupting Alicia's musings about the holidays. Johnny was gulping down the pureed chicken and vegetable baby food from the end of the spoon John was offering him. Alicia loved to watch her husband feed their son. She could already see a strong resemblance between them. Johnny wiggled his tiny feet clad in a blue onesie from under the high chair. He made some gurgling and giggling sounds as he ate.

"He seems to really be enjoying that. You're doing a great job, Dad." Alicia gave a spoonful of the same food to Carol who slurped it right up.

"You're not doing too bad yourself with our little girl." John smiled and, although Alicia could still see the worry lines around his eyes, they were less pronounced. After his outburst and crying spell, he'd slept well. Alicia had tended to the babies and let him have his much-needed rest.

"It isn't too difficult, John. Both our kids are hearty eaters like us."

John's grin widened. He wiped Johnny's mouth with his puppy bib. "What's on the agenda today, Mrs. McKinney? Are you going to the library?"

Alicia fed Carol another spoonful. "Yes. I have to, John. I'm feeling a lot better. Johnny only got up once to have his diaper changed last night, and Carol slept the whole time. I think that baby tooth that was erupting finally came through."

"Nice. They're growing up." John patted Johnny's head. "I think he's had enough."

"I also need to break the news to Sheila that I won't be around next week."

"She'll be glad about that. She's got plenty of help now, and she'll want you to have the vacation Pamela gifted you."

"What are your plans?"

"Not sure. I'll probably head to the paper to work on next week's issue after Kim gets here. Andy wrote a few stories. I have to edit them. Maybe I'll do some Christmas shopping later, and I'd also like to spring the news about our trip on Dad. I know you're worried about his being upset that we're not asking him and Betty to watch the babies, but I know he'll understand. I might stop at the library around lunch if you'd like to go out with me. We could hit Casey's or that new place in Cobble Corner. I hate to patronize the diner's competitor, but it's good to try new things once in a while. I'm sure Casey won't mind. His business has picked up so much since Chef Harold started cooking dinners."

"Lunch sounds good, John, and I've been curious about that Italian place, La Bella, I think it's called."

"Yep. Right next to the bakery, so if people aren't into cannoli or spumoni for dessert, they can grab something from Claire's."

***

After Kim showed up in tight jeans and a red Christmas sweater decorated with Santa elves, Alicia gave her the rundown on the twins – what they'd eaten, when they'd had their diapers changed, how they were feeling/behaving.

"Carol has a bit of a sniffle, so just keep an eye on her. I hope she's not coming down with something."

"It's probably just the weather, but I'll watch her," Kim promised.

John had put on his coat and given both kids a kiss on their foreheads. Walking to his wife, he enveloped her in a hug and kissed her lips. "Stop worrying, mama. They're fine. Have a great morning. I'll see you at noon."

Alicia smiled. She couldn't help being concerned. Every time she left the babies, she worried something would happen. Although Carol wasn't exhibiting any of the symptoms of the virus in the schools, she was keeping her fingers crossed that she wasn't developing it or some other illness.

After John left, as she put on her own coat, she said to Kim, "You'd better not take them out today just in case they're starting to get sick. It's pretty chilly."

"I won't, but it's sunny, Mrs. McKinney. Sometimes it's nice for them to get some fresh air."

"Let's see how they are tomorrow, Kim. Thanks again for taking such good care of them."

She kissed both kids in about the same spot John had, leaving a light pink lipstick mark on the top of their heads. Wiping it off with a napkin, as the babies giggled, she found herself even more reluctant to leave.

Being a working mother was difficult. But she knew staying home with them the whole day might drive her crazy as much as she would love it. Besides, her work at the library was fun and very interesting, so unlike her work on Long Island. She thought she would find the pace in Cobble Cove too slow, but as the town grew, more patrons flocked to the library for reading material or other informational needs. Their audio section had also expanded. Sheila was wonderful to work for, and the new Board of Trustees was supportive and appreciative, often leaving cookies or other home-made goodies for the staff in the employee's lounge.

Alicia tried not to look back as she took the short walk to work. It was brisk out, and the wind whipped her hair.

She could feel her cheeks reddening and was glad she'd taken the gloves from her pocket and put them on.

Donald and Jean were behind the Reference desk as she entered. Alicia was glad to see Jean was back. Vera, the full-time clerk, was at the Circulation Desk checking out some books for a patron. The library was already open because Sheila allowed Alicia to come in an hour later on certain days when she needed to wait for Kim. In exchange, Alicia often worked after five to help the librarian on the evening shift. John usually relieved Kim in the afternoons when she went to her classes.

"Looks like a full house today. Glad to see you back, Jean. How are you feeling? Is Jeremy better?" She approached the reference desk.

The dark-haired woman in her late thirties smiled. "He's much better and back in school. I'm taking the morning shift. Sheila thought you might not be coming in. Were you sick yesterday, too? She said you went home early."

"No. I'm fine. I actually need to speak with her. Is she in yet?"

"In her office," Donald replied. He had caught the Christmas spirit and was wearing a holiday tie over a white shirt and green vest.

"Thanks. I'll stop there on my way to check in. Nice tie, by the way."

Donald looked down at his chest and fingered the material that looked like silk but may have been a blend. "Thank you. It was a gift from Roger last year."

The patron at the Circulation desk walked away carrying her checked-out books in a library bag.

Vera joined the group. "I think we should all start dressing in holiday clothes. It'll add some spirit to this place." She wore a red sweater over gray slacks and a wreath pin with matching earrings. Her blondish-gray hair was short and curly. She also wore horn-rimmed glasses that she insisted were only for reading but that she never took off. In her sixties, the short spunky widow who had moved to Cobble Cove a year ago, had become good friends with Edith and Rose and was an active member of the Christmas Fair Committee. She was also responsible for many of the decorations now gracing the library's windows and walls.

"I'd be up for that," Jean said. "The new clothes shop in Cobble Corner has some nice holiday stuff. I picked up a hat, scarf, and mitten set for Jeremy over the weekend and noticed they're selling lots of Christmas sweaters at a decent price."

"Gotta check that out," Vera said.

Alicia wondered if now was a good time to mention her upcoming trip, but she thought she should speak with Sheila first. "I'll be right back, folks. I still haven't checked in."

She made her getaway taking the stairs behind the Reference Desk up to the staff lounge. Sheila's office was up there, but the director also spent a lot of time at the Reference Desk.

Alicia was about to knock on the closed door of the office wondering why it wasn't open as usual when Walter, the library custodian, stepped out. She almost collided with him as he walked into the hall in front of her.

"Whooo. Sorry, Alicia." Walter's balding head was covered with just a strand of gray hair. His eyebrows were thicker, the same texture as Ramsay's but lighter in color. He was also taller and not as fat, but he could definitely benefit from more exercise and less food.

"That's okay, Walter. What's up? Are you working this morning?"

"Yes. They're having a special Children's program today. It's "Sneaky Story Time.'"

Alicia had forgotten that, once a month, they brought Sneaky down to the Children's Room where some of the youngsters got a chance to read a book to him and pet him. She figured that's what Sheila was discussing with Walter, but why behind closed doors?

"What time does it start?"

"In about a half hour, but I have to help Laura set up. Why don't you come by? We're pretty well staffed today."

"I think I'll do that."

"Good. See you down there."

As Walter walked toward the stairs, Alicia peeked into Sheila's office. Walter had left the door slightly ajar. Sheila sat behind her desk, her red head bent over the keyboard typing into her computer.

Alicia hesitated. She didn't want to disturb her, but Sheila noticed her. Without looking up, she said, "Come in, Alicia. I thought you'd take another day, but I'm glad you're here. I hope you had a good rest yesterday."

"Yes, thanks, Sheila."

"Have a seat."

Alicia took the chair next to Sheila's desk. It was a wooden one with no arms that might have a match at the elementary school.

"There's something I need to tell you, Sheila."

Sheila's green cat eyes assessed Alicia. Although they'd been through so much, and Sheila had proved to be a true friend to both John and his father, Alicia still felt the woman's gaze a bit perturbing. She looked down at her hands that she'd placed in her lap and was unconsciously tearing back a cuticle. Besides the hair styling, she badly needed a manicure. Her fingernails were unpainted, chipped, and some were broken.

"Alicia, what is it?" Sheila's voice changed to one of concern rather than questioning. "Is there a problem?"

"No. It's . . . Well, it's about that gift I received from Pamela."

"Oh? Was it something you disliked or already have? I'm sure she would understand if you told her."

"No, that's not it. Sorry, Sheila." Alicia knew it was best just to come right out with it.

"Pamela gave John and me a week's vacation in New York in the honeymoon suite at the Park Lane Hotel."

Sheila was silent a moment and then she let out a low whistle. "And that's bad, why, Alicia?"

"Aren't you upset that I'm taking vacation with such short notice?"

Sheila smiled, showing perfect teeth, another feline attribute. "I'm thrilled you and John are finally getting some much-needed time away. I think Pamela gave you two the best gift ever. I wish I'd had the money and thought of it first. The honeymoon suite at Park Lane. My gosh, you'll be in heaven. And the city is so festive this time of year. I've gone on shopping trips during the Christmas season and have some great memories of all the store windows and the Rockefeller Center Tree. Mind you, I stayed at a friend's apartment while I was there. I can't afford the hotel costs. My husband and I did spend one weekend in New York once."

Sheila's voice turned wistful. "You'll just love it. You have my blessing."

"Thanks for understanding." Alicia wasn't sure she felt relieved. Everyone seemed to think this trip would be so good for her and John. Yet, she still had reservations. Was it because she'd be leaving the babies for an extended time, or was something else bothering her? Before she could explore those thoughts, Laura came rushing up the stairs in her three-inch heels, her long blonde hair flying as she hurried down the hall. The sound of excited children floated up behind her.

"Morning, Sheila, Alicia," she said as she passed the office. "It's time for the star."

"You'd better go help her," Sheila said. "I have some things to get back to, but I'm glad we had our talk.

Remember, have fun and don't worry about this place while you're gone."

Even though Laura was rushing, she overheard Sheila's comment and came to a halt. "Fun? Is that possible for a new mom?"

Laura was only in her late twenties, but she had four younger siblings and was often the caretaker for some of them, as her parents both worked long hours. They lived in Carlsville, and Laura commuted the short drive to Cobble Cove each day in her red Taurus. She shared it with her sister, Lily, and sometimes was dropped off by her. She'd graduated last year with her library degree after working nights as a clerk at her home library.

When the position came up for a children's librarian in Cobble Cove, she was one of dozens of applicants who had seen the ad listed in the paper along with the previous news articles about the construction of the new Children's Wing. Sheila, trying to curb her impulsiveness, interviewed Laura twice before offering her the job. One of the factors in her favor was her knack with and love of cats because Sheila already had the idea for the Sneaky Story Time.

"Alicia and John will be in New York next week for a long overdue vacation. They'll be staying at the Park Lane Hotel in Central Park."

"Oh my God!" Laura exclaimed. "Lucky you, Alicia. That's awesome."

Alicia had gone out into the hall to join the younger librarian.

"It was a gift from my sister-in-law. John is all gung ho about it, and I can't blame him because we've both been pretty stressed these past few months, but I'm a little nervous about leaving the twins. Part of the gift is that Pamela is coming here to watch them, but I'm still concerned."

"That's totally normal. My mom still worries about me and my brothers and sister. I think she will when we're fifty."

Alicia winced. She'd turned forty-four in October but had no mother to look after her, having lost hers about the same age as Laura.

The bustle downstairs grew louder.

"Oh, I've got to get him. I don't need help, Alicia. I can handle Mr. Sneaky."

It was then that Alicia remembered the vet appointment. "I'll come with you just in case, Laura. You remember Sneaky has his physical with Dr. Clark tomorrow, right?"

Laura paused, her hand on the knob of the staff lounge. "Oh, no. I forgot all about it. What time?"

"I think it's around noon. You could call and check."

A worried expression crossed Laura's face. "Lily needs my car tomorrow. She's got a class. We'll have to reschedule."

"You can use my car," Alicia offered. "I hardly have use for it now that I walk everywhere in town."

"I wouldn't feel comfortable driving someone else's car."

"I'll go with you. We could do it on our lunch hours. It probably won't take very long."

"Sounds good. Thanks."

Laura opened the staff lounge, and Alicia followed her in flicking up the light switch next to the door. The room into which they walked was cozy with a few tables covered by red and green holiday tablecloths that Vera had recently purchased in town, and chairs similar to the one in Sheila's office that she'd promised to replace soon with padded ones. There was a small refrigerator and a counter with coffee maker, mugs, and sweeteners.

Laura continued through the room to the back door framed by a cat flap. She put her finger to her lips.

"Shhh. He might be sleeping. That would be great. We can catch him unaware."

She opened the door slowly and tiptoed through. Alicia followed on her toes, as well, the squeals from downstairs reaching a crescendo as the two women entered the storage/cat room.

Sneaky was indeed sleeping, nestled into the cat bed they'd moved from under the local history collection downstairs; but, like most felines, he was alert to the slightest noise. As Laura and Alicia entered the room, one brown ear flap lifted and Sneaky's left eye opened a slit.

"Uh, oh. He's heard us." Laura bent down and unlocked the cat carrier. Sneaky, hearing the familiar sound, jumped up from his bed.

"Oh, no you don't, Mr. Sneak," Laura said. She signaled to Alicia to block the exit as she ran across the room and scooped up the cat in one fell swoop. Then, rushing back to the carrier, she pushed him in and secured all four hinges that closed the door.

"Amazing," Alicia said. "You're such an expert at catching cats. I had one before I married my first husband, and my mom and I always had such a difficult time getting him to the vet. We had to close all the rooms in our house, and he would still run under the couch."

Laura laughed. "I've had lots of practice. I grew up with a house full of kitties, and I've also done animal rescue. Mr. Sneak is no match for me."

She picked up the case as Sneaky began to meow, his bellows mixing with the children's wails from below. "Let's get down there before some of those kids start throwing up from excitement."

Alicia, abandoning her guard post by the door, followed Laura and the caged cat to the Children's Room. Parents, mostly mothers and a few fathers, were lined up around the room as their children, ranging in age from two to five, sat in a circle Indian-style around a chair. Jean was handling crowd control and had selected and arranged some picture books on a cart next to Laura's seat.

As soon as Laura entered the room carrying Sneaky, the group went wild. Jean, assisted by some of the parents, had to restrain the children from opening the cat carrier. Sneaky had quieted down but had scuttled to the back of the box. Alicia knew it would be difficult to extract him until the noise level dissipated.

Laura excused herself as she carried Sneaky to her reading chair and placed the carrier beside it. She put a finger to her lips in the stereotypical librarian "shushing" gesture.

"Quiet down, children. Sneaky will be too frightened to come out if you are loud."

Alicia noticed Walter on the other side of the room. He was ready to clean up any mess the cat or the kids might make. Donald and Vera were also looking on from the sidelines, ready to return to their posts at Reference or Circulation if any patron needed them. Alicia was surprised Sheila wasn't there, as she usually attended all library programs. She wondered what the director was working on that might be so important.

Laura sat in the center chair.

"Okay, kids. If this is your first time at Sneaky Storytime, let me go over the rules. I have a few books to share with you this morning. After I read them, I will allow you to come up, one at a time, to pet Sneaky on my lap. You will have to be very quiet, or he will run away." She looked toward Walter who took his cue and drew closed the room dividing panels. Since the panels were opaque, Donald and Vera could still keep watch on the front desk.

"One other announcement before we begin," Laura continued. "Sneaky is also having a special guest today. He will be joining us in a few minutes."

This was a surprise to Alicia. Who could be the cat's special guest? Laura's words were met with claps and yaaays from the kids.

***

After Laura read the three books that Jean had chosen, each of them featuring cats and dogs, and had interacted with the kids by asking them questions, she asked for a volunteer to help her open Sneaky's carrier.

Jean, who had gone to stand by Alicia, whispered, "I wish Jeremy could be here. He's older than these kids, but he loves Sneaky."

"Maybe Sheila will consider doing something after school for the older children," Alicia suggested. "Do you have any idea who the special guest is?"

Jean shook her dark head. "Nope. Laura's keeping that quiet."

A freckle-faced little girl wearing a polka-dotted jumper was chosen to do the honors. She ran over to the carrier when Laura picked her.

"Now be very quiet, Angelina," Laura said. She bent down next to the girl. "I'll undo the bottom latches while you open the top, okay?"

Angelina nodded. She was taking this job seriously. As they opened the carrier, Sneaky tentatively put out a paw. Laura instructed Angelina to step back as she tapped on the carrier, and the cat's head appeared. The kids screeched happily, but Laura put a finger to her lips to silence them. Sneaky, ever the performer, walked out, tail high, surveying his audience. Laura scooped him up and sat back down in the chair.

"Thank you, Angelina, you can be the first to pet Sneaky and then, one at a time starting with Nicholas, you can each have a turn. Parents may take photos if they like."

Jean whispered to Alicia, "See that girl, Angelina. It was nice of Laura to let her go first. She's having a tough time of it."

Alicia didn't know many of the children who had recently moved to Cobble Cove. She glanced at the girl again. She was quite tiny and thin, but she looked happy and well adjusted. "What do you mean?"

Jean continued in a low voice, turning to face Alicia. "Angelina has leukemia. She comes from the city. Her parents couldn't afford living there any longer. It's possible she may need a bone marrow transplant in the future. Edith and Rose are talking about a fundraiser near Christmas to help the family."

"How awful. I would never know it. She doesn't look sick."

"Yes, so sad. She's in remission now." Jean directed Alicia's attention to one of the young women standing behind the circle of children. "That's her mom, Patty, over there. She teaches Kindergarten at the school."

Alicia hadn't seen the petite brunette before. She made a note to visit the school soon, maybe attend a PTA meeting. It was never too early to get started with the twins entering pre-school there in just a few years.

Jean continued talking about the ill child's parents. It seemed the story only got worse. "Angelina's dad, Gary, is working for Duncan at the grocery. He got laid off from his corporate job years ago and hasn't been able to find anything else."

Alicia couldn't help thinking of Tiny Tim and a Christmas Carol. Maybe there was something that could be done for these poor people beyond a church fundraiser. As reluctant as she was to seek the aid of her sister-in-law especially after John had warned her that he no longer was accepting Pamela's charity, Alicia wondered if there could be an exception in this case. Just thinking about anything like that touching the lives of her own family made her shudder.

***

As each child had a chance to spend time with Sneaky and mothers and fathers came up to click shots with their cell phone cameras, Alicia was amazed at how well behaved the cat remained on Laura's lap. After the last child took her turn, Laura put Sneaky back in the carrier.

"Walter, can you please open the doors now? Our guest should be here."

There was a loud murmur from the children as Walter drew back the panels. Alicia looked toward the front doors as Mac and Fido came through the turnstiles. She should've known. The special guest was none other than her father-in-law's golden retriever.

The kids went wild again as Mac led Fido into the room.

"Settle down, children," Laura said in her calm, even voice. "Mr. McKinney will let each of you have a turn with Fido as you did with Sneaky."

Mac smiled. He looked toward Alicia and winked.

"Good morning, kids. Fido is honored to be a special guest here today." As if agreeing to his master's statement, Fido let out a short bark. The kids squealed in response.

Laura moved Sneaky's cage out of the way, and Walter wheeled the book cart to the side and then pushed the chair next to it.

"Line up one at a time and, after you pet Fido, you may leave with your parent. Photos can also be taken."

Alicia knew that Jean was taking pictures, too, with her digital camera to share with John for the paper. They didn't have a program director at the library yet, but Sheila was talking about hiring one if the position was approved by the Board at the next meeting.

When the last child had spent time with Fido and most of the children and parents left waving to the pets as they exited the room, Donald and Vera returned to their desks. Jean was busy putting away the picture books. Alicia, still thinking of Angelina who had blown kisses to the animals after she'd been picked up by her mother and was being carried from the library, jumped when she felt a nudge on her shoulder and turned to see Sheila behind her.

"You missed another great Sneaky Storytime," she told the director. "Fido was a special guest today."

"I know." Sheila looked a bit frazzled, unusual for her regular put-together appearance. A few stray strands of red hair were out of place over her gold headband as if she'd run her fingers through them.

"I have to talk to you a moment, Alicia. Do you mind coming to my office?"

"Of course not." Alicia wondered if Sheila had reconsidered giving her vacation time the following week. "I just want to say goodbye to Mac first."

"Sure." Sheila stepped away. "Take your time. I'll see you upstairs."

Laura already had Sneaky back in his case and passed Sheila on her way to the stairs. "I think Sneaky wants to go back to bed. He's had a busy morning."

"He was great. So were you. I used to do story times at my library on Long Island when I first worked there. It's hard to keep the little ones' attention. I give you credit, and you also have to deal with a stubborn feline."

Laura grinned. "I love animals and kids. It isn't that difficult if you know how to handle them."

As Laura headed for the stairs, Mac ambled over to Alicia with Fido. She marveled at her father-in-law's ability to control the dog and keep his balance with the cane, but Fido seemed used to obeying his master, and he kept pace with his elderly owner.

"Hi there, Alicia. That was lots of fun. It's great that the library provides young ones interaction with animals."

"Yes, and Sheila is always sure to warn about allergies in her advertisements."

"I didn't hear a wheeze or a sneeze in the group." Mac displayed his dimple "I saw John at the newspaper office a little while ago. He says he's taking you to the new Italian place for lunch."

"Yes. I wanted to try it. Would you like to join us?"

"No. I have some other plans, but thanks for the invite. I'm going to lunch with John and Ron Ramsay tomorrow at Casey's."

"I'm helping Laura take Sneaky to the vet tomorrow. Not that she needs much assistance, but her sister is borrowing her car, so I offered to drive."

"Nice of you. Okay, catch you later, Alicia."

She smiled as Mac led Fido through the library turnstiles and out into the sunny, cold day. Her expression changed as she recalled that Sheila was waiting to talk to her privately upstairs.

***

Sheila's door was open. As Alicia stood in the doorway, she looked up from some papers on her desk. "Come in, Alicia. Please close the door behind you."

Alicia tried to read the director's face. It was somber, but not angry. She sat in the school room chair feeling like a student in the principal's office.

"Let me get right to the reason I asked you here." Sheila regarded her with her cat-like eyes. "I have a dilemma. Bonnie called in sick tonight, and I don't have a librarian who can work until nine. I know you have the babies to worry about, but I also know John is usually home in the evenings. Would it be too much trouble to ask you to fill in? You can take a longer lunch today and come back at two if you want."

Alicia was relieved. Sheila wasn't asking her to give up her trip next week. "Not a problem. What's wrong with Bonnie?"

Alicia's face darkened. "I had a feeling she might not come in tonight."

"Is she sick? Did she catch the virus that's going around?"

Sheila hesitated and then lowered her voice. "Alicia, this is confidential. I know I can trust you to keep this quiet."

She spread both hands across her desk blotter displaying her long, red nails. "I had to have a talk with Walter this morning. There was an incident last night."

Alicia was surprised. Although she'd had to write several incident reports about abusive patron behavior at her home library, she'd yet to write one in Cobble Cove.

"What happened? Was Bonnie hurt?" She couldn't imagine any of the town residents attacking the young part-time clerk.

Sheila shook her head. "Not physically, but I'm afraid she's very upset."

"Did it involve a patron?"

"No." Sheila's green eyes were veiled.

"It seems Bonnie called me after her shift last night. I've given you all my home number in case of emergencies. Since Jean only worked until six, Bonnie was alone after that. She told me," Sheila paused and took a deep breath. "She said Walter made a sexual gesture toward her."

"No." Alicia was shocked. Although she didn't know the custodian well, she knew he was quite devoted to his wife, Gloria, who'd recently served her and John at Casey's.

"That was my reaction, but I don't think Bonnie would lie."

"May I ask what Walter did?" Alicia couldn't contain her curiosity.

"It was just suggestive," Sheila waved her beringed fingers. "He said a few things to her. I don't want to go into detail. I had a talk with him. He says she took it the wrong way, that he was only kidding with her, but I can't have that. Now she's called in sick, and I think she's afraid."

"Is Walter working tonight?"

"Yes." Sheila's eyes widened. "No need to worry, Alicia. I'm sure he wouldn't bother you. He seemed quite chastised. I don't know what to do about Bonnie, though. I might take a drive to her house later and have a chat with her. I'm not taking any action against Walter, but he's been warned. I'm sure I won't have any trouble replacing him."

For Gloria's sake, Alicia hoped Walter wouldn't be fired. But if what Bonnie said was true? Something had to be done about it. Alicia knew through her own experience that some men put on an innocent front when it came to activities behind their wife's back. What if it happened with a female patron? Alicia knew Sheila was thinking the same thing.

"Well, thank you for working tonight, and I apologize for such short notice, Alicia. I'm planning to suggest we hire a guard as well as a program director at Thursday night's Board Meeting, and I may change Laura's hours so she works from one to nine. Most of the kids don't come in until after school, anyway, but don't you worry too much about this matter. You're going on a nice trip and need to put all of this aside until you get back, so you can enjoy yourself."

Alicia couldn't help worrying as she went back to the reference desk to relieve Donald for a break.

Chapter Five

John arrived a few minutes before noon. He met Alicia at the Reference desk, a smile on his face.

"Good afternoon, library folks."

"Hi, John," Donald said. "Picking up your wife to take her to lunch?"

"Yes, Sir. We're trying La Bella. We both like Italian food."

"I've eaten there with Roger. It's very good. Teresa and Salvatore make delicious pasta. I'd recommend their lasagna, and the Italian cheesecake is to die for." He rolled his brown eyes.

Vera laughed. "I've eaten there, too. It's family run. Their daughter, Lucia, is the waitress, and their younger son, Vinnie, buses tables after school. He's in the same grade as Jeremy. I love the paintings on the walls, and they always have Italian music playing."

"Sounds like that place you took me to once with the singing waiters and waitresses," Alicia told John.

"The music isn't live," Vera said, "but it's atmospheric."

"Let's see for ourselves," John suggested as he helped Alicia slip on her coat. "See you all later."

"I have some extra time for lunch today, John, because Sheila's asked me to work tonight. I hope that's okay with you."

"No problem. I don't have any plans. I'll enjoy having the babies to myself for some daddy time." He winked.

***

It was a short walk from the library to the town Green. Alicia remembered touring Cobble Corner with John when she first came there never imagining she'd end up living so close to the quaint hub of the village. People waved to her as they passed. Some of the shop keepers were outside decorating their store fronts. When they passed by the Grocer, Duncan and a slightly shorter man were hanging garland over the display of deli platters and festive fruit and vegetable trays in the supermarket's window. Alicia assumed the man was Gary, the father of the poor little girl with Leukemia who had been so sweet handling Sneaky at the library.

"Nice job," John commented as Duncan attached the last strand of silver, red, and gold garland to the window. His employee greeted them. Up close, Alicia could see the man had a bit of stubble on his square-shaped chin and dark circles under his eyes; like John had developed staying up at night with the twins and struggling to write their book. He had a friendly look, and Alicia could see some faded freckles by his nose similar to his daughter's. There was a solid look about him.

"I don't believe we've met." He extended a hand to John. "I'm Gary Millburn. My wife, Patty, works at the Fairmont School." He paused, his voice lowering a pitch. "We have a daughter in Kindergarten there."

John smiled. He didn't know about Angelina. "Nice to meet you, Gary. I'm John McKinney, and this is my wife, Alicia."

The man smiled, showing slightly crooked teeth. "A pleasure." He shook Alicia's hand. His shake was strong and warm. She looked into his gray eyes and saw a hint of pain there. It appeared the same as what she'd seen in John's before he told her about his first wife's death.

"So now you've made the acquaintance of my new man," Duncan said, a bit of tinsel stuck to his fingers. Duncan wasn't obese, but one might call him "chubby." He had a round appearance like her friend, Gilly. Alicia thought he might make a nice Santa if John wasn't playing that role in the Christmas fair.

"How's business?" John asked.

Duncan clapped his hands together to remove the tinsel. "Getting busy. Gary and I have been setting up holiday platters. Would you and Alicia be interested in anything?"

"Not today, but maybe after we come back from New York. We're taking a trip there next week."

"Nice. I always like the city near Christmas."

"Dunc, sorry to interrupt, but did you want me to put up that tabletop tree by the deli counter?"

"That would be great, Gary. Thanks."

"Nice meeting you folks. Have a good day."

As Gary went in the store, Duncan turned back to Alicia and John. "He's a good worker. It's great to have the extra hand. Wendy used to hate the long hours I put in here, and now I can spend more time with her."

"Great. I guess we should be going. I'm taking Ali to lunch at La Bella today. It's the first time we've been there."

"You'll like it. Terry and Sal's food is authentic I-talian," he emphasized the first letter. "Very tasty. Enjoy, guys."

Duncan waved to them as he went back inside the store to join Gary.

***

La Bella was next to the bakery a few doors down from the grocery. Claire was outside stringing lights through the evergreen by the door.

"Hi, John, Alicia," she said as they walked by. "Happy Holidays! Can I interest you in some cookies or a cake?"

"Hi, Claire. We're going to lunch next door first, but maybe we'll pick up something for dessert," John told the baker.

Claire stood back from the tree and tossed her blonde curls. "Sure thing. I just baked a batch of Christmas cookies this morning, John. You can give the twins a small bite of them. How are those darlings doing, by the way?"

"Getting big," Alicia answered. "I don't think they're quite ready for cookies, but they seem to enjoy baby food fruit and applesauce, so I think they may be developing a preference for sweets."

"I'm sure they will be big customers of mine soon."

Like Duncan, Claire could afford to lose a few pounds, another victim of working with food all day. Dressed in a red turtleneck sweater and green corduroy pants covered with a white baker's apron, Alicia noticed how tight the garment stretched across Claire, exposing some unflattering bumps.

"I can just see the dental bills now." John laughed.

***

La Bella was already decorated to the nines with holiday trimmings. Two toy soldiers stood at opposite ends of the entranceway greeting customers in their bright painted uniforms. A 6-foot fir filled with ornaments and topped with an angel graced the vestibule. Red, green, silver, blue, and gold Christmas balls hung from the high ceiling inside. The front desk had a smaller decorated tree on it, next to the menus.

A pretty, dark-haired young woman smiled as they entered. "Ciao. I'm Lucia Romano. Please call me Lucia, and welcome to La Bella." She walked out from behind the stand with two menus. "Two for lunch? Would you like a table or booth?"

"A booth would be nice. Thank you," Alicia said. The girl was about her height with dark, Southern Italian looks.

She led them through the restaurant to a booth beside a window that looked out on the court that faced the gazebo and the center's Christmas tree. Low instrumental music played soothingly in the background of the wood-paneled room. Paintings on the walls featured Roman architecture, the canals and gondolas of Venice, and the Sistine chapel.

Alicia slid into the right side of the booth, while John sat across from her. Lucia handed Alicia and then John a menu.

"There are some specials for lunch. My father is making Penne Ala Vodka and our custom dish, Romano Carbonara. It's linguini in a red sauce with mozzarella and red peppers. Everything is served family style. Take your time, and I can take your drink orders first if you're ready."

Alicia glanced at the menu, which had a separate page for drinks, both alcoholic and non-alcoholic. She noticed a large list of wines.

"Would you care for some wine with lunch?" John asked looking over the selections.

Alicia didn't normally drink even at dinner, but she felt like she needed something to soothe her nerves from that morning.

"I think that would be nice, John. Maybe a glass of red. That usually goes well with Italian food."

"Excellent. I'll bring over a bottle of vino." Lucia stepped away as a few more diners filed in.

"I'll try the house special," John said putting down his menu and unfolding the white table napkin to drape across his lap. "What about you, Mrs. McKinney?"

Alicia smiled, but it was halfhearted. "Since they serve everything family style, maybe I should split with you. I'm always up for a challenge."

A twinkle lighted up John's eyes. "That you are."

There was a carafe of water filled with ice cubes on the table. John offered to fill her glass.

"I'll wait for the wine, thanks."

"Alicia, is something wrong? Tell me about your morning. Did something happen that upset you?"

She had to give him credit for always being able to read her so easily, but the fact was she wasn't all that difficult to read especially when she was worried.

"There were several things, John."

Before she could continue, Lucia was back with their bottle of wine, a basket of assorted rolls, and slices of warm bread. There was also a small tub of olive oil for dipping.

"Are you ready to place your orders, or would you like more time?"

"I think we're set. The lady and I will be sharing your house special, Romano Carbonara."

"Good choice." Lucia jotted down their order on the white pad she took from her apron. "Would you also like an appetizer?"

"I think we'll skip that for now." John looked over at Alicia. "Unless you want something, Ali?"

"No, I'd like to enjoy the meal, and the bread is more than enough to start."

"That's fine. I'll bring your order in just a few minutes, although we use fresh pasta, so it does take a bit longer to cook unless you're in a rush."

"We're not in a rush," Alicia replied.

"Okay then. Enjoy the music and talk while you wait. Thanks again for choosing La Bella for lunch today." Lucia walked away to a table in the back to take another order.

John poured Alicia wine and then filled his glass. "Have a sip and then please continue, Ali. I want to hear what happened at the library today that seems to have upset you. I'd also like to know why your schedule was changed so abruptly. That's not like Sheila. She's so organized."

Alicia did as John suggested, savoring the red liquid as she tried to relax. The low notes of an Italian melody played in the background.

"It was Sneaky Storytime today," she began. "And, by the way, your dad brought Fido as a special guest for the children. They were ecstatic."

John smiled over his wine glass and passed her the bread basket along with a few rose-shaped pats of butter. He munched one of the bread biscuits. There was an unlit candle next to it that she assumed was lit at night when the lights of the restaurant were dimmed. It would be romantic, and she made a note that it might be a nice date night for them when Kim watched the babies.

"I saw him earlier, and he took the news about our trip well. Having Sneaky at the library must've been fun."

"Yes. For both the kids and Mac." Alicia put down her glass.

Cutting open her roll and slathering butter inside, she said, "But Jean filled me in about one of the little girls who was first to pet Sneaky. We actually met her father today, Gary, the man now working for Duncan."

"Oh?" John looked surprised. "What did Jean tell you about his daughter?"

"She has leukemia."

"Gosh, what a shame." John's eyes clouded. His mother had died of cancer as had both Alicia's parents.

"The treatments are very costly. That's why they moved from the city. She's in remission now, but she may need a bone marrow transplant in the future. It's so sad."

Alicia started to choke on her words, just thinking about the cute girl with the freckles. "The church committee wants to hold a fundraiser for her at the Christmas fair, but I was thinking maybe Pamela could help . . . ."

"No." John said the word softly but firmly. "I can't ask my sister to do anything else for us or anyone in this town. I'm sure that girl's parents wouldn't accept the charity either, although the fundraiser might be okay."

"What's the difference how they get the money, John? They're in need. It could mean the difference between Angelina living or . . . . ." Alicia was unable to think of a five-year old in a coffin being lowered into the ground.

"Sorry, Ali. I know how you feel, believe me. But if we start asking Pamela to give to everyone in Cobble Cove who needs money, she'll be broke herself. Kim and Andy are struggling to make their tuition payments. Dora and Charlie have the upkeep on the inn. Your co-worker Donald told me he's having problems with his car and may need to buy another one."

"But, John, this is a child whose life might be cut short. It's so awful." Tears started to form in her eyes. "I know Pamela would be happy to help Angelina."

"Alicia, please."

As much as John could read her, she could also tell when he'd made up his mind about something. He took a swallow of his wine and another biscuit.

"Let's discuss this further another time. But speaking of my sister, she called earlier today. I had dropped home for a few minutes, and Kim had the message for me. She'll be arriving Saturday morning."

When Alicia nodded, still perturbed from their talk about Angelina, he said, "I hate it when you brood, honey. If it makes you feel any better, I'll consider speaking to Pamela about the kid when we get back from our trip."

"Thanks, John, and I do understand what you mean about everyone needing money. For all we know, Pamela might be in debt. A lot of rich people are because they live beyond their means. She's so generous she might be giving away too much."

"Exactly. That's what I'm afraid of, Ali." John finished his wine and biscuit. Alicia's glass remained half full, and she'd hardly touched her roll.

"What else happened this morning? Why are you working late tonight?"

A wave of queasiness washed over her that felt a bit like the morning sickness she'd suffered with the twins, but she knew it was from nerves and not pregnancy. Should she tell John about Walter? She decided that information was too confidential to share even with her husband.

"Bonnie's out sick tonight, and they don't have anyone to work."

"Why doesn't Sheila hire another librarian? If we lose Kim or I get a full-time job, you'll have to reduce your hours and the library will be even shorter staffed."

John had talked about looking for full-time work recently, so Alicia knew he had a good point. "She might be bringing that up at the Board meeting, John. I guess we'll know more on Friday."

Lucia appeared then at their table with a heaping bowl of linguini in red sauce. She laid it carefully in the center of the table along with a large serving fork.

"These also come with our house salad, guys, so I'll be back with that."

"Thank you," John told the waitress.

She returned in a few minutes with the salads and then headed back to the kitchen for the orders of the people at the back table.

John divided the house salad--lettuce and assorted greens, black olives, sliced tomatoes, and cucumbers doused in creamy Italian dressing—into two bowls for them to share.

"It sounds like you didn't have a good start to your day."

Alicia's stomach had settled a bit, and she managed to eat a bit of salad. "You could say that. Oh, and Laura needs me to help her bring Sneaky for his annual vet visit tomorrow. Her sister is using her car, so I'm driving them."

"No worries. Just be sure to remove the car seats before you take the car. The babies aren't allergic to cat fur, but it might be tough to fit Sneaky's carrier in there with the two seats in the back. I can do it for you when I get home if you'd like. I really should speak to dad about bringing Fido to Dr. Clark. He used to take him to Dr. Pinkerton in Carlsville, but now that we have a town vet, it might be a better idea to see her."

Alicia finished her salad and pushed the plate aside. "Thanks for taking care of the car seats, John. I can check if Donna has any openings for Fido this week if you want."

"Thanks, but it can probably wait until we get back from New York. Fido's in fine health despite his age, and I would need to help Dad bring him. I'll be busy the rest of the week preparing for the town hall meeting and having lunch tomorrow with the new and improved Ramsay," he winked. "I also have a job interview on Friday morning."

This was news to Alicia. She gasped. "You do? Where?"

"At Columbia. A friend of mine called me the other day while you were at work and told me there's a position there teaching in the journalism department. He thought I might be interested. There's a lot of competition, so I'm not that confident I'll be chosen, but I thought I'd give it a shot, anyway."

Alicia was surprised and a bit concerned that John hadn't mentioned this sooner. "It's a long commute into the city, John. How would you manage it?"

"Let's eat, Ali, before the food gets cold." John began to scoop the linguini onto her plate.

"No you don't, Mr. McKinney. Answer my question." She directed her gaze at him. He immediately put the serving fork down.

"I thought about that, and like I said, it's a long shot. But if I get it, I might have to stay there during the week and come home on weekends. We would need to make some adjustments, but the pay would be so much more than I'm making in Cobble Cove from all my little jobs."

Alicia had completely lost her appetite. She looked around for Lucia.

"Get the waitress. I want to leave."

"Ali, it's not as bad as it sounds, and it probably won't be necessary."

"Then why are you even going on the interview? John, we have two young babies. Even with Kim and your dad, I can't manage without you."

Alicia thought of Sheila and how she had raised her daughter alone after her husband died young, also of Jean who was the single mom of Jeremy. She didn't know how they did it, but their circumstances were due to necessity and not a spouse's whim. She became angry. She didn't like being put on the defensive, but she couldn't help it.

"You are so darn stubborn, Mr. McKinney." She stood up from her chair. "You refuse your sister's help when she's happy to give it, and now you're thinking of deserting me when I need you the most."

Tears began to form behind her eyes, but these were hot and not the cold ones she'd almost shed for Angelina.

John got up and put his napkin on the table. Lucia, coming out of the kitchen, came over to them.

"Is something wrong? I can get you another dish if you're not happy with that one."

"No. That's okay," John said, throwing some bills on the table. "I hope this covers our lunch. My wife is not feeling well, and I need to take her home. We'll be back another day."

Alicia grabbed her coat, put her arms through the sleeves, and walked ahead of him without a word. John apologized again to Lucia and followed Alicia past the festive Christmas tree and out through the garlanded door.

When they were outside, Alicia turned to him. "I don't have to be back at the library yet, but I might as well check in early."

"No." John took her arm. He gently, but firmly, backed her against one of the sentinel toy soldiers.

"You haven't even had lunch, nor given me time for an explanation. I want us to go up to Cove Point and talk. It's not too cold, and we're dressed warmly."

Cove Point featured a lovely view of the town. It was a special place for them, and Alicia didn't have the heart to go there now where those good memories might be clouded.

"I can't, John. Don't ask me to do that. I'm not in the mood to talk."

John sighed. "Look at me, Ali."

She turned and saw the regret and love in his eyes. He pulled her close and kissed her tenderly on the lips. A few stray snowflakes drifted down on them.

"Believe me, I don't want to leave you, but this is something that might be best for both of us and the babies, too. I know you can't see that now, but I have to give it a try. Don't be mad at me, Ali. Please."

Even though she heard the sincerity in his voice, she pushed away from him. "This might be a good opportunity for you, John, but I wish you would've consulted me before you agreed to the interview. I am your wife, after all."

John sighed. "Let's go to Cove Point. It's snowing a little, but I think we'll be able to talk better there."

He glanced behind him as a few diners headed into the restaurant.

Alicia still wasn't happy about going to their favorite spot while her anger still simmered, but, rather than make a scene in front of La Bella, she followed him across the Green noticing that most of the shopkeepers were no longer outdoors. The day had turned chilly, and many of them were probably having lunch or manning their stores to serve their lunchtime customers.

Taking John's "secret" path, which she now realized most Cobble Cove residents were aware of, they climbed the hill together to their special spot.

"Let's sit by the rock," John said referring to the large stone that overlooked the best vantage point of the village and cove. Alicia pulled her coat closer around her as the wind, picking up velocity, whipped through her clothes and blew her hair across her face.

"Maybe this wasn't a good idea, John."

"We won't be here long. I just need to clear my head a bit. This is the place where I can do that."

He beckoned to her to join him on the rock. His hair was also tousled, and it gave him a boyish, devil-may-care look.

Alicia took a seat on the boulder and glanced around. The snow was still intermittent, tiny wet flakes hitting the air every so often. To her right, she could see the village, the houses and businesses as well as Cobble Corner. Both dirt and highway roads wound through the town dotted by winter bare trees and some evergreens. There were many more houses now. John and his father had managed to keep up with the growth, and Mac still handled much of the real estate sales. They had formed "McKinney and Sons Realty" after Pamela deeded the town with construction money. As sales ebbed off, John stepped back to work on their mystery series. He hadn't returned. Another project uncompleted. She could understand his frustration.

For a few minutes, they sat quietly together, his arm around her to help warm and shelter her from the wind. The town below them, despite its expansion, was still the quaint village that reminded her of a Thomas Kinkade painting. It bustled more now but was never crowded. She glanced down at the roofs of the stone and brick buildings and thought about the new people living and working in Cobble Cove—Leslie Dalton, the school nurse; Jean and her son Jeremy; Laura and Lily and their family; Walter and

Gloria; the Romano's from La Bella; and, of course, Patty, Gary, and Angelina.

John took a deep breath from beside her, exhaling a cloud of cold air. "Can we talk some more about the interview, Ali? I want to make sure you understand why I'm doing this."

She turned to face him. His cheeks had turned red. She imagined hers were, too.

"I do, John. I just didn't expect it when you told me. You made me feel left out."

"I know." John took his arm from her back and rubbed his hands together. He hadn't worn gloves. Neither had she. Her hands were in her pockets.

"I'm sorry I didn't tell you sooner. I guess I was afraid you wouldn't take it well. I also apologize for ruining our lunch. I'll make it up to you in New York. There are some fine restaurants there."

Alicia turned her gaze to the left out toward the cove. The water was dark and rough. There wasn't a boat in sight.

Although she still felt upset, Alicia decided to let the subject go for the time being. "You said Pamela's coming Saturday morning. I guess we'll have some time to go over things before we leave. I'm hoping to do all our packing Friday night."

"I'll help. You know I don't pack much, but I realize you women like to take the kitchen sink or rather the bedroom closet with you on vacation." He smiled.

"I'm not that bad. It's just good to have extra clothes, just in case. Remember the bind I was in when I only packed for a weekend in Cobble Cove and ended up staying in town longer?"

"If you run out of clothes, you can purchase some in the city. I'm planning to buy you a few things, too. I'm sure Sheila and Pamela can both give us great advice on where to shop." Sheila was known for her trips into the city to purchase her fashionable outfits, and Pamela had an apartment there.

"I thought we were on a budget. Prices are high in New York."

"I can splurge on my wife a little." John replaced his arm around her. "I know you're cold, but it's such a pretty sight down there. It refreshes me. I love this town, Ali, and I love you. I'm not leaving either of you."

He placed his finger under her chin in the familiar, affectionate gesture and tilted it up to look at him. His touch was cold, but still managed to warm her. They looked into each other's eyes, and then his lips were on hers, warming her whole body. She felt her anger melt. The kiss lasted until they came up for air and then John broke away, his face red from passion now instead of the cold.

"I think I should take you back to the library. I have to get home, so Kim can make her class."

Alicia got off the rock, her legs a bit wobbly from a combination of their romantic interlude and sitting on the hard surface in one position for a length of time. She glanced at her watch.

"Yes, it's almost time for me to get back. I'll be home to check on you and the babies later when I take dinner. I'm sorry I can't be there tonight."

"Like I said, it'll be a daddy's night for me." John slid off the rock next to her.

As they headed down the hill, Alicia caught a glimpse of the man she saw near the gift shop after she bought Kim's earrings. He was walking away from Cobble Corner in the direction of town.

"Do you know that man, John?" she asked pointing her finger toward him.

"I can't see him that well from this distance but he doesn't look familiar. Why?"

"He seems to be hanging around town. I noticed him when I was shopping yesterday. He looked at me when I passed, but he didn't return my smile. I thought that was odd."

"Don't you know better than to smile at strange men when you're a married lady, Mrs. McKinney?" John grinned, but Alicia felt another sharp gust of wind rush through her. It wasn't the only thing that caused her to shiver. The man in the trench coat had turned down their street.

Chapter Six

Back at the library, the rest of the afternoon went quickly and rather smoothly for Alicia even though she still felt somewhat uneasy about her second encounter with the Cobble Cove stranger. When Donald was on a break and Jean was helping Vera put up some additional holiday decorations in the reading room, Sheila came by the Reference Desk.

"How did it go with Bonnie?" Alicia asked. She hadn't seen the director since she returned from lunch.

"She'll be back tomorrow." Sheila glanced over her shoulder and lowered her voice. "I promised her she wouldn't be left alone at the desk at night. I'm sure she just took things the wrong way, but I want to make sure she's comfortable here. She's a good employee. I'm not writing Walter up. He's had a warning, and I think that's all that's necessary at this point."

Alicia nodded. Walter was changing some light fixtures in the children's room and couldn't hear them.

"So, how was your lunch?"

Alicia averted her gaze. "It was nice," she replied. "I didn't have much of an appetite, though." John had offered to take her to Casey's on the way back for a quick burger, but she'd declined, and her rumbling stomach reminded her she'd have to wait for dinner to refill it. She considered grabbing a snack from the vending machine in the staff lounge when she went on her fifteen-minute afternoon break. If she was lucky, Jean would have brought in some of the delicious muffins she often baked for Jeremy to share with her co-workers.

"That's too bad," Sheila said. "After seeing Bonnie, I picked up a cake from Claire's bakery that I put out upstairs. I guess you won't want any, but you can bring a slice home to John when you go to dinner. Maybe the twins could have a taste, too."

"You sound like Claire and Gilly trying to fatten my kids up." Alicia laughed.

"Growing babies can afford the calories. I won't touch the stuff myself." She gave a short laugh. Sheila's trim figure attested to her deprivation of sweets. She was about an inch or two taller than Alicia, which also helped.

Donald and Jean returned to the desk. "What's that I hear about a bakery cake?" Donald asked.

"Now don't you go eating half of it, young man." Sheila waved a finger at him jangling one of her rings. Donald was known to devour break room desserts, but was thin despite his high caloric intake, which frustrated Vera and Jean who both had a hard time keeping their weight down.

Donald grinned. "Sorry, but it's hard to resist Claire's cakes. I used to stop there on my way home and pick one up for Rog and me to share, but he's on a health kick these days and won't allow the stuff in the house."

"Good for him." Sheila turned around and faced the front door. "I'm going back to my office. You guys can squabble over the cake. Just don't get any blood on the floor or I have to pay Walter extra for cleaning it." Another short laugh echoed through the air as her heels clicked toward the staircase.

Donald stuck out his tongue and made a face. "She's a party pooper."

Alicia's stomach rumbled.

"Sounds like you could use some of that cake, Alicia. Why don't you go on your break now?"

"That's a good idea, but don't worry, Don, I'll be sure to save you some."

***

Laura was upstairs when Alicia got there. The black forest cake, one of her favorites, was already missing three slices. A chocolate covered knife sat next to it on a serving plate. A few paper plates, plastic forks, and napkins were also on the table.

"The devil made me do it." Laura laughed, licking some chocolate from her fingers. She tossed an empty paper plate with a few crumbs and a balled-up napkin into the trash can near the table.

Alicia laughed as she cut herself a large piece. "I don't care if the devil makes me do it. I'm starved."

Laura lifted a blonde brow. "I thought you were going to La Bella for lunch. Italian food always fills me up."

Alicia didn't want to explain to the young librarian what happened, so she told her the same thing as Sheila. "I didn't have much of an appetite at lunch, so I guess I'm making up for it."

"That's what happens to me. Then I go to the gym to try to burn it off, but it would take three hours there to do that."

Alicia felt no sympathy for the girl. When she was in her twenties, she could eat almost anything without gaining an ounce but now, being in her forties and having gone through pregnancy, the pounds seemed to come on if she went one calorie over her daily allowance. Luckily, all the walking around town seemed to help, but she knew she could easily tip the scales if she didn't curb her sweet tooth. Now she just dug into the dessert, savoring the syrupy cherries and chocolatey devil's food cake.

She swallowed and said, "Sneaky Storytime was great today. Having Fido as a special guest was an added bonus for the kids."

Laura smiled showing teeth that, like Kim's, should've been restrained by braces years earlier. "It was Sheila's idea. She's still lukewarm around Sneaky, although I know she has a soft spot for him. As for Fido, she and Mac are good friends and that extends to his dog."

Alicia nodded.

"Jean told me the sad story about Angelina." She threw away her empty plate so she would avoid going back for a second slice of cake.

Laura's blue eyes clouded. "Yes. I feel so bad for Angie and her parents. My family is lucky that none of us has any major illnesses. Lily has asthma and mom's arthritis is getting worse, but, knock on wood," she tapped the table, "No cancer or heart disease and no one has ever needed a kidney or bone marrow transplant like poor Angie. Medical costs are astronomical when you don't have insurance. Patty's plan with the school doesn't cover that type of thing and neither does Gary's grocery job. The Christmas Fair committee is trying to raise funds for them, but it'll probably only amount to a pebble in a bucket."

Alicia sighed. "I was thinking that. I spoke to John about asking Pamela to help those poor people, but he's right that his sister can't be expected to save the world if you know what I mean. She's done so much for us and the town. Is it definite that Angie will need a bone marrow transplant?"

"It's a matter of time. She may look good right now, but that could change suddenly. She goes to a doctor in New Paltz regularly to check her numbers. I hate having blood tests, but she's a real trooper."

Alicia glanced at the clock in the break room. She'd been up there longer than her allotted fifteen minutes, but most of the library workers didn't keep to the limit.

"I have to get back. I'm working tonight, so I'll be taking dinner in an hour and then returning."

"That stinks. Sheila wants me to start working nights, too, but I'm not sure I can manage it. I usually watch my brother Henry once or twice a week when my parents work a late shift. He's probably old enough to stay home alone, but mom would worry, and no one else can usually do it."

Alicia knew the youngest Carson child was twelve years old and in seventh grade at the Fairmont School. In another two years, he would have to commute elsewhere unless they opened the high school they'd been planning to build for two years.

"That's tough. Maybe Sheila will hire someone else."

"I certainly hope so. The Board meeting is Thursday. I think that's on the agenda." She lowered her voice. "There's another reason I'd rather not work late. I don't mean to frighten you, but this strange guy spooked me the other night when I was shopping in Cobble Corner after work. As I came out of the gift shop, he was there smoking. It smelled like a joint, and he looked like he was high. He stared at me with glassy eyes and started to follow me to my car. Luckily, there were people in the parking lot and a man was loading some packages into the trunk of the car next to mine. When the weirdo saw him, he turned around and went back toward the stores."

Alicia's stomach began to knot, and she was glad she'd already had cake because her throat had gone so dry she could hardly swallow. She listened in shocked silence as Laura continued her tale.

"I could be wrong, but I think he had his eye on my bag. He may have wanted to mug me. Little did he know I maxed out on my credit cards and now only carry cash in small enough denominations that I won't be tempted to overspend." She smiled wryly. "Sorry to vent, Alicia. I'm probably just being paranoid. I should get back to the Children's Room. It starts to get busy now with the kids coming out of school."

As Laura began to walk away, Alicia wanted to call her back. She wanted to tell her that she had seen the same strange man. She would've done so had she been able to speak; but before Alicia could clear her tight throat, Laura was already downstairs.

***

The rest of the afternoon flew by. Alicia didn't have time to dwell on the disturbing thoughts that Laura's story had provoked. When she went home to dinner, she was surprised and thankful that John had cooked his special chicken dish. It was a recipe his mother had passed down to him that included tasty herbs from what was once Mac's garden. She could smell the aroma of the simmering chicken as she walked through the door.

"Hi, honey," John greeted her as she came into the kitchen. He was wearing her blue checkerboard apron. The twins were seated in their high chairs at each end of the table.

Alicia tossed her coat on one of the kitchen chairs, went over to give John a kiss and then kissed each of the babies.

"That looks delicious, John," she said stepping over to the stove where chicken slices slathered in a mushroom sauce simmered. There were two other pans on the stove, a pot of green beans and one of mashed potatoes.

"I wanted you to have some sustenance before you work tonight. Have a seat, and I'll serve you and the twins. Too bad they can't have any of this stuff yet." He eyed the baby food jars next to Johnny and Carol's plates.

"Oh, John. You didn't have to go through all this trouble."

"No trouble. I like to cook. You know that."

Alicia liked to cook too, but she hated the cleanup and never seemed to have enough time to experiment with recipes.

After John brought their plates over that were scooped with potatoes, green beans, and chicken pieces, she and John took turns feeding the twins. She loved seeing Carol take small scoops off her baby fork. Next to John, Johnny was licking his spoon. In addition to the baby food, they both gave the babies a taste of mashed potatoes.

"I have some sort of good news," John said. "The interview at Columbia has been rescheduled until after we get back from our trip."

Alicia concentrated on feeding Carol, pretending to ignore John's comment.

"Ali, did you hear me? You're not still angry about the interview, are you?"

"No, John. It's fine. It won't matter if you go to the interview today or tomorrow, next week or next month. It's the fact you're going at all that's the problem."

"I thought I explained that."

Alicia handed Carol back her fork and turned to her husband. "Let's not discuss this now. I don't want to get into another argument over a meal. You're doing what you have to do, or at least what you think you have to do."

"Okay, Ali. Subject changed. How were things at the library this afternoon?"

She hesitated before replying. "Nothing unusual. Sheila brought a cake from Claire's bakery, and I'm afraid I had to have a piece because it was my favorite, Black Forest. It didn't make a dent in my appetite, though, but I'll have to walk back to the library briskly now to burn up all those calories." She didn't mention what Laura had told her about the strange man in Cobble Corner. Even though she considered it too much of a coincidence that she'd seen the man herself again just that afternoon with John, she knew he'd probably dismiss both their concerns as imaginary.

"I like my wife with a few extra curves." His words were light, but she felt he was still upset over her discontent with his decision to go ahead with the interview at

Columbia. She couldn't pretend to be happy about it, although now her mind was troubled by other things.

***

After dinner, John offered to walk her to the library because it was dark, but Alicia didn't want the babies to go out at night.

"I'm perfectly fine, John. You were the one who said there's hardly any crime in Cobble Cove. It's only a few blocks, and I have a warm coat."

"You could take the car, Ali. I really don't like you walking after dark."

"All the homes are already lit up for the holidays, so I'll have lots of light to illuminate my path."

"That reminds me. I still have to put up our lights. I'll try to do that soon." He paused. "And, okay, I'll let you go yourself, my stubborn lady. I love and hate that about you."

He kissed her goodbye.

"You're pretty stubborn yourself."

***

They were at the front door. "I'll put the babies to bed before you get home. It should be quiet at the library tonight with everyone out shopping."

Alicia hoped he was right, but quiet wasn't necessarily good. She might end up being alone with Walter. And, even though Sheila was convinced Bonnie had taken his overtures the wrong way, what if she was wrong? Alicia knew the custodian probably wouldn't be dumb enough to try anything again after Sheila's warning, particularly with her. Teasing a young clerk was quite different from coming on to a married woman. Just the same, thinking about Walter as well as the man she and Laura had seen hanging around town Alicia regretted her decision to walk to work alone. She felt a tingle of fear as she headed toward

Bookshelf Lane, the warm, safe light of her house receding into the shadows behind her.

Chapter Seven

Donald was at the reference desk giving a tall brunette a computer pass when Alicia entered the library. Vera was replenishing books from the holiday display by the door.

"Is it five o'clock already?" she asked, glancing at the clock over the circulation desk. "I still have a couple of minutes. I wanted to finish this display. The patrons are grabbing up these books before I can put them out. I have to admit I've been reading some of them myself. Debbie Macomber always writes a new Christmas story each year and occasionally so do Fern Michaels and other popular romance authors. There are cozy mysteries with holiday themes, too. Sheila told me to be sure to put aside one of Leslie Meier's books for Jean to deliver to Mabel."

Mabel was the homebound patron who always requested mysteries. When Alicia first started at the library, she was put in charge of homebound deliveries. That was Jean's job now.

Donald handed the brunette the yellow slip with her computer log in and stepped away from the desk. "Hi, Alicia. Things haven't been too busy. There's nothing pending for tonight."

"Thanks, Donald. See you tomorrow." She noticed he had already gotten his coat from upstairs.

"Gotta run, so I can get dinner going before Roger gets home. I'm making a vegetarian dish tonight. I copied it from a cookbook. Rog is on a vegetarian kick now. He may even go vegan. I'm a carnivore, so it's not that easy. I have to sneak my cheeseburgers when I can." He laughed.

As Donald headed for the door, Alicia looked around for Walter.

Vera finished the display. "Bye, Donald. Alicia, I'm going upstairs for my coat and then leaving. You'll be alone for a few minutes. Walter's having his break." That explained why the custodian wasn't in sight.

"No problem." Alicia glanced around the room. There was only the lady who'd just signed up for computer use in the recently added computer room and a few other patrons browsing the aisles for books and videos. One elderly man sat reading a book in the reading room. She thought of Mac and wished he'd drop by, but he didn't go out nights much anymore, even with Fido at his side. Although his real-estate business was dropping off after last year's boom, he spent nights keeping records and filing paperwork. He still used the rare manual typewriter that he'd moved from the storage room to the cottage. John had suggested buying him a PC for Christmas, but she knew he'd be resistant and that it would probably just sit and gather dust. It wasn't that Mac was a technophobe, but he tended to cling to the past. He refused to buy a cell phone and didn't even own a microwave.

Vera returned wearing her puffy brown coat. "Bye, Alicia. Have a good night."

"Bye, Vera. See you in the morning." Alicia watched the older woman exit through the glass doors and head for her car in the parking lot.

A few minutes later, Walter strolled by the desk. Alicia was working on a cart of damaged books. Sheila had taped Alicia's name to it with a note to check if any of the items should be repaired or reordered. That was another job Mac still handled. Sheila sent him books with broken bindings that he taped and returned to the library in suitable condition to be put back on the shelves.

"Hi, there, Alicia," Walter said leaning against the reference desk. "Looks like it's going to be a slow night tonight."

Alicia tried to keep calm as she turned to him and not think about what Sheila had said. "Yes. I think so, too, Walter. People are probably in the stores." She looked back at the books. The computer patron logged off and left wishing them a good night. She was followed by a few other patrons. Only the elderly man remained reading in the other room.

"Have you done all your Christmas shopping?" Walter asked. "I still have to find a gift for Gloria. She's not easy to shop for. Every time I buy her something, she returns it." He waved a hand through the thin, gray strand across the top of his head. At least they were on safe ground if he was talking about his wife.

"Most people have trouble shopping for their spouse. I'm still figuring out what to get John."

"I'm sure you'll find something nice in the city next week. Gloria tells me you guys are taking a holiday there. Great time to visit with the tree up in Rockefeller Center and all."

Alicia wasn't happy the word was spreading about their trip. She still felt uneasy about leaving the twins, and she didn't want the whole town to know they were going away. John probably wouldn't care. He'd just consider it the Cobble Cove grapevine at work again.

"It'll be nice," she replied keeping her eyes focused on the books as she checked the wear and tear, stains, or other conditions noted on the small slips Sheila had left in them.

Walter finally got the message she wasn't in a talking mood. "Okay, I'll let you work and take a stroll around. If you need anything, I won't be far."

She tried not to read anything into the crooked smile he gave her. She berated herself for the way her heart began to race as the man in the reading room got up, hobbled out on his cane, and left the library. It was just her and Walter in the building now, and it was only six o'clock. How would she spend the next three hours there with him and not drive herself crazy with worry? The phone rang just then, causing her to jump.

"Cobble Cove Library, good evening. How can I help you?"

"Alicia. It's Gilly. I tried you at home, but John said you're working late."

"Gilly!" Alicia sighed with relief at her friend's voice. "I had to fill in some hours here. It's quiet, though, so I can talk."

She glanced around looking for Walter, but he had headed into the Children's Room. There was no one in there, but a sign directed any patrons needing help to the Reference Desk.

"Great! All the boys are on sleepovers tonight at friends. I can't believe I have one night to myself." She laughed. "The problem is I'll have to return the favor one day, and I dread the thought of adding even one more kid to this crazy place."

"They're growing up, Gilly. Pretty soon, you'll be missing them."

"I know I will." She paused. "Are you and John ready for your New York second honeymoon?"

"It's not a second honeymoon, Gilly, even if we are staying in a honeymoon suite."

"Nonsense, sweetie. It will be even better than the first. I could hear the excitement in John's voice when I asked him before I called you. He's planning some naughty stuff with you."

"Oh, stop!" Alicia knew the way her divorced friend's mind conjured up elicit scenarios from all the romances she read.

"Remember, you have to stop here first to pick up that special nightie I have for you."

Alicia made a note that she would have to buy Gilly and her sons' gifts before the end of the week and add them to her packing list.

"I'll be sure to do that, Gilly. Is that why you're calling, to remind me about the X-rated outfit you're giving me as a present?"

Gilly's laugh was raucous. "You're too much, Alicia. The nightie isn't X-rated. It's just a bit evocative. Don't you know that certain things are better left to the imagination?"

"In your case, everything is left to the imagination."

"I'll ignore that remark because I love you, honey. The actual reason I'm calling is that I wanted you to know I received a canvas letter today. It's from Sheila."

"Whoa!" Alicia was stunned. "Sheila sent you a letter about a position here?" *Why hadn't the director said anything about that?*

"It's actually from the Board, but Sheila's name is on the letterhead."

"I didn't know they were looking for another clerk. I thought they were addressing the hiring of another librarian at Thursday's meeting."

"Maybe they need a clerk, too. The letter says that it's just an inquiry if I'm interested. If I am, I'm supposed to mail it back and then I'll be contacted again to schedule an interview."

"How strange." Alicia would have to ask Sheila about it the next day.

"Don't worry, Gilly. I'll check with Sheila and clear this up. She should've said something to me about sending that to you, and she should know that you couldn't possibly consider the job."

The line was quiet a moment.

"But I can, Alicia. Since you left the library here, it hasn't been the same. I miss talking with you, not just on the phone. I also could use a change. I'll need time to get my house ready to be put on the market and take the boys out of school, but if Sheila is willing to wait, I'd love to take the position over the summer."

"Gilly, are you sure?" Alicia was surprised, but she considered that maybe it was Gilly's time to leave the past behind and start anew somewhere else as Alicia had two years ago. The house Gilly had shared with her cheating husband probably still held too many memories for her. If things went right and Gilly moved to Cobble Cove, Alicia would have her closest friend nearby and another babysitter for the twins.

"Yes, honey. I'm definite. I'm sending back the letter tomorrow."

"I'll let Sheila know. It would be great having you here, Gilly."

"You bet. I'll be able to help you woo your husband on date nights while Aunt Gilly watches your darling babies."

Alicia laughed. "You're the one who's too much, Gilly, but I love you, also."

***

As Alicia hung up the phone, Walter strolled by the desk again. He had a broom with him and was sweeping up crumbs one of the patrons left on the floor despite the fact there was no eating allowed in the library. She went back to checking the damaged books. No other patrons had entered the library since the old man left.

"You might consider closing early tonight," Walter told her as he emptied the crumbs in the wastebasket by the desk." I don't think anyone else will be coming here."

Alicia looked at the clock. It wasn't even seven. "I don't know. We always seem to get those patrons who arrive five minutes before we close to sign up for a library card or who have fines on their card that need to be cleared."

"So they'll just come last minute tomorrow night," Walter said. "Sheila should actually change our hours during the holidays."

"It doesn't matter what time we close. People will still come right before you lock the doors."

"You're probably right about that." Walter moved closer to the desk. Alicia was thankful the book truck stood between them. He hitched up his jeans, his stomach hanging over his belt.

"I guess you've heard what Bonnie said about me to Sheila."

Alicia now felt trapped behind the book cart instead of protected by it. She couldn't look at the custodian but tried not to sound nervous.

"I don't get involved in office gossip."

"Good for you." Walter stepped back, and she inhaled a breath of relief. "Just don't believe it. Bonnie took it the wrong way. Heck, I'm a happily married man. I don't flirt with girls young enough to be one of my daughters."

Alicia realized she didn't know if Walter or Gloria had kids of their own. They'd moved to town alone, but it was possible their children were grown and living elsewhere. She wanted to ask, but decided against it when Walter reached for his broom again.

"I'm going upstairs to sweep the staff lounge. I've already cleaned some of the fur from the children's floor that was left over from Storytime. Sneaky and Fido both seem to be shedding."

"Pets usually do that in the fall, so they can get their winter coats."

"In my experience, they shed all year. I have nothing against animals, but I don't like cleaning up after them. I'm glad Laura handles the litter box now. I made it clear to Sheila scooping the library cat's poops wasn't in my job description."

He gave her a crooked smile again and then walked toward the stairs with his broom.

***

The rest of the night passed slowly but uneventfully. A few patrons drifted in close to nine o'clock, but they only wanted to check out a few books and videos. Luckily, Alicia knew better than to close the registers early. Walter had not reappeared by the front desk. She assumed he had finished his cleaning and was relaxing in the staff lounge watching sports or news on the small TV kept up there.

Alicia's book-truck project had been completed an hour ago. She'd added notes with instructions to discard, mend, or replace each book. Sheila could check it in the morning. She yawned. The big hand inched toward twelve. *Why were the last few minutes at work the longest?*

She heard the jangle of keys and realized Walter was there to lock the doors after she left. Her doubts about him subsided as she'd had time to think things over. What he'd said about being a married man and that Bonnie took his words the wrong way echoed in her mind. He approached the desk.

"I bet you're ready to go home to the husband and kids."

"Yes." Alicia had hung her coat behind her on the chair at Reference and was slipping it on. "I hadn't planned on working tonight, but Bonnie called in sick." She almost bit back her reply as she realized what she was saying.

Walter's thick brows knitted together. "I hope she comes back. I didn't mean to frighten her."

"I'm sure you didn't." Alicia suddenly felt sorry for the custodian. "Sheila said she had a talk with her, and she'll be in tomorrow."

"That's good to hear. Sheila's a nice lady."

Walter looked at the clock. It was finally nine o'clock. "Time to go. Would you like me to drive you home? I can lock up quick."

Alicia hesitated. She had no reason to refuse the kind offer, but she hadn't allowed John to accompany her to the library, so why should she let Walter take her back?

"Thanks, but I'm fine, Walter. My home is just 'a stone's throw away' as my husband always jokes."

Walter nodded. "Fine. I'll lock up, turn off the lights, and be out of here right behind you."

He waited while Alicia walked out into the dark, cold night before switching off the interior lights.

Luckily, some of the light posts that still graced Cobble Cove streets and were adorned with garland this time of year provided illumination for her as she headed down Bookshelf Lane. In the distance, she could hear some Christmas music. Straining to hear the melody, she realized it was coming from the direction of Cobble Corner. *The shops must be keeping late hours for the holidays, she thought.*

Just as Alicia was about to turn on to Stone Throw Road, she heard footsteps behind her. No one else seemed to be on the road except her. The footsteps were muffled by the music coming from the shops, but she had good hearing. She began to walk faster. The steps behind her increased to match her pace. She was afraid to turn, but as the music swelled away, she heard someone breathing.

She was just a few doors from her house, John, and the twins. She had to make it there before her pursuer caught up to her. She didn't dare turn around. There was less light on this segment of road. Whoever was following her could easily hide in the shadows. She was tempted to take her cell phone from her purse and call John, but there wasn't enough time. If she paused, her pursuer would surely catch her. He was only a pace behind. Somehow, she managed to reach her door, panting and stumbling as John opened it.

"Ali, what's wrong? What happened?" He grabbed her as she fell into his arms.

"John, there's someone behind me . . . ."

It was only as she crossed her home's threshold into her husband's embrace that she dared to look back, but the outside light John had left on for her shone only on the empty walk.

"Come in, honey. You're shivering. I'll make you some tea. The babies are asleep. We can talk."

John pulled her the rest of the way in the house and closed the door. She noticed he locked it behind him, something he almost never did.

She tried to control her breathing.

"Did you see him, John? He was so close. I think it's the man we saw leaving Cove Point. Laura's seen him, too." It was only when she knew that she was safe that Alicia voiced her true fear.

John led her to the rockers by the lit fireplace.

"Let me get that tea for you, Ali. Please sit and try to calm down. I didn't see anyone. Maybe it was a possum or another night creature. They can be loud but hide from humans."

"No, John. It was a person. There was someone behind me. He followed me from the library. I think it's that stranger who's been hanging around town." Alicia was still shaking.

"Alright. I believe you. From now on, no more walking alone at night. I told you I was worried. It's usually pretty safe, but we have a lot of new people in town. It only makes sense that crime will increase. That's why they're considering hiring a sheriff for Cobble Cove. I'll definitely bring this up at the meeting tomorrow. I just hope Ramsay is the right man for the position. He wasn't all that helpful last time."

That didn't make Alicia feel much better. "I know zebras don't change their stripes too quickly or whatever that saying is, but Cobble Cove needs protection for its residents. Are there any other applicants?"

"I'll tell you after I get the tea. Warm up by the fire, and I'll be right back."

***

When John arrived with a tray of Alicia's favorite chamomile vanilla herbal tea, she finally had her breathing under control, and the shivering had subsided.

"Thanks, John."

"Now tell me exactly what happened." He sat in the opposite rocker and regarded her through troubled blue eyes.

"I'm not sure. I left the library and, as I was walking down the street, I began to hear footsteps following me. I didn't see anyone, but when I started walking faster, the footsteps quickened, too."

"And you didn't notice anyone else on the road?"

"No. I heard some music from Cobble Corner. I figured the shops were still open, but the sound of the footsteps was right behind me. I know it sounds crazy, and I should've looked back, but I panicked. I just wanted to get to the house."

"You did the right thing, Ali. I'm sure there's a reasonable explanation, but the main thing is you made it home okay."

Alicia took a sip of tea. The firelight and the warmth of the liquid began to calm her.

"Laura told me a story about a strange man she saw in Cobble Corner. His description matches that of the guy I've noticed. That probably was on my mind as I walked home even though I wasn't consciously thinking about it. I hate to admit it, but maybe my imagination did run away with me. Now tell me who else is running against Ramsay."

John smiled. "No one. That's the problem. We haven't exactly advertised the job, but Casey opened his mouth at the diner one night when Ramsay was there and, the next thing you know, we got an application from him."

"So why don't you advertise now?"

John took the second cup on the tray and brought it to his lips, blowing it a little to cool the tea.

"It's almost Christmas, Ali. We would have to wait until after the holidays."

"So what's the rush? Even though I still think that man Laura and I have seen around needs be checked out, there haven't been any crimes in Cobble Cove lately, at least I haven't read of any in the *Courier*."

"So you do read your husband's paper."

"Of course, John. And, yes, it's contained more news and less ads since Kim and Andy are helping."

"The gossip features are still strong, but the interns are doing a good job. I hope they can handle it by themselves while we're away."

"It's only for a week, but what about the work on my office? Did you talk to Andy about that yet?"

"Yes. He's happy to help. He seemed eager to do it. I think he was feeling a bit indebted to us."

Alicia took another sip of tea. "This will work out best for all of us, John."

"Are you feeling better?" John's eyes were full of concern.

"I'm beginning to calm down. It was such a scare."

"Ali, you're safe here. I'll make sure of that. Why don't we go upstairs? You've had a long day, and I think the babies are out for the night. Kim said they didn't have an afternoon nap today, so we may be in luck." He winked.

Now that the adrenaline of her fight or flight response had worn off, Alicia felt the weariness creep back in. She yawned as John led her to the bedroom, both of them peeking into the nursery as they passed by.

They changed into their night clothes, and then lay together in the dark, only the light from the baby monitor and their alarm glowed in the room.

John stroked her hair as he nestled her head against his chest.

"I think you need to rest, no matter how much I'd like to take advantage of the twins sleeping."

"I'm tired, John, but I could use some comfort."

"That I can definitely provide." He grinned and let her hair go. A strand of chestnut fell against the pillow, a touch of honey on the milky case.

Then they were touching, hugging, kissing. It was as if they'd been away from one another for days instead of just a few hours. Alicia forgot her fears about being followed and her concerns about the Columbia interview, as John pulled her nightgown over her head and tossed it on the floor next to her. He then slipped off his undershirt and slid out of his pants, throwing both garments in the opposite direction. They embraced and melted into one another.

"Oh, John!" Alicia gasped. She pulled him closer. From what seemed like a distance, she heard him groan and then what sounded like something ringing.

"Darn!" John stopped abruptly. He was breathless and angry. "Not again. Why didn't I turn off that phone, but who would call at this hour?"

He slid off Alicia.

"Just let it ring, John." Alicia's body was still quivering in anticipation.

"Sorry, Ali. It could be important, and it might wake the babies." He pressed his lips to her forehead with a scowl of disappointment.

The ringing continued.

"I'll get it." Alicia rolled over toward the phone.

"It better not be someone selling something or Mary Beth again." John's voice was tight.

"Hello," Alicia said.

A young male voice she didn't recognize at first replied. "Is Mr. McKinney there?"

"Just a moment." She covered the receiver with her hand. "John, it's for you. I think it's Andy."

"Andy?" John was already out of bed putting his pants back on.

"Andy, is that you?" John's anger had dissipated. Alicia heard Andy's anxious voice through the phone but couldn't make out his words. Andy had called once before at this hour with a breaking story when Cobble Cove Stables had caught fire. Luckily, it hadn't spread, and the horses were all fine including Starburst, the pony Pamela had gifted the babies. The twins would soon be old enough to ride her.

"Okay. Hold on. I'll be down in a few minutes. Have the police been called?"

Alicia glanced at the clock as John put down the receiver. It was almost eleven.

"What's going on?" She had already slipped her nightgown back on.

John's face was grim. "There's been a robbery in one of the shops in Cobble Corner. I'm sorry, Ali. I have to get down there." He started dressing.

"Oh, my God! Which store?"

"The gift shop. They closed at ten, but Irene came back because she forgot something. She found the door lock picked and even though the register still had a little money in it, the jewelry case was smashed and empty. She called 911. Andy was driving home from school when he passed by and saw all the commotion. He phoned me from his cell."

"How awful!" Alicia thought of Kim's earrings and the other lovely items in the glass case by the register. She got off the bed and rolled her feet into slippers.

"You go back to bed, Alicia. I have to go there, but I'll be back as soon as I can."

"I won't be able to sleep, John. I'll wait for you downstairs."

She followed him, taking a quick look in the nursery at the sleeping twins who were making sleepy noises as they turned in their cribs. So innocent. Unaware that even in a small town like Cobble Cove, there were bad people who did bad things.

She walked John to the door as he pulled on his coat. "Lock up when I leave, Ali." His voice was firm, and then his lips were on hers for a quick but intense kiss.

"I'll make this up to you." He looked down at her, his blue eyes sharp with a mingling of passion and regret.

Chapter Eight

Alicia didn't know what to do with herself while she waited for John. She paced back and forth in the living room and then decided to go upstairs to check on the babies again. Seeing they were safe and still sleeping, she went back down and got herself another cup of tea. She considered something stiffer, but she wasn't a drinker. She chose tea because coffee would keep her up the rest of the night when she had to go to work in the morning.

She sat staring into the fire hardly tasting the drink, her mind racing with possibilities. What if the person following her had been the one who broke into Irene's shop? Could it have been the strange man she and Laura had seen hanging around town? Even though Alicia's pursuer had turned down Stone Throw Road behind her, he could easily have gone in the opposite direction after running away. The shops had been open while she walked, but they would've closed shortly afterwards. But who would steal from poor Irene? There were too many questions, and Alicia realized her only choice was to wait for John and some answers. Maybe they'd even caught the culprit by now.

She checked the clock again and saw it was only an hour since John left. Just as she'd put away her empty tea cup and was about to make another round upstairs, she heard John's car pull into the driveway.

Rushing to the door, she flung it open. John walked in, his face somber. He hung his coat on the rack by the door and then walked with her to the chairs next to the fire. His face told her he knew she would want the details, but he wasn't happy about relating them.

"Ali, it was bad. The shop was full of glass from the broken jewelry case. Irene was in tears. The officer who came from New Paltz tried to calm her down and suggested she take something to sleep tonight, but I doubt she'll follow his instructions."

Alicia recalled how, not too long ago, she'd suffered the same feeling of violation when she'd seen her burned down house. Even though Irene hadn't lived in the shop, she'd worked there every day, arranged its counters, and decorated it for the holidays. Now that special place wouldn't be the same to her. Had she been at the store when it was broken into, what would've happened? Did the robber carry a gun or knife?

"Do they have any clues? What are the police doing about this?"

John shook his head. "They took some notes and tried to get some prints off the register but, of course, Irene's would've been on it, and it's more than likely the robber wore gloves. Besides the jewelry, not much money was actually taken. Andy and I helped sweep up the glass. I don't think this will be a priority case. No one was injured."

"But John, if Irene was in the shop when . . . ." Alicia let her words trail off, but John got the gist of her thoughts.

"She wasn't. She locked up at a little after ten. There were still carolers in the village, so she spent some time listening to them and also stopped to pick up some muffins in the bakery. Claire was just about to close. By the time Irene got back to her car and realized she'd left her car keys in the shop, everything was closed and the carolers had gone home. She walked back to the store and saw the door wide open. She must've gotten there only a few minutes after the robber."

"Oh, my God!" Alicia could imagine Irene's terror upon seeing her shop broken into, glass on the floor, and the register open. "This must be the first time one of the shops in Cobble Corner has been burglarized. Will you be writing it up in the *Courier*?"

"Andy took notes for the story, but I'm hesitant to run it. On one hand, it might bring out any witnesses if there are any and warn others to take stronger safety measures, but it also might give the wrong ideas to some loonies out there. There's nothing worse than copycat criminals."

"I bet you wish the days of front-page headlines featuring women breaking heels on the church steps or people winning big at Bingo were still here."

John grinned, but his eyes stayed serious. "I thought about what happened to you tonight. I hate to think Cobble Cove is becoming a dangerous place to live."

"John, is it possible the person who followed me broke into the gift shop?"

"Maybe. Maybe not. But I wish you'd looked behind you. I know it's dark on this road, and you may not have seen much. I'll bring up replacing and adding more street lights on Stone Throw at the meeting Friday."

"So you believe that someone was after me?"

John sighed. "Ali, I don't know. I didn't mention it to the police. Maybe I should've. I still don't think much will be done until we hire our own sheriff. Even more reason that motion should be passed at the town meeting."

Alicia suddenly remembered Gilly's call earlier that night. "I forgot to tell you, John. Gilly called me when I was at work and told me she received a canvas letter from Sheila for a job at the library. I found it strange because Sheila didn't say a word to me. I have to ask her about it tomorrow. Once she hears about the gift shop burglary, I'm not sure Gilly will still be interested in moving here."

"I don't think one incident will scare her off, Ali. Not after dealing with three boys. I'm sure she misses you, and it would be a great thing for both of you if she relocates to Cobble Cove."

Alicia stood up. "Let's go to bed, John. Not that I will sleep well the rest of the night, but we do have to get up tomorrow. I feel so bad for Irene. I'll have to stop by the shop after work and talk with her. Do you know if it will be open tomorrow?"

"It's cleaned up, but I think she plans to close it until the weekend. She has to make a report to the insurance company, so she can replace the jewelry."

John got up and took Alicia's hand. "I don't know if either of us are in the mood for picking up where we left off, but it sounds like the twins are still sound asleep. I promise to take the phone off the hook this time."

There was a glint in his eye as his voice thickened with pent-up passion.

***

Although Alicia was still wound up, she found herself stirring at John's touch as they lay in bed together. Making love helped her forget, for the moment, the concerns of the night.

Afterwards, they drifted off together in one another's arms until the alarm and two babies crying woke them at seven o'clock. Alicia jumped up automatically, while John turned, his eyes still closed.

"Give me a minute, Ali, and I'll come help with them," he murmured groggily.

Alicia was used to this regular morning scenario where she would rise first, go to the nursery and spend some time with the twins before John would get up and join her. Then the two of them would carry the twins down to the kitchen, prop them up in their high chairs, and the family would eat breakfast together.

In the light of day, Alicia tried to convince herself it had all been a nightmare – the heavy, quickening steps behind her as she turned down Stone Throw Road and then the call from Andy shortly afterwards alerting them that Irene's store had been burglarized.

The smiling face of her babies as she entered the nursery, calmed her thoughts. She busied herself changing their diapers and clothes, talking and playing with them as she did so. Carol was starting to make sounds that were close to words, while she had the feeling Johnny would be the quieter one, the thinker like his dad.

When John joined them, she was on the floor with the twins tickling their tummies and coaching them to roll over. They hadn't yet mastered the motor skills to crawl.

As soon as John entered, Carol and Johnny rolled over in his direction.

John picked both of them up, one in each arm, something Alicia now had difficulty doing because of their size.

"Why don't you get dressed, Mother, and I'll take care of these two?"

Alicia left him with the babies and got ready. Then she gave John a turn in the bathroom.

At the breakfast table, John served Alicia eggs and toast while she fed the twins baby food and gave them their bottles. Then he made up a plate for himself.

When they were all seated, John brought up the plans for the day. "I know you're going to the vet with Laura at lunch, Ali, and I'm meeting Dad at Casey's to eat with him and Ramsay." He grimaced. "Even though I'd like to see this town better protected, I still can't believe that cop will be the best one suited for the job."

"So what are you doing the rest of the day?" Alicia asked spooning Gerber 1st Foods peaches into Carol's mouth and wiping the yellow dribble around her lips with her bib.

John was doing the same with Johnny who was licking his baby spoon clean.

"I'll be at the newspaper office this morning working with Andy. As much as I dislike doing it, we have to run the robbery article. After lunch, I'll come home to relieve Kim and try to do some writing if the babies will let me. It won't be long before they stop taking their afternoon naps altogether, and then we'll be in trouble."

He looked back at Alicia with a smile that showed her he was kidding. He was a great father and all too happy to spend time with the twins.

"I thought you were waiting until our trip before attempting to write again, John." Alicia was worried he'd become despondent and have another outburst while she was at work.

"I'm not pushing it, Ali, but if the ideas come, I'm going to take advantage of getting them down. Don't worry, I've got a handle on it now. I'm confident I'll get past this block, if not here, then in New York."

Alicia was hesitant to bring up his pending job interview scheduled for when they returned, but she had a feeling he would be preparing for that, too. She'd promised him she would cope if he was offered the position; but after the happenings of the previous night, she was less sure she'd be able to do that. She could hardly imagine staying in the house alone with the twins five nights a week.

Having finished feeding Johnny, John dug into his own eggs and toast. She pushed hers aside.

"What's wrong, Ali? Not hungry?"

She avoided his eyes. "I'll have something on break at work. I don't have an appetite right now."

She knew John saw through her excuse, but he didn't comment. Instead, he got up and cleared the breakfast dishes.

"I'll wait for Kim. You're taking the car today, right?"

Alicia heard the barely concealed relief in his voice and realized he was worried about her walking to the library after last night's experience. She was sure she could face the streets of Cobble Cove in daylight and could use the fresh air, but she needed the car to take Laura to the vet at lunchtime.

"Yes. I need to have the car with me today. I wish I could walk. It looks like it's going to be nice."

"I took out the car seats yesterday, so there's room for Sneaky's carrier."

"Thanks."

John leaned over and kissed her. "Try to keep your mind off last night, honey. You have my number programmed into your cell if you need anything. These things are bound to happen, especially near the holidays when people are frantic for some extra cash."

He was referring to the burglary, but what about her pursuer? Was he after money, too? She carried very little cash and just one credit card.

She stood up and gave Carol and Johnny kisses. John walked her to the door and helped her into her coat.

"I'll see you tonight, Ali. If Sheila asks you to work late again, I'll shoot her." He laughed, but she could see the worry in his eyes. She realized he was taking her experience just as seriously as she was, but didn't want to alarm her.

"Bye, John. Good luck with Ramsay."

Chapter Nine

Thanks to Cobble Cove's infamous "grapevine," word had already spread through the community. When Alicia walked into the library, Sheila, Donald, and Laura were huddled by the front desk talking with a patron about the robbery.

"Cobble Cove used to be such a safe place except for that incident two years ago, but that happened on Long Island and just spread here," the elderly woman said.

"Crime happens everywhere, Mrs. Hynd," Sheila told her. "It might be someone passing through. The Cobble Corner shops are really not protected well. They don't even have alarm systems."

"But how would the robber know that unless he was a local?" Donald interjected.

"I saw some strange guy hanging around Cobble Corner the other night. I wonder if he's responsible for this," said Laura.

"You don't even live around here, how would you know if he was a stranger?" Donald countered.

As Alicia walked to the desk, the group quieted and turned to her. Donald finished checking out Mrs. Hynd's books. Alicia noted the circulation desk was empty, so it looked like Bonnie hadn't returned. Jean would have to take that post when she came in at eleven, but who would work that night? Alicia knew John would not be happy if she was asked to fill in again, especially after her experience the night before. Should she say anything about that to Sheila?

"Good morning, Alicia." The director walked over to her, the heels of her boots clicking across the library floor.

"Hi, Sheila."

"You look a little bit frazzled. Is everything okay?" Sheila appraised her with wide green eyes.

She might as well be truthful. "I didn't sleep well. John got a call from Andy about what happened at the gift shop and had to rush out there."

"I figured as much. The news is all over town. Why don't you go upstairs, hang up your coat, and get settled? Have a cup of coffee or tea in the lounge for a few minutes. The desk is covered. Bonnie is working the night shift today. I've given Walter a day off and called in Gladys. I'm opening up a position as a part-time night cleaner for her with the Board tomorrow night."

Gladys used to clean the library on Thursdays before it expanded, and Sheila had hired Walter as a full-time custodian. Gladys still worked on Thursdays, but it looked as though Sheila now saw the need for her to work nights.

"Come upstairs, and I'll fill you in," Sheila urged heading for the stairs. Mrs. Hynd took her books and thanked Donald. She passed Alicia on her way out and smiled.

Laura headed back to the Children's Room stopping Alicia with a tap on the arm. "Remember today's Sneaky's vet visit. Jean is going to cover my room at twelve, and Donald said he can wait until one if you go to lunch then."

"That's fine. I have my car, so we can go directly to Dr. Clark's."

"If the appointment takes too long, I'll cover," Sheila offered. "I usually eat at my desk and can do that anytime."

"Thanks." Alicia followed Sheila upstairs as Laura went to the empty Children's Room. There was no

Storytime scheduled for today, so patronage probably wouldn't pick up until after school.

"I can use another cup of coffee myself," Sheila said as they entered the staff lounge. She poured herself one as Alicia hung her coat up in the closet. Then Sheila took a seat at a table. Alicia joined her after also taking a cup of the reviving liquid. She usually only had one cup in the morning, but she was still feeling the effects of last night.

"I'm glad to hear you're giving Gladys more hours, but Walter was fine last night. I think you were right that it was just a misunderstanding between him and Bonnie."

"I hope so." Sheila stirred a packet of sugar into her coffee. "I just don't want her being uncomfortable. I'm still asking the Board to hire another clerk and possibly a librarian. I don't know how much of the budget we can spend. The treasurer should have those figures."

Now was the time for Alicia to mention Gilly. "Have you sent out canvas letters yet, Sheila?"

Sheila looked into her coffee cup. "How could I? I haven't even had the positions approved."

"That's strange. Gilly called last night and said she received one."

Sheila raised her head. A smile played across her lips.

"It was supposed to be a surprise, but I should've guessed your friend would've been too excited to keep it from you. I was pretty sure the Board would approve the clerk position. I actually had planned to present it to them before Bonnie's incident. I realize it will take time for Gilly to sell her house and get her kids transferred to school here, but I'm not expecting to hire anyone overnight. I thought it would be great for the two of you to be together again."

"Oh, Sheila. You are so kind."

Sheila raised a red eyebrow. "I also know about John, Alicia. He told me about the job interview at Columbia."

Alicia was surprised and slightly hurt. Why had John told Sheila before her? She knew the two of them were friends, but she was John's wife. She suddenly realized that Sheila had thought of hiring Gilly when John told her he might be away five nights a week in the city.

"Naturally, I wish him well," Sheila continued confirming Alicia's thoughts. "But I know the value of a close friend. Although he's not sure he'll get the position, I'm quite confident he will." She took a sip of coffee.

"When I first married, my husband travelled a lot. I was at home with our baby daughter. It was tough. My parents had moved away to Arizona to a seniors' complex. Dad loved to golf, and he enjoyed the community. They were both sick of the New York winters." She smiled. "I didn't really have a lot of girlfriends. If it wasn't for Mac and John, I would've really felt alone when my husband was away. And after he passed, well. . ." Sheila spread her hands displaying her rings, a sadness entering her eyes. "I can never repay them for all their support."

Since Sheila seemed to be confiding in her, Alicia felt she could share the events of the previous night. "Sheila, there's something I have to tell you about last night. I know you heard what happened at Irene's gift shop, but something happened to me, too."

Sheila's red eyebrows rose again in question. "It wasn't Walter, was it? You can tell me the truth, Ali. You don't have to protect him. I gave him a warning, and I need to know if he dared to ignore it."

"No. Walter was fine. I already told you that. It was after I left the library." Alicia took another sip of coffee, but the warm liquid turned cold as she recalled the footsteps behind her hurrying to meet her pace as she turned down the darkened street.

Sheila sensed her alarm. "What happened, Alicia?"

"I had just left the library when I felt that someone was following me. I heard their footsteps, and when I walked faster, they did, too. I could hear their breath so close even above the music from the shops. I was relieved when I got home and John was at the door."

Sheila's hazel eyes darkened to a deep green. She pushed her mug to the side of the table almost knocking it off the rim. "Did you report this?"

"What could I report? When I got home, the pursuer disappeared. I never saw him. I was too afraid to turn, and some lights were out on Stone Throw Road. John has promised to bring up their replacement at the town hall meeting on Friday."

"Hmmm." Sheila drummed two long red nails on the festive tablecloth. "I wonder if this person who followed you was the one who broke into the gift shop." So her thoughts mimicked Alicia's.

"You believe that someone was after me?"

Sheila stopped drumming. "Of course I believe you, Alicia. A woman's intuition should never be doubted. If you felt someone was behind you, I'm sure someone was, but the question is why?"

Before the conversation could go any further, Jean came into the lounge.

"Good morning, Sheila, Ali. I know I'm early, but Jeremy got to school on time for once, and I couldn't sit around the house any longer looking at all the housework I should be doing." She grinned as she hung her ankle-length gray wool coat in the staff closet after pocketing the matching gloves.

Alicia recalled Mac's turn on the adage, "The early bird catches the worm." John's father liked to say, "The early bird has more chances of catching the worm." She wondered what he thought of the burglary news.

Sheila stood up. "I guess we all should be getting to work. I have to prepare the agenda for tomorrow's meeting, so I'll be in my office the rest of the morning. If anyone needs anything, just buzz me upstairs."

She went to the sink and cleaned out her mug before replacing it on the wooden rack next to the sink. Alicia joined her there and did the same. She was a bit disappointed that they hadn't been able to finish their discussion about her mysterious pursuer and the possibility that he'd also been the one who'd stolen jewelry from Irene's shop.

***

The morning passed quickly as Alicia answered phones and assisted patrons with requests for information, books, or other materials. She focused on her work, trying to forget the previous night's incidents, but people kept bringing up the robbery. Every patron that entered the library began their queries with, "Did you hear about what happened at the gift shop last night?" or "Any word on whether they caught the robber who broke into Irene's store?" or "How is Irene holding up? If it was me, I'd close my shop and move out of here," this from a tall woman with a wide-brimmed hat covering her eyes; toting a bunch of mysteries to the circulation desk a few minutes before noon.

Vera just nodded as she checked out the woman's books. The lady kept going on and on about the dangers now lurking in Cobble Cove. Alicia couldn't help notice the bloody designs on the book covers as Vera placed them into a library bag and handed them to the woman.

After the hat lady left, Vera and Alicia both let out a laugh, and it felt good to lighten the situation.

"Next thing you know, Mrs. Wexler will be saying there's a murderer in our midst," said Vera when she caught her breath and pushed up her glasses that had slid down her nose.

Donald came over to the desk. "Don't laugh. Rog is concerned that this is just the beginning of a crime wave here. He told me this morning to check my wallet when I went into town and be sure to keep my car locked."

"It's that type of panic that starts copycat robberies," Vera pointed out. "The best thing to do is go about our daily routines in the same manner."

"I think you've all been reading too many mysteries." Laura had joined them from the Children's Room trading places with Jean to take her lunch break. "Although I still consider that man I saw in Cobble Corner very suspicious."

"Ready to take Sneaky to Dr. Clark's?" Alicia asked trying to change the subject. She wasn't in the mood to talk about her experience again.

Laura nodded. "Let me get my coat from upstairs, and then I'll put him in his carrier."

"Vet visit today?" Donald asked. "Lucky you than me. The last time I tried to help Laura get that cat into his box, I ended up with scratches all over my arms."

"You need to know the tricks," Laura said. "I don't really need Alicia to help today. I just need her car because my sister is using mine."

"Ah. Well, good luck to both of you. Sneaky looks so sweet when he's curled up sleeping in his bed, but he always keeps one eye open and is plotting to take over the world with his fellow felines. They've already taken control of the Internet."

Laura tapped Donald's arm. "Stop that! Cats are awesome. I've lived with them since I was a little girl."

"Then they've already brainwashed you." Alicia knew Donald was actually fond of cats and was just teasing the young children's librarian.

"Let's get going," Laura said ignoring him. "I know Sheila said we could have some extra time, but I don't want to be late. Our appointment is twelve-fifteen."

Alicia glanced at the library clock. It was already noon. She thought about John meeting his father and Ron Ramsay at Casey's for lunch and wondered if John would see the obvious change in the retired detective that Mac mentioned.

It was as she turned to head for the stairs that a male patron walked into the library toward the reference desk. Donald had gone back to his post and greeted the man. Alicia was startled to see that the patron was Ramsay. He was thinner than she remembered, but his dark, bushy hair and eyebrows were just as prominent. There was a scent, not unpleasant, wafting off him, a mixture of spicy musk cologne or aftershave. What gave him away, because he was dressed in civilian clothes, baggy brown pants and a tan vest over a checkered brown and white shirt, was his deep booming voice. But instead of the rude comments he'd been known to issue, he addressed Donald politely.

"Good afternoon. I'm on my way to a lunch meeting so don't have much time, but I was wondering if you could help me, sir?"

"I'd be happy to. What can I assist you with?"

Alicia wanted to hear the rest of the exchange, but Laura nudged her. "C'mon, Ali. We have to go."

As Alicia followed Laura upstairs, they passed Sheila's closed door. She imagined the director was still at work on the board meeting's agenda because her light was still on.

"Who was that man who just came in?" Laura asked as they both got their coats from the staff lounge. "You seemed surprised to see him. Do you know him?"

"I did, yes. He's the man who wants to run for sheriff."

"Get out of here." Laura's blue eyes opened wide.

"John and Mac are having lunch with him today. John hasn't seen him since he moved to town after retiring from the police force on Long Island. Neither have I, but we both heard he's changed from the nasty cop we remember."

"Really?" Laura seemed intrigued. "I'd love to hear more about that, but let's get Sneaky first."

She motioned for Alicia to stand guard outside the storage room/cat quarters as she opened the door and switched on the lights. Then, taking a package of cat treats out of her coat pocket, she shook the contents and called, "Sneaky. Where are you? I have some goodies for you." It sounded like she was a mother calling her baby, and Alicia imagined that's how she sounded when talking to the twins.

Alicia glanced into the room and saw Sneaky rolled up on his cat bed. When he heard the jingling of cat treats, he awoke with a start. She watched as the cat's ears became erect and the sleepy cat rose slowly, arching his back in a stretch. Laura patiently waited by the door, shaking the treat bag off and on until the cat approached, rubbing against her lower legs. She put two pieces down, and Sneaky gobbled them up.

When Sneaky finished his treats, he meowed and looked up at Laura, fully awake now. Laura sealed the bag and put it in her pocket.

"You'll get more if you're good at the vet's office," she promised as she slid him into his carrier.

Sneaky made a cry of objection as Laura swung the carrier out of the room.

***

When they arrived downstairs, Ramsay was already gone. Donald sat at the desk chatting with Jean. Alicia regretted she hadn't had a chance to observe the new Ramsay. She was curious as to what the man was looking for at the library and what John would report about him that night.

Laura jostled the carrier toward the exit oblivious to Sneaky's cries of confinement. Alicia walked in front with her keys ready to open the car.

"See you guys later," Laura called over her shoulder. "Wish us luck with our impatient patient."

"Just watch your fingers when you open that cage," Donald warned.

Jean chuckled. "Don't worry. Laura's got that tiger under control."

***

Dr. Clark's office was in her house on Marble Lane in the new development west of the shops. The house itself was of moderate size but large enough for the practice, Donna, and her pets. She had three rescues – a greyhound and two cats.

Alicia tapped on the office door using the cat-shaped bronze knocker. Donna Clark, her cinnamon-colored hair in a bun atop her head, answered immediately.

"Come on in, Ladies. My receptionist just went to lunch, but I'm all set to see you. Bring Sneaky back to the exam room."

They followed her through the carpeted front office where a few plastic chairs sat empty. The vet's waiting room was hardly ever vacant, but it was lunch hour, so they had come at a good time.

The pale blue walls of the exam room featured framed prints and photos of cats and dogs. Laura hefted the cat carrier on to the metal table. It was typical of cats to prefer to remain caged once they got used to their captivity and made fusses to be removed. Sneaky was no exception, but the vet deftly pulled him out while closing the case in one quick motion.

Laura smiled. "Good job, Dr. Clark. He's a fast one."

Donna squinted her gray blue eyes as she used some instruments she carried in her white smock to examine the cat's eyes and ears. Then she squeezed his mouth open to look inside.

"He looks quite healthy but is due for his rabies shot. I'll also need a weight on him." She picked Sneaky up and laid him down on a scale that Alicia thought she could've used for her babies when they were smaller. The dial registered fifteen pounds.

"Oh, my. He can afford to lose a little weight. Does he eat scraps?"

"His room is right outside the staff lounge," Laura replied. "I think some of the staff smuggles food to him. Even though Donald makes all those cat jokes, I think he's the biggest offender."

"That's not good," Donna said. "Today's cat food is specially formulated for feline needs. I would restrict him to that and cut back a bit on his dry food." She was petting Sneaky who was beginning to purr, finally adjusting to his new surroundings. "I'll go get the shot. Just watch that he doesn't make a run for it."

While they waited for Donna's return, they heard someone knocking at the door.

"Maybe we should get that since the receptionist is out," Laura suggested.

Alicia kept her hand on Sneaky who didn't look like he would vault when Laura opened the outside door, but she wanted to be prepared just in case he tried. She heard a woman and young girl's voices as Laura let the visitors into the waiting room.

"Thank you," the woman said a bit breathless. "I don't have an appointment, but I hope Dr. Clark can see us. My daughter is worried about Muffin. She hasn't eaten for two days, and Angie was so upset she didn't go to school today. I also had to take off work."

"Sorry to hear that, Mrs. Millburn. I'm here with my co-worker and Sneaky for his annual physical."

Alicia thought it was safe to leave Sneaky for a minute and stepped out of the exam room to peek into the waiting area. Patty Millburn stood there next to her daughter who held a cat carrier similar to Sneaky's. A low meow echoed from inside. The little girl looked pale and frightened.

"Is Muffin going to die, Mommy?"

"No, Angie. I'm sure Dr. Clark can do something for her. Go put Muffin down and have a seat. We just have to wait until she finishes with Miss Carson and her friend. Sneaky's here having his exam."

"Sneaky?" The girl's eyes lit up momentarily. "Can I see him?"

"When they come out."

Mrs. Millburn led her daughter to a chair. Laura headed back to the exam room as Alicia turned and saw Dr. Clark return with a needle for Sneaky.

"Is someone else here?" she asked.

"I just let Mrs. Millburn and her daughter in with their cat, Muffin," Laura said walking back into the room. "They were hoping you could see them. Muffin hasn't been eating."

Donna shook her head, and a strand of cinnamon loosened and fell across her forehead. In a low voice, she said, "Of course, I will. That poor little girl. She has enough to worry about."

She turned to Alicia who was closest to the exam table. "Please hold Sneaky while I administer the shot."

Alicia held Sneaky's hindquarters while Donna quickly inserted the needle into his tail.

"We don't give rabies injections in the back anymore because of the slight chance of vaccine site sarcoma. The formula is safer nowadays, though."

Sneaky made a short cry, but Donna had already removed the needle. "Good boy. He can go back in his carrier now." She helped Alicia slide him back in and closed the door.

"How old is Sneaky?" Laura asked.

"Judging from his teeth, I'd say he's about eight, which is starting middle-aged for cats, although many indoor ones are living until twenty today. Siamese cats are known for their longevity; so if you take good care of him, he should live a long life. Just be careful with the treats."

Donna handed the carrier back to Laura. "I know you ladies need to get to lunch, and I'd like to check Muffin now. It was nice seeing you both. Sneaky doesn't need to come back for another year unless he has a problem, of course, but I think Fido is due for his annual. Please let Mac know he should schedule an appointment."

"I will," Alicia promised.

"Thank you," Laura added.

Donna walked them both out to the waiting area where she motioned to Angelina and her mother.

"Hi, there. Please bring Muffin in, and I'll take a look at her."

"There's Sneaky," Angie said, her serious expression changing as she ran to Laura and looked inside the carrier. She tried putting her hand in to pet him, but Laura restrained her.

"Be careful, honey. He just had a shot."

"Can you take him out for me to see?"

"Angie, no, sweetie," her mother said. "The ladies need to leave now, and Dr. Clark has to see Muffin before her other patients arrive."

Although the waiting room remained empty, Mrs. Millburn's words seemed to have the desired effect on her daughter. She rushed back to Muffin's carrier and picked it up.

"Let's go then, Mommy. We want Dr. Clark to get Muffin better."

"I'll do my best," Donna said. "I also have a lollipop for you in my office, Angie."

The girl's face brightened, although Alicia could tell she was still very concerned for her pet. She followed the doctor eagerly to the exam room carrying Muffin's case.

Mrs. Millburn walked behind her. "Take care, ladies. See you at the library."

"Good luck with Muffin," Laura said. "I hope she feels better soon."

Alicia caught a glimpse of a pretty red tabby inside the case Angelina carried.

As she walked out into the chill December air silently praying that the little girl wouldn't lose her pet, Alicia's cell phone buzzed. She saw the caller was John. As Laura pushed Sneaky's cage into the back seat, Alicia placed the receiver to her ear and fumbled in her purse for her car keys.

"Hi, John. We're just getting out of the vet's office. What's up?"

John's voice came through the cell. "Perfect timing then, Ali. I was wondering if you and Laura have time to join us at Casey's?"

Alicia got behind the wheel. The time on the phone said twelve-fifty. They had been at the vet for less than an hour, and Sheila had agreed to let them off until two.

"I don't know, John. We have to bring Sneaky back to the library. It might be rushing things."

"You have to eat. I doubt Casey will be busy mid-week, and we have reservations. He shouldn't have a problem adding two more."

Laura probably figured out the conversation because she said, "We can make Casey's. You can just pull up in front of the library, and I'll run Sneaky in. I'll check with Sheila, but I'm sure she'll let us go."

"Okay. We'll be there within fifteen," Alicia told John.

She could almost see him smile through the phone. "See you then, honey."

She turned off the phone and started up the car. Sneaky was beginning to cry for release again, but both women ignored him.

As Alicia drove down Book Shelf Lane, she found herself eager for another chance to see the reformed cop.

Chapter Ten

Alicia pulled up in front of the library while Laura carried the box with the yowling Sneaky inside. She returned in less than five minutes empty handed and smiling.

"Boy, you're quick."

"Bonnie's here, and she gave me a hand. She took Sneaky back to his room. Sheila was at the desk, and she said we could take our time."

"How does Bonnie seem?"

"She's fine. She won't be working nights now. They want Donald to do a few. They asked me, too, but I can't do more than one. That's all that's in my hiring agreement, anyway. If they hire new staff members, it'll help a lot. Who knows how long that will take."

Alicia restarted the engine. "I'd rather not work nights either. John was a little upset last night when I did." She didn't add that she was even more upset after her episode with a pursuer.

"I don't know the whole story, Alicia, but I think something happened between Walter and Bonnie Monday night. Sheila's acting strange around him, and I know she called him into her office yesterday morning."

Alicia couldn't break the promise of secrecy she'd made Sheila, so she simply said, "Who knows, Laura. It's a good idea to have a clerk and librarian work at night, anyway. I don't know how Sheila and Mac managed with a staff of two all those years. Of course, the library was open less hours back then."

Laura was still creating her own hypothetical scenarios. "I think it's strange, Alicia. I've never worked alone yet, but I'd find it pretty creepy with just me and that custodian around. He's very quiet, but that's what they say about serial killers after they've committed ten murders."

Alicia laughed. "Have you been hitting the mystery section again, Laura?" She turned up the hill toward Casey's, hoping to get there soon, so the conversation would be finished. She was afraid they'd start discussing the man Laura thought followed her in Cobble Corner, and Alicia wasn't ready to relive her own frightening experience.

"I'm not saying he's a Charles Manson or anything, but it's types like those who are harboring dark secrets. If they ask me to work by myself in the building at night, I'm requesting that Gladys be the custodian on duty."

"How do you know about Charles Manson, Laura? I thought you were too young to recall anything that happened before 1990."

"I once considered becoming a lawyer and took a criminal justice course that discussed crimes of the past."

"Really?" Alicia was surprised. John had also taken law courses at Columbia before switching to journalism.

"Yes, but I'm happier being a children's librarian. The kids are so much fun. I'm sad about Angie, though. She's such a sweet girl."

Alicia parked in the diner's lot. "I know what you mean, Laura. It's terrible when a child is ill, and it must be even worse on her parents since she's an only child."

Laura's blue eyes became watery as if she were about to cry. She took a tissue out of her pocket and wiped at them. "Let's go meet the men. "I'm sorry, but I just can't talk about this anymore."

Alicia followed Laura as she headed for the front door of the diner. She could well understand how someone, especially a young woman as emotional as Laura, would be frustrated and sad about Angelina's situation. She, herself, found it difficult to fathom. If one of her twins was ever diagnosed with a serious condition, she wouldn't know what to do.

***

The three men were seated in the back of the restaurant. John was looking toward the door, and he waved to them. That wasn't necessary because Gloria, seeing Alicia and Laura enter, ushered them to John and Mac's table. As she led them to the back of the restaurant, she murmured to Alicia, "Packed for your trip yet?"

In all the activity of the past days, Alicia had pushed the plans for New York to the back of her mind. "I haven't even started," she admitted.

Gloria handed them each a menu as they sat down. John had pulled out the chair next to him for Alicia, and Laura sat on the other side near Ramsay, who looked like a third wheel sitting next to John's father. Up close, Alicia could indeed see the change in him. The detective was definitely thinner. His angular face, clean shaven for a change, showed it and he seemed to have lost his double chin. She still smelled the scent of his aftershave, but it wasn't masking any unpleasant odors.

"I'll be back to take your orders unless you want to place them now," Gloria said. "I know some of you are on your lunch breaks from work."

Laura glanced at the menu. "I'll just take the grilled cheese, my usual order when I come here."

"And I'll have the grilled chicken salad," Alicia added. She was glad Casey now had more variety on his menu and was even offering salads.

"What do you guys want?" Gloria asked, her pen poised over her pad.

"I think I'll just go with the cheeseburger and fries," John said. "You, Dad?"

"Same for me unless you have PB&J here, although it wouldn't be the same as mine."

Gloria grinned. "I should have you share your recipe with us, Mac. It might gain us more customers." She turned to Ramsay. "And what would you like, sir?"

Alicia noted Ramsay was fidgeting in his chair. She recalled how impatient he used to be and realized he still had to make an effort to control his hyperactivity.

"The grilled chicken salad, like Mrs. McKinney, please." He handed her back the menu. Alicia guessed he was still watching his weight. She was curious to see what other personal improvements he'd made in two years, and what had spurred them.

Gloria gathered the rest of the menus and walked toward the kitchen. She came back after dropping off their orders and brought water and a basket of rolls to the three businessmen sitting at the table behind them.

While they were waiting for their food, John started the conversation. "So, Ali, how did it go at the vet's? Did Sneaky get a clean bill of health?"

She laughed. "That and a rabies shot."

"Ouch!"

"He took it like a trooper."

"As long as he didn't pee on Dr. Donna." Mac's toothy grin showed his dimple.

"Oh, Dad!"

"By the way, Fido is due for his appointment," Alicia said. "You might want to call and schedule it, Mac."

Her father-in-law paused and then replied, "I'll do that when Betty and I get back. I was planning to tell you sooner, but I forgot. We're headed to Smugglers' Notch while you and John are in New York."

Alicia was shocked. "You're going skiing in Vermont?" Both Mac and Betty walked with the assistance of canes.

Mac's grin widened. "We may give it a go, but there are more things to do at a ski chalet than ski."

"Good for you, Dad." John winked. "I'm glad you and Betty are hitting it off."

Alicia thought it was time the old man found a companion of the opposite sex. She was also relieved that now she wouldn't have to worry about hurting his feelings by having asked Pamela and Kim to watch the twins.

"When are you leaving?" she asked.

"I have to be here for the Town Hall meeting Friday night, so it won't be until Saturday morning, Alicia. I also have a favor to ask. I know Pamela's watching Carol and Little Mac, but I was wondering if she could look after Fido, too. I considered boarding him with Dr. Donna, but he wouldn't do well in a cage. He could also help guard your house while Pamela's there alone with the twins. Are you okay with that?"

"Of course, Dad," John replied. "I hope Pamela doesn't mind. I don't know how she feels about dogs, but she's very fond of horses."

"Maybe I should call her," Alicia suggested. "I'll do that tonight. I'd like to speak with her, anyway."

"Sure." John turned to his father. "We'll let you know, Dad, but don't worry about Fido. Just enjoy your time with Betty. You both deserve it."

"What about you guys?" Laura asked. "If anyone needs a vacation it's you two. Your week in the city sounds totally awesome. I wish I could get away somewhere nice, but I'd rather go on a cruise. My sister and I always wanted to do that. One day," she mused.

Ramsay sat through this banter without a word. Alicia felt she needed to include him. "Detective Ramsay, how have you been? I saw you at the library this morning. Was Donald able to help you?"

Ramsay's eyes were still beady but less assessing than they used to be. "Yes. I was looking for some information about the shops."

"You mean about the robbery?" Laura asked.

Ramsay was about to answer when Casey came out of the kitchen and approached their table. "Hi, folks. Everything okay here? Is Gloria taking care of you all?"

"Hi, Casey," John said. "Yes, we've already placed our orders. Gloria's doing a great job."

"Then be sure to tip her well. I get a cut of all tips. Just kidding." He patted the back of John's chair just missing his shoulder. "How are you and the lady? Babies behaving?"

"The twins are great. Growing up fast."

Casey had never married and probably couldn't relate, but he twitched his salt and pepper moustache into a smile and peered at them through the thick lenses of his glasses. "Kids tend to do that. Oh, well. Enjoy them before they're teenagers. I'd wager one of those was responsible for the break-in last night."

Alicia flinched.

"That's not what I think," Ramsay put in from his side of the table. All eyes turned toward him. He hadn't said it loudly, but his deep voice tended to boom. *He might've made a good radio announcer if he hadn't gone into police work, Alicia thought.*

"Hmmm. What do you think, officer?" Casey asked leaning on John's chair.

"I'm not an officer anymore," Ramsay reminded him. "I retired two years ago, but I'm hoping to take the sheriff position here if the town approves it on Friday."

"Is that so? I'd give you my vote. We sure need some police protection here now." Casey was on the town board along with John, Dora's husband Charlie, and a few other male residents of Cobble Cove, as well as a few women including Sheila, Edith, and Rose.

"Thanks."

"So what's your thoughts on the crime then, Mr. Ramsay?"

"Inside job."

Alicia was surprised. Except for Irene, the only other gift shop employee was Irene's daughter, Maggie, a young single mother with a two-year-old son. She only helped at the store on Saturdays, Irene's day off.

"By inside, I mean a resident," Ramsay clarified before Alicia could comment. That was just as unimaginable. Alicia couldn't picture anyone from town breaking into the gift shop and smashing the jewelry case to steal the expensive items within.

"Interesting, and why do you say that?" Casey probed.

Both men waited for his reply, but Laura was drinking from her water glass and checking her cell phone. Alicia was surprised she wasn't taking the opportunity to mention the man in Cobble Corner to Ramsay. She wanted to say something about her own experience but wasn't sure this was the time. A look from John told her to remain silent. Maybe he had plans to talk to Ramsay privately.

"I've looked into some things. I'd rather not go into details right now. If I'm put on the case, I'll share my findings with the cops currently investigating."

"I see." Casey didn't look satisfied with the answer. "Well, I hope they catch whoever did it. I feel so bad for poor Irene. I don't even know if she'll reopen after this, but she's been here for years without an incident."

Gloria came with their meals. Casey stepped back while she served them.

"I'll leave you all to eat. Have a good day now." He walked back toward the kitchen.

As Gloria served them, she said, "I heard part of that. I don't have any notions about who committed the robbery, but I would feel safer if we did have a law enforcer here.

I'm not on the town board, but I would vote for you, too, Mr. Ramsay."

Ramsay still hadn't brushed up on his manners enough to thank her, but he nodded as she placed his chicken salad plate in front of him.

"I'm not predicting the outcome," John spoke from beside Alicia, "but I think you have a good chance, Ramsay, in light of what happened last night."

"Hindsight reactions are always faster than foresight ones," Mac added philosophically. "That's why so many people drop dead from not taking care of themselves properly."

"I quit smoking," Laura chimed in abandoning her phone for a moment. "That was after my uncle died of lung cancer. He'd been a smoker all his life."

"That's what I mean. Sometimes people need a wake-up call to get moving." Mac picked up his burger and bit into it.

Alicia saw Ramsay wince at these words and wondered why. Then they all began eating and chatting about other topics until it was time for Alicia and Laura to return to work.

Back at the library, they found Sheila at the Reference Desk. She had filled in for Alicia when Donald went to lunch. Bonnie was at the Circulation Desk. The curly-haired brunette with owl-shaped glasses greeted them as they entered. "Hi, Alicia. Hi, Laura. I heard you guys took Sneaky to the vet during lunch."

"Welcome back, Bonnie," Laura said. "Yes. He did super, and he has a clean bill of health."

Alicia wondered about the outcome of Angelina's cat, Muffin. There wasn't another Sneaky Storytime scheduled until next week, and it was unlikely she'd see the girl before then to ask.

"Good to hear." Bonnie seemed her old chipper self as she took some returned Christmas and Hanukkah books from a cart and shelved them on the holiday display.

"Are you feeling better?" Alicia inquired.

A shadow crossed the girl's face a moment, but she shrugged it off. "I'm fine. I just told Sheila I can go back working some nights. I really don't mind. I'd hate to have you all put off your own schedules to fill in for me."

Sheila, after handing a patron a computer pass, came over to them.

"I've redone the schedule, and Bonnie will work the three nights that Gladys does; Mondays, Wednesdays, and Fridays. Tuesdays and Thursdays will be rotated between Donald and Jean. I would rather use you on weekends in the Children's Room, Laura. I know you have trouble juggling transportation with your sister and need to watch your younger brother some nights. I also know it's tough for Alicia to do a night shift because of her twins. If I manage to convince the Board to hire more help, the schedule will be more accommodating for everyone, but it will take time to add new staff. I ask for everyone's patience in the meantime."

"Thanks," Laura said. "I'll bring my coat upstairs, check Sneaky while I'm there, and then head back to Children's. Is Jean there now?"

"Yes. She got in while you were at lunch and will be in the rest of the day." Sheila turned to Alicia. "Why don't you go upstairs with Laura, too, and get settled? I'll wait at the desk until you return. Donald will be back any minute. I'm almost done with the agenda but have a few more reports to finish in my office later."

Alicia nodded and followed Laura upstairs.

***

When Alicia arrived back at Reference, Donald was already there, and Sheila was gone. She hadn't seen or heard her go back to her office, but she must've done so quietly.

"How was lunch?" Donald asked. "I saw Laura bring Sneaky back, so I see you all survived his sharp claws including Dr. Donna," he said with a grin using the nickname Mac and some other people gave the vet.

"Stop that, Donald, and, yes, Sneaky was quite well behaved except for a bit of dramatic wailing on our drive. Lunch was good."

"That cop was there, right? The one who came in earlier asking about the gift shop."

"He's not a cop. He was a detective, but he's retired now," Alicia corrected.

"He said he's running for town sheriff. We certainly can use one now."

"That's the general consensus. He's changed quite a bit from when I knew him, so maybe it'll work out."

Alicia busied herself with stamping date due cards. She couldn't believe it was almost mid-December already. They were collecting food donations for the holidays to offset patron fines, and there was a Toys for Tots bin to the front of the main entrance for donations to needy children. She thought about Angelina and wondered if she might pick her up something small in the town's toy store when she shopped for the twins.

"Ransey, or whatever his name was, told me he almost croaked two years ago."

Donald's words drew her attention. She stopped stamping.

"Really? What did he say happened?" She was curious that this might be a clue to the radical changes in Ramsay's behavior and appearance.

Donald tapped some keys on the reference computer keyboard. Alicia saw a Facebook wall pop up and knew Donald was checking his social media sites again. She refrained from doing that at work, but Sheila didn't seem to mind as long as it didn't take anyone away from helping patrons.

"Guy said he had a heart attack," Donald continued as he entered his day's status. "The doctors warned him he wouldn't make it if he continued on the same path with his diet and type A personality. I guess it spooked him. Rog is always after me about eating better and exercising more. But people tend to be complacent about that stuff until something happens."

Alicia thought of Mac's saying about hindsight and foresight. Her father-in-law liked using euphemisms that were often true. Now she knew why Ramsay had decided to turn over a new leaf.

***

The rest of the day passed uneventfully. Edith and Rose dropped in around four asking for more decorating books. Edith was determined that the robbery would not affect the revival of the Christmas Fair in two weeks.

"Bad publicity before our fair is poor timing," she said, "but I used to work in PR, and I know that publicity of any kind is good because it draws attention."

Alicia knew firsthand about the advantage of bad publicity. People flocked to Cobble Cove to see the place where all the drama occurred. When Pamela donated money to revitalize the village, some people decided to stay and make it their home.

Alicia didn't know much about Edith and her sister except that they were very active on church and town committees and were known as the town's "cousins," a nickname coined for them many years ago. They helped Dora and Charlie at the inn after more rooms were added, and the place began booking up with tourists. The Christmas Fair brought in even more visitors, so the cousins had to create an additionally festive atmosphere at the inn and in the town square this year.

Rose, the quieter cousin, said in a low voice, "It's a shame about Irene. People shouldn't gain from another's loss."

Alicia thought the shy sister was a deep thinker like Mac.

"Hopefully, they will catch the perpetrator," she said. "John and I are going away next week, but we'll be back by the time the Christmas Fair opens."

Alicia was actually starting to look forward to the trip. She hated to admit part of the reason for her new-found enthusiasm was wanting to escape the memory of being followed and the news about the gift shop. She needed some cheering up and time alone with John. When she returned, she hoped things would be back to normal in charming Cobble Cove.

Chapter Eleven

When Alicia got home that night, John was waiting with dinner on the table. He'd made spaghetti with meatballs and homemade sauce using some of Mac's herbs. She smelled it simmering on the stove, a blend of basil, oregano, and tomato. The babies were propped up in their high chairs waiting to eat. Carol was fiddling with her baby spoon while her brother was playing with the blue rattle Betty had given Alicia at her baby shower. She'd given Carol a matching pink one that also lay on her table.

"Uhmmm. That smells good."

John smiled. He was wearing the white apron they shared when cooking, although he did most of the job on weeknights, while she cooked over the weekends. It was an arrangement that had been working well for them, but if he was hired for the position in New York, that would change. Alicia wasn't looking forward to cooking dinner after work, but it was another concession she might have to make for their family.

"How was your day, honey?" John asked after kissing her lightly on the lips.

"Nothing exceptional happened after lunch. I did find out what's up with Ramsay, though." She tightened the bib around Johnny's neck that was coming loose.

"Did you?" John's blue eyes lit up with interest. "Let's talk about that over dinner. I'd love to hear the story."

He turned off the burner under the sauce pan and ladled some of the aromatic mixture over heaps of spaghetti and meatballs on two plates he brought to the table. Then he sat and began cutting up a meatball and winding a few strands of spaghetti over a small fork for Johnny.

"John, you know the twins can't eat spaghetti yet," Alicia told him. She took some baby food jars from the cabinet.

"You baby them, Ali. Johnny can at least have a bite of meatball." He unwrapped the spaghetti strands, placed them aside, speared a small piece of meatball on the fork, and passed it to his son. Johnny opened his mouth and bit it off.

Alicia didn't see him chewing. She rushed over. "He could choke, John."

John grinned. "He's fine, even though he's gotten some sauce from the meatball on his mouth." He took a napkin and wiped red dribble off the baby's chin.

"I see you've been reading Dr. Spock again, Dad."

"Please leave my favorite Star Trek character out of this." John took back the fork and, with a mock frown, reached over and commenced feeding Johnny from one of the baby food cans. "I just wanted to try it, but I'll follow Mom's advice for now." He winked.

"I just wonder what you feed them when I'm not home."

John put his finger to his lips. "They promised me they won't tell."

Alicia shook her head. When they'd finished feeding the twins, they began to eat their own dinner.

"So, tell me, Ali. How did Ramsay make his awesome metamorphosis from smelly rude cop to clean-cut Old Spice sheriff wannabe?"

Alicia laughed. "His aftershave is quite pungent but not unpleasant."

She took a slice of the garlic bread John had left by her plate and bit into it. When she finished chewing, she said, "Donald tells me he and Ramsay had a conversation when he came into the library looking for information about Cobble Corner and its shops. Ramsay told Donald he'd had a heart attack and was warned by his doctor that he needed to make a change or he might not live much longer. Looks like he took that advice to heart literally."

"Interesting. I can understand that frightening someone into changing."

John wound some spaghetti over his fork and ate it. Some sauce dripped down his mouth, and he grabbed a napkin to wipe it. "I'm worse than the twins making a mess when I eat. Maybe you should get me a bib, Alicia."

"Now I know what to buy you for Christmas."

"Ha, ha." John's dimple showed in his cheek. "I'll consider that when shopping for your gift in Manhattan next week, Mrs. McKinney."

At the mention of their trip, Alicia remembered she had to call Pamela.

"John, I still need to check with Pamela about taking care of Fido. I promised Mac I would ask her. He seems sure she won't mind, but I want to make sure it's okay with her."

"That's not a bad idea, Ali. I could call her, but I know you haven't had a chance to speak to her about the trip. I need to do some things after dinner, so you can call from your office or the bedroom if you want."

John considered Mac's old room Alicia's office even though it was still more of a storage room until it was renovated.

"What are you doing after dinner, John? You're not going out, are you?"

"No." He took the last bite of food and pushed his plate away.

"First, I'm going to do the dishes because we've done as good a job as the twins on these plates. Then I'm taking these guys up to the nursery and having a Storytime with them. I enjoyed our daddy night last night, and I think I need to spend more time with them."

"You spend more time with the twins than I do," Alicia said; but, as soon as the words were out of her mouth, she realized why John was starting to feel guilty. He knew that if he got the job at Columbia, he would not be seeing his children most of the week.

"I guess quality time is what's important, Ali. I'll keep them occupied while you talk to Pamela. Afterwards, you can have a turn with them if I haven't put them to sleep yet." He smiled. "Of course, I wouldn't mind a bit of attention later myself."

She laughed. She knew exactly what type of attention he was referring to.

***

After she helped John transport the babies upstairs and given all three of them a kiss, Alicia went back down and dialed her sister-in-law.

Pamela answered on the fourth ring. She sounded breathless but, unlike Gilly who always answered that way because she was multitasking her household work and dealing with her three boys, Pamela had been in the middle of exercising.

After she picked up and knew it was Alicia calling, she said, "Hi, there, Alicia. I was doing my cardio. I alternate it with my yoga practice every other day. Nice to hear from you. All ready for New York?"

Alicia could imagine the tall blonde on the other side in what probably was a home gym. When she'd first met her, Pamela had a riding crop in her hand and was preparing to ride one of the horses in the stable next to her house. The second time she'd been painting. It seemed her rich sister-in-law had a variety of interests and the leisure to participate in them.

"Sorry to interrupt your workout, but I was calling about the trip."

"You haven't changed your mind, have you?"

"No. In fact, I'm looking forward to it very much. It was quite generous of you to make all these wonderful accommodations and reservations for us."

"Nonsense." Pamela's breathing had slowed to a more even tone as she cycled down from the aerobics.

"I know you and John never really had the honeymoon you deserved. I should've done this long ago, but now is a good time since I'm available to watch my darling niece and nephew and give you two a break. I always had paid sitters for my daughters and, of course, Mom used to watch them when she was alive. It really helped for me to get away for some 'me' time. My husband couldn't take the pressure of twins. He was never home and then he was gone completely." Alicia could hear a bitter tone enter Pamela's voice, so she didn't probe.

"Well, thank you for your thoughtfulness. John is very eager to go. He's been a bit down lately about our book which he seems stuck on writing."

"I'm sure that will clear his head, but no working on this trip. It's your honeymoon, after all." Pamela gave her usual short laugh. "I told John I would be arriving on Saturday morning around eleven. Is that good? You can't check into the hotel until three, anyway, although they may have your room ready if you get there earlier."

"That's fine, Pamela. I'll go over everything with you when you get here, but that's not why I called."

"Oh? Is something wrong?" She sounded concerned.

"Not exactly. It's just that Mac is also going away with Betty while we're gone. I don't know if John told you that Kim and Andy will be around if you need them to help with the babies. Kim's our regular babysitter. She and Andy are also going to work on converting Mac's old room into an office for me."

"Hmmm." Pamela paused. "I don't mind them stopping by to work, but I don't need them to help with the twins. I want to spend a lot of time with them. They grow so fast, and I don't get to see them much."

"I understand, but if you need a break, don't hesitate to ask Kim."

"I certainly will. It's interesting about Mac and Betty. Who would've guessed? Where are they going?"

"To Smugglers' Notch."

Pamela's laugh was full blown now. "That sly old father of mine. Good for him. You only live once."

"Actually, why I'm calling is that since Mac will be away a few days. He wanted to know if you wouldn't mind watching his golden retriever, Fido."

"I recall Fido and, of course, I wouldn't mind his staying here. I grew up with dogs and also cats. Unfortunately, I travel so much that I don't currently have time for pets. I have people to care for the horses."

"I just wanted to make sure you weren't allergic."

"Not at all."

"Great! One other thing, Pamela."

Alicia wasn't sure she should mention the previous night's occurrences, but she figured Pamela might hear about it another way, so she added, "There was a robbery here yesterday. Someone broke in and stole some jewelry from Irene's gift shop. The police are investigating but haven't made any arrests yet." She didn't mention the person who seemed to be following her after she left the library or the man hanging around Cobble Corner who Laura thought was strange.

"They probably won't. Robberies are common this time of year. People are pretty strapped for cash. Didn't Irene have a security system?"

Alicia recalled the state-of-the-art one Pamela had in her Brookville home that included an intercom for visitors and a locked gate a mile from the entrance.

"No. Crime isn't that common here, Pamela."

"Crime is everywhere nowadays, Alicia. Small towns are no exception, but I'm not afraid. I know Fido isn't much of a watch dog, but I've been trained in Karate and hold a black belt, so no one will mess with me."

Alicia thought it might not be a bad idea to ask Pamela for some self-defense lessons in the future. There were so many aspects of her sister-in-law about which she was still learning.

"I'd better get back to the twins now. John is reading to them. Did you want to say anything to him?"

"No. We spoke yesterday. If he wants to give me a ring before Saturday, I should be home, or he can call my cell. He has both numbers."

"I'll tell him."

"Thanks for calling, Alicia. I'll see you Saturday."

"Thank you, Pamela. We both really appreciate it."

***

After hanging up with her sister-in-law, Alicia joined John in the nursery. As she walked in, she saw John crawling on his knees attempting to give Johnny a piggyback ride. Carol looked on with glee awaiting her turn from her crib.

"What are you doing, John? They can't even crawl yet."

"I can hold him up, Ali. See?"

Alicia watched nervously as John tried again to get the baby up on his back. Before the baby fell, she ran over and picked him up. "I think it's Mommy's time now."

John grinned. "You want a ride?"

"I was referring to taking over and spending some time with my children before they go to bed. Have you read any stories to them yet?" Alicia asked as she sat with Johnny in the rocker by the window next to the bookcase.

"We didn't get to that." With a strand of gray-tipped hair falling over his eyes from his exertion, John still looked boyish.

"Too busy playing, I guess."

"Play is very important for kids—of all ages. After you finish reading them bedtime stories, I have a few games I'd like to play with you, Mrs. McKinney."

Alicia smiled but didn't comment. Instead, she asked, "Can you bring Carol over here, John, and a few books from the shelves? They like *Twinkle, Twinkle Little Star* and *Rock a Bye Baby*. I love the illustrations in the picture books Gilly sent. I can't believe she saved them from when her boys were young, and they aren't even dog-eared or torn which is a surprise, considering how rambunctious her kids are now."

"Boys will be boys, but Johnny's actually the tame one. Carol is the mastermind behind all pranks. I think she takes after her mother."

He brought his still giggling daughter over to Alicia who settled her on the other side of her lap. Then he took the two requested books and laid them on the small table beside the rocker.

"Why do you insist on these second-hand books when we have practically a whole library of new ones from Pamela?"

"These are the ones they like, John, and I was never a prankster as a child."

Maybe she preferred Gilly's books because it was a way of keeping her friend close, even though they were miles apart. If the new clerk position was approved at the meeting the following night, Gilly might become her neighbor again in a few months.

"I don't know about that. You librarians aren't the quiet, thinking types you're stereotyped as, at least not in my experience." John was still in a childish mood.

"Can you also dim the lights on your way out, John?" Alicia asked preferring not to spar words with him. The babies, seeing their books, were becoming fidgety on her lap. Carol was reaching for *Twinkle, Twinkle*, its cartoonish yellow star catching her attention.

"I'll lower them, but I wasn't planning on leaving. I want to hear a bedtime story, too." John positioned the switches by the door so that the room was in partial darkness and then he sat Indian style in front of Alicia on the floor, his feet tucked under him, his long legs bent at the knees.

Alicia had to laugh. "Okay, children," she emphasized the word 'children.' Let's begin with *Twinkle Twinkle Little Star* and then we'll let Johnny choose one."

Carol cooed in pleasure as Alicia opened the book. She found it difficult keeping both kids balanced on her knees.

"Why don't they sit by me?" John suggested. "Then you can show us all the pictures, and I can keep them still." Before she could reply, he was up and gathering the babies in his arms. "This'll work better, Ali."

"Yes, but who will keep you still?" She couldn't resist the urge to tease him.

"Good one. I'll get you back for that later."

Alicia was glad John had the knees for getting up and down so easily. If it was her, she'd need someone to help her up. Getting old wasn't easy, and she was still only middle-aged.

"Okay. All set, Momma. Please read to us," John implored. Carol was tapping his knee while Johnny was starting to pull brown tufts of rug from the carpet.

"No, Johnny," John said taking the rug pieces from his son's chubby fingers before he put them in his mouth.

Alicia began as soon as they were settled. Afterwards, she and John took turns putting the twins in their cribs and kissing them goodnight.

As they went next door to the bedroom, John said, "That was nice, Ali. I love hearing you read. Maybe we should consider you doing the female voices on our audiobooks."

Alicia knew she probably wouldn't have the time to do that, but she was glad of the compliment and even happier that John's words indicated that there would be more of their mysteries forthcoming. He was no longer questioning his ability to continue to write and, even though she knew he hadn't penned any words yet in their next book, she figured he was now hopeful that he would do that soon. She only worried that he might be pinning too much on their trip to the city.

While they both changed for bed, Alicia said, "Pamela's agreed to dog sit Fido while she's at our house, John, but did you know your sister has a black belt?"

He turned to her as he pulled the covers over to get into bed. "I still don't know Pamela well, but it doesn't surprise me. Finding out I had a rich sister two years ago really threw me for a loop. I hope I'll get the opportunity to get to know her and her daughters better in the future."

"Maybe she can stay a little longer after we get back. If Kim and Andy manage to finish my office, we can put a cot in there for her to stay, or maybe Dora would have room for her at the inn. It would be nice for the twins to attend the Christmas Fair with us and their aunt."

John turned off the bedside lamp. "That's a very smart idea, Ali. Now, come here, and let's begin our games."

Alicia giggled like her baby daughter as he pulled her close and began tickling her. All fears from the previous night were momentarily erased from her mind.

Chapter Twelve

On Thursday afternoon, Alicia filled in the rest of her co-workers about her upcoming trip, but it seemed Sheila or Laura had already spread the word. Alicia broke the news to Donald when she was alone with him at the reference desk.

"Lucky you," he said. "But I hear your father-in-law is going away, too. He and Betty to a ski chalet no less. I've always wanted to do that with Rog, but he's too afraid he'll come back with a broken leg."

So word about Mac's trip had also spread.

"I don't think they'll be doing much skiing, Donald. I didn't know you skied."

Donald glanced away from his Facebook wall. "I don't, but I'd love to curl up with Roger in front of a roaring fireplace, and I absolutely adore cheese fondue." His expression was wistful.

Alicia laughed. "I don't think a ski vacation would be for me. I'd be with Rog worrying about breaking a leg. I'm clumsy as it is. You know how many books I drop each day. But the real sticky point is the cold. I think I'd prefer a cruise to a secluded island instead."

"Maybe Pamela will gift that to you next." Donald winked. "She may even have a house on one."

"I don't think my sister-in-law is quite that rich."

"What's Mac doing with Fido, bringing him along or boarding him?"

Alicia knew Fido would probably enjoy romping in the snow at a ski lodge. She recalled the fun he'd had tagging along next to John with the snow blower when he cleared the library walk after the unseasonable storm that changed her life two years ago. Of course, watching a dog was probably the last thing Mac wanted to do when spending time with his newfound lady love who just happened to be a reformed homebound and the director of the library board.

"Fido's staying at our house. John's sister is keeping an eye on him and the twins."

"Good deal." Donald clicked on a link and studied its contents.

"I'll be right back," Alicia said as she stepped away from the desk. Vera was usually the clerk who pulled damaged books to be checked, but she decided to take a glance through the books herself since it wasn't busy. She would also keep an eye out for duplicate titles that were taking up much-needed shelf space. Even though the library had expanded a year ago, the discarding process had to be ongoing to make room for new titles. As in one's home, there was never enough space.

As she rounded the stack near the reference desk, Alicia noticed Walter. He had come in just an hour earlier because he was working that night during the board meeting. He had started his new schedule immediately.

"Hi, Alicia," Walter said as he saw her turn the corner. He held a long strand of red garland in his hand.

"Sheila wants me to hang this up. Would you mind helping? I'll get a ladder, but I need someone to hold it while I tape it around the stacks."

"Sure. I was trying to find something to keep me occupied. It's so quiet today."

"People are probably shopping, although I don't know if many will be hanging around Cobble Corner." He shook his head, bobbing the single gray wisp of hair covering his skull. "It's a shame about Irene. I hear she may close the gift shop."

"I didn't know that." Alicia wondered how the shopkeeper was recovering after the robbery, but she hadn't been privy to this piece of news.

"That's what Gloria says. Anyways, let me get that ladder. Thanks for your help."

He bounded away, his tall, gangly shape disappearing toward the newly installed elevator that was much welcomed by the handicapped and had been added at Betty's suggestion. Although she and Mac were quite spry with their canes, other Cobble Cove elderly residents were not in as good shape, some using wheelchairs. In compliance with ADA law, it was one of the first changes Betty implemented when she became a library trustee. The ladder was kept in the storage room that doubled as Sneaky's cat room.

After Walter returned with the ladder and Alicia helped him hang the garland over the stacks, she spent the rest of the afternoon checking the shelves for discards and then rejoining Donald at the desk, so he could take his afternoon break.

The rest of the day remained uneventful, but Alicia couldn't help thinking about Irene. She also realized it was only two days before she and John would be leaving for New York, and she hadn't had a chance to pack, write a list for Pamela, or pick up a gift for Gilly and her sons. As she prepared to leave work, an idea came to her. Maybe she could stop at Cobble Corner, do some shopping, and check to see if Irene was around.

Alicia still wasn't comfortable walking home from the library after dark and, because of the time change, night already set in by five p. m. But she told herself she had to get past this irrational fear. She had her cell phone in her coat pocket and would try to stay in the lit areas that were occupied by people. Five o'clock at night wasn't late. Most shops closed at nine for the holidays; some even later. The shopkeepers hadn't changed their hours, although she heard from John that some merchants were planning to install alarms or other security measures since the gift shop break in.

On her way out of the library, Donald offered to drive Alicia home, but she declined. She thanked him, but told him she was doing some shopping first. She wondered if John had said anything about her experience to any of her co-workers, but she didn't know when he'd have had the chance. Donald headed off to his car, and she turned in the direction of Cobble Corner.

As she walked, she called John on her cell and told him she would be a few minutes late. She didn't mention why, and she figured he might think she was tied up helping a patron at the library or doing some last-minute task for Sheila. If she told him she was going to Cobble Corner, she was afraid he might become alarmed.

The path to the shops was well lit, and there were people driving and walking past her as she travelled it. When she got to the square, she was delighted to see the bright Christmas lights strung on the shop windows and on the trees that bordered the area. The gazebo also shone festively, although the evergreen near it was dark, awaiting the tree lighting ceremony on the first night of the upcoming Cobble Cove Christmas Fair. She hoped the burglary would not put a damper on that event. While Edith was probably right that headlines, both good and bad, were a source of publicity, Alicia was still concerned that the gift shop robbery might deter some people from attending the fair or shopping in the stores. Yet, there seemed to be quite a few people strolling through the square with packages and bundles in their arms.

Alicia considered which shop to check for a gift for Gilly. She didn't want to keep John and the babies waiting too long for dinner. Since the gift shop was likely still closed, she had to think of another place that might sell something her friend would like. A couple of new shops had opened during the expansion of the town—the toy shop that was added to the children's clothing boutique; the candy and chocolate shop that had the most delicious fudge that John couldn't resist; and a ladies clothing store.

Alicia decided to try the clothing store. Gilly wasn't very fashion conscious like Sheila or Pamela, but she could probably use something new. Most of her budget currently went to her sons' expenses. Although they didn't wear as many clothes as a daughter would, they still needed sports gear, sneakers, and other clothing items. Once boys started sprouting up, they grew quickly. Gilly's eldest son, Danny, was approaching his teens now, so that change would be taking place soon.

As Alicia entered Chloe's Closet, the name of the clothing shop, a bell tinkled over the door. A woman about Alicia's age came to greet her. A red silk headband, like one Sheila might wear, held back the storekeeper's long black hair. She wore a red tunic over dark leggings. The shirt was accessorized with a red and green holly-patterned scarf, and the leggings fit smoothly into fur-cuffed calf-length boots.

"Good evening. I'm Chloe Gibbons. Welcome to Chloe's closet. Are you looking for anything particular I can help you with?"

Alicia glanced around the store. One side featured racks of business-like clothing – suits, dresses, skirt sets along with some evening clothes. The other was full of more casual wear – jeans, slacks, t-shirts. The store seemed to cater to women in their twenties and up. She wondered if there were any plans to open a men's clothing store in Cobble Cove in the future.

"I'm actually shopping for a friend," Alicia replied. "My name is Alicia McKinney, and I live nearby. I'm visiting my friend from Long Island over the weekend, and I wanted to bring her a Christmas gift."

Chloe smiled, and she noticed the lady had tiny but white teeth. "Is your friend about your age and size?"

"She's a year younger and about a size higher."

"Is she a working woman?"

"Yes. She has a part-time job in a library, but she's also a mother of three and doesn't like to dress fancy."

"Does she like accessories? We have scarves, purses, gloves, and other items in the back. We also have pajamas and nightgowns."

Alicia thought of the naughty holiday negligee Gilly said she was giving her and smiled.

"I'm not sure. She doesn't dress up much. I usually see her in an apron. She bakes a lot. At the library, she just wears jeans and sweatshirts."

Chloe nodded, thinking. "Hmmm. Let me see. We have a variety of sweatshirts with different graphics and sayings. The college students like them. Let me show you."

Alicia followed Chloe past the register and toward the back of the store. She joined her by a rack of tops with cute illustrated sayings. Alicia browsed through them spotting a light blue colored shirt with a frazzled-looking cartoon lady wearing pink fuzzy slippers like Gilly wore. At the lady's feet were a baseball, toy rocket, and a miniature race car. Words in large black letters proclaimed, "Mother of Boys." The top next to it had the similar image on pink with a doll, ballet slipper, and jewelry box. This one said, "Mother of Girls." Alicia pulled out the "boys" sweatshirt.

"I think this will be perfect for my friend," she said.

Chloe smiled. "That's part of our holiday sale. Bring it to the desk. I'll ring it up for you at twenty per-cent off and add a free gift box."

Alicia was happy she'd found something for Gilly in a short time and even saved some money on the purchase.

"Thank you so much," she said after she'd paid, and Chloe handed her a bag containing the top and a festively-decorated gift box inside a shopping bag with the words "Chloe's Closet" written in fancy script.

"You are very welcome. Please come again, and Happy Holidays."

As Alicia exited the store, she remembered that she wanted to take a quick look at Irene's shop before she left Cobble Corner. She glanced at her watch and saw that her shopping trip had only taken twenty minutes. She could afford to spare five more to check out the gift shop. Her stop at the toy store for gifts for Gilly's sons might have to wait for another time.

Making her way across the square, Alicia also passed the grocery store. She considered picking up some dessert for dinner as a way to make up for being late that night, maybe some holiday cookies or a cheesecake. She could get those at Claire's Bakery, but the grocers was on her way, and she'd noticed last time they were at Duncan's that he'd put out some displays of holiday baked goods.

When she entered the store, Gary was there at the counter checking out a tall blonde woman she recognized as Bridget Stafford, the school principal, even though she'd only met her once when she came to the library to take out some crochet books. Angelina stood at her father's side helping the principal pack her purchases into brown grocery bags.

"Hi, Alicia," Gary said as Mrs. Stafford pushed her shopping wagon from the aisle, wishing them all a happy holiday and telling Angelina she would see her in school tomorrow.

"Hi, Gary. I notice you have a little helper with you today."

Angelina smiled, and it tore at Alicia's heart.

"I'm helping Daddy because Mommy is wrapping presents at home. I think she got me a lot of gifts this year, and she told Santa I'm being good, so I should get a lot of stuff from him, too."

Alicia wanted to ask about Muffin, but she figured things had gone well because the girl was far from sad. Angelina answered her unspoken question.

"My bestest gift is Muffin being all better. Dr. Clark gave her medicine, and she's eating her cat food again."

Gary laughed. "She'll be fattened up again in no time, Angie, and there is no such word as bestest. Best is all you need to say because it means the most." He turned to Alicia, "Is there anything we can help you with? Are you shopping for dinner tonight?"

"No, just something nice for dessert."

"What do you think we should recommend to Mrs. McKinney and her family?" Gary asked his daughter.

"How about the cherry cheesecake you brought home last night, Daddy?"

"That sounds good, Angelina," Alicia said. "I was thinking of a cheesecake."

Gary smiled as Angelina ran to the back of the store to the bakery section, her stubby little legs racing at top speed. He didn't caution her about running. *There were too many other fears he had for his daughter besides falling,* Alicia thought.

Angelina returned carrying a see-through box containing the cake garnished with layers of syrupy cherries in sauce. She handed the package to Alicia.

"Thanks so much, sweetie. This looks delicious."

Gary rang up the charge, and Alicia paid. She withdrew an additional dollar from her wallet. "This is for Angelina for her help choosing our dessert."

The girl's eyes lit up. "Daddy, can you give me quarters for that, so I can get a toy from the vending machine?"

"Sure, Angie. Did you thank Mrs. McKinney?" He took the bill, added it to the register, and handed his daughter the change.

"Thank you, Mrs. McKinney. Daddy has the bestest, uh, I mean best vending machines," she corrected herself.

Angelina ran to the three, bubble-shaped machines lined up against the wall across from the checkout aisles. It seemed the girl had an abundance of energy and that was a good sign.

"Thanks again, both of you," Alicia said as she carried the grocery bag with the box of cheesecake toward the door. She wondered if Duncan was planning to install any security measures yet or whether he had ignored the panic some of the other shopkeepers were experiencing after the robbery.

"Best to your husband and the twins," Gary called after her. Angelina was busy inserting the coins into the vending machine slots and twisting the metal wheel to extract one of the toys within the plastic bubble.

Chapter Thirteen

Alicia wanted to go directly home, but she wasn't far from the gift shop and could cut across the square to head over to Stone Throw Road once she passed it. She noted that neither Gary nor Chloe had mentioned the robbery. Either they were doing their best to keep from thinking about it or weren't that concerned over it.

As she walked, she noticed the number of shoppers traversing the paths to the stores had thinned. Although the area was brightly lit, she felt a sensation of unease as she headed toward Irene's shop. Then she saw him. That same man. He was smoking a cigarette by one of the artfully designed Cobble Corner trash cans. He wore a long gray overcoat over grungy jeans and when he saw her, he stepped out of the shadows.

The sound of a pebble rolling under foot in the silent square. The absence of carolers singing. The wind whispering through the trees rattling the hanging lights. The cool dark stare of the cigarette smoker. She gripped her red wool coat tighter against the chill that had nothing to do with the temperature and quickened her pace. She looked back over her shoulder several times to make sure the stranger hadn't moved, but he was still smoking by the trash bin under the overhang of one of the vacant stores. She berated herself that she was getting just as paranoid as Laura about strangers, but with the happenings of the last few days, it was probably natural to be anxious when encountering someone unfamiliar especially the weird man she'd noticed hanging around Cobble Cove on several occasions.

She jumped when her cell phone chimed from inside her pocket. Retrieving it, she saw she'd received a text. It was from John.

"All ok, Ali? When should we expect you home?"

She waited until she was standing outside the gift shop before she texted her reply, "On my way. Sorry for the delay." She kept the phone in her hand for comfort.

The shop was dark. A "closed" sign hung in the window. What had she expected, the door wide open welcoming visitors?

She turned to make her way back when she literally crashed into someone. The woman seemed even more startled than she. It was Maggie Palmer, Irene's daughter.

"Oh, my gosh. So sorry. Ms. McKinney, I believe."

They had only met once because Maggie had only recently been working Saturdays at the shop for her mother. She was in her late twenties with a son not much older than the twins. She'd come back to live with Irene after her brief marriage ended in divorce when her husband, the drummer in a rock band, ran off with the lead singer. Maggie was quite attractive with a head full of auburn ringlets and emerald eyes.

"Yes, and you're Irene's daughter." Alicia wondered what the woman was doing there, even though it was odder that she was visiting the closed shop.

"I'm Maggie. I just came by to get some things my mother needs." She took a key from the pocket of the brown cape she wore. "Mom just can't bear to come back here herself. She's still in shock over what happened."

"I can imagine. I was so sorry to hear about it."

"Why don't you come in with me? We can talk inside. It's rather cold and dark out here."

Maggie opened the shop door and switched on the lights. Alicia followed her. She inhaled sharply at the sight of the nearly empty store. More than half the shelves were empty. Boxes stuffed with merchandise lined the aisles, and the space that the jewelry case once occupied was bare.

"Be careful where you step," Maggie warned. "There are still some small pieces of glass they may have missed when cleaning up."

Alicia could see a few slivers and shards around the checkout desk where the register gaped open and empty, its drawers a hungry mouth.

"The robbers didn't do all this," Maggie said in answer to Alicia's thoughts. "Mom is clearing out the place. We're closing."

So the rumors were true.

"I'm so sorry, Maggie. Maybe they'll catch the burglar. The town is possibly voting in a new sheriff tomorrow night."

"It doesn't matter. Neither does the fact that the insurance will cover most of our loss."

She faced Alicia, her green eyes large, brighter than Sheila's and more jewel-like than feline. "You don't know everything about my mother. This isn't the first time she's been violated. You're new to this town, and your husband left for a few years before he came back here. I grew up in Cobble Cove with Mom. I only moved away when I met Eric, and he turned out to be a cheater and a liar."

Her voice rose on the last words, but then she stopped and bowed her head. Her shoulders began to shake. Alicia went to her and hugged her.

"It's okay, Maggie. When my house was set on fire, I felt the same way—angry, sad, and violated. The pain never goes away, but it lessens. If it wasn't for the fire, I may never have decided to return to Cobble Cove with John. I know this may sound cruel now, but things happen for a reason. I had trouble accepting that when my father-in-law said it, but it's true."

Maggie looked up and wiped her eyes on her cape sleeve. She pulled back from Alicia.

"You don't understand. It's not that simple. I have to get some things for my mother and then I have to go."

She walked toward the back of the store where a curtain separated the public space from the employee's area. Alicia knew she'd been dismissed. Maggie had rejected her attempt at consolation.

"I'll leave you then. I need to get back home, anyway, but please give my regards to your mother. I wish her well whatever she decides to do and you, too."

Maggie hesitated a moment but didn't reply. Instead she parted the curtain and went to retrieve whatever her mother had requested from the storage room. Alicia left the shop feeling frustrated and hurt. She didn't even notice that the man with the cigarette was gone.

***

Feeling low, Alicia slinked down Stone Throw Road not even listening for footsteps behind her. She was so absorbed in her thoughts. But as she came upon her house, she was dazzled by a display of brilliant red and green lights. The bushes out front were strung with holiday bulbs, and there was even an illuminated red-nosed reindeer and Santa pulling his sleigh full of gifts. She smiled. John had done an impressive job. She thought he was waiting until they got back from New York, but she guessed he'd changed his mind.

The door was open; and as she came in with the cheesecake and Gilly's gift, John greeted her with a grin.

"Welcome home, Mrs. McKinney. The twins have seen the light display and approved it. I fed them already because they seemed hungry, but your dinner is staying warm in the crockpot. It's stew."

Alicia could smell the aroma of the garlic, rosemary, and basil herbs John often used in cooking. Her stomach rumbled.

"Smells delicious. Thanks so much, John. I'm sorry I took so long. The lights are beautiful. They surprised me."

She put her coat on the rack by the door after John took her packages.

"What are these?"

"Be careful with the grocery bag. I brought cherry cheesecake from Duncan's. He wasn't there, but Gary and his daughter were tending the store. They said hello."

"Yum. Now I know why I married you."

He gave her a kiss on the cheek. "What's in the other bag? Is that from that new clothes store? Did you get something for us after dessert?"

"John!" she laughed. Her mood had definitely lightened. "This is Gilly's gift. It's a sweatshirt."

His grin widened showing the dimple she found so attractive.

"She gets you a negligee and you get her a sweatshirt. I love it!"

They walked together into the kitchen where the babies sat in their high chairs around the table making some sounds as if they were communicating to one another in baby talk they both could understand.

"How did you manage to get those lights up yourself?" she asked after he'd ladled some stew on to her waiting plate and she'd given the twins kisses.

"Dad dropped by, and I enlisted his help. I wanted to get them up before we left and it got too cold, and you'd mentioned it was too dark on this street. I told him about Fido, and he was relieved. He'll be bringing him over Saturday morning. It might be a bit early. He and Betty are both morning larks and they want to get on the road as soon as they can."

Alicia smiled. "Was Betty with him?"

"No. She was packing. I know you need to get started with that, too. I can help if you want."

"I'm a bit tired, John. I'll save that for tomorrow night when you're at the town hall meeting."

"Good idea. That's another reason I wanted to put up the lights tonight."

He had placed the cheesecake box on the counter next to the refrigerator. "Mind if I open this? I think Carol and Johnny are ready for dessert."

"You mean you're ready for dessert? I know it's your favorite. Go ahead. I'll have mine when I'm done with the stew. It's very tasty, John. My compliments to the chef."

She spooned a bit of the meat, potatoes, and vegetables into her mouth. The herbed sauce blended with the other ingredients deliciously on her tongue.

"Thank you, ma'am." He cut the cake and brought two slices along with two jars of baby applesauce to the table.

"I see Johnny and Carol eyeing the cherries. I wish they could have a bite of the cake, but I know you'll scream if I even suggest it." John smiled.

"They can't have it yet, John, but they love applesauce."

"Would you like some coffee or tea with this, Ali? I have hot water on."

"I'd rather not have coffee at this hour, but tea's fine. I'll get up and make myself a cup after I finish dinner. I'm not an invalid."

She thought of Mac and how he managed to do all sorts of tasks even though he needed a cane to assist him when walking. He'd even helped John string their Christmas lights.

They fed the twins and then, as Alicia began eating dinner, John started on his dessert.

"I thought you got caught up at the library," John said taking a forkful of cheesecake.

"I wanted to get Gilly a gift before our trip." She didn't mention that she was also curious about the gift shop.

"I'm sure she would've understood if you hadn't had the time, but I'm glad you found something." He finished his cake. "Anything else happen at work today or during your shopping trip?"

She hesitated. Should she tell him about Maggie? If she didn't, she knew he'd read her omission on her face. "I also wanted to see the gift shop. I'd heard it was closing."

"I could've told you that."

"I forgot you're up on town news."

"That's my job as editor of the *Cobble Cove Courier*."

"Do you know if Irene is leaving town?"

"I don't know everything."

"I ran into her daughter." Alicia knew her voice had changed; become touched with the sadness she'd felt earlier before seeing the holiday lights John had added to their home.

"Mary or something?"

"Maggie. She opened up the shop because she had to get some things there for her mother. The place is nearly empty now. She was upset."

"I don't blame her."

John took his empty plate and put it in the sink.

"It was more than that, John."

Alicia finished her stew and brought the plate up to her husband. She looked into his blue eyes.

"She said something about her mother being violated before. I didn't understand what that meant. Do you know anything about Irene's past?"

John lowered his head, and now she was the one who recognized omission. "John?"

He walked back to the table. "Have your cake, and I'll tell you."

At the table with the babies, busying themselves gabbing in baby talk again, John related the story about Irene.

"Dad told me all of this, and I think we should keep it to ourselves."

Alicia nodded.

"Irene's parents now live down south. I'm guessing that's where she'll head now. The family originally came from Queens. They also had a shop there. Irene helped them run it, as Maggie was helping her at the shop in Cobble Cove." He paused and took a sip from his water glass.

Alicia waited for him to continue. Her cheesecake remained uneaten on the table.

"Irene was about Maggie's age when two masked men broke into their store. There wasn't much in the register, so the men decided to take her."

"Take her? Oh, my God! John, they kidnapped Irene?"

"Well, she was in her twenties, but, yes, I guess that's still the term. They took her hostage. They left a note for her parents for the amount they wanted for her return. If they contacted the police, she would be killed."

"How much did they want?" Ali had lost her appetite completely and pushed away her plate.

"More than they had." His blue eyes darkened. "But she was their only daughter. They liquidated all their assets including savings for her college. Her father gathered the denominations they requested in unmarked bills and brought the bag to the meeting place they contacted him with. Remember, this was twenty-five years ago, Ali. There were no cell phones, and her parents were too panicked to consider consulting a detective or having the kidnapper's calls traced."

He took another swallow of water. "They got her back and never found the kidnappers. Her parents had to close the store. They moved here to Cobble Cove in the hopes of a simpler life and opened the gift shop. They ran it until they retired and moved to Florida and then Irene took over."

"What a sad story," Alicia said. "I can't imagine having to face that type of ordeal. How did Irene recover?"

"I'm sure she had therapy. You know that even I needed to talk to someone for years after my wife died."

"I would never have guessed she'd gone through all that. She seems so positive, so happy every time I shopped at the store. But now I understand why she's decided to close the gift shop and leave town. The burglary must've brought back all that horror she experienced."

"It's worse than that, Ali." John looked down at the festive tablecloth on the kitchen table as if studying the holiday design.

"What do you mean?"

"Irene was kept captive for three days before her parents could get the money together. During that time, they raped her."

"Oh, no! John, that's horrible."

Alicia was aware that Irene was a single mother like her daughter, but she never questioned Maggie's father. As she put together the pieces, she exclaimed, "Don't tell me, John. Is that how? . . . ."

"Yes. Maggie's father was one of the kidnappers. Irene never saw their faces. They wore their masks around her and kept her tied up most of the time. When they raped her, they also blindfolded her. I don't know how Dad managed to get these details, but I know he was a friend of Ben Mallory's, Irene's father. Both Irene's parents were devout Catholics, so they wouldn't even consider an abortion for their daughter."

"What a terrible story."

"The truth is that people aren't safe anywhere nowadays, Ali. You hear of shootings on a regular basis, and they take place in small towns as well as large cities. If someone is crazy and you're in the wrong place at the wrong time, your life is in danger. It's something we all have to face in the world today, unfortunately."

He looked over at the twins who had quieted down and seemed to be nodding off in their high chairs.

"As parents, I know we feel that we have the capability as well as the responsibility to keep our kids safe, but that's not really true. It's scary."

Alicia got up and threw her piece of cake in the garbage.

"I can't eat anymore, John, and the babies look tired. We should bring them upstairs."

"I'm sorry if this disturbed you, Ali, but I thought you needed to know."

He started unfastening the high chair strap from Johnny as she took Carol out of her seat.

"I understand, John. It's just difficult for me to comprehend. I know how I felt two years ago when I thought someone was threatening me at the library and then the fear I had of you being implicated in a murder. There were all the unanswered questions that I thought I couldn't face, but it was all well worth knowing. The truth is always best no matter how uncomfortable it makes someone."

Despite Alicia's painful memories, she knew she was blessed to have John and the twins especially since they'd come so late into her life. She just hoped that the safe haven she'd started to consider Cobble Cove for herself and her family wasn't in jeopardy of being threatened.

Chapter Fourteen

Alicia hardly slept that night thinking about Irene, but she must've managed to sleep at some point because; as she woke, images still floated in her mind – the man in the gray coat with the cigarette dangling from his mouth, masked men, Maggie's angry green eyes, glass on the gift shop floor, Irene standing behind the gift shop counter handing her the bag containing Kim's earrings.

She jumped up. Kim's earrings! Andy hadn't given them to her yet. How would she feel about receiving them now after the robbery? The gift box clearly said "Cobble Cove Gifts."

"What's the matter, honey?" John rolled over to check his alarm. "Darn, it's time to get up. Are you okay?"

"I had some strange dreams. I don't recall them, but I keep seeing pieces of them in my mind. They're all connected with Irene and the burglary and also what you told me last night."

"That's what the subconscious does – weaves a tale from our day's or past experiences."

"They made me think of Kim's earrings. Maybe you should talk to Andy about putting them in a different box before he gives them to her."

"Ali, he got them . . . you got them before the robbery. No one will suspect him of stealing the jewels. The bill is on your credit card."

"That's not what I meant, John. If Kim knows they're from the gift shop, she may feel bad about wearing them. She might even consider them unlucky."

John grinned. "You women worry too much." He began to get out of bed.

"I think I hear the twins. We should get down to breakfast. I'll make some pancakes this morning if you're up to it. I know Carol and Johnny love when I flip them."

Alicia wasn't happy about the way John changed the subject.

"Are you seeing Andy today?" She persisted still sitting against her pillow.

"Yes. I'm going to the newspaper to do some editing before we leave. Tonight's the town hall meeting, and then Mac will be dropping off Fido tomorrow morning. I think Pamela is arriving around noon depending on what traffic she hits."

"I'll pack while you're at the meeting. If I know Sheila, she'll probably let me leave early today to get started."

John was already at the bedroom door.

"Try not to dwell on what we discussed yesterday, Ali. I want us to enjoy our time away and take a breather from this place. One incident doesn't make Cobble Cove a hotbed for crime. What happened with us two years ago started on Long Island, so it doesn't really count. This is a safe place, honey. It's unfortunate that the burglar targeted the gift shop. Irene was just unlucky."

Alicia got out of bed and put on her slippers to join him in taking the twins downstairs.

"What I don't understand is why Irene's parents didn't put in security measures in the gift shop after what happened to them in Queens. When they retired and moved from here, Irene didn't either."

"I think they felt safe in a small town. I know that's not true anymore. You still need to be wary. Dad keeps his door open all the time, and so do we most of the time."

"We may have to start locking it. I'm planning to do that when you're not home and I'm alone with the twins."

He walked to her standing by the bed and put his arms around her. Looking into her eyes, he said, "Ali, you're a strong lady. I saw that in you when we first met at the inn. If locking a door makes you feel safe, then go ahead, but I'd like to think this was just some burglar passing through town who just randomly chose a place to rob. When things settle down, Cobble Cove will return to the tranquil and sometimes boring village it is."

Alicia smiled. "Thanks, John. You have a way of putting my fears into perspective."

"That's what husbands are for. C'mon. I want to heat up the griddle."

***

As Alicia left for work, after eating John's delicious cinnamon apple pancakes, he kissed her at the door and promised her he'd have a chat with Andy.

As she walked toward Bookshelf Lane, she couldn't help thinking of Irene. Alicia knew the gift shop owner lived near the library. When she picked up her favorite novels, she always commented to the staff how she enjoyed walking there. However, as John always liked to point out, most places were just "a stone's throw away" in Cobble Cove.

Alicia had never been to Irene's house, but she knew she could find the address in the library computer's database. When she'd first come to town, all library functions were done manually. Pamela's grant changed all that. Every patron who applied for a card was now entered into the library system, and details about them as well as the books they had checked out or owed could be gathered by a staff member.

Throughout the morning, Alicia contemplated looking up Irene's address and paying her an impromptu visit to check on her. She wasn't doing anything in particular for lunch. Since John was busy at the newspaper office and finishing up all his other projects before their trip, she wouldn't be seeing him until after work and then only until he left for the town hall meeting that night. Kim didn't have a class on Fridays, so she could watch the twins the whole day. Alicia would probably have enough time on her lunch hour to see Irene and then drop home to visit Kim and the twins. If she was lucky, she could have a bite to eat, too.

Just before noon, Sheila came downstairs. Alicia hadn't seen her all morning and figured she was wrapping up information from the previous night's board meeting. Her thoughts about Irene had taken her mind off what may have transpired at that meeting.

"Hello, Alicia." Sheila smiled. She wore black leggings this morning inside high-heeled boots. Her yellow top was the one Gilly had sent. She'd accented it with a Christmas scarf of gold bells against a dark background.

"I want to fill you in on what was decided last night about our new hires."

Alicia changed her screen where she'd looked up Irene's address. She'd already jotted it down on a piece of paper and put it in her purse.

"What did the Board decide?" She held her breath.

Would her best friend actually be moving to Cobble Cove in the summer? Was it safe for her to do so? She shrugged those thoughts aside. As John pointed out, the robbery had most likely been a fluke. The town would soon be peaceful again.

"The Board voted unanimously to hire a new full-time librarian, a new part-time clerk, and a public relations director." She paused on the last word, her red eyebrows rising. "We're also going to contract with an outside security firm to have a guard here in the evening hours."

Alicia realized that decision had been made as a result of the gift shop burglary. Having a guard around in the evening would also add an additional person in the building, so Bonnie or anyone else working the night shift would not be alone even if someone called in sick.

"Sounds good." Alicia wanted to ask about Gilly, but before she had the chance, Sheila added, "I've already received Ms. Nostran's signed reply of interest, and I'm more than happy to wait until her children are out of school in June for her to join us."

"Thanks so much, Sheila."

Alicia felt her spirits rise. She'd needed a boast since John had related Irene's awful story.

"One more thing." Sheila was leaning against the reference desk, her long red nails resting on the counter. "I want you to go home after lunch, start packing, and spend some time with your babies before you go on your trip tomorrow. There's nothing that can't wait a week."

Now she would have plenty of time to visit Irene.

"I appreciate that, Sheila."

"My pleasure. Enjoy your trip."

Sheila turned to Donald on the other side of the desk." You can take lunch now, too, Donald, and I'll relieve you until Jean arrives."

Donald signed out of his Facebook page.

"Cool. I'll get going then. See ya, Alicia. Have fun in the city."

The rest of the staff wished her a good trip as she left the library.

***

Turning in the opposite direction from her street, Alicia headed toward the address on the paper she'd taken from her purse. She just hoped Irene hadn't left town already.

The talk about her had died down. If people knew what Alicia now did about Maggie, she was sure it would still be on the airwaves.

As she grew closer to her destination, a man approached her on the sidewalk. It was the same man she'd seen smoking by the gift shop the previous night and hanging around Cobble Cove the past week. He wore the same gray coat and, up close, she could see some thick stubble on his face from a trimmed beard or one he was hoping to grow. His gray eyes surveyed her a moment, and then he smiled out of one side of his cigarette-less mouth and walked past her in the opposite direction. She felt a chill as they crossed paths. She told herself that the fellow must be a Cobble Cove resident and was simply walking home or to work, as most people in the town did, but she couldn't quite shake the feeling that there was something sinister about him.

Irene's house turned out to be a small brick ranch in a cul-de-sac. It reminded Alicia of Mac's cottage before it was expanded. She wondered if there was enough room there for Irene's daughter and grandchild. She knew they lived with her, and she worried, as she approached the door, that Maggie might be home. After their confrontation in the hollowed-out shop, she wasn't eager to see the young woman again.

Her fears were laid to rest when Irene answered the door. At noon, she still had on a robe. Dark circles lined her eyes, and she looked as though she had aged ten years in the space of the four days since Alicia last saw her.

"Alicia." Even her voice was weak.

"I came to see how you were doing, Irene. Is it okay if I come in? I'm sorry I didn't call."

Irene didn't question how Alicia had found her address. She opened the door.

"Maggie just went to pick up some lunch for me and Toby." Toby was Maggie's two-year old son. "You can join us if you'd like. She always gets extra."

Alicia figured Irene wasn't eating much. She appeared thinner as if she'd lost a few pounds. It looked as though she hadn't been out of the house in days even to grocery shop. Alicia knew that type of apathy that came with depression. She'd experience it herself after her first husband's death.

"Thanks, but I have to get home to start packing for my trip tomorrow. Sheila's given me the rest of the day off." She stepped into the house.

"That's nice of her. It's good to get away. I'll be leaving myself next week for my folks in Florida."

Alicia had feared Irene would be moving quickly, but she hadn't expected it to be that soon.

"I'm sorry you're moving. We'll miss you." She meant that.

"I'm not moving. I'm just going down for a week to canvas things out. Maggie and Toby aren't coming. They're still dealing with the police and insurance company."

Irene led Alicia into the living room. Similar brown boxes as those in the gift shop were scattered about the room spilling their contents, while a bunch of toys were also littered about.

"Excuse the mess. I haven't been in the mood to clean, and Maggie is a bit of a clutterer. It doesn't help that this place is so small. Toby hardly has room to play. It'll be different when we find something in Florida."

"I'm so sorry about what happened," Alicia said as Irene moved a toy block off a chair.

"Have a seat. Do you want any tea or something else to drink?'

"Please, Irene. I can't stay."

She remained standing. As she wondered where Toby was, the little boy wearing blue-striped pajamas came down the hall from what she presumed was his bedroom. He was rubbing his eyes and tousling his sandy hair with the fingers of his right hand. He held a teddy bear in the crook of his left arm.

"I see you've finally risen, young man," his grandmother said. "You need to go to sleep earlier, but I know it's not easy in this house with your mom playing music until midnight."

She sighed. "My daughter still has all those rock albums of her ex. I think she should've burned them, although now she has them in digital form, too. I remember vinyl records and 45's."

"Gramma," Toby said waddling toward Irene. "Teddy woke me up. He had a bad dream."

"Oh, did he?" Irene scooped Toby up in her arms. "Toby, this is Mrs. McKinney. She works as a librarian at the library."

"Hi, Mrs. Mac."

"McKinney," Alicia corrected. "I have a son and daughter younger than you."

The boy smiled, his hazel eyes twinkling. She could see a bit of Maggie in him.

"I'll leave you two to your lunch then," Alicia said aware Toby's mother might be arriving any minute. "I just wanted to stop by and say hi on my way home."

Although Irene's house was not on the route to Stone Throw Road, it wasn't exactly a lie.

"That was sweet of you." Irene sat with Toby on her lap in the chair she'd emptied for Alicia. "I hope you have a good time in New York. I haven't been back there in years."

Alicia thought of Irene's experience at her parents' shop in Queens and understood why she hadn't visited there in such a long time.

"Thank you. I hope to be back before the Cobble Cove Christmas Fair opens. Since you said you'd only be in Florida a week, maybe you can join us there one night. We're bringing Carol and Johnny. I'm sure Toby will love it. Santa is coming."

She knew her husband would have a special treat for Toby when John dressed up as Santa in the chair by the Cobble Corner gazebo.

"Santa!" Toby's eyes lit up brighter.

"Maybe we'll make it," Irene said. "I haven't been out much since . . ." she paused. "Well, things should be back to normal by the time we both return."

She looked down at her grandson. "You'll have to be extra good to me and Mommy to see Santa when we get back."

Toby nodded solemnly. "Yes, Gramma. I will."

"Say goodbye to Mrs. McKinney now. Thank you again for coming, Alicia."

"Bye, bye, Mrs. Mac." He waved. Alicia didn't correct him this time.

***

As Alicia hurried away from Irene's house in the hope she wouldn't run into Maggie on her way home, she felt bad that she was avoiding the gift shop owner's daughter. She had every right to grow angry at the violation of her mother's shop, and it wasn't Alicia she'd been angry at, but the circumstances. How hard it must've been for Irene to break the news to Maggie that she'd been conceived in violence instead of love. How long had she known, and how had she reacted? The two of them seemed quite close, which was understandable.

To Alicia, Irene as well as Sheila, who had raised her daughter alone after her husband's sudden death, were remarkably strong women. Despite John's belief in her strength, Alicia felt emotionally like a weakling compared to those two ladies. She had been frightened off by imaginary footsteps and a shady looking man who was probably a friendly neighbor, while they'd faced real tragedy. Even her experience with her first husband hadn't been a true trial. She had been so naïve and trusting. Then when she'd found what appeared to be evidence of John's involvement in a murder, how could she not have realized it was intended for blackmail? She berated herself all the way home chanting in her mind, shoulda, coulda, woulda. The past was over. She'd cut loose from it when she'd made the decision to move to Cobble Cove. Now she had to work on becoming the woman John believed in, his faith in her never faltering, even when she'd turned her back on him.

Chapter Fifteen

Kim was at the house when Alicia arrived home. She was reading the babies a book in the nursery when Alicia came up the stairs. As Alicia entered the room, she saw the babysitter in the rocker with the twins. Kim was displaying a picture book and making finger movements as she acted out the characters' actions. Alicia had seen Laura do the same thing during Children's' Storytime's. She also sang and involved the kids with questions and other activities to keep them focused and entertained.

As soon as she walked into the room, Carol and Johnny turned around and Kim paused in her reading.

"There's Momma," she told the twins. "Hey, Mrs. McKinney, are you home for lunch?"

"I'm home to stay. Sheila gave me the rest of the day off to finish getting ready for the trip. I'm glad it will also give us a chance to go over things. I haven't had much time to write too many instructions, but you may have noticed I put up the hotel's main phone number and address on the refrigerator along with our cell numbers. After we're checked in, we'll call with our room phone."

Kim smiled and placed the *The Three Little Pigs* book down.

"Don't worry. Everything will be fine. I'll be here tomorrow around noon to meet Mrs. Morgan. Andy said he can come, too. He's going to start working on your office with me. It'll be all ready for you when you get back from New York."

Alicia picked up her twins, feeling a slight twinge in her back as she did so. They were getting to be a bit heavy to carry, although Kim seemed to have no problem. The advantages of youth.

"Sorry I interrupted your story, kids," she told them as she placed them back in their cribs. They didn't seem to object. Carol was playing with a strand of her hair, curling it around her fingers as she often did, but Johnny felt wet, so she asked Kim if she could help her change him.

"You don't need to stay since I'm home," she said as they put Johnny on the changing table, and Kim grabbed a diaper from the box on the shelf.

"But you need to pack. I can watch them, so you can do that."

"I was thinking of packing tonight while John is at the town hall meeting. It'll give me something to do."

"I don't mind staying, really."

Alicia knew the girl could probably use the time to shop or study. The end of the college term was close, and reports would be due soon along with end of semester exams.

"No, you go ahead. You'll have plenty of time with Carol and Johnny next week if you can steal them away from their aunt."

"Okay. If you insist. I do have to prepare for some finals."

After changing Johnny and putting him back in his crib, Alicia took some cash from her purse and handed it to Kim.

"I'm paying you for the full time. Use it for Christmas shopping or something for yourself. John has probably worked out an arrangement to pay you and Andy for your time next week. I think he mentioned he'd give you some money before we go and the rest when we get back if the room is complete."

"It will be. Once Andy gets started on a project, he doesn't quit."

A light came into Kim's eyes as she mentioned her boyfriend. Alicia knew the young man was a bit like John in his persistence to complete a task. It was a good quality, but could also be frustrating if the task proved too difficult. She thought of John struggling with his writer's block and hoped their trip would refresh him and clear his mind.

She walked Kim downstairs.

"Maybe I'll finish reading to the twins later," she said as Kim slipped into the furry white vest she used instead of a coat, swinging her ponytail over the collar.

"Why don't you rest? Traveling is tiring, and John told me your father-in-law is coming early tomorrow morning to drop off his dog. I hear he's a golden retriever. I can't wait to meet him. I love animals. I wish we had pets. When I'm older and move away from home, I'm planning to have a house full of them."

"Pets certainly are great. I'd love Carol and Johnny to grow up with them. Sneaky is here sometimes, but maybe when they get a little older, we'll ask Dr. Clark if she knows where we can adopt a kitten from a shelter."

"There's one in Carlsville, but Mrs. Whitehead told me when I visited the library once that Sneaky just turned up there. She said that's how people get a lot of their pets— they just come into their lives at the right time."

Thinking back about the cats of her childhood, Alicia had to agree.

"Yes, that happens with many of them. Sometimes you have to look a bit before the one that's especially right for you comes your way. I remember the cat I had before I married my first husband. His name was Floppy. I picked him out of a litter of gray and white kittens at a pet store with my mother when I was in high school. He seemed the friendliest and came to me when I approached his cage. Unfortunately, after we brought him home, we discovered he was sickly. He had asthma and then developed diabetes. I ended up giving him insulin shots twice a day. I had to learn to do that because my mother was afraid of needles. But it actually helped bond me and Floppy. He lived until he was almost fifteen when I had to put him to sleep to stop his suffering. It was the year before I met my first husband. He never cared for animals and we both worked, so I never thought about getting another pet. The toughest part is saying goodbye to them."

Alicia still felt pain at the memory of her loss.

"How sad." Kim opened the door. "Andy has a dog and likes cats, too. If things work out between us, I'm sure he won't object to us keeping pets in our house. Cats are a bit easier to care for when you work, but I'll probably be home with the babies." She smiled. "I know it's hard when you lose a pet, but I'm sure the joy you get from them is worth it."

"It must be because there are millions of pet owners."

"Yes, but not all of them treat their pets like kids. I wouldn't want to be the type of owner to neglect my pet. Then it wouldn't be right for me to have one."

Alicia thought of Gilly and how she babied her beagle, Ruby. To some people, pets were like their children.

"I agree, Kim. Like kids, you shouldn't have them if you aren't ready for the responsibility."

"Absolutely. Okay, Mrs. McKinney. I'll see you tomorrow.

"Thanks, Kim. Good luck with your studies."

***

After Kim left, Alicia went back to the nursery and spent the rest of the day with the twins. She enjoyed having this special mommy time with them. Each day, she marveled at the amazing changes in them. Not only were they maturing physically, gaining weight and growing, but they were beginning to master complex concepts. It wouldn't be long before their babbling would turn into words, and, as John alleged, Carol was definitely the mastermind of naughtiness. As Alicia played with them, peekaboo games with their stuffed toys, changing her voice to make Johnny's teddy talk and Carol's doll sing, she thought back to the day she discovered she was pregnant.

Although she and John did not think their chances of having a family was possible at their advanced ages, she'd stopped birth control the day John proposed. She actually thought of it as his second proposal, the first taking place on top of Cobble Point that day in December when he'd told her he'd been cleared of murder. Then on New Year's Eve, at the stroke of midnight as they celebrated at Dora's Inn, the place they met, John made it official. Charlie also took that opportunity to propose to Dora. That May, both couples took their vows at the church in Cobble Cove and had a garden reception at the inn.

Six months later, Alicia missed two periods. Afraid to mention anything to John, she made an appointment with a gynecologist who confirmed she was pregnant with twins. Alicia announced the wonderful news to John when they had Thanksgiving with Dora, Charlie, and Mac. She would never forget the look of astonishment and joy on her husband's face as he paused over his turkey dinner. They had so much to be thankful for that year. They still did.

Her little ones grew sleepy in her arms after she'd finished reading to them, and she gently placed them in their cribs. Carol curled up next to the red-headed doll Sheila had given her, and Johnny hugged his teddy as he closed his dreamy blue eyes. It was afternoon naptime, so Alicia was able to do some packing, start a list of instructions for Pamela, and even cook dinner before John got home. She was happy to surprise him with the meal since he'd been the chef the past few nights.

***

John left for the Town Hall meeting at a quarter to seven that night. He dressed in a gray suit, even though the meetings were usually casual with Casey supplying beer, wine, and soda along with some snacks. The Town Hall Board was the second most influential committee in Cobble Cove besides the library. The members included John, Casey, Dora's husband Charlie, Sheila, Edith, and Rose. They met once a month usually on a Friday to discuss town concerns that were addressed to them and voted on resolutions to these issues. The main topic on the agenda that night was the hiring of a town sheriff, and Ramsay had been invited to attend to introduce himself and what he could offer them in the way of protection for their community.

As Alicia busied herself finishing packing, her mind wandered to what was transpiring at Town Hall. She agreed that Ramsay had changed since his medical scare and that Detective Faraday on Long Island had always believed his previous partner to be an excellent cop, but would Ramsay be a good fit in the small town of Cobble Cove? Since the gift shop robbery, she was certain people were pushing for a local law representative, and she herself would feel safer knowing there was someone else to call besides the police, miles away in New Paltz.

Just as she had zipped up the last suitcase, realizing she'd over packed as usual, the babies began crying from upstairs. They had taken a second nap after dinner, which wasn't that common for them, especially as they were getting older and requiring less naptime. She feared they were coming down with something, even though Carol no longer had the sniffles. John said she was just worrying too much.

She decided to bring the twins downstairs to wait with her for their father. John had lit the fireplace before he left. It added a warm glow to the parlor. She set up the playpen with some of the twins' toys, so they could play within sight of her. She also warmed up their milk bottles and took turns giving each a drink. She wiped both their mouths with their bibs afterwards to clean off their white "moustaches."

Laughing, she hugged them to her. "You kids are so funny."

Carol giggled and Johnny, the quieter one, smiled showing what might be the start of a dimple.

John had been at the meeting over an hour, but Alicia figured the meeting might run late. John had told her not to wait up for him, as Mac and Betty would be dropping Fido off early the next morning. But she knew the babies weren't tired, and she really didn't want to sleep upstairs alone. She had to admit she was still a bit on edge from her fright a few nights ago and from seeing the man in the gray coat again when she'd visited Irene.

Sitting by the fire with the babies playing in their playpen, Alicia suddenly heard a noise outside. At first, she thought it was John's car. He had taken the pickup to the meeting because he was giving a ride to Casey, whose car was in the shop getting repaired. It was an old, half dead 60's Thunderbird, but Casey insisted it was vintage and vowed he would never part with it. John said it was a piece of junk.

The noise outside was more of a rustle than a car engine. The night had turned windy, so Alicia told herself that was the source of the sound. But when she heard the doorknob turn, her heart quickened.

"Who's there? John, is that you?" she called out, but she knew it couldn't be John. He had locked the door when he left and told her he would open it with his key when he got home so as not to disturb her or the twins.

Alicia went to the door. The sound stopped. She switched on the outdoor light, which she should've done earlier and looked through the window and keyhole. If someone had been there, they were already gone. Maybe it was one of those people selling things door to door or a kid raising money for their school, but then why hadn't they knocked? Then she noticed the Christmas display was dark. She thought John had left it on. He had shown her the remote that would turn it off and on that he kept near the door. The lever was up, but the lights were dark. She would have to ask him about it when he came home. She checked to make sure the door was still locked and then went back to the babies.

***

When John finally came through the door around eleven-thirty, he was whistling softly, a habit he'd picked up from his father. She had already put the babies to sleep in their cribs.

"Ali, what are you doing up? I told you not to wait for me."

Then he noticed the look on her face. "What's wrong? Are the babies okay?"

"They're sleeping, John, but I think someone tried to break in. I heard someone at the door, but when I went to see who was there, they were gone. I had forgotten to leave the outside light on, and the Christmas lights don't seem to be working."

"What?" John was halfway out of his coat. "Those cheap bulbs. Duncan promised me they'd work all winter if I wanted to keep the display up that long."

He walked to the shelf where Alicia had left the remote switch after trying it, and fingered the control. "Nope. You're right. They're dead. I'll have to ask Dad about it in the morning. We tested them. You saw them when you came home."

He had a puzzled expression. Hanging up his coat and replacing the remote on the shelf, he walked over to his wife. "Let's go sit by the fire, and you tell me what happened tonight. Everyone's on edge in town, but maybe they'll relax more after we swear Ramsay in this spring."

So the town had voted to hire the retired detective for their sheriff.

Alicia followed John to the rockers. "I'm glad to hear we're going to have a sheriff, but why does it take so long to put him in office?"

John sat in a rocker, and Alicia sat next to him in the other. "It's a process, honey, lots of red tape, but he was chosen unanimously. Of course, no one else was running and considering the recent crime, it was pretty obvious he'd be picked." he grinned grimly. "But back to you. You said you heard someone at the door?"

"Yes. They turned the door knob. I'm just relieved it was locked."

"Do you want to report it? We're leaving tomorrow, but it might be a good idea to have someone keep an eye on the house since you've had other encounters in the area so far."

Alicia considered John's suggestion. "There's really nothing solid we can point to, but I think we should warn Pamela and Kim. Even though Ramsay's not yet official, maybe you should also mention this to him."

"That sounds like a good idea, honey. I'll call him right now."

After John got through speaking with Ramsay, he said, "He offered to come over and check the door for prints, but he said that if it was anyone trying to break in, they'd probably have worn gloves. He promised to watch the house while we're away."

"Good. What else happened at the meeting?" Alicia was more than happy to put aside her fear with John sitting next to her and the babies sleeping safely in their cribs.

"The usual. . . They're purchasing more computers for the school. The newspaper was commended on its coverage of the gift shop burglary. I have to let Andy know about that. He was the one who wrote the piece."

Alicia hadn't even read it. She loved to read each week's paper, but she'd avoided the one with the front page photo of Irene in tears standing on the glass spattered floor of her shop.

John paused. "There was one other item before we broke for refreshments."

Alicia noticed the darkening of his eyes and heard the note of caution in his voice.

"What was that, John?"

"Charlie got up and informed us that they're putting the inn up for sale after the holidays."

"Oh, no." The Cobble Inn was close to Alicia's heart, as the place she'd met John and where she and Dora had shared breakfasts in the quaint kitchen. They'd also celebrated every Thanksgiving there as well as their joint wedding reception. Dora made her own sweet smelling soaps and lotions and also grew herbs like Mac. The inn had expanded, and Edith and Rose had been hired to help with the influx of visitors. The holiday season brought even more.

"I don't understand, John. They're doing a booming business."

John lowered his eyes. "Dora's not feeling too well lately, Ali. She and Charlie aren't young. They think they'd be better off down South in a retirement home. They'll get a nice nest egg when they sell."

"I don't believe this." Alicia's mind was racing, trying to recall any indication that Dora had come to this decision. When had she seen her last? She'd been so tied up with her work at the library and taking care of the babies.

"Dora's not sick. Is she, John?" Alicia feared her first friend in Cobble Cove might have cancer or another disease.

"No. Other than some arthritis, she's fine. I know we'll miss them, Ali, but remember Dad's favorite saying, 'everything happens for a reason.'"

"I just can't imagine Cobble Cove without her."

"Someone else will take over the inn, and it'll still be here for us."

"It won't be the same."

John got up. "Why don't we go to bed? We have an early day tomorrow. I'm sorry I was so late. After the meeting was over, the women got to gossiping and the men gabbing with each other."

"So what else is new on the grapevine?" Alicia was still thinking of Dora. She'd have to talk with her when they returned from New York.

John helped her from her seat. "We'll talk upstairs. I want to check the twins."

As they went to the nursery, John slipped in as Alicia stood in the doorway. She watched him kiss Carol lightly on the cheek and Johnny on the forehead before joining her in the hall.

"Out like two lights. What did you do to them, Mommy?"

"We played. I gave them their bottles and then had them out in their playpen while I waited for you."

After they'd changed into their night clothes, John let Alicia lay against his chest. "There was one item of interest on the men's grapevine."

She laughed. "Fill me in." She knew some of the men were worse gossips than the women.

"Well, actually, this was told to me in confidence by Casey when I dropped him home. It seems Gloria's been acting oddly lately. She's come to work late, which is unusual for her. Casey thinks it's Walter. He said she wore a long blouse the other day, but he could see a black and blue bruise under it."

"That's awful. Does Casey suspect Walter beat her?"

"I think so. He said he's seen Walter come into the diner drunk, and when he's eaten there with Gloria, he depletes Casey's liquor supply."

Hearing this news, Alicia wondered if Walter might've been drunk the night Bonnie made her accusation against him.

"Maybe Sheila should be told."

"I don't think so, Ali. If she catches him drinking at the library, that's a different thing. But this is just Casey's word."

"But you know about Bonnie, John, and why Sheila took Casey off the job for three nights during the week."

"More hearsay. Look, honey. I'm sorry I brought all this bad news home with me and that you had another scare. We're going to have a wonderful trip tomorrow. It'll be just the two of us in Manhattan during the holidays in a honeymoon suite. We've got tickets to Radio City, and I'm planning to buy you some nice things in the stores. I really think this will be good for us. I'm beginning to feel excited. Let's put this place behind us and concentrate on having fun."

She snuggled closer to him. "You're right, John. We deserve some time together, and I'm looking forward to it, too."

But even though she tried to put her worries aside, Alicia couldn't help thinking about Irene, Maggie, Angelina, Gloria, and Dora, as well as the two scary episodes she'd experienced – the footsteps behind her as she walked home from the library and the door knob turning while John was at the Town Hall meeting. Along with these thoughts, was the image of the man in the gray coat that kept popping into her mind. As she lay with John, she wondered if she should've mentioned the man while Ramsay was on the phone. She was about to tell John now, when she noticed his eyes were closed and heard low snores emanating from his mouth.

Chapter Sixteen

When Alicia finally fell asleep, she had a strange dream. She hadn't had one this unusual since the ones she'd had two years ago while staying in what used to be an upstairs guest room of the library. This time, she was walking down a dark street. She wasn't sure if it was Stone Throw Road. Footsteps sounded behind her. But, unlike the real life experience, she turned her head. A man with a black ski mask over his face followed her, his long gray overcoat flapping as he advanced. She ran, and he disappeared. Then she heard caroling from the distance. No singers were in sight, just the drifting melody that sounded like a recording. She realized she was in Cobble Corner and straight ahead was the gift shop. Her footsteps led her there.

When she touched the door, it slid open, as if waiting for her. It was dark inside, but she could see glass scattered on the floor, large jagged pieces, how the shop must've looked before it was cleaned up after the burglary. She slept while her mind processed these things. The dream led her to the checkout desk. The masked man stood there holding Angelina against his chest, a large shard of glass at her throat.

"No," Alicia yelled. "Leave her alone."

The man smiled from behind the mask, his yellowed teeth glinting in a spotlight that suddenly shown around him. Angelina looked terrified, but Alicia knew she was too scared to utter a sound as the man inched the glass toward her neck.

Alicia stood in their path. She kept her voice firm. Showing fear would only feed this deranged man's hunger for control. "Let her go. Take me. I know you've been following me."

The man released Angelina who backed away with a cry. He approached Alicia.

"Show me who you are."

Alicia's voice broke. She knew he meant her harm, but she had to make him reveal himself. She had to find out who her enemy was, so she could learn how to fight him.

The man began to lift the ski mask. She was going to meet her assailant. But as he pulled it off, she heard John's voice.

"Ali. Are you okay?"

She looked toward the shop door, but no one was there. Someone was shaking her. She thought it was the masked man. She struggled to be free.

"It's alright, Ali. You're just dreaming."

She opened her eyes and saw John next to her in bed.

"Oh, John." She took a deep breath. "It was horrible."

"It must've been. You were shaking and saying some strange things."

He put his arm around her.

"I was in Irene's shop. Someone followed me there. He was wearing a ski mask, but he had on the same coat as the man I've been seeing around town. He had Angelina, and he was threatening to slit her throat with a large piece of glass. I convinced him to take me instead but to show me who he was first. He was about to remove his mask . . . Then you woke me."

She shivered even though the room was warm.

"Oh, honey. When you have a nightmare, you go all out." John tried to make light of the situation. He kissed her cold cheek.

"You'll sleep much better in New York and only dream of our passionate nights." He grinned.

"Sorry, sweetie. I know you were really frightened, but it was only a nightmare. You've had some things on your mind. Your subconscious made up a storyline. I must say it was quite creative. I wish I could remember my dreams. I might work them into our next mystery."

"I know you're right, but it seemed like a message. That may sound crazy. Like you said, dreams are a reflection of your thoughts and experiences while you're awake that your subconscious puts together like a puzzle with different pieces in different places. I've been seeing this man around town. Laura's seen him, too. I think it was him behind the ski mask. I should've said something last night when you spoke to Ramsay. He might be the person who followed me and possibly broke into the gift shop. I saw him hanging around there smoking after I bought Gilly's gift, and he passed me on the street yesterday. You saw him when we left Cove Point."

John's brows knit together. "We could mention this to Ramsay, but it's not proof of anything, Ali, except that you were thinking about this guy and he ended up in your dream." He reached out and smoothed back a strand of her hair that had fallen across her face. "I know you're worried about everything that's been going on, and I don't blame you. But you can't let your imagination start playing tricks on you. Leave the detecting up to Ramsay and the officers in New Paltz."

He glanced at the alarm clock. "Come downstairs with me. I'll make us and the twins some breakfast. I'm glad you woke me because Dad and Betty should be arriving soon."

Alicia's fears weren't totally assuaged, but she got out of bed and followed John out of the room.

***

John prepared scrambled eggs. He made enough for Mac and Betty, and they arrived as he was adding some slices of bread to the toaster while he started the coffee maker. Alicia answered the door to the tapping she recognized as her father-in-law's cane. The elderly couple stood on the doorstep with Fido between them like one of their children. Alicia knew how pets could be substitute babies. Gilly regarded her beagle as her fourth child, and now that John was grown and Betty's own kids were tragically lost, the dog had bonded with Mac and Betty.

"Good morning." Mac's smile was wide. "It's a beautiful day for travel. How are you, my dear?"

He and Betty wore matching light blue ski pants and parkers.

She didn't suspect he noticed the remnants of worry on her face.

"I'm fine, Mac. Why don't you and Betty come in? John has made scrambled eggs this morning, and there's enough for all of us to share."

"When are you going to start calling me dad?" Mac asked, his blue eyes twinkling. "You've been married to my son over a year now."

He led Fido, sniffing the air, into the house. "I hope there's enough food for Fido, too."

"We know you'll give him some of yours. That's how you keep so trim," Betty said ambling in with her cane.

She turned to Alicia. "Hi, Alicia. Thank you for asking your sister-in-law to watch Fido while we're away. I'm sure the children will enjoy playing with him."

It was true Carol and Johnny loved Fido when he came to visit. As soon as the dog bounded into the kitchen almost knocking over John with his arms full of plates, Carol and Johnny wiggled in their high chairs. Carol put out her arms to pet the dog.

"They're eating now. If they touch Fido, they will have to clean their hands."

"I'm on it," John said holding a wet rag. "They're just eager to see their fur friend."

"Can I help you, John?" Betty offered.

"No, thanks. Just have a seat."

"John used to cook all the time with his mother," Mac said sitting in one of the extra chairs John had added to the table. Betty sat in the other. "I wasn't allowed in the kitchen except to make my PB&J sandwiches."

He grinned again. "So are you two ready for your wild weekend in New York?"

Betty tapped his arm.

"C'mon, honey buns, you know what young people do on second honeymoons."

Betty laughed. "You're such a tease, Jonathan."

Jonathan? Alicia didn't realize Betty was calling Mac by his full name now.

John placed the two egg plates on the table in front of his father and Betty. "I'll be right back with ours, Ali, and some toast and coffee for everyone."

As he made his way to the stove, Fido looked up at him with his big brown eyes, one paw extended in full begging mode.

"Whoops," John said deliberately dropping a piece of egg on the floor. I'm so clumsy."

Fido eagerly gobbled it up.

"You'll be mopping that floor, John," Alicia said with mock firmness as she went to give him a hand with the toast and coffee.

"I always clean up after I cook."

John finished filling their plates and brought them to the table along with the twins' baby food. Alicia poured coffee all around and passed the plate of toast.

"Are you guys all set for your weekend at Smugglers' Notch?" John asked as they were eating. His grin matched his father's.

"You bet. Betty and I may even attempt the slopes."

"You're kidding, right?"

Mac speared some egg onto his fork. "I am not. You only live once, son."

"I just don't want to see the two of you with matching casts in the hospital."

"Don't worry. I'll keep him tethered to our room," Betty said with a matching twinkle in her eye.

"Brought along that nightie I like, huh?"

Alicia wasn't a prude, but she was becoming uncomfortable with the conversation. She remembered the Christmas lights and changed topics.

"Mac, the lights you helped John put up yesterday were lovely, but they didn't seem to be working last night."

John poured himself another cup of coffee and offered it around the table. Mac declined and then answered Alicia.

"I'll have a look before we leave. John's mom and I used to have awesome displays each year. Remember, John?" His eyes took on a sadness at the mention of his dead wife.

"Yes, Dad. You guys did a great job decorating the house. All my pals in the neighborhood were jealous."

Alicia could imagine a young John. so proud of his parent's handiwork, boasting to his friends.

Fido lay under the table waiting for the next scrap to fall his way. The twins had baby food smeared chins. It was a happy morning, and Alicia could almost forget her frightening dream and the reality of her doorknob being turned the night before.

*** *

After they'd all eaten, Betty helped Alicia do the dishes while John mopped the floor and cleaned the babies' mouths. Mac went outside to check the Christmas lights. When he returned, he was no longer smiling.

"Looks like you guys have a prankster hanging around. Maybe one of the eighth-graders from Fairmont."

"What do you mean, Dad?" John put the mop back in the dust closet and turned to his father.

"That was no defective bulb. A few of the wires were cut. Looks like they did it with a blade of some sort. I hate it when kids get destructive. I wouldn't expect that here, though."

Alicia almost dropped the plate she was washing. "Mac, are you saying someone deliberately turned off those lights?"

"Yep. Sorry, Alicia. I can't do anything about them now, but I'll replace them for you as soon as we're back. You won't be at home, anyway."

So there had been someone at their door last night. "Why would someone do that?"

"I think Dad already stated the reason, Ali. Vandalism is always senseless."

John came over to the sink and helped the women put away the dishes. Then he turned back to his father.

"Dad, Ali thought she heard someone outside last night. She actually said they tried the doorknob. I've asked Ramsay to watch the house while we're away, but do you think we should file a report with the police?"

Mac paused, considering John's question.

"Nah. Nobody was harmed. It would just tie us all up here and ruin our vacations. I would just have Ms. Morgan keep the doors locked. She's used to security from up on the North Shore. Besides, she'll have a watch dog to guard her." He looked down at Fido who was still scouting under the table for food scraps.

Alicia remembered Pamela's gated entrance with its intercom, but their locks were far from high tech, and she was even less confident of the protection an aging golden haired retriever would offer her sister-in-law despite the fact he was able to lead them to his missing owner during a snowstorm two years ago.

"I hate to leave town at a time like this," she said. "First, the burglary at the gift shop and now this."

John tried to soothe her. "I know you're worried enough about us leaving Carol and Johnny, but everything will be fine. I have total faith in my sister."

Alicia was amazed at how confident John sounded. He'd only known Pamela the last two years; after it was revealed Mac had a child with a woman he'd loved before he married John's mother.

"I'm still not happy about leaving like this."

"Alicia's got a point," Betty said. She had gone to the twins and was playing with them with the rattles she'd given them before they were born. If anyone knew how quickly danger could strike, it was Betty who had lost her whole family during a pleasant summer night's stroll.

"I'm sorry to cause all this worry," Mac said. "I should've told John privately. Women tend to blow things up."

Betty didn't like that. She pointed Johnny's blue rattle at Mac and shook it.

"Now you listen, Jonathan. This is not just feminine fancy. There's nothing wrong with taking precautions. The world can be an evil place, even in a small town like Cobble Cove. I know it's wrong to lock up your life and hide from fear like I did for too long a time. But there are measures you can take for safety."

"I think Dad's right and that we should just let this be until we get back, and I'm not saying that just because I'm a man." John smiled. "I agree with you ladies completely, and I'll definitely warn Pamela, but we'll only be away for a week. I doubt that troublemaker will strike again."

Alicia recalled how people had suggested her house fire was set by juveniles and how she'd refused to believe that theory until they'd arrested the kid responsible.

"Okay, John," she relented. "But when we get back, we should do something – install an alarm system maybe. I know a lot of the Cobble Cove Corner shops are planning to do that now."

John sighed. "We'll talk about it, Ali. Now C'mon, Pamela is arriving soon."

He put his arms around Alicia as his father, Betty, and the twins looked on and planted a very loud kiss on her mouth.

"That should shut you up." His blue eyes twinkled as she swatted at him.

***

After Mac and Betty left, giving Fido some farewell pets and still teasing one another like an old couple about the differences in how men and women viewed various things, Alicia brought the twins into the living room and set up their playpen while they waited for Pamela.

Alicia laughed as John stopped the twins from pulling the dog's tail as he walked by the playpen, but it seemed they were having fun and even Fido didn't mind the light yanks.

She left John to referee them and went down to her soon-to-be office to make one last check of the list she'd be giving Pamela. When the phone rang, she was surprised to hear Laura on the other end.

"Alicia, I'm sorry to bother you before you leave for your trip. I actually called to wish you a nice one, but there's something else I thought you should know."

Laura didn't sound like her usual bubbly self. In the background, Alicia could hear some of her siblings squabbling over something.

Laura paused. "Hold on a second, Alicia. Yes, Lily, you can borrow that shirt. Just please don't forget to return it like you did last time."

She came back on the line a few minutes later. "She's always taking my stuff and keeping it. It doesn't help that we share the same room."

Having been an only child, Alicia couldn't sympathize. "What's wrong, Laura?"

Laura sighed, but it wasn't from exasperation with her younger sister. "Patty called me last night. Angelina's in the hospital."

"What?" The girl had looked fine when Alicia saw her at the grocery store just two days ago.

"She's had a relapse. Patty was frantic. They'll know in a few days if they have to start the bone marrow transplant search, but she and Gary don't have the money. They had placed their hopes on the funds raised from the Christmas Fair but that's not starting for another week and it probably won't be enough."

"Oh, my God!" Alicia's heart sank. More bad news before their trip.

"I wish we could do something. John won't let me ask Pamela, and it's true we can't keep relying on her."

"I'm sorry if I upset you, Alicia. I figured you'd want to know."

"It's okay, Laura. Please keep me posted. You have my cell. If anything happens while I'm gone, call me. I don't mind, really."

The thought of the little girl fighting for her life in a hospital bed clenched at her heart. It wasn't fair. Why was medical care in this country so astronomically high?

After Laura promised to keep Alicia informed of any changes in Angelina's condition, Alicia took Pamela's instruction list and left the room. As she stepped out into the hall, she heard John whooping with pleasure and watched him, down on his knees, racing Fido while the twins laughed from their playpens.

"Boy, these kids have a weird sense of humor, Ali."

John noticed the expression on her face and came to a halt. Standing up, he asked, "What's wrong?"

"Laura called. Angelina's in the hospital."

"Gary's little daughter?"

"Yes, and Patty's. She'll be out of work for a while. I wonder who will teach her classes."

"What a shame. It must be awful having a chronically ill child."

"I can hardly imagine."

"She shouldn't have told you the news before we left. It's just going to add to your worry, and there's nothing you can do. We've discussed this already, honey."

She looked into his deep blue eyes and saw the empathy there.

"I know. Okay, maybe we should get these kids to calm down a bit before their aunt arrives, and I think Fido's about had it. He's no pup anymore."

John agreed, and the two of them gathered up the twins, Carol still giggling and Johnny flashing his father's dimple, as Fido rolled over catching his breath from racing.

They brought the twins up to the nursery and changed them. As soon as they'd placed them both in their cribs to play with a few toys, the phone rang again.

Alicia jumped, worried it might be Laura, but John reached the bedroom phone first. She watched his face as he mimicked that the call wasn't from her. Judging by the loud rambling chatter coming through the receiver, she knew who it was.

"Yes, Mary Beth," John confirmed the caller's identity. "We're leaving in a few hours. I'm waiting for my sister."

John held the phone away from his ear as the cacophony of words spilled untethered from the other end. "I understand. Yes, Mary Beth. I will do my best. I think so, too. Thanks for calling."

He stuck out his tongue and hung up the phone.

"She's pushing for that first chapter again, I bet," Alicia ventured.

"More than that, Ali. She says that we're breaking our contract. If we don't come up with something soon, she has a legal right to cancel our agreement."

"Oh, John." She walked over to him. "How much time do we have?"

"Not much. She wants it before Christmas, the sooner the better."

Alicia hated to see John pressured this way, but she had so many other things troubling her.

"Don't worry. I think I'll be able to produce what she's looking for after the trip."

"John, you can't pin your hopes on that. If it's a matter of losing our publisher, I've already offered to write the first chapter."

"I know, Ali, and I appreciate that, but I need you to give me more time, too. Please have faith in me."

Alicia recalled the time she'd doubted John and he'd come through. She only hoped their time away would clear his writer's block, but she wasn't as confident it would as he was. She nodded.

"Of course, John."

"And if it doesn't work out, I can send Ms. Simmons a box of coal for Christmas or maybe something from Sneaky's litter box."

Alicia laughed as he grabbed and kissed her.

"Let's go downstairs and wait for Pamela. I don't hear anything from the nursery, but we can check the twins first. I have a feeling they're down for a nap after all the activity with Fido, even though I did all the work." He exaggerated being out of breath, although he was in great shape.

Sure enough, as Alicia and John peeked into the nursery, they saw both twins curled up around their toys – Carol hugging her doll and Johnny with his teddy—fast asleep. Downstairs, Fido was also slumbering, his breathing slowed down, his flanks rising and falling as he lay by the fireplace.

***

Wh>hen a rap sounded at the front door, Alicia expected it to be Pamela, but opening the door and seeing Kim there, she remembered the babysitter had promised to stop by to meet her sister-in-law.

"Hi, Kim." She hesitated as she took in the girl's appearance. Loose strands of brown hair fell out of her ponytail, and her blue eyes were red and watery.

Kim walked into the house without greeting Alicia. She looked around as if she'd never been there before.

"Is something wrong, Kim?" Alicia had to ask her. The girl looked dazed.

The question brought a tide of incoherent sobbing, and Alicia grabbed Kim as she fell against her chest. John had gone back upstairs to check the babies, and he must not have heard Kim's entrance.

"Let's go sit down, and you can tell me all about it."

Alicia knew women Kim's age were prone to dramatic episodes, but after the events of that morning, she prepared herself for more bad news.

Kim took a seat in a rocker by the fireplace, walking around the still sleeping dog. She'd brought a small tissue pack from her jean's pocket and dabbed at her eyes. Alicia sat in the chair across from her.

"Would you like some tea or something? Have you had breakfast?"

"Nothing, please. I'm not hungry." Kim gulped back tears.

Alicia hoped she could calm down the girl. She really didn't want Pamela to meet her in this condition.

"Tell me what happened, Kim. Is it your family? Is someone sick?"

"No." Kim waved her hand and a Christmas bracelet jangled off it, an ironic reminder of the merry season. "It's Andy."

Ah, Alicia thought, a lover's quarrel.

"Did you two have a fight?"

"It's worse than that," she sniffled. "He's acting so strange. He hardly talks to me, and I don't know what I've done."

"Did you ask him?"

"Of course." She swallowed.

"He won't tell me. He says everything's fine, but it isn't." Her voice rose. "He hardly looks at me. He hasn't asked me to a movie or anywhere all week."

Alicia considered the minds of men.

"You don't think he has someone else, do you?"

"I don't know." She wailed, and Alicia was afraid the sobbing would resume, but Kim caught herself and took a deep breath.

"He said he won't be able to help me work on your room while you're away. He made an excuse. He said his father needs him to do some stuff at home."

"And you don't believe him?" Alicia worried that Kim's lack of trust in Andy would hurt him and their relationship as her lack in John almost did.

"I know he's lying. I can tell."

Before Alicia could reply, she heard John's footsteps on the stairs, and he joined them.

"Is Pamela here yet?" He paused as he saw Kim in the rocker.

"Oh, Kim. Hi. I guess you're here to meet my sister."

Kim nodded.

Alicia thought it was best to talk to John privately about the situation.

"Kim, I need to talk to John about our trip a minute. You wait there for Pamela, and I'll be right back. Or, if you want, you can go upstairs and check on the babies. I think they'll be sleeping a while. John had quite a romp with Fido earlier, and the kids exhausted themselves laughing at them. As you can see, Fido's still out cold, as well."

Kim chose to remain seated by the fire staring into it. She hardly acknowledged Alicia leaving the room with John.

In the kitchen, John asked, "What's wrong, Ali?"

"Didn't you see her? The way she looked? She's all broken up over Andy. She thinks he's avoiding her."

Alicia had lowered her voice, so Kim wouldn't hear from the other room.

"Hmm. I should talk to him."

"We're leaving in a few hours. What did he say to you yesterday when you worked with him at the paper? Did he mention Kim?"

"He didn't mention anything. He didn't show up."

"What? You never said anything about that."

Alicia leaned on the sink counter. John stood in front of her.

"I didn't think much of it. This time of year people are busy. I put the finishing touches on this week's paper and figured Andy had worked out a schedule with Kim about coming here next week to do your office."

"I think that project is off. Maybe that's what this is all about. Was Andy keen on it when you discussed it with him?"

John looked down.

"I wouldn't build too much into this, Ali. Andy had to work off those earrings. I gave him a way to do that."

"The earrings. Maybe he's guilty that they were one of the ones from the gift shop."

"No, Ali. You're playing psychiatrist again. Don't do that. Kim and Andy are young. They have all sorts of issues going on in their lives. This could be something very simple."

"So I guess I'm not getting an office for Christmas."

"I wouldn't discount it. I'll bet they'll be kissing and making up tomorrow. That's typical of these young romances." He smiled.

"Now let's go back out there and wait for Pamela. Everything's going to be fine, but the sooner we're out of here, the better in my opinion."

He walked to her and tilted his chin up with his finger in the familiar way that made her heart lurch. "I have some extra special plans for us in New York, Mrs. McKinney, and nothing is going to ruin them."

Alicia only wished she was as confident as her husband. Black clouds seemed to have gathered around their home that morning, daring them to leave.

Chapter Seventeen

Both Kim and Alicia had calmed down by the time Pamela arrived. She breezed in, her ash blonde hair in a stylish bob, carrying a case that appeared surprisingly light considering the wardrobe Alicia imagined she owned. She'd parked her red sports car behind John's pickup because Alicia mentioned they'd be using her Ford to drive into the city.

"Sorry I'm late, folks," Pamela said as John took her coat and gave her a kiss on the cheek. "That traffic on I-87 was horrid this morning."

She made a face that temporarily wrinkled her brow. Alicia wondered if John's older sister had ever had a face lift. If not, she'd aged very well or the expensive beauty products she used had lived up to their claims. Her skin appeared as youthful as her twin daughters who were in their early thirties.

"Sorry your drive was so difficult, Pamela. Maybe we can all sit down and have lunch. Kim's here, and I want you to meet her."

Kim had gone upstairs to watch the babies, Fido at her heels, having recovered from his play session with John.

"That sounds wonderful. I must say you are looking well, Alicia. After I gave birth to Cynthia and Caroline I was a mess. It took a year and constant visits to the health club before I got my shape back."

"It's all the walking," John said hanging up Pamela's coat. "We hardly use a car here even in winter."

He turned back to his sister. "I made breakfast, so maybe Ali wouldn't mind taking care of lunch. There are cold cuts from Duncan's in the fridge. What would you like?"

Pamela smiled showing perfect white teeth. "I don't eat much meat nowadays, especially not the processed kind. Would you have any salad?"

"Sure thing. I stocked the kitchen with lettuce, tomatoes, and other vegetables. I wasn't sure what dressing you like, but there's a variety to choose from."

"Thank you, John. You look great, too." She turned to Alicia. "Where are my nephew and niece? I can't wait to see them."

"They're upstairs with the babysitter. I'll take you up. I can carry your bag. Do you have more cases in the car?"

Pamela fidgeted with her designer purse and extracted a set of keys. "Yes, would you mind getting them, John?"

"Of course not." He took the keys and headed out the door.

As Pamela followed Alicia to the nursery, the sound of high-pitched laughter echoed down the hall. Alicia dropped Pamela's bag in the bedroom and then joined her sister-in-law watching Kim tickling and blowing raspberries on the babies' bellies as they lay on the floor with Fido prancing around them, trying to figure out what all the excitement was about.

"You must be the babysitter," Pamela said entering the room.

"Yes." Kim's tears had dried and only a slight trace of redness rimmed them. It was good to see her having fun with the twins.

Kim stood up. "And you must be Ms. Morgan, Mr. McKinney's sister."

"I am, but please call me Pamela."

"I'm Kim."

Kim walked around Fido, just as Alicia picked up the twins and put them in their cribs.

"Fido's a good dog, but one of them might tease him by accident. You have to be careful with animals."

"My sister-in-law is quite a worrier," Pamela said to Kim. "The kids are having a ball and that dog is lovely. Do you mind if I pet him?"

The twins, back in their cribs, started to cry and hold out their small, chubby hands to Fido.

"Of course not," Alicia said trying to soothe her children. "He's going to be keeping you company while you're here next week."

She had an impulse to tell Pamela about the lights, but she hoped John would fill in his sister later and make sure she took the right precautions during her stay.

"I look forward to that and becoming more acquainted with my adorable nephew and niece."

Pamela went over to Fido. "Here, boy. Sit, boy. Aren't you handsome?"

Alicia was amazed at how Fido followed the commands. She knew Mac had given the dog some training, but she was surprised how he responded to Pamela's instructions.

"Have you ever had a dog?" Kim asked Pamela. "We don't have pets at our house, but we used to have cats and dogs. Then they got sick and it cost a lot to take them to the vet, so we didn't replace them after they passed."

"Pets are expensive," Pamela said. "We used to have quite a few when the girls were young, but I travel so much now that it wouldn't be fair to them. The only pets I currently have are my horses, and I pay people to care for them at my stables. By the way, how is Starburst? When will the babies start riding her?"

"Who's Starburst?" Kim asked as Pamela stroked Fido's golden fur.

"Starburst is the pony that Pamela gave the babies before they were born. He's at Cobble Cove Stables now, and John visits her occasionally. We plan to start the twins riding when they're a little older, probably two. They should really walk before they get in the saddle."

Pamela let out a short laugh. "I was born riding, but I understand."

John stood in the doorway wheeling a large suitcase, his arms full of two others. "You didn't tell me you were moving in, Pamela." He grinned.

***

They all went down to lunch which Kim helped Alicia prepare. John was catching up with Pamela. They spoke of happy things – the babies and Pamela's daughters who were still taking classes in Europe. Pamela mentioned that Caroline had a crush on her French teacher and that Cynthia was considering changing her major yet again to Egyptology. John almost choked on his coffee when she said that.

"Your daughter wants to study King Tut and the pyramids? What type of job will that lead to?"

John had confided in Alicia that he thought his sister's girls were a bit old to still be traipsing around the world trying to find themselves.

Pamela smiled as she fed Carol a spoonful of baby food and wiped her niece's mouth with her bib. "This certainly brings back memories. Thanks for letting me feed her, Alicia. I should take a turn with Johnny, as well."

"Both our kids are good eaters," John said. "As soon as they're old enough, I can't wait to try them on our family's special PB&J sandwiches."

Pamela still hadn't replied to John's question about her daughter Cynthia's new choice of study, but Alicia figured he wasn't about to probe. He had already finished his lunch and fed Johnny as well as Fido, who sat under the table diving for the scraps he sent the dog's way like his dad did.

"Ladies, I have an errand to run before Alicia and I head out. I'm sure she has some things to discuss with you two." John stood up.

"Leaving us to the cleanup, are you?" Alicia joked half serious. She wondered where John was going, but she was glad that she'd have some time alone to go over things with Kim and Pamela.

***

After John left, the three women cleared the table, and Pamela took the babies into the living room where Alicia had left the playpen from the night before. Fido bounded after them, eager to play, but Pamela persuaded him to sit by the fire with a few firm commands that he obeyed and was rewarded by her stroking his golden head. Alicia's sister-in-law definitely had a way with dogs.

Pamela and Kim discussed their plans for the following week as the twins played with their toys, occasionally reaching for Fido, but giving up as the dog remained at Pamela's side.

Alicia offered Kim and Pamela some tea and, when they both refused, she pulled a chair out from the kitchen to join them by the fire keeping her eyes and ears peeled on the babies even though they were restrained in their playpen. She hoped Pamela could manage on her own, but remembered that she'd raised twins herself; and, with Andy possibly off scene, it was likely Kim would have more time to devote to helping Pamela, too. Alicia regretted her office might not be complete by the time she returned, but it wasn't a priority project.

When Pamela brought up the work that was scheduled to be done on Mac's old room, Kim skirted around the subject.

"We don't want to disturb the babies with all the noise of hammering as we put up shelves and stuff," Kim said. "Maybe if you take the twins out one day, we can get to it."

Alicia noticed how Kim still used "we" when speaking of the job, as if she hoped Andy would come around.

Alicia gave Pamela and Kim the details of where she and John would be staying along with their cell numbers and a few instructions about caring for Carol and Johnny.

"Don't worry about a thing," Pamela told her. "Just enjoy my gift. You two need a second honeymoon, and I need some time with my nephew and niece."

***

When John returned, Kim had already left, saying she had some things to do that day, and Pamela had helped Alicia move the suitcases to the door. The twins were back upstairs playing with toys in their cribs. Fido was sleeping by the fire.

"Hey, all set, Ali?" John said as he came to the door.

While he seemed happy enough, Alicia noticed a shadow around his eyes as if something disturbed him. She told herself she was imagining it after all the troubles they'd learned of that morning. She was now determined to set those issues behind her as they left on the trip, although she still wanted to let Pamela know about the Christmas lights. She wished she'd told Kim, too.

As John loaded the cases into the car, she found an opportunity to be alone a few minutes with Pamela.

"We don't have great locks on these doors," she told her sister-in-law, "but you might want to use them at night. I already mentioned the gift shop robbery to you, but someone also turned the doorknob and cut the wires of our Christmas lights last night."

Pamela didn't look concerned.

"Those things happen everywhere, Alicia. No need to worry about me. I have a black belt, remember?"

"I just wanted to let you know."

Pamela came over and hugged her. Alicia caught the scent of her expensive perfume.

"Don't worry, dear. I will keep your children safe."

***

After Alicia and John said goodbye to everyone and both took turns kissing Carol and Johnny, they were finally off in Alicia's car. John had removed the car seats and left them in his pickup.

He drove, as Alicia checked off the things in her mind she may have forgotten. At the last minute, she had grabbed Gilly's gift off the bedroom nightstand where she'd left it wrapped and ready to bring with them because they were stopping at her house on the way to the city. She regretted she hadn't bought the boys anything, but had placed a few dollars for each of them inside cards.

"We're running a little late," John said, "I know we're hitting Gilly's first, but it won't matter if we end up in the city by nighttime. It'll be all lit up and waiting for us."

Already, she could see a difference in her husband. His shoulders were relaxed, his eyes calmer as they watched the road. She hated to ruin his mood, but she had to ask the question that had bothered her since he'd come home from his mysterious errand.

"John, where did you go before? You looked a little upset when you came home."

He maneuvered the car to pass a slow driver in the right lane. They were headed for an exit entrance ramp onto the highway.

"I was afraid you would ask, Ali, and I can't lie to you."

His voice had changed from excitement to one of concern. "I went to Andy's house. I wanted to find out why he wasn't at the paper the other day and have a quick chat with him about women."

A fleeting grin touched his mouth. "I didn't get the opportunity to do that."

"You mean he wasn't home?"

"Right. His mother said he was out with a friend. I didn't like how she looked when she said it, and then she invited me in for some coffee. I wasn't going to accept because I knew we had to leave soon, but she seemed to want to talk. As a reporter, I'm keen at observing people. I told her I only had a few minutes. She was alone because Andy's brother was also out, and you know she's a widow."

"Yes." Alicia mouthed the one-word reply because she wanted to hear the rest. She had a feeling John was building up to something she wouldn't particularly like.

"Well, I took a seat in her kitchen, and I was right that she was eager to talk. She needed someone to confide in." John made a right onto the exit and then continued.

"She said Andy had been acting strange all week. He'd been very quiet and his mind seemed to be elsewhere. At first, she put it down to his finding the gift shop vandalized. But then Kevin came over."

"Kevin?" Alicia had never heard the name before.

"I don't think I ever mentioned him to you because he wasn't worth mentioning." John's grin was now grim. "He and Andy went to high school together. He came to the paper once. They used to be buddies back then, but Kevin got into some trouble with drugs. Andy wasn't into that type of thing."

"What type of trouble, John?"

"He was selling the stuff. They caught him dealing at his old high school in Carlsville. His parents bailed him out, and he promised he'd turn over a new leaf, but Mrs. Phillips doesn't believe that. She isn't happy that Andy is hanging out with him again."

Alicia tried to process this information. She thought of Betty and Ramsay, how both of them had made dramatic personality changes, but it was true some people couldn't sustain their self-improvements like those who lost weight only to gain back the pounds and even more. Her father-in-law would probably have his own twist on the saying, "A leopard can't change its spots."

"Anyway," John added keeping up with traffic, "I tried to console her that I knew Andy well enough that he wouldn't get involved with drugs, but I'm not too sure. He's a good guy, but his family is suffering financially since the father died, and Mrs. Phillips hasn't been able to find a job. She also has some health issues, and her medicine is costly. She confided in me that Andy may not finish college. She says he refuses to take a loan, and they've almost depleted his college savings. There isn't even anything left for Alan to attend the university next year."

Alicia could imagine the appeal of extra money if it were offered to Andy, even if its source wasn't legal. But she wondered why the young man would take a chance that way rather than seek a student loan. She thought of John and his stubbornness when it came to asking his sister for more money, not only for them but for Angelina. On the other hand, John would never consider doing anything illegal for cash. He would much rather take a job away from his family five nights a week than do that. She winced at that thought, and John seemed to interpret it as her reaction to what he'd told her.

"I'm sorry, Ali. I didn't want to worry you with this, but you asked. I'm just hoping we can put all of this behind us this week. It doesn't look like Andy will be around to help Kim work on your office, but I promise I'll give her a hand next week when we're back. It'll be done by Christmas."

"But, John, Andy was working it off for you for the earrings."

"I know, but I'll forget about that for now. I still mean to talk with him. I'm probably old enough to be a father figure to him since his own is gone."

Alicia had no reply to that. Maybe John could talk some sense into the young man, but often those attempts backfired. If Andy left the paper, John would have to hire another assistant, especially since he'd be away in the city most of the week. *If* he landed the job he was interviewing for after their trip.

"Let's change the subject. Are you still giving Gilly that godawful sweatshirt?"

Alicia laughed, and it lightened her mood. "Oh, John. I think she'll love it."

"Hmm. I'll love the nightie she gives you."

He smiled, and this time it was genuine.

Chapter Eighteen

Alicia called Gilly from her cell phone when they were fifteen minutes away. She felt a mild homesickness as they pulled up to the ranch house so similar to the one she and Peter once shared in what felt like ages. In the last two years, she'd been back to Long Island a few times to settle the details of her insurance claim. The bank had taken over what was left of her burned-down home, and it was rebuilt and sold to an elderly couple. She had no desire to see it now. She'd cut loose those old threads when she married John and moved to Cobble Cove. Yet the sight of Gilly standing in the doorway with her dog Ruby at her side brought back so many memories. John had once said that you didn't realize how much you missed a place until you returned to it. That was true, but it was even truer about a person.

Alicia was out of the car as soon as John parked it, running up Gilly's walk as her friend opened the door and ran out, the beagle running with her. John stood back as the two women embraced, Ruby circling them and yipping, excited by the commotion.

"Gilly, it's so good to see you. I've missed you so much." Alicia felt tears well in her eyes.

"Same here, honey. Why don't we go in the house?" She looked over at John. "Don't act like a stranger, handsome. Come join us inside."

John grinned as he followed them into the cluttered, yet cozy, kitchen. A bunch of Christmas-shaped cookies stood on a platter in the center of the table. There was a six-foot tree in the living room decorated with handmade ornaments. Alicia figured the boys had made them with Gilly or their Boy Scout troops. The air was scented with evergreen and cinnamon. Alicia felt instantly at home.

"Have a seat, you two, and help yourselves to some of the cookies I baked with Danny. I hope you brought photos of your babies. I am just dying to see them."

Alicia and John sat at the table. John took a gingerbread man cookie, but Alicia declined.

"I have a bunch of pictures in my wallet, but I left the cards and your gift in the car. I'll go get them."

"No, Ali. I can do that," John offered. "You start catching up with Gilly." He wiped the crumbs off his mouth.

"He's still such a hunk," Gilly said with a wink as John went out the door. "I wish I was spending time with someone like that in New York."

"Oh, Gilly. I hope you meet someone. Maybe you'll have some luck in Cobble Cove. Are you decided about the job?"

"Wild horses wouldn't keep me away. It'll take time for the boys to adjust, but they'll keep in touch with their buddies through Facetime, and I'm sure they'll make new friends. You said they have a school there now."

"Yes. It goes up to eighth grade, but there's still talk about opening a high school in the next few years. Danny is going into seventh next year, I imagine." Danny was Gilly's eldest son.

"Speaking of the boys, where are they?"

Alicia looked around. A pile of mismatched socks and assorted sweatshirts were tucked away in a corner. A few notebooks and a bike helmet were tossed on a chair. It looked like Gilly had tried to neaten up, but hadn't been successful.

"Billy and Mike are at a Boy Scout meeting. I'll be picking them up in about an hour. Danny went to a friend's house for a sleepover. And, yes, he'll be going into seventh grade. He's looking like his dad every day, but thank goodness, he hasn't inherited his personality."

Gilly took a Santa cookie from the plate, broke it in half, and gave a piece to Ruby who was begging by her chair.

"You sure you don't want any cookies, sweetie? I can put on coffee or tea, too."

"No, thanks, Gilly, unless John wants something. It's starting to get dark, and we still need to check in at the hotel."

Gilly smiled. "Eager to get to your honeymoon suite, I see. While John is getting the stuff from your car, let me go get your special gift."

She jumped up, but Ruby didn't follow her. Instead, she came to Alicia's side, her brown eyes wide.

"You are as bad as Fido," Alicia told the dog as she fed her a piece of a Christmas tree cookie and ate the other half. She was more nervous than hungry, but a little sugar might give her some sustenance for the rest of their trip.

John came back at the same time Gilly returned to the kitchen. Both laid their gift-wrapped boxes on the table. The boxes were about the same size, standard clothing boxes. Alicia's featured cute snowmen and snowballs against a blue background. The bow was also blue.

"You go first," Gilly prompted. "I'll look at the pictures after we open our presents." She eyed Alicia's purse that John had handed her when he'd laid down Gilly's gift.

"If you insist," Alicia said as Gilly moved the gift to her side of the table.

"This paper is so cute."

Alicia tore it open along the taped corners, but Gilly exclaimed, "Just tear it open like the boys do. I'm not saving the paper."

Alicia ripped the rest of the gift wrap, splitting a few snowmen apart. Gilly took the paper and tossed it aside as Alicia lifted the lid of the uncovered box and the tissue paper that covered the garment it contained.

"Oh, my God!" Alicia said pulling out the sheer lace nightie of bright red.

Gilly laughed. "Happy Honeymoon."

John looked as though he was about to blush.

"And there's more. Look underneath."

Alicia followed Gilly's instructions and found a small book. A reprint of the *Kamu Sutra.*

"You are crazy," Alicia said, "but I love you." She got up and hugged her friend.

"Put it to good use. I also have something for John."

"I don't wear nighties. I sleep in the buff," he said surprising them both. That wasn't exactly true. John wore pajamas or at least their bottoms most of the time, in case he had to run to tend to the babies.

"It's not clothing."

Gilly reached into the pocket of her Christmas sweatshirt and pulled out a small version of Alicia's gift with the same wrapping paper and brought it over to him.

"I think you'll like it."

"You didn't have to, Gilly. Alicia's gift is good for both of us."

He grinned as he took the box. Ripping it open in one quick tear, he uncovered a thin, rectangular box. Alicia watched as he fingered the lid open and revealed a shiny silver pen nestled in a satiny case with the Cross name and logo.

"It has your initials. I know you use the computer to write your books, but I thought a nice pen might be handy to jot down notes or ideas when you're on the go."

"Thank you, Gilly."

John showed the pen to Alicia. "JM" was inscribed in gold against the silver. "That was very thoughtful and stylish, too." He looped the pen over the flap on the breast pocket of his plaid shirt." "I imagined it would be something, uh, less discreet."

"You have a dirty mind, Mr. McKinney." Gilly tapped him.

"This from the lady who gave my wife a see-through nightie and a copy of an Oriental sex manual."

Gilly ignored him and glanced at Alicia. "So show me those adorable baby pictures."

"Not until you open your gift." Alicia brought three envelopes from her purse. "And these are for the boys. There's some cash for each of them. I thought they might like to pick out something for themselves."

"Good idea. Thank you." Gilly took the envelopes and put them aside as she reached for her gift. Opening it, she took out the sweatshirt and smiled. "How nice. This is something I can wear around the house and also at work."

"I found it in the new clothes shop in Cobble Corner. I think you'll like the place."

"You know I'm not much of a shopper, Ali."

"I would prefer Alicia shop in the kind of place you bought that nightie," John interjected. "I guess you removed the tag, but it looks like a Victoria Secrets type of item."

Gilly rolled her eyes. "I think you like that gift more than she does."

"Well, my pen is rather nice, too, but it won't keep me warm at night."

Now Alicia was the one to tap his arm. "I think I'll bring out those photos for you to see now Gilly."

***

Alicia and John arrived in New York around six p. m. The city was lit up and bustling. Alicia was glad she'd asked John to drive as she sat on the edge of her seat. He maneuvered the narrow taxi and people-filled streets to reach their destination up town.

"New York drivers," John exclaimed as a car passed him without signaling and the cab in back of him blared its horn. People carrying totes and packages were crossing at the light.

"What does he expect me to do, plow into them?"

"Take it easy, John. I know you're not used to driving in the city anymore."

Alicia wondered how he would cope getting around Manhattan if he got the job at Columbia, but he would be staying there, most likely in university housing, and would probably use the subway or walk if he had to get somewhere. This definitely wasn't a driver-friendly place.

They made it to the doors of the Park Lane Hotel in one piece. John happily handed the keys to a valet parking attendant as a bellhop in a red velvet jacket loaded their bags on a suitcase trolley.

"Welcome to Park Lane" the gray haired man said as they followed him into the building.

John had produced their reservations, and the man smiled. "I'll get these right up to the honeymoon suite for you, sir." He waited a moment as John fished in his pocket for a tip.

Alicia went to the check-in desk as John tipped the bell hop. Both men and women in business suits stood in line, a few also wore cocktail and evening attire. The desk was strung with red and gold garland, and there was a large Christmas tree by the fireplace in the corner where a few guests mingled at tables in the lounge. All around there was brass, glass. and crystal. The atmosphere exuded wealth and refined culture. Alicia felt a little out of place, but the thirtyish receptionist smiled warmly as she handed Alicia two room key cards.

"Enjoy your stay with us, Mrs. McKinney. The elevators are around the corner. You take the one that goes up to the forty-fourth floor."

John was at Alicia's side then, and she handed him one of the room cards.

"Let's go on up and see what awaits us in the honeymoon suite, my bride."

***

Their room was subdued and quite stylish in hues of red and gold. Classy would be a good word to describe it. The suite contained a sitting area with a couch that faced a large, flat-panel TV/DVD player as well as a king-sized bed. Oversized picture windows looked out upon the city's buildings. The lighting could be dimmed to set the mood for lovers and although there was a writing desk, there was no phone or computer. For storage, the room contained a closet and one Cherrywood dresser. There was another cabinet near the bed that contained a fully-stocked bar – wines and liquors of all varieties along with glasses, goblets, and flasks.

John whistled softly. "My sister knows how to pick hotels."

"Our bags are here already," Alicia noted. The suitcases had been placed unobtrusively in the corner near the closet.

"Unpacking can wait, but we really should try the bed to see how comfortable it is." His grin told her he had another idea in mind than testing the bed's mattress.

"What about dinner?"

"There's a few nice restaurants in this hotel according to the brochure," John said picking up the hotel directory from the end table by the bed, "but maybe it's best we have room service tonight. I'm not in the mood to get dressed up formally, and I want to take you to a nice place for dinner tomorrow night after the show at Radio City. Remember, Pamela gave us some gift certificates along with our reservations."

Alicia had forgotten the plans. "That sounds good, John. I'm a bit tired from the drive myself and would rather relax tonight."

"Perfect. Why don't we get undressed and lay down a bit before we eat?"

"Okay. I'll check out the bathroom and freshen up first."

Alicia found two white cotton guest robes hanging on a hook behind the bathroom door. There was a tub with shower, toilet, and a bathroom vanity with a hairdryer and makeup mirror. Everything was rimmed with gold giving the room a gleaming, heavenly essence. Alicia felt as if she'd walked into a dream. There were bottles and jars of shower gels, shampoos, body lotions, and other toiletries on the shiny counter. Alicia thought of Dora's homemade soaps at the inn and felt a bit nostalgic. She wondered if the new innkeeper would replace those with store-bought ones or ones supplied to hotels that were cheap enough to be taken away by guests without concern.

As she slipped out of her clothes and donned one of the robes, she heard John moving around outside. She didn't want to keep him waiting too long.

She stepped out of the bathroom and saw John on the couch leafing through some newspapers and magazines that the hotel had left on the table. He had changed into his own robe that he must've retrieved from his suitcase.

The drapes at the long windows of the parlor were open to the glittering New York skyline. A nighttime view of Central Park beckoned from the bedroom.

"Hey, Ali." He glanced up. "There's some pretty interesting reading material here. International publications, some in other languages. A little strange they would be in a honeymoon suite, but this hotel caters to business people, too."

He dropped the magazine he was holding on to the table. "I was just trying to keep occupied while I waited for you."

He walked over to her, and she felt a blush start at the way he was looking at her, his blue eyes full of passion.

"Shall we?" He invited glancing at the bed's turned-down sheets.

When she averted her eyes, he laughed. "You're still a bit shy with me, Ali, even after carrying my babies and my name for more than a year. Come on. Have some fun with me. It's our second honeymoon."

Unexpectedly, he swooped her up in his arms. She let out a squeal.

After he carried her to the bed, he walked back across the room to Alicia's tote where she'd stuffed Gilly's gift and retrieved the red negligee. "No need to use that hotel robe when your friend has gotten you such a nice gift." He handed her the nightie as he lowered the lights and pressed a button on the alarm clock, that began to play some soft piano music, next to the bed. "Don't worry. I didn't program it to wake us, but I found a nice station I thought was romantic."

As Alicia removed the hotel robe, John took it from her and placed it on the chair by the window. Then he undid his robe and tossed it on top of hers. She almost gasped at his unclothed body. She had a fleeting thought of Gilly and how she often referred to John as Mr. Hunk. There was no doubt Alicia's husband had aged well despite his sedentary work and without the help of a health club.

Before she could slip on the silky red nightie, John joined her in bed. "Maybe you won't need this after all," he grinned, flinging the gown to the floor where it fell in a heap on the room's amber and gold carpet.

The next moments erased all her concerns of the last few days as John's lips and body pressed against hers. They tumbled over the sheets together. It was just her and her husband in this romantic fantasy away from all the troubles back home, away from their sweet babies who were demanding and yet so rewarding, away from memories of her first disastrous relationship and of the destruction and death that followed.

Chapter Nineteen

Alicia awoke in the unfamiliar bed as light filtered into the room. They had forgotten to close the curtains before going to sleep, but it didn't matter because they were on a top floor of the hotel with only the birds flying around outside to see them entwined together on the soft sheets. Alicia felt slightly embarrassed at the memories of the night before, but she also felt warm and very alive. She took a deep breath, and John opened his eyelids at the sound.

"Hey, beautiful. How do you feel this morning, the second day of our second honeymoon?"

"I feel awesome." She stretched. "We didn't even eat last night, you know."

"Who needs to eat?" he grinned. "But if you want, we can have a big room service breakfast or go downstairs. The show isn't until tonight, but maybe we can do some shopping today or tour a museum. I know you're probably eager to visit the New York Public Library."

She was glad he hadn't put Columbia on their itinerary. She was still a bit upset about the prospect of his taking that job, but she understood and needed to come to terms with it on her own.

"I think I'll start by unpacking and then get dressed, John."

"Wait one minute." He pulled her back as she started to rise from the bed. "You can stay here with me a little longer."

***

After making love again, they unpacked their cases, dressed, had a quick breakfast in one of the hotel's restaurants, and spent the day like tourists, even though John had lived in the city and Alicia had visited with Peter on several occasions. They took the subway and got off at different stops where they browsed small bookstores and poked into antique shops. They even came across one of Manhattan's cat cafes on Hester Street.

"Oh, look, John," Alicia said gazing in the window of Meow Parlour. "There's a Siamese like Sneaky." A cat with chocolate tipped ears and muzzle stared out at them through its sapphire blue eyes.

"Don't get any ideas, Ali. Those cats are up for adoption. But if you'd like to have some lunch there, it's about that time." He glanced at his watch.

"We might consider a cat when the kids are a little older, and I definitely would like to rescue one."

"We may end up taking Fido one day, too," John pointed out. "Not that Dad is going anywhere fast, and Fido is no pup either."

"Maybe Fido needs a girlfriend like your dad. Since he's found Betty, he seems even spryer than ever. Do you think they'll marry?"

John ignored the question. He was looking through the glass of the store beyond the large "Meow" sign in the window.

"Ali, I don't think they serve lunch here, but I remember reading in the *Times* when they first opened that they're connected with a bakery around the corner where people can pick up muffins or cookies and bring them back here to eat. Would you like to do that? Then we can discuss Dad and Betty or whatever else you'd like."

John subscribed to the New York papers, so he kept up with what was going on in the city. He also shared some of the news in the *Cobble Cove Courier*, although most of the paper covered local events and happenings.

"I don't mind. I'm not that hungry right now, but I could use a small bite of something."

"Okay. Remember, we're going to a nice restaurant before Radio City tonight, so lunch can be light."

They took the short walk to the Meow Parlour's Patisserie, a French styled bakery, on Ludlow Street. It was a small place crammed with delicious baked goods from brownies to a variety of cookies and macarons, many of them cat-shaped. The shop also sold drinks – hot chocolate, iced tea, a variety of other teas, sodas, and raspberry lemonade. Alicia ordered a Rosemary & Cornmeal with Apricot Jam cat-shaped cookie and herbal tea, while John chose a brownie with hot chocolate.

"No cat-shaped cookie for you?" Alicia asked as they walked back to Meow Parlour. John held the takeout bag. Alicia carried the drinks.

John grinned. "I think those are overpriced."

"Everything is overpriced in the city."

"True. Okay, let's go mingle with the kitties."

They walked into the café. A woman of Asian descent greeted them with a smile. A red tabby sat on her shoulder. It was almost the same shade as her short hair despite the fact she was of Asian descent.

"Welcome to Meow Parlour. We take reservations, but we do allow walk-ins. You're in luck. There are seats available. Follow me."

She led them to a table by the window where a striped tabby watched New Yorkers stroll by from its vantage point on a ledge. Behind the table was a cat tree where two other felines perched.

"I see you picked up some items from our bakery," the receptionist noted, eyeing the bag from the patisserie.

"Yes. The cat-shaped cookies are adorable," Alicia said.

"They're delicious, too." The lady smiled again as the cat on her shoulder jumped off and scurried to join some of his friends on the cat tree.

"Whoops, there goes Charlie. By the way, all these cats are rescues and may be adopted, but we have strict rules. If you're interested, I can give you some information."

"No. Sorry," John said. "We're not local. We're from upstate on vacation here this week."

"I see. Well, we still could arrange something, but if you want to play with any of the cats, you need to sign a release."

"A release?" John's eyebrows rose.

"We're very cautious about how the cats are treated, and we also have to protect ourselves in case a visitor is bitten or scratched, although these cats are quite tame. I'm sure you understand."

Alicia nodded. "Of course. I don't think we plan to play with them, but thank you for the information."

"Very well. Enjoy your food." She walked away as lithely as the felines scattered about the room.

***

After an interesting half hour spent eating among the cats, Alicia and John left the cat café to head back to their hotel. They'd spoken about the plans for the rest of the week, but Mac and Betty hadn't entered into the conversation again. Alicia supposed John was happy for his father, but maybe a bit sad about someone replacing his mother.

"I know you'd like to get back to the hotel, but I still want to shop a little more to see if I can find you a gift. I've been keeping an eye out, you know."

Alicia had sensed John peering over her shoulder when they'd gone through the antique shops and small stores on their walk around the city. She'd made no purchases, as items were either too high priced or just not to her liking.

She didn't need any kitschy souvenirs or a knickknack that would just sit on their shelf gathering dust.

"What about stopping in here?" John suggested as they approached a jewelry store with a display of necklaces and earrings in its windows.

Alicia thought of the stolen jewelry from Irene's gift shop and hesitated. "I don't know, John. Those items are probably costly."

"I don't mind spending some cash on my wife. It'll be a memento of this special time together. I still plan to give you something else for Christmas. Let's go in."

Before she could object, John was holding the door open for her. A bell tinkled as they entered, and a man in his sixties wearing bifocals, striped suspenders, and a Santa's cap came through an aisle toward them.

"Good day. If I can assist you with anything, just let me know. I'm Martin Tinker. Welcome to my shop."

"Hello, Mr. Tinker," John said. "We're the McKinney's, and I'm looking for something nice for my wife. She's not easy to find a gift for."

"Most women aren't." He looked at Alicia through his thick lenses as if trying to size her up. "You look like a locket lady. Am I right?"

"A locket lady?"

"Yes. You seem a bit old-fashioned. You aren't wearing a lot of jewelry, nothing gaudy or expensive."

He glanced down at her wedding band and diamond engagement ring. The band was plain gold with their initials and wedding date engraved inside. John had a matching one. The diamond was also conservative in comparison to today's standards. Alicia had chosen it after John urged her to replace his first wife's ring.

"I've never owned any lockets," Alicia told the shop owner.

"Then you should. Come, young lady."

Having turned forty-four two months ago, Alicia didn't consider herself young anymore, but she followed Mr. Tinker to the back of the store. John walked along behind her.

"Wait here. I have something I think will suit you very well."

Mr. Tinker stepped behind a curtain that led to the storage area and brought out a silver box. Opening it, he handed her an oval locket on a sterling chain.

"This is on special today."

He turned to John. "That piece has a history. When I first opened this shop with my wife thirty years ago, I was handling the purchases. We didn't argue much in those days, as we hadn't been married long and had two young children. But we got into a tiff one year. I believe it was around Christmas time."

The man tapped his brow as if trying to dislodge the memory. "Vivian, that was my wife's name, said I was buying the wrong stuff. She said I was only looking for value and not meaning. We weren't doing great business, so I challenged her to do the buying. Next thing I know, our jewelry was selling like hotcakes." He smiled showing a gold crown on his upper molar.

"The odd thing is she wasn't buying things so different than the items I chose. They were less fancy, I suppose, but what was ringing up our register was the stories she attached to each item. My wife was a great storyteller. As the customers came in, she matched them up with certain pieces that she said reflected their character. She gave me some lessons, and the business flourished. Even in these times of online shopping, this place does well. It's the personal touch that still matters."

"So what's the history of this locket?" Alicia asked.

The man turned back to her. "My wife purchased it a month before she passed away five years ago. She had cancer and died a quite painful death. Our children are grown and maybe one day one of them will take over this store."

Alicia had lost her own parents to cancer, and John's mother had succumbed to that terrible disease as well, so she empathized with Tinker's loss.

"But getting back to the history of the locket. After my wife gave it to me, I didn't put it out for sale. I kept it in the back room. I was so involved in spending our last days together that I never really looked at it. After she passed, I finally brought myself to examine it. When I did, I realized why she gave it to me. I kept it as a memory of her for comfort, but I'm ready to let it go now."

"Are you sure?" Alicia felt hesitant about taking away the old man's reminder of his wife. She knew John had held on to his wedding ring and even worn it for many years after his wife died in childbirth.

"Yes. I don't need it anymore, but I have a feeling you do. Call it intuition."

"How much do you want for it?" John asked. Alicia wondered if he doubted the shopkeeper's story and considered it a sales pitch.

"I don't know what Vivian paid for it and it is sterling silver, but I want it to be affordable. Give me fifty dollars for it, and I'll even gift wrap it."

"That's very reasonable." John reached out and took the locket from Alicia. He opened it and, looking inside, a smile touched his lips.

"I agree this is perfect for Ali. And, yes, please gift wrap it. I don't want her to see the inscription until she opens it for Christmas." He handed the man a fifty-dollar bill from his wallet.

Alicia wondered what could be written on the inside of the locket, but she didn't press John. When they were out on the street again, John holding the small red and white package in the Tinker's Jewels bag, she said, "I thought this wasn't going to be a Christmas present, but a souvenir of our trip."

"I changed my mind, and it can be both. I think you'll like it, Ali, but I want part of it to be a surprise. Do you want to go back to the hotel now?"

"I think we should. I still haven't called Pamela, and I'd like to check on the babies before we go to dinner and the show."

"Great idea, but I'm sure they're having a ball together."

Chapter Twenty

Not only did Pamela assure Alicia that all was fine with the twins when she called, but she put them on the line. Carol came on first, giggling as though her aunt was making funny faces. Alicia found it hard imagining her sophisticated sister-in-law doing that, but she knew there was a side of Pamela she was still discovering. Johnny was more reserved, but she could hear him tapping on the phone, and then Fido joined in barking.

"See, I told you. It sounds like they're having a party," John said from beside her. He could hear the raucousness through the receiver.

"Would you like to talk to your children or sister?"

He shook his head. "No. Just send my love. I'm going to take a shower and change for dinner."

He went to the closet and removed one of the dress suits he'd brought along for some of the fancy places Pamela had reserved for them. Tonight they were headed for Delmonico's, a well-known steakhouse in the financial district. Since Alicia had only eaten a cookie at the cat café, she was already hungry.

After kissing the twins through the phone and saying goodbye to Pamela with the promise of calling again the next day, Alicia gathered her own clothes for the evening. She chose a scarlet velvet dress that would accentuate her figure and bring out the shades of red in her chestnut hair.

When John was done in the bathroom, she showered and changed into the dress, redid her makeup, styled her hair in an upsweep, and added simple, but classy, jewelry.

"You look lovely," John said as she joined him in the bedroom, his blue eyes lighting up to complement his gray suit and blue and gray striped tie.

"Thank you. You're not bad yourself, Mr. McKinney."

***

John hailed a waiting taxi outside the hotel, and they snuggled in the back seat like newlyweds, which, according to John, they were because this was a second honeymoon.

Delmonico's was housed in a pillared building on Beaver Street south of Wall Street. The card Pamela had included with their vacation gift raised the maître d's eyebrows and put a smile on his face when John handed it to him.

"Right this way, Mr. and Mrs. McKinney. There's a special table reserved for you." He led them into the wallpapered and wood-paneled main dining room to a corner table that featured a white tablecloth and shiny mahogany-backed chairs. There was a small shaded lamp in the center that let off a golden glow. Although surrounded by other tables, theirs was set back a bit to provide some privacy.

"The waitress will be with you in just a moment." After pulling out a chair for Alicia, the maître 'd handed them both menus and walked to the front of the room.

Alicia glanced around. There were a few couples and business people seated at other tables, but the restaurant wasn't crowded. She noticed a few paintings gracing the walls. They featured diners at tables throughout different time periods from Victorian through current day, their clothing distinguishing them from other decades.

John followed her eyes. "This restaurant is a landmark. It's been around since the 1800's."

Alicia looked back at him. "Have you eaten here before, John?"

He smiled. "No. I read the history on the menu." He pointed his finger below the dessert listings.

"So what would you like, Ali? Even though this is a steakhouse, there are a lot of other items available."

Alicia glanced at her menu. She caught her breath at the price listings, even though she knew Pamela had picked up the tab.

"I think I'll have the Delmonico, their signature steak," she said after perusing the choices. Alicia wasn't a big meat eater, but she enjoyed a nice steak once in a while.

"I'll order the Prime New York Strip," John declared moving his menu off to the side of the table. "What about an appetizer, Ali? Would you like to share one with me?"

"Just one of the salads would be nice, John."

When the waiter arrived, they placed their orders and then spent time talking until their food came. Their steaks were both large and filling, but they still found room for dessert, a classic cheesecake for John and a slice of apple pie ala mode with a scoop of vanilla ice cream for Alicia. They had coffees and also shared after dinner glasses of wine.

When they were done with dinner, John asked, "Ready for the show, Ali?" His eyes danced in the light from the table lamp. She felt as if they were the only two people in the restaurant.

"Yes, if I can get up."

Although the meal was covered by Pamela's gift, John left a nice tip on the table and then took Alicia's arm after helping her into her coat. He nodded and smiled to the waiter as they passed him on the way to the door.

Outside, John hailed them another cab to take them to Radio City.

When they were left off, a few snowflakes were beginning to fall.

"It's snowing," Alicia exclaimed.

"Yes, but it's not too cold." John took her hand as they joined the crowd entering the building.

Alicia felt like a young girl sticking her tongue out to catch a few flakes.

John laughed. "Ali, I think this trip is agreeing with you. I knew it would."

Alicia smiled. She'd never had such a magical evening, and the night wasn't yet over.

***

Alicia had seen the Christmas Show at Radio City with Peter when they first married, but the experience was different with John. She enjoyed watching him observe the Rockettes performing their various dance numbers while he occasionally muttered terms of endearment in her ear throughout the first part of the show.

At intermission, when she returned from using the restroom after luckily only waiting in line five minutes, she found John at one of the concession stands buying an ornament featuring the Rockettes and 'Radio City Spectacular' written across the red, white, and green ball.

"This will look nice on our tree, don't you think, Ali?"

"You are into kitschy souvenirs, John, and I thought only women fell for those."

"I want us to remember everything about this trip," he said suddenly turning serious. "I'm so glad we're getting this chance to reconnect with one another."

She wondered if he was referring to the challenges of parenthood that often tired them so much they hardly had time to talk or whether he was thinking of their upcoming separation if he got the job at Columbia.

The rest of the show was dazzling and festive, ending with the Santa Claus finale with the dancing girls. When the lights came back up, John placed a quick kiss on her lips.

"Thanks for joining me tonight, Ali. Let's go check out the tree."

They filed through the crowd exiting the music hall out into the street that was now covered in a white dusting of snow. The falling flakes were a bit thicker, and a few clung to John's hair, whitening the touches of gray at his temples.

The huge live tree at Rockefeller Center was a wondrous site.

"Beautiful, isn't it?" John asked her as they held hands gazing up at it along with a crowd of people including many kids who scrabbled to get up close to view it.

"Yes. It sure puts one in the mood for Christmas."

John let go of Alicia's hand a moment and pointed in the direction of the ice rink where people were skating. "We have a date there tomorrow, remember."

Alicia was hoping John might change his mind about that part of their itinerary. "I haven't skated in years, John."

"Don't worry. If you fall, I'll catch you. Just think of my dad and Betty on the ski slopes, and I'm sure you'll gain courage." He grinned.

"I can't imagine." But she could. She pictured the old man and woman in hospital beds with their legs in casts, and her in the bed beside them.

"I guess it's time to get back to Park Lane and our very comfortable king-sized bed," John said close to her ear, his words rising on the smoke his breath produced, the invitation clear in the huskiness of his voice.

Without replying, she took his hand again, and they walked toward a waiting line of cabs.

***

John surprised Alicia on Sunday when she woke to find him up in bed using Gilly's pen to jot some story ideas on the hotel's note pad.

"I think this trip has broken through my writer's block as I'd hoped it would."

He read her the plot synopsis he'd written for their second mystery, and they spent some time bantering back and forth about the details as they'd done for their first book. It felt good, and Alicia could tell a weight had been lifted from John's shoulders.

Later that morning, Alicia called Pamela before they were leaving to ice skate and was assured all was fine on the home front. Both John and his sister warned Alicia that calling again was unnecessary. Everything was under control.

They had a fun time at the ice rink, and Alicia did indeed fall a couple of times, but John was always at her side to help her up. They laughed afterwards over hot cocoa and cookies. The streets were still coated with snow, but no additional accumulation occurred. They spent their night wrapped around one another making love into the wee hours of the morning.

***

Although most of Alicia's thoughts were on John and the stronger love bond they were forging on this holiday, there were also moments her mind turned to the problems at home – Irene escaping to Florida after the burglary; Angelina in the hospital facing a possible bone marrow transplant that her parents might not be able to afford; Dora ready to sell the inn and move away with Charlie; Kim and Andy fighting; Andy's mother's suspicions about his reunion with a young drug dealer; and Casey's confiding in John about his fears Gloria was being physically abused by Walter.

Alicia also still worried about the vandalism of their Christmas lights by someone who'd also tried the door and the unidentified person who had followed her home from the library. Even in New York, she imagined she spotted the man in the gray coat, but it always turned out to be just one of the millions that walked the city streets. Then, of course, there was her motherly concern for the twins. She trusted her sister-in-law and Kim, but she missed her children terribly and couldn't keep them far from her thoughts.

John seemed to read her feelings when, on Monday night, after another nice meal at one of the restaurants near their hotel, he said, "I know you're enjoying our time together, Ali, but I sense you're starting to miss the kids. I realize that's only natural. I miss them too, but I'm not in a rush to go home. Maybe I'm being selfish wanting you all to myself this week, but we really needed this."

He looked into her eyes, and she had to agree. She felt like she was in a snow globe and could stay with John in that safe magic world forever, but she knew that wasn't possible, nor was it possible to totally take her mind off her precious babies.

"I know, John. This has been the best gift I've received besides Gilly's naughty nightie."

John laughed. "Yes, we've gotten lots of use out of that, although most of the time you haven't worn it." He winked.

"We still have lots to do this week – the museums, a carriage ride through Central Park, a Broadway show, the New York Public Library, maybe the 9/11 museum if you don't find it too depressing," he ticked off the remainder of the Itinerary Pamela had suggested to them. "Too bad F. A. O. Schwartz closed down. I would've loved to buy the twins some gifts there, but maybe we can pick up something for them at Toys R Us."

***

That night, as they lay together in bed sipping some complimentary champagne room service delivered while they were out, Alicia's cell phone buzzed.

"Let it go to voicemail," John said. "It's probably an advertiser."

"What if it's important? It could be Pamela."

A hundred emergencies popped into Alicia's mind. She jumped out of bed self-consciously grabbing the hotel robe and slipping into it hurriedly as she scrambled for the phone that she'd left charging on the bureau.

"Darn! I missed it." She looked at the display. A sense of déjà vu flashed through her as she recalled Gilly's call about her house fire two years ago, but that had been in the early morning. It was nearly midnight. They'd gotten into the habit of staying up late, as they no longer had a reason to rise early. They were on 'vacation time' as John called it.

John sat up in bed. "Who was it?"

Alicia checked the display again. It read, 'Kimberly Pierce.'

"It's Kim." She held her breath as she hit redial. Why was Kim calling her at this hour?

When the call went straight to voice mail, Alicia tried to keep her voice calm as she recorded a message for Kim to call her back.

"Don't worry, honey," John said taking the phone from her and laying it by the bed. "Maybe she had another fight with Andy and wants to talk to another woman about it."

"I don't think she'd interrupt my second honeymoon to do that."

Alicia waited for the phone to ring again. But when it did, she jumped. John handed it back to her and listened as she spoke to the girl.

"What's wrong, Kim? Speak slower. I can't understand you. What? The babies? Pamela? Fido? Oh, my God!"

Alicia's world began to spin. Kim was almost incoherent, but she could make out some of what she was saying. Piecing together the garbled sentences, she realized her children had been kidnapped and their aunt shot. Fido had also been injured in the foray.

"I'm so sorry, Mrs. McKinney." Kim gasped for breath between sobs. "I'm in the hospital waiting for news about Mrs. Morgan. Dr. Clark has Fido."

"Give me the phone, Ali." John reached over as Alicia crumpled onto the bed crying.

"Kim, what's going on?"

Through the rush of her tears, Alicia saw her husband's face whiten at the news Kim was relating to him. John seemed torn between comforting Alicia or the girl who was in hysterics on the other end of the line.

"Kim, listen to me. Where are you? You have to calm down."

Alicia rolled herself into a ball on the bed, her loud sobs wracking her body. John sat next to her and put his hand out to comfort her as his other held the phone steady.

"Call your parents or someone you know, Kim. You shouldn't be alone. Ali and I are coming right back."

Chapter Twenty-One

Alicia was amazed at how John managed to pull it all together, helping her pack, arranging for the valet to retrieve their car, and driving at a speed that was just enough over the limit to get them to Cobble Cove as quickly as possible without fear of a ticket.

She had finally stopped crying as John urged her gently but firmly through the motions of composing herself to get through the two-and-a-half-hour ride to Carlsville Memorial Hospital where Pamela had been taken.

John was very quiet as he drove, keeping his eyes on the road and his foot on the gas, but she saw how hard his fingers dug into the steering wheel and how deeply furrowed his brows were drawn as he concentrated on getting them to their destination. She'd seen him this determined once before when he'd been searching for his dad in a snowstorm.

As they drove north, the roads were clear, and the cars crossing the bridge from Long Island to upstate New York were minimal. At two in the morning, they didn't have to face rush hour traffic.

After John hung up with Kim, he'd received a call from Ramsay on his cell phone. He'd explained to Alicia that Ramsay would be waiting for them when they got to the hospital to fill them in on what had transpired in better detail than the panic-stricken babysitter. He'd held her tight as she cried and told her that they had to be strong and face whatever it was that had happened. They couldn't fall apart. The lives of their children were dependent on them.

Alicia knew he was right. She gathered what strength she had left and told herself everything would be okay because John would make sure of that. In what seemed like another life she had trusted a man who hadn't deserved her belief in him. When John came into her life, he taught her to believe in herself. They could get through this together. She knew that in her heart as much as her mind reeled with the shock and pain of what lay before them. Her babies were gone, her sister-in-law admitted for a gunshot wound. Her whole world had turned upside down in a matter of minutes. But there was John, silent at the wheel, her rock, the one thing she could cling to in the face of this horror.

***

As they rushed into the hospital, Alicia immediately spotted Ramsay. He was standing next to the entrance talking on his cell phone. The sight of him that, in the past had revolted her, now brought hope to her heart. As soon as the detective saw them, he clicked off his phone and hurried over. His face was grim.

"Glad you're here. Your sister is okay, but they won't allow me in to see her. Her blood pressure is a bit elevated, which is not surprising considering what she's been through. They're keeping an eye on her, but they might let you in for a few minutes."

He turned to Alicia. "Your babysitter is with her brother. They want to give her a tranquilizer. She's in a bad state."

Alicia now saw Kim sitting with her older brother, Carter in the lounge. The young man with the same shade of brown hair and a thin moustache had his arm around her. Kim was staring straight ahead as if in a trance. Her ponytail had opened and her long straight hair fell loose and straggly over the sides of her face.

"I should go to her."

John nodded. "I'll talk to the sheriff."

Ramsay's eyes lit up at the title. "I'm not quite official yet, McKinney. The authorities from Carlsville informed me of that. They have a unit working on this, but they said I'm allowed to assist."

Alicia walked over to Kim and Carter as Ramsay took John aside and spoke in a hushed voice, another unusual trait for the previously boisterous detective.

Carter rose as he saw Alicia. They'd only met once before, but she'd liked the young man who, a year older than Kim, was the eldest member of the Pierce family.

"Mrs. McKinney. I'm glad you're here. I'm so sorry about what happened. Kim is all torn up about it."

Alicia slid in the seat next to Kim that Carter had vacated.

"I'm going to get a soda. Would you like something? How about you, Kimmy?"

Kim raised her red, bloodshot eyes. "No, thank you. Hi, Mrs. McKinney." Her voice sounded raw from crying.

Alicia declined refreshment too, even though her throat ached from her bout of tears and emotion.

When Carter stepped away, Alicia asked gently, "Can you talk about it, Kim? Ramsay is filling in John, but I'd like to hear your version if you are able to tell me."

Kim sniffed. Her voice still cracked as she spoke, but she seemed to have gained a bit of control either from her brother's presence or Alicia's.

"I got this call around eleven on my cell. I thought it was Andy, but it didn't sound like him. The ID was blocked, so I couldn't tell who was calling. It was a man." She paused. "He knew my name. He told me to go to the McKinney's' house." It sounded as if she was reciting from a script, and Alicia figured she'd already been questioned several times by the police.

"What else did he say? Did he mention the babies?" Alicia's voice broke as she spoke of her children, but she held back her tears. She knew if she started crying, Kim would join in, as well.

"No. That's all he said."

Alicia looked over at John and Ramsay. They were still talking in the corner. Ramsay was gesticulating with his arms, as was his usual mode of speaking when he was excited. She wondered what he was telling her husband.

"They asked me what he sounded like, but the call was so short it's hard to remember."

Kim continued. "I think he had a cloth or something over his mouth to disguise his voice. It sounded muffled. He could've been young or old. I didn't recognize it."

Alicia turned back to her. "Kim, I can imagine how awful this was for you, but can you tell me what happened when you got to the house?"

"The door was open. The lights were also on, so I thought Pamela was up. I called to her, but then I saw the dog."

"Fido?"

"Yes. He was acting strange. He didn't even bark when I entered, and he was chasing his tail, acting goofy. His eyes looked odd like they were glazed over or something. I called upstairs to Pamela. The house was strangely silent. When I got to the top of the stairs, I saw her."

Kim's pale face whitened even more as she related the rest of the terrible tale. "She was on the floor outside the nursery. There was blood all over." She covered her face with her hands as if to block out the memory of the sight.

"They told me later that head wounds bleed a lot. I'm very squeamish about blood. I can't even donate it because it makes me sick. I almost threw up. I couldn't tell if she was alive. I dialed 911 on my cell and also called Dr. Clark because it seemed like something was wrong with Fido. Then I went into the nursery and found the note."

"The note?" Alicia hadn't realized the kidnappers had left a note.

"The police have it. It was in Johnny's crib." Kim sniffled, and Alicia saw tears gather in her brown eyes. "It was pasted letters and words from a newspaper. It might've been from the *Cobble Cove Courier*."

"What did it say?" Alicia's heart was thudding.

Tears slid down Kim's cheeks. "It said, 'One Mil for each kid. We will call with instructions.'"

"Oh, God!"

John was at her side then and Carter had also returned with his soda and two cups of water.

"I think you girls need this." He placed the cups on the table by Alicia's chair.

"I'm going to try to get in to see Pamela," John said. "They say she's awake but a bit weak, and they're trying to bring down her blood pressure. She was lucky. It was a surface wound, but it knocked her out. The bullet nicked her skull and there was a lot of bleeding, but it could've been way worse." He lowered his eyes at the thought. "They've been trying to question her, but the doctors aren't letting them in the room. Do you have her daughters' contact numbers? I thought she left them with you."

"They're in Europe. I doubt we'll be able to reach them. She's going to be okay, right?"

"She should be, thank God, but they want to keep her for a few days to monitor her."

"Do you think they'd let me in to see her with you?"

"I'm not sure, but I think it's best you stay here with Kim and her brother. I won't be able to stay with her long."

Alicia nodded. "Okay. I guess Ramsay told you about the ransom note?"

John's eyes darkened. "Yes. I'm prepared to deliver anything they want."

"But we don't have two million dollars, John." Alicia kept her voice low despite her rising panic for fear the other people in the waiting room might hear, but she realized most of them were probably absorbed in their own emergencies.

"Let's not talk about it now, Ali. I'll be right back." As he walked away, Ramsay came over to them.

Alicia started to stand, but Carter urged her to stay in the seat. He took the one on the other side of his sister. Between them, Kim sat crying into her hands, her shoulders shaking intermittently.

"I'm so sorry I got her started again," Alicia told Carter.

Kim's brother put his arm around his sister. "Not your fault. This has been traumatic for her. I offered to take her home, but she won't leave."

Andy should be with her, Alicia thought.

Ramsay stood before them, leaning his trimmed-down body against a nearby pillar.

"I'll tell you all what I shared with Mr. McKinney. There's a team working on this. They're specialists in kidnapping cases. All communication goes through them. They took Miss Pierce's cell phone and will take Mr. McKinney's and yours, as well. They put a trace on your house phone."

He looked over at Alicia though his thick brows.

"We're a little puzzled as to why they called Ms. Pierce. We're thinking they wanted her to contact you so you would return from your trip, but they could've called you directly. We'll know more when Mrs. Morgan is able to tell us exactly what happened last night."

Alicia suddenly recalled the lights being cut and her stalker. "Did John remind you about the Christmas lights and the person who followed me from the library last week?"

"He did. I'm going to share that information with the head of the investigating team. Also, we think there might be a connection between the gift shop burglary and the kidnapping."

Alicia had considered that. "You mean you think the same person is responsible for both?"

"Persons. This looks like a two-person job to me."

Alicia thought of the man in the gray coat. She'd never seen him with anyone else, but that didn't mean anything. "Before we went away, I saw a strange man in Cobble Corner and also on the street a few blocks away. My co-worker has seen him, too."

Ramsay's thick brows rose. "What makes you say he was strange, Mrs. McKinney?"

"I don't know. There was just something odd about him. He appeared to be hanging around the neighborhood."

"Can you describe him?"

After all the times Alicia had brought up an image of the man, she was suddenly at a loss to form his face in her mind. "He wore a long gray coat. He was about John's height. He's a smoker. He walked right by me, but I can't recall his features. I think his hair was dark. He had a lot of stubble on his face. I'm not sure of his age, under forty, I'd say. Maybe as young as twenty-five."

She saw the doubtful glance Ramsay gave her, and she couldn't blame him. Now she knew what the term "unreliable witness" meant. "We'll look into that, too. Would you like something for your nerves? Miss Pierce won't take anything, but the nurses can get something for you."

"No. Thank you." She shook her head.

John rejoined them just a few minutes later. "I should call Dad. I hate to interrupt his trip with Betty, but he should know about Pamela and the twins."

"How is your sister?" Carter and Kim had moved over, so John could sit next to Alicia.

"Weak but putting up a good front. She told me a few things. We'll talk later."

It seemed John didn't want to share his sister's confidence with the others. Ramsay didn't push. He gave them some privacy as he went to speak with a group of officers who had gathered by the front desk. Alicia supposed those men were in charge of the investigation.

"I have Dad's number at the chalet, but they took my phone. I shouldn't use yours either. They're going to ask you for it, too. I can try to make a call from the desk. There's also a pay phone in the lobby, one of a last breed of them since everyone has cell phones."

"Are we allowed to go home?" Alicia wasn't planning to leave Kim, but she wondered what state their house was in. She knew it would be trying for her to enter that place and find the nursery empty.

"They've already dusted for prints and taken samples of stuff. I'm not sure if the blood is cleaned up. They're testing the ransom note. Would you like me to take you home? You must be exhausted."

"No. I'm staying here with you." Alicia touched his arm.

"I'll call Dad and come right back then. You sit tight, hon."

He gave her a quick kiss on the cheek and then went to the desk where Ramsay and the other officers were still conferring about the case.

A tall, dark-skinned cop took John aside, and Alicia saw them shake hands. She assumed he was one of the men assigned to the kidnapping. After the clerk at the desk handed John the phone, the tall man walked over to Alicia.

"I'm Detective Stryder," the man introduced himself extending his hand. "I'm in charge of your case, Mrs. McKinney."

Alicia stood up and shook the black officer's hand. She didn't know what to say. 'Nice to meet you' didn't seem to cut it under the circumstances.

"So sorry about your children and your sister-in-law." The man's dark eyes seemed sincere. "We have some top men on this case. We're hoping to get your kids back soon. Your husband told us about the Christmas lights and your experience walking home last week. Sheriff-elect Ramsay filled me in about the man in the gray coat. Is there anything else you think we should know?"

Alicia was glad he wasn't chastising her for not reporting either incident earlier or the information about the stranger loitering in town. If they had, maybe Carol and Johnny would still be safe at home. "No. I'm sorry."

"Okay. We'll question you again later. You might remember something else then. Right now we need your phone in case the kidnappers call. We'll return it after this is over." Alicia reached into her purse and handed it to him.

"Thank you." He patted her shoulder. "Try to stay strong. We've made this case a priority." He walked back to his fellow officers as John hung up the phone and returned to Alicia.

"Dad's on his way. He was glad I called and calmer than I expected. He asked about Fido. I didn't have the heart to tell him. I need to check with Dr. Clark to see how the dog is doing. It sounds like he was drugged, but he's old. I hope he pulls through without any lasting effects."

Alicia had forgotten about Fido. "Poor Mac. His grandkids, daughter, and his pet."

"All family," John said. "Fido is special to me, too. He didn't deserve this."

His voice edged into anger. Alicia knew it was toward the kidnappers and not her. She could tell John was close to the end of his rope from worry and lack of sleep. He'd held it together so far, but she sensed he was close to collapsing.

"Sit with me, John." She took his hand as he lowered himself into the chair at her side. They huddled together, with words unspoken, both sharing a similar grief.

***

The hours ticked by like a time bomb. Alicia had read somewhere that the longer kidnapped victims were missing the less chance of them being recovered alive. She couldn't contemplate losing her babies, and she could just imagine what John was going through. Memories of his first dead child were likely going through his mind.

At times, he got up to pace the room, stopping at the nurse's station to inquire about Pamela who remained in stable condition but was still weak from loss of blood. Her blood pressure was not yet back to a safe number. A brief check with the vet revealed Fido was recovering from his ordeal. Dr. Clark said he'd been fed marijuana to keep him quiet and was still a bit tipsy, but not in any danger.

***

At noon, Carter asked if any of them were hungry and offered to go down to the cafeteria to bring them back some food. John said he needed to stretch his legs and would help. And, even though no one had an appetite, it was important for them to keep up their strength.

While the men were getting the food, Betty and Mac hobbled through the hospital doors. The old man spotted Alicia right away.

"My dear, are you okay?" he asked his face full of concern.

Betty came over, leaned her cane against the pillar where Ramsay had stood earlier, and hugged Alicia as she stood. "We came as fast as we could. This is just awful."

Alicia realized Betty had gone through an even more harrowing experience when muggers had killed her own children and husband sixty years ago in the city.

"John's getting lunch," Alicia said avoiding their sad eyes. "Last we heard, Pamela's holding her own. They're limiting visitors, though."

Mac nodded. "They'll let me in. Betty, you stay here with the ladies. I'll go ask. When John gets back, let him know I'm here."

Betty sat in John's seat and took Alicia's hand. She looked over at Kim who had stopped crying, but still had her head in her hands.

"I'll keep them company, Mac. Please send Pamela my wishes for a quick recovery."

"I will. Thank you, Betty." Mac walked off thumping his cane toward the desk to ask to see his daughter.

**

After John came back with the sandwiches they ate tastelessly and Mac returned with something for himself and Betty, although neither of them touched it, Ramsay came to share some news.

"Stryder tells me they got a call. It came through on John's phone."

Alicia gasped. "Did they trace it?"

"No luck. It's from a blocked number. The call Ms. Pierce received came the same way. We think they're using disposable or what we call burner phones. The calls are also very short so even harder to trace."

"What did they say?" John asked. Mac had told them there was no change in Pamela, and she was sleeping when he visited.

Ramsay raised his bushy brows. "I'm not at liberty to discuss that here."

He signaled John and Alicia to follow him. They walked behind him through the hospital doors. Stryder nodded as they passed and joined them. The four stood in a circle out in the cold air. Alicia hadn't bothered to grab her coat. She took in a chill breath and braced herself.

"They want the two mil delivered to a location atop Cobble Point," Stryder said. "They said you knew where that was."

His attention was directed on John. "They want it at midnight tonight, all unmarked bills in a bag. They said you could get it from your sister. They warned you not to send cops to the rendezvous point, but all kidnappers say that."

Before John could reply, Ramsay added, "We have a plan. We're going to ask you to go up there, but Stryder and I will be hiding right behind. There'll be some backup cops from his team, too. We'll fill the bag with counterfeit money. As soon as the kidnappers come into sight, we'll take over."

"What about my children?" John asked. "If there are two of them, as you think, one of them will be holding them. If they sense a setup, they might . . ." he paused glancing at Alicia knowing she would understand what he was imagining.

"They're after the money," Stryder said. "They know you want your kids back and won't risk anything funny. We can only hope they react as we expect."

"It's too dangerous," John said. "I want to go alone."

Alicia gasped.

"We can't allow that." Stryder gave John a stern look.

"Then what about the money? I think I can get it from Pamela's account. I spoke with her. She already has a line for me on it."

"Did she tell you anything about her assailants?" Ramsay had taken a step closer to John.

"She said there were two as you suspected. They both wore ski masks. She didn't get much of a look at either man. It happened very fast. She woke up when she heard footsteps on the stairs. She rushed to the nursery, but the man in the hall stopped her before she could get to the twins. She caught a glimpse of his partner in the nursery standing by the cribs. The man guarding the door took out a gun and aimed it at her. She didn't have a chance to protect herself. She remembers nothing else until she awoke in the hospital. Luckily the shooter either had poor aim or wasn't a professional, but the nick she got from the bullet still caused her to faint and lose a lot of blood."

"We'll need to question her when they allow us in," Stryder said. "Sometimes things come back even after somebody's been knocked out."

"There isn't time." John's voice was urgent. "You see what they've done to my sister. The babies are defenseless. Pamela urged me to give them what they want. I can get to the bank now."

"No." Ramsay's exclamation was strong. "You can't do that, McKinney. You would be sacrificing your sister's money as well as your babies' lives, not to mention your own. Listen to Stryder. He has experience with cases like these."

"Thank you, Ramsay," Stryder acknowledged the compliment.

"You have to leave this in our hands, Mr. McKinney. I know that's hard to do, but in circumstances like these, you're stuck between a proverbial rock and a hard place. Our team has safely returned children to their parents in many cases."

"And in others?" Alicia saw the hardly disguised angst on John's face.

"We don't have one-hundred per cent success rates, Mr. McKinney. Nothing's guaranteed."

John broke down as Alicia feared he would. The stress of the past hours crumbling his reserve.

"That's bull, Detective. My children's lives are at stake. I'm the father, and my decision needs to be considered. I'm getting the money, going up there alone, and making the payment."

He turned to Alicia. "Stay here with Dad and the others. I'll be right back." As he strode toward their car in the parking lot, Ramsay headed after him, the thinned-down officer was finally able to keep pace with John's long strides.

Stryder looked at Alicia silently questioning why she wasn't trying to stop her husband. But she knew better. John had once told her the frustration he'd felt when the doctors broke the news to him that both his wife and child had perished in childbirth. She knew he was thinking he had a chance to do something now that would make a difference, and who was to say he was wrong?

She watched as John pulled out of the parking lot, Ramsay standing in the wake of the car, and turned and walked back through the glass hospital doors.

Chapter Twenty-Two

When Alicia came back inside, Mac and Betty were talking with Kim and Carter. They looked up at her as she rejoined them.

"Where's John?" Mac asked.

She was hesitant to tell him. "He left for a few minutes. He'll be back."

"We're leaving ourselves," Carter said. "I'm taking Kim home. We'll check in to see how Pamela is doing and what's going on with you folks. I hope everything works out."

Alicia tried to smile, but it took effort. "Thanks, Carter. Try to get your sister to rest."

Kim sniffled and hugged Alicia. "Please let me know what happens. I feel responsible. I know they took your phone, but borrow another one if you have to. It's important you contact me if . . .." she paused at a loss for words, but Alicia understood. She hugged her back.

"I promise, Kim, and you promise to try to relax. I hate to see you like this, and it's not your fault. In fact, because of you, Pamela and Fido both got the care they needed as quickly as possible and should be fine . . ."

Kim looked back at her through smeared mascara. She ran a hand through her hair, searching for her missing pony tail holder and then decided to forget about it.

"I hope you're right, Mrs. McKinney." She seemed about to say something else, but let her words trail off as

Carter took her arm. Neither of them seemed to have the courage to mention the twins.

***

After Kim and Carter left, Betty offered to get everyone something to drink. Alicia wasn't sure the old lady could manage carrying drinks and handling her cane at the same time, but she had a feeling Betty wanted to give her and her father-in-law some time alone.

"I could use another glass of water, Betty. Thank you." Alicia had finished the cup Carter had brought to her earlier, but her throat still felt tight and dry.

"And, you, Jonathan?"

"Scotch on the rocks might be the ticket at a time like this, but I'll go with water, also. Thank you, dear."

As Betty hobbled away, Mac said in a hushed voice, "She just wants to give us some privacy. We both were wondering what Ramsay and that black cop were talking to you and John about. Did the kidnappers call?"

"Yes. They want a lot of money. John thinks he should give it to them. Pamela okayed it. But the police want to set up a ruse. John's afraid it'll backfire. He wants to handle it all himself."

She kept her voice low, so no one else in the room could hear. She noticed Ramsay and Stryder were still outside waiting for John to return.

Mac's eyes, so similar to John's, took on a worried expression.

"My son is quite stubborn, as you've probably learned by now, Alicia. I understand his motives, but there are times you have to put your trust in others. You know the saying, 'no man is an island.' John Donne, the poet, coined that euphemism in 1624, and it continues to be true. To put my own twist on it, I say, 'no man or woman should float their boat alone.' I'll talk to John, for what good it might do, but I don't want to see him sink because he refuses to grab hold of a life preserver."

"It's so hard to know what the right thing to do is in this situation." Alicia could hardly believe that just two days ago she and John were skating happily in Rockefeller Center and now they were faced with confronting kidnappers with guns.

Mac placed his wrinkled hand over hers and patted it.

"My dear. Life is full of many trials. When you get to be my age, you'll realize that. My heart aches knowing my dear grandchildren are in jeopardy, but I also know that there is still hope. Hang on to that and your love for my son, and it'll pull you through."

Betty appeared with their waters, one of their fellow waiting room visitors assisting her.

"See," Mac said as the young man placed the glasses on the table and Betty thanked him. "Even if you don't seek it, help often comes when you need it."

Betty looked at him with a puzzled expression, and Alicia found herself able to smile despite her sadness and fear.

***

John arrived back a little later. Alicia saw Ramsay and Stryder corner him outside and watched him exchange a few words with them before walking through the glass doors toward her. He didn't look as angry as before, but just as dejected.

"I can't get it, Ali." he said to her as he plopped down in the chair at her side. "The bank won't process that amount as quickly as we need it. They say it'll take several days."

"Maybe it's for the best, John. I've been speaking with Mac. He thinks you should go with the plan Ramsay and Stryder have in mind."

John made a fist out of both his hands and squeezed them together, turning the knuckles white. "I may have no choice, Ali. This can't go wrong."

"Calm down, son." Mac spoke in the same gentle tone he'd used with Alicia. "There are things we have no control over, whether for good or bad. That's life, I'm afraid, so don't struggle against it."

"Stop being philosophical over this, Dad. We're talking babies here."

John started to raise his voice, and a few people in the waiting room turned to see what the commotion was about. Noticing this reaction, he quieted down but resumed his retaliation against his father that Alicia recognized was his frustration talking.

"I'm sick of having my hands tied. Do you have any idea how I feel?"

"Yes, Son, I do. You need to be the hero. Well, John, I hate to burst your bubble, but heroes don't always win and sometimes they get killed, especially in those sappy westerns."

Betty observed their argument but kept her mouth pursed.

"I'm getting out of here." John stood up. "I need some fresh air and you and those cops to get off my back. I need to figure out to what to do to save my kids."

As John rushed off, Mac leaned on his cane preparing to follow him, but Betty held him back.

"No, Jonathan," she whispered. "Let him go. I know what he's feeling. I went through that myself. He's not mad at you. He needs some space to think. He'll do the right thing once he has a chance to work it out himself."

Alicia agreed with Betty. She had no idea where John was going or how long he'd be gone, and she knew she had no reason to feel deserted, even though a part of her wondered why this was the second time he hadn't considered her when he stalked off.

***

To pass the time until John returned without going insane, Alicia decided to inquire at the desk if Angelina was a patient there. She didn't know if the girl was still in the hospital, but she remembered Laura mentioning before she and John left for New York that this was where Angelina had been admitted. Maybe visiting with the young girl would take her mind off her own troubles.

When the head nurse confirmed that Angelina was indeed a patient there and Alicia asked if she could visit her, she was given the room number.

"I'll be back in a little while," she told Mac and Betty. "There's someone else here in the hospital I want to see. I won't be long."

"Take your time," Mac said. "We'll be here in case John comes back. I may stop in again to see Pamela if she's up by now, but Betty will wait if I'm able to do that."

***

As Alicia made her way to the children's ward, her heart ached as she passed the doors of kids strung up to wires and tubes. The lights in the corridors seemed too bright, too harsh. Even the Christmas decorations seemed garish. In a few weeks, it would be Christmas, and many of these young patients would still be here, some fighting for their lives. Others might have already passed on, bringing grief to their parents during what should be a jolly season. It was too sad to contemplate.

The nurse made her wear a scrub suit over her clothes, as well as a mask to prevent contaminating the kids who were sensitive to germs from their chemo.

Angelina's room was in the Children's Oncology section. As she approached the door, Alicia saw a bald child sitting upright in the adjacent room, a chemo patient laughing as his mother read him the story of *The Grinch who Stole Christmas.*

She was suddenly nervous to enter Angelina's room. The door was open, and she saw Patty sitting in a chair by the bed, her back to the door. Gary was standing at the foot of the bed speaking softly to his daughter. Both wore the same scrubs and a mask, but she still recognized them.

Alicia feared interrupting the family, but Angelina noticed her and called out, "Mrs. McKinney. Are you here to see me?"

Alicia felt as if she'd been caught in an illegal act, but Angelina's bright face gave her courage to enter.

"Hi, Angelina. I'm actually here because my sister-in-law was admitted earlier, but I'd heard you were also here, so I thought I'd drop by."

"Weren't you on a trip? Did you come back because of your sister-law?"

Out of the mouth of babes, Alicia thought.

"Please come in," Patty said standing. "You can have a seat right here. It's so nice of you to come."

Alicia saw the dark circles under Patty's eyes and the haggard look of her husband, who forced a smile as Alicia approached Angelina's bed.

"No, please stay seated, Mrs. Millburn. I can stand."

"Take the seat. If you don't mind, I'd like to go grab a quick bite to eat. We've been here all morning. Do you want to come too, Gary?"

"I'll stay. You go get lunch. I'm not hungry."

"Are you sure?"

"Yes, Pat. I'm fine." His shadowed eyes belied his words.

"What about you, Mrs. McKinney? Would you like anything?"

"I just ate, thanks, and please call me Alicia."

"Call us Patty and Gary, too. I'll be back in a little bit."

***

After Patty left, Gary said he was going to the nurse's station to ask a question. He promised to return soon.

Alicia saw that Angelina had already eaten. An empty juice box sat on her tray along with a few crackers and part of a sandwich.

"Are you sure you don't want more of that?" Alicia asked the girl. "I'm sorry if I interrupted your lunch."

Angelina pushed the food aside. "You didn't. It's been sitting here awhile. I just don't have an appetite."

"Sorry to hear that. How do you feel otherwise?"

"Pretty stinky. I heard Daddy talking to the doctor before, and I may need a marrow bone transplant."

"That's bone marrow transplant, honey."

"Yes, one of those." She looked up at Alicia, her brown eyes wide. "I'm kinda afraid of it, but I want to get better. Daddy says it's a very expensive operation. He told Mommy it could cost almost a million dollars, and how in the world could we afford it?"

Alicia knew medical costs were astronomical and were almost impossible to pay without decent insurance, but she never realized how expensive Angelina's procedure would actually be. She doubted the girl was exaggerating.

A fleeting thought passed through her mind. *What if Angelina's father was so desperate to save his daughter he'd resort to kidnapping?* Gary probably knew John's sister had money, but Pamela told John two men had worked together to take the twins. Did Gary have a brother or another male relative who might've helped him? She tried to erase the scenario her mind was conjuring as Gary walked back into the room.

"I got you a chocolate bar from the nurse's station, sweetie," he said handing her a Snickers bar. "Your favorite."

"Daddy, I told you I'm not hungry."

Alicia watched as Gary's smile faded. "Maybe later then, Angie. Have you and Mrs., uh, Alicia, been having a nice chat?"

"We haven't had much time to talk. I don't even know what's wrong with her sister-law."

Alicia didn't want to lie to the girl, but she didn't feel like discussing the kidnapping with her and her father.

"She had an accident, but she'll be okay," Alicia said thinking it was partially true. Pamela had not intended to be shot. If she'd had more time and hadn't been facing a gun, she may have thwarted her attacker with her karate moves.

"Good. Does it cost a lot to make her better?"

"Angie, you don't ask questions like that."

"But, Daddy, you're always saying how much money it's costing you when I'm in the hospital."

Gary sighed and looked apologetically over at Alicia. "I think it's time for you to take your nap, so why don't you say goodbye to Mrs. McKinney now? I'm sure she'll visit again."

"But I'm not tired, Daddy."

Alicia knew she was being dismissed, so she was glad when Patty returned.

"Your mom's here now, Angelina. I'll be back as your dad said. My sister-in-law will probably be here for a few days."

Angelina looked resigned. "Okay. Maybe you can be my donor."

"Angelina!" Patty had gone back to the chair next to the bed as Alicia got up.

"But you said they have to look for someone who matches up with me, and it would be nice if Mrs. McKinney was my match."

"I already explained to you how that works," Patty told her daughter. "Usually a brother or sister can be a match, but since you're an only child, a registry of people from all over the country will be used to match you up with a donor."

"So, why can't they check Mrs. McKinney?"

"Angelina, I'd love to be your donor, but there are some strict rules involved," Alicia said. "When I go back to work, I'll try to find some information at the library for you that might help you understand better."

"Thanks. I wish I could go to the library with you. I miss seeing Sneaky and Fido at Storytime."

The mention of the pets made Alicia recall that Fido was at the vets recovering from being drugged, and no one had checked on him.

"You'll see them soon, Angelina. But you have to get well first, so try to eat your food and get lots of rest."

The girl lay back against her pillow. "I'll try. I hope your sister-law is better soon, too."

"Thanks, Angelina. So do I."

***

On her way back to Mac and Betty, Alicia inquired about Pamela at the nurse's station. She was told there were no changes in her condition, but that the doctors were no longer allowing anyone in to see her.

"A cop demanded to talk to her and got her a bit upset. Her pressure skyrocketed again," the blonde nurse confided. "You'd think they'd leave the poor woman alone after what she's been through."

Alicia nodded in agreement, wondering if it had been Ramsay, Stryder, or one of Stryder's men who had been so pushy.

When she arrived back in the waiting room, Stryder was there talking to her father-in-law and Betty. He stopped when he saw her and walked over.

"Mrs. McKinney, I'm glad you're back. As soon as Mr. McKinney returns, I have something to share with both of you."

Alicia tried to read his face. *Was it bad news or good?*
"Did they call again?" she asked figuring his news had to do with a communication with the kidnappers.

He bowed his head, his expression neutral, one that detectives and doctors learned to wear when talking with those emotionally involved with the outcome.

"Yes. We have it recorded, and the hospital has a private room in which we can listen to it. I wish your husband hadn't raced off, and I'm not too happy about Miss Pierce leaving either. I had hoped all of you would stay together. I couldn't contain Mr. McKinney, but Ramsay went after him. He's been in touch with me, and he's trying to bring him back."

So it looked like it hadn't been Ramsay who had disturbed Pamela. She looked over at Mac and Betty. The old couple were beginning to show signs of weariness.

"Is it okay if they go home?" she asked. "They look pretty worn out."

"We're not going anywhere," Mac said, although Betty had looked hopeful at Alicia's question.

"Pamela's no longer allowed to have visitors, so why don't you two leave and take a break? You can join us here in the morning." She thought that, by then, the fates of Mac's grandchildren would've been decided, but she still couldn't mouth those words.

"She might take a turn for the worse overnight," Mac said. "She isn't out of the woods yet. If high blood pressure isn't controlled, it can be a dangerous thing. I need to be here. I wasn't here for her all those years I denied my paternity. You and John have other matters to deal with."

Before Alicia could argue the issue any further, Ramsay and John came through the hospital doors. Stryder strode over to Ramsay and took him aside to talk while John walked to Alicia.

"I'm sorry about leaving you behind before, Alicia, and Dad," he looked over at Mac, "I apologize for letting the stress get the best of me and behaving how I did toward you. You were only looking out for me as you always do."

Mac nodded, obviously not feeling a reply was needed.

"Where did you go, John?" She was glad he was back to his normal self, but she wondered what decision he'd come to while he was away.

John sat next to her. The strain showed on his face, but his voice was calm.

"First, I went to Casey's to grab a few beers to drink away all of this." He waved his hand. "But Casey wasn't there. Gloria said he came down with that bug that's going around and won't be at the diner for a while. She was running the place herself, but the lunch crowd was thin. She said Casey actually gave her the go ahead to close the place for the week if it got too hectic for her."

That didn't sound like Casey to Alicia. The man was a workaholic. She thought a fever wouldn't keep him away for more than a day.

"So I decided not to drink and went for a walk to clear my mind instead," John continued. "I ended up at the newspaper office and hoped I'd find Andy there, but it was empty. It's a shame he isn't at Kim's side at a time like this." That was exactly what Alicia felt.

"I also stopped at the library. I think Sheila saw through the same story I told Casey about why we came home early. I had to make something up because Ramsay warned me not to talk about our situation. I told her you were missing the kids too much. She gave me that look that says she thinks I'm lying through my teeth, but didn't comment. She said you should still take the rest of the time off. The other staff members sent their regards."

"The last stop I made was at the vet. I wanted to check with Dr. Clark. I'm happy to say Fido's back to his old self. He was up and about when I got there, and he even recognized me. I felt bad about leaving him, but it's best he stays with her until this is all over."

Alicia caught a tear at the edge of John's eye and realized how close he was with the dog that was his pet as much as his dad's. But John had forgotten he hadn't told Mac about Fido.

"What's that about Fido? He's at the vet?" Mac had overheard their conversation.

"Sorry, Dad. I didn't want to alarm you. Fido was fed some marijuana by the kidnappers. After Kim called the police, she was alert enough to call Dr. Clark who took him to her office and checked him out."

Mac grinned. "That old boy is tough like me. Thanks for saving me the concern, John, but if I can handle all of this, I think I could've handled that."

"The main thing is he's going to be okay, and I'm sure Pamela will be, too. She's inherited your stubbornness, as have I."

That widened Mac's smile to show his dimple.

"Can you come with us now, Mr. and Mrs. McKinney?" Stryder and Ramsay had rejoined them.

"Where are we going?" John wasn't there when they'd told Alicia about the private room.

"We've had permission to use the hospital's conference room and equipment for our work here," Ramsay explained. "We have something we want you both to hear."

Chapter Twenty-Three

Stryder led them through the hospital corridor to a back room accessed through several swinging doors, the last of which said, 'staff only.' Ramsay trotted along. Despite his lighter weight, he was still heavy on his feet. Both officers were silent, not indicating any hints as to what they were about to reveal.

The puke green room into which they were taken was about the size of a large closet with fold-up metal chairs stacked next to a long table. Stryder arranged a few of the chairs in a line and invited them to sit. He placed John's phone on the matching metal table.

"We've recorded all the calls made to Mr. McKinney's cell," he explained. "I've edited out the parts that aren't relevant. Ron, Sheriff Ramsay, has already listened to it."

Ramsay still responded with a smile at being addressed by his unofficial title.

"The latest communication from the kidnappers is short, but we thought you should hear it. Again, the trace failed. Listen to the voice and see if either of you recognizes it. We think he used a voice synthesizer to change it; but maybe you can make something out of the pattern of speech, if it's someone you know."

Other than her brief thought about Gary, Alicia had so far considered the kidnappers to be strangers. Ramsay's belief that she or John might know them was disconcerting.

Stryder reached out and, taking the cell phone in his hand, tapped the screen a few times. The room was quiet except for their breathing. Ramsay's was fast and raspy as if he was agitated while John's was shallow and slow as if he was holding it. Alicia was aware of her own along with the heartbeat that drummed in her ears. She felt a bit faint. She was about to hear the voice of one of the men who'd kidnapped her children.

"Tonight at midnight. Be there alone with the money. Once we get it and verify it's all there, we'll deliver the kids." The audio clicked off.

Alicia was somewhat relieved when she didn't recognize the voice that spoke through the speaker of John's phone, but she could understand what Ramsay meant about it possibly being disguised. To her, it sounded like a morphed recording. The deep voice was erratic and unreal.

"I don't like that," John said before anyone else could comment. "He's not even indicating when or where he'll return the babies. He and his partner could just take the money and run."

"That's where we come in," Stryder said. "If you let us assist you, we can arrest him. Odds are his partner will be easier to catch. One of them must be the mastermind; the other the follower."

John sighed. "I already told you I've changed my mind and will allow you to accompany me when I go to Cove Point. I'll bring them the bag full of the counterfeit money you'll supply. I don't really have a choice about that now."

"What if he's carrying a gun?" Alicia asked, thinking of how Pamela was shot before she could make any move to defend herself.

"We're supplying your husband with a bullet proof vest," Stryder replied, "but we'll have him in sight the whole time. We'll also equip him with a listening device, so we can hear what's going on."

That didn't inspire much confidence in Alicia. Pamela had been shot in the head.

"Did either of you recognize his voice?" Ramsay asked.

They both nodded no.

"He changed it," John said. "The tone, the inflection, the pitch. Even if we knew him, we wouldn't be able to identify him from that audio."

"There's something else we need to tell you." Stryder pocketed the cell phone. "I have to keep this a little longer."

"Detective Stryder and I have been doing some investigating, and we've dug up a few things," Ramsay said. "But we also need to ask you a few questions before we come to any conclusions from our findings."

"Shoot," John said and winced at his own choice of words.

Stryder picked up the story. It was interesting to see how well he worked with Ramsay, and Alicia wondered if the Cobble Cove sheriff-elect missed his old partner, Faraday, at all.

"Ramsay filled me in on what happened to your first husband, Mrs. McKinney, and also what transpired when you first came to Cobble Cove two years ago."

Alicia felt a tingle touch her spine and work its way up her back. Why was Stryder bringing this up?

"You understand we had to keep our inquiries discreet," Ramsay added. "I suggested we speak to some people in town and check a few records. I told Detective Stryder that whoever is responsible for this had to know something about your relationship with Pamela Morgan. They knew you had a source for the money."

"Ramsay thought we should look back at the incident involving Maura Ryan."

Alicia listened intently as the two men spoke in tandem. She watched John observing them, as well.

"We went over Maura Ryan's file again. We had some cooperation from White Plains."

Ramsay cleared his throat. He directed his beady eyes on Alicia, but they weren't accusing. "I don't think you're aware, Mrs. McKinney, that Walter Langley, the custodian at your library, was Maura Ryan's foster father."

"Oh, no." The tingly sensation up her spine intensified. Suddenly, it all came back to her.

"We spoke to your director," Stryder continued. "She wanted to know why we were asking about Mr. Langley, but we made sure she wasn't connecting our questions with you in any way. She told us he'd been disciplined by her after a complaint of sexual harassment by one of the female clerks. She also told us he didn't report to work yesterday despite the fact she'd called his house to ask him to take over the night shift because the female cleaning woman was out sick. We checked in with his wife at the diner that you went to earlier."

Stryder looked over at John. "She says she doesn't know where her husband is. He's been gone all weekend. He left the house Friday night and hasn't been back. She didn't seem worried, though. I gathered from our talk that they're going through some sort of marital difficulty."

Alicia was piecing all this information together. Could Walter have turned their doorknob and cut their Christmas lights Friday night and then gone back yesterday in cover of darkness to break into the house with some man he'd hired to help him? When she'd left the library to walk home all alone that night they'd worked together, he could easily have followed her. Casey had mentioned to John at the Town Hall meeting that he was concerned Walter was beating Gloria. Bonnie's complaint against him made sense in the light of Maura Ryan's accusations if he was indeed her foster father.

"We need to more thoroughly question Mrs. Langley," Ramsay said. "But, in the meantime, we have an alert out for her husband. It seems too much of a coincidence that he moved here after the papers ran the story about what happened to his foster daughter in Cobble Cove. The information about John and his sister was in those stories, as well."

John fidgeted in his chair. "I guess you also suspect Langley of stealing the jewelry from Irene's gift shop?"

"We do," Stryder agreed. "But those jewels weren't valued at two million dollars."

"Something seems wrong," John said. "If he intended to kidnap our kids, why hit the jewelry store first? It doesn't add up."

"The big question is where is he now?" Ramsay asked.

"Maybe with his partner," Stryder suggested. "I have a feeling he's the one in charge and will be the one making the pickup tonight. Oh, and by the way, Gloria told us he has a gun. She says it's licensed and that he uses it for protection. We're in the process of getting a warrant to check their house, but she tells me it's been missing since he left and that she thinks he has it with him."

"Curioser and Curioser," Ramsay mused. Another surprise from the reformed detective. Alicia didn't know he'd read *Alice in Wonderland*.

"I want to go with John tonight," Alicia suddenly said. The idea had come to her in a flash. "If Walter is really the one responsible for this, I think I can speak some sense into him. I also want to be there in case they bring the babies."

"Out of the question," Stryder said. "It won't be safe for you, Mrs. McKinney. We can suit you up too, but it'll be difficult to keep an eye on both of you. They only wanted one of you to deliver the money."

"But I have just as much at stake in this as John, and there are two of them. Just because I'm a woman, you think I run more of a risk."

"Please, Ali. The detectives are right about this. I won't let you go, either."

Alicia got up. Her spine no longer tingled as she stood tall. What had come to her on the spur of the moment seemed the best thing to do. She could be just as stubborn as John.

"I'm going back to Mac and Betty if you're done with us, detectives. But I plan on being there tonight, not in the background hiding, but by my husband's side. We went through childbirth together and we can go through getting our kids back together, too." She strode out of the room leaving John and the two officers staring after her.

Chapter Twenty-Four

The more Alicia thought about it, the more determined she became to stay by John's side when he delivered the counterfeit ransom money on Cove Point that night. Even though the police were trained in situations like these, they could not protect John as close as she could. If the kidnapper was Walter, as they suspected, he knew her and would not be alarmed at her approach as he would by a cop or someone unfamiliar. The two of them delivering the cash made sense, but no one except Betty supported her decision.

"If this is what you really want to do, don't let the men change your mind," Betty said after Alicia had discussed her plan with her and Mac. "As much as I'd hate to see anything happen to either of you, regret is a terrible thing."

Stryder and Ramsay came over to them. John avoided her gaze.

"Listen, we're taking a break for a few hours. If you folks want to go home and rest before tonight, you should do that. We have men outside both your houses, so you don't have to worry."

Alicia wasn't looking forward to stepping back into the empty house with the bloodstains near the nursery, but she and John had been up for over twenty-four hours, and they could use some rest, even if they couldn't sleep. Mac and Betty seemed just as exhausted.

"The nurses tell us Pamela's blood pressure has begun to drop. They don't foresee any issues tonight, but if anything changes, they'll call you, Mr. McKinney," Ramsay told Mac.

Stryder handed John two cell phones. "These are for you and your wife. You can borrow them until I return the others. We'll meet up around eleven at the sheriff's office. It shouldn't take much time to outfit you with the vest and a listening device."

Alicia noticed Stryder was still not including her in their plans. She also remembered John mentioning that Ramsay's unfinished office was located in an empty building between town hall and the *Cobble Cove Courier*. It was a short walk from there to Cove Point.

"We'll be there," John said. She wasn't sure if that meant he had changed his mind to have her accompany him or whether he thought she'd stay with the police while he confronted the kidnapper atop the mountain.

***

As they all walked out to the parking lot, Mac said that he wanted to stop at the vet to pick up Fido. He didn't like the idea of the dog spending the night in a cage, especially after his hallucinogenic experience.

Betty hugged Alicia. "Remember, Alicia. You stick to your guns. I wish both of you luck." Mac made a face behind Betty, but she ignored it.

When they were driving home, John said, "You really can't come tonight, Ali. I'm sorry, but I'm putting my foot down. If something happens to me, and believe me I'm going to take all precautions to prevent that, I wouldn't want Carol and Johnny to lose their mother, too."

Alicia stayed silent. There was no use arguing about this. She would find a way to change his mind, even if she had to run up the mountain after him.

It was difficult to walk into the house. The silent giggles of Carol echoed through the walls while Johnny's chubby hands shaking his rattle played like a video in her mind.

"Can we sleep downstairs, John? I don't want to go up there." She was dreading the vacant nursery.

"We can't avoid it forever, Ali, but if it makes you feel any better, you can use the couch. I doubt I'll sleep, but I might recline in a rocker."

"We haven't even eaten dinner."

"I doubt there's anything in the house. Maybe we can have something delivered. I bet those cops over there are sharing a box of pizza." He directed her eyes across the street at an unmarked car where two men sat peering through dark sunglasses.

"Donuts, too," Alicia remarked, recalling Ramsay and Faraday's favorite breakfast at the Long Island precinct. She and John once spent a lot of time there in what seemed ages ago.

"Come here, honey." John sat down next to her where she'd collapsed on their sofa. He cupped her face in his hands. "I know how difficult this is for you to stand by and watch me take my life and our children's lives in my hands while you do nothing, but this is how it has to be."

She looked into his blue eyes. "John, I need to be with you tonight. Please. We're a team. Those babies are part of both of us. Let me be there."

She thought he would continue to argue with her, point out that she might end up being more of a hindrance than a help. Instead, he let out a long breath. "Okay. I'll tell them I want you to come with me. They won't like it, but tough."

"Oh, John!"

He took her in his arms. "God, I hope I'm doing the right thing and not just pandering before your stubborn ways."

She smiled. "I love you."

"Once this is all over and the kids are back, we'll take another vacation – all four of us. Maybe to Florida. I know they're a little young, but all kids and adults love Disney World."

"That sounds wonderful, but all I want is our family to be together again."

She thought of the Christmas Fair scheduled to open next week and how she'd looked forward to taking the twins, how their eyes would light up as John, posing as Santa, would take them on his lap in the chair by the Gazebo, how Carol would laugh at his cotton beard and Johnny might pull it. Now it looked like those plans could be discarded if tragedy hit Cobble Cove, as it did when she and John first fell in love.

***

They ended up with pizza like the cops watching their house. Neither of them could finish one slice. "There's so much left, John."

"Save it for tomorrow. We'll have more of an appetite once the twins are back."

The reminder that the babies were gone brought tears to her eyes. She wiped her face with the sleeve of her blouse. "I can't stop thinking of them. Do you think they're being fed, their diapers changed? Oh, God, what if they're being abused?" With Walter's track record, there was a high probability of that, and it made Alicia nearly wretch up her food.

"Try not to imagine that, Ali. Stryder tells me they took some baby food with them and also a box of diapers along with their playpen. He'd asked me what was left in the house. They cared enough to take some provisions, so let's assume the twins are being well cared for."

Alicia knew the police had made a thorough check of their home, but it made her uncomfortable that they'd been through her things. As for the kidnappers treating the twins well, she doubted anyone who would drug a dog and shoot a woman in the head had much compassion.

***

The hours seemed to tick by slowly. John suggested they try to nap. Alicia lay on the couch while he sat by the fire in the rocker. The house was too quiet.

Alicia recalled the night of the snowstorm two years ago that she'd spent alone with Sheila in the library. So much had happened since then, but she felt as if she was coming full circle. The audio recording, a missing man, so many questions.

"Would tea help you sleep?" John asked when he noticed her tossing and turning.

"No, but thanks, John."

He gazed into the fire that she knew he'd lit in the hope of lulling them to sleep with its crackling, golden glow.

"I can't think beyond midnight tonight, Ali. I don't know what we're up against. If Walter really is one of the men involved, he's held a grudge a long time, but this isn't vengeance for his foster daughter's death. It's pure greed. In a way, I'm glad I couldn't withdraw Pamela's money. Stryder assures me the bills look realistic. He won't be able to tell."

"Do you think his partner will be with him?" Alicia rolled over again to look at John.

"Yes. Somewhere. He'd want him for backup."

"What about Carol and Johnny?"

"I don't know." John's reply was almost a moan. She shut her eyes and somehow fell asleep.

***

John was shaking her. "Ali, get up. It's almost time to go."

She was groggy. It was still dark out. Then she remembered and opened her eyes wide.

"I was tempted to let you sleep." The strain was clear on his face, but he managed a weak smile. "I'm glad you got some rest. None for me, but it doesn't matter."

He took her hand, and she got to her feet. "I told the officers in the patrol car that we would walk. They still need to keep an eye on the house, and the cold will help wake you."

As John helped her into her coat, she started to shake.

"You're not even outside, and you're shivering already."

"It's nerves," she said. "I know I'm doing the right thing, John, but I'm still afraid."

He slipped into his own coat. "That makes two of us."

***

The temperature had dropped, and their breaths frosted the air as they walked toward Cobble Corner. The shops were closed, but the lights decorating their windows and the trees on the Green provided illumination on the path. The town's tree lighting, scheduled for the opening of the Christmas Fair next week, had not yet taken place, and the large evergreen stood dark against the black sky.

"Feels like snow," John said trying to start a conversation.

Alicia wasn't up to talking. She was still shaky.

"Hey. Somebody's at the newspaper, or maybe I just left the light on when I was there earlier."

Alicia followed John's eyes to the yellow strip around the *Cobble Cove Courier's* door. Who would be there so late at night? She knew John had worked to get the next two weeks' issues done before he left for New York. There was no reason for Kim or Andy to be at the office, and they were the only other people who had keys besides John.

"Let me check it out. Wait here, Ali."

John went to the door and tapped. He waited a few minutes, and then used the doorknocker again. Alicia began to worry. What if someone had broken in and was robbing the office as they'd done the gift shop? They didn't have time to wait for an answer. They had to meet the detectives in less than ten minutes.

John reached into his pocket for the office key but then tried the doorknob before using it. "It's open," he said turning the knob. I'm going in, Alicia. Stay there."

A sense of déjà vu hit her again. A similar scenario had happened before, John entering his father's cottage when the old man was missing and telling her to wait while he checked things out. But this time, when John stepped into the silent room that released a foul odor mixed with musty newsprint, he didn't find a healthy old man reflecting on his life but a very dead body sprawled across the floor.

Chapter Twenty-Five

John bent and rolled the man over, uncovering a gaping bloody hole in his chest. When the body was on its back, Alicia gasped at the man's face. It was Walter.

John felt for a pulse at Walter's wrist and then at his throat and shook his head. "He's dead, and he's stiff, probably been gone awhile. Ali, go next door and get Stryder and his men."

Alicia ran on wobbly legs to the new sheriff's office. A group of officers stood around the unfurnished room, Stryder and Ramsay among them. She noticed half a wall was pale blue while the rest of the room was still an ugly gray. A paint bucket stood in the corner, and she caught a whiff of the smell. The scent of death still lingered in her nose, and she almost wretched at the combination of the two pungent odors.

"Mrs. McKinney, what's wrong?" Stryder approached her. "Where's your husband?"

She could barely speak. "He's next door at the paper. He, We . . ." She felt the tears of shock threaten and knew what Kim must've felt finding Pamela.

"There's a body. It's Walter. He's been shot."

Stryder's face changed. He issued a few orders to his men. A group of them including Ramsay rushed out the door. Alicia followed.

***

When they arrived at the newspaper office, Stryder examined the body the same way John had and came to the same conclusion.

"It's obvious what's happened here. Langley's partner either became greedy so he knocked Langley off to get all the money or got cold feet and threatened not to go through with the pickup."

"We have to notify Langley's wife," Ramsay said.

Stryder agreed. "Is the diner still open? Maybe you should go there first and see if she's there. I'll stay here. I have some questions for Mr. McKinney about his assistant, Andrew Phillips. When we were checking things, we learned he's been hanging out with a drug dealer. It's very possible he's involved in this."

Casey often kept the diner open until two or three in the morning for the bar crowd. Alicia didn't know if Gloria would do the same since she was running the place herself while Casey was recovering from a virus. John said the waitress might even consider closing for a few days.

As for Andy, Alicia hoped Stryder was wrong in his suspicions, but the young man's actions lately had been questionable, and he and Kim were the only ones besides John who could've unlocked the office. Another strike against Andy was the fact that Fido had been drugged during the kidnapping. If Mrs. Phillips was right that her son was associating with a drug dealer, it was possible that's how he obtained the marijuana to nullify Fido. Alicia had never seen Andy's friend, Kevin Tucker, and even though John had, his recent view of the man when they were at Cove Point was from a distance and after many years. She wondered if Tucker was the man who wore the gray coat and if he was involved in the town's crimes including the kidnapping of her precious twins.

Ramsay hurried off with a few men to Casey's restaurant, while Stryder took John aside to discuss Andy. Alicia stood outside by the door, taking in gulps of the cold night air to clear away the awful distaste in her mouth. She still felt nauseous. What were they going to do now? Was Walter's partner still planning to pick up the money in an hour?

A few minutes later, Stryder's cell phone buzzed. He must've had it on speaker, because she heard Ramsay's agitated voice on the other end.

"The diner's closed and there's a sign in the window that it won't open again until next week. Should I go to Langley's house?"

"Yes," Stryder said. "Report back as soon as you find Mrs. Langley. She may be in danger."

It wasn't long before Ramsay called back with the information that Gloria wasn't home.

"Damn!" Stryder exclaimed. "Langley's partner must have her, or maybe she's dead already. Okay, come back here, Ramsay. We'll need to work out a backup plan."

As soon as Stryder hung up the phone with Ramsay, John's cell, which the detective carried in his other uniform pocket, signaled an incoming call.

"Jesus." He looked at the display. "It's him."

Alicia ran to John's side averting the body still blocking the doorway. The two of them listened as Stryder played the new message, the mechanical voice delivering an ultimatum.

"Last chance. Six a.m. same place. Real money. No cops or the children die."

John's face paled. "What now? I can't get the money for a few more days."

"That's not going to be necessary, Mr. McKinney, because we're going to catch this guy before morning. I'm sending men to Mr. Phillip's house. If he's not home, we're going to track down his drug dealing friend, Mr. Tucker. There's nothing more you two can do tonight. One of the officers will walk you home, and we still have men watching your house."

"That isn't necessary. We'll be okay," John said. "It isn't far."

Stryder raised his eyebrows. "You sure?"

John nodded. "C'mon, Ali. The detective is right. We might as well go home."

Alicia was surprised John had handed matters over to the police so easily. She still felt sick and dizzy. She just wanted to lie down and wake up when this nightmare was over.

***

As they walked toward their house, John said, "We're not far from Casey's, Ali. I know it's late, and he's still recovering from being sick, but maybe Gloria's with him. If we find her, I'll call Stryder on the borrowed cell."

"I don't know if that's a wise idea, John."

"I understand how upset you must be over all this and probably exhausted, but it won't take long."

Alicia followed him the few blocks to the beige, two-level ranch on Slate Street. She'd never been to Casey's home and was surprised the bachelor had such a large house.

As if reading her mind, John said, "Casey took over this place when his parents moved down South. He's been talking about moving to a smaller house, but I think he's attached to this one."

"It looks like no one's home." Alicia noted that the house was dark and even the Christmas decorations out front were unlit.

"He's probably sleeping. I'll knock, anyway."

As John tapped at the door, Alicia thought she saw someone watching from behind a curtain. After a few minutes, she was about to suggest to John that they leave, but the door silently swung open.

Gloria stood framed against the darkened entryway.

"John, Alicia. What are you doing here?"

Alicia thought they could ask her the same thing, but John was probably right that she was taking care of Casey.

"Can we come in, Gloria?" John asked. "We're sorry to bother you so late, but we have something we need to tell you. Is Casey asleep?"

Alicia wondered why John wasn't calling Stryder, but she realized he might prefer to break the news to Gloria himself. Even though it seemed she and Walter hadn't had the best marriage, Gloria would still be quite upset hearing of his murder.

Gloria hesitated. "Yes, Casey's sleeping. He's still running a fever. I don't think you should come in. I'll speak with you outside."

As Gloria stepped through the door, Alicia saw she was dressed all in black, a black sweater over black jeans. She even wore black leather boots that, although adding an inch or two to her height, were not heels but square wedges in a unisex design.

"I really don't know how to break this to you," John said.

He stood facing her and was level with her chin. "The real reason we're back from New York is because our kids have been kidnapped. The police think Walter was one of the kidnappers, but he was working with someone else. They suspect it's my assistant Andy or his drug dealer friend."

He paused as Gloria took in his words, a strange light entering her eyes. Alicia wasn't sure if it was disbelief or shock.

"Alicia and I were supposed to deliver the ransom money tonight, but we found Walter's body in the newspaper office. I'm sorry. They think his partner killed him, and you might also be in danger. The police have been trying to find and warn you. I have to let them know." He reached for the cell phone.

"Put that down." Gloria's voice had changed, deepened. From her pocket, she produced a gun.

John dropped the phone. "Gloria?"

"Walter didn't kidnap your kids. I did. Me and Jim. Now you've bumbled it all up because you didn't follow instructions."

She waved the gun toward John who took a step in front of Alicia to shield her.

"Why, Gloria?" John asked. "Casey's my friend. I thought you were, too."

His voice was steady, but Alicia knew he was as frightened as she. She felt frozen in place. She had left the house without the other cell phone that Stryder had given her. She didn't even have a purse that might contain a weapon to protect them.

Gloria smiled, but there was no happiness in it.

"We're no friends of yours. Jim's in love with me."

She laughed, and the sound was eerie.

"I should've gotten rid of Walter long ago, that sniveling idiot. Always going after our foster daughters and even that library clerk. But when he found out about me and Jim, I had to do something. All we wanted was the money to start a new life away from this hick town. The only reason I convinced Walter to move here was because of what happened to Maura. I suggested that maybe he could seek some sort of revenge, but he wasn't smart or gutsy enough to take any action. I didn't care that Maura got herself killed, but your sister's money would buy me a ticket to the life Walter never provided. Taking a job as a custodian. No brains in his head to do anything but assault little girls and clean up garbage."

She spat out the words.

"I just didn't have a plan until I met Jim. Then it all came together. He was the one who gave me the idea about the kidnapping. He kept talking about how cute your kids were. I have to admit he gave me some grief when I first brought it up after hearing you were going away. Luckily, I used my charms on him and explained how easy it would be. I promised him we wouldn't hurt the little brats. After we broke into your house, he complained again because I shot your rich, stuck-up sister. I told him it was in self-defense. Then I let him take care of your little darlings while I made those calls that I knew the police were listening in on. I disguised my voice, so they thought I was a man, clever, huh?"

Alicia watched John edging closer to Gloria. Was he planning a way to overcome her?

Gloria must've been thinking the same thing, because she waved the gun again and said, "One step closer, John, and you'll be in the hospital alongside your sister. I hear she's recovering, but you might not be as lucky."

"Gloria, please put down the gun. The police are all over Cobble Cove. They're searching everywhere. It won't take long for them to get here. In fact, Ramsay already went to the diner and your house. This is sure to be his next stop."

Alicia knew John was bluffing to gain them some time. She had no idea where Ramsay was now. He possibly had rejoined Stryder at the newspaper.

Gloria kept the gun raised. Alicia decided to help John by asking the woman some questions.

"You said Casey is taking care of the babies. Are they in the house, Gloria?"

"Yes. I couldn't bring them to my place. Walter didn't know what we were up to until right before I shot him."

"How did you get in my office?" John had figured out Alicia's plan and began questioning Gloria to keep her talking.

"That pimple-faced assistant of yours. He came in the diner right after you left yesterday. I told him I wanted to check something in last week's newspaper and asked him if he could please open the office for me. I had already planned to put Walter's body there. I'd shot him that morning and, even though I'd cleaned things up and avoided answering Sheila's calls checking to see why he didn't report to work, I needed a place to dump him. I thought leaving him in the newspaper office would be ideal. It would direct suspicion toward the kid."

Her voice was maniacal, and Alicia wondered if the woman was crazy or on drugs. That would explain what she did to Fido, but it appeared she also suffered from the same type of mental illness as her foster daughter.

"After Andy did as I asked, I told him I wasn't sure of the date of the article I wanted, so I might be awhile. I suggested he go and promised to lock up after I left. Then I called Jim and had him help me bring the body here. I left the light on and the door open intentionally. I knew the cops would be around tonight, but I didn't expect you to find Walter. It doesn't matter. John, do you think you'll find a faster way to pay if I kidnap your wife, too?"

She took a step back into the house and called, "Jim, darling. You can come out now. I need some help."

Casey appeared in the doorway. He looked haggard, and Alicia nearly believed he was actually sick.

"What's going on, Gloria? I was downstairs with the babies. I don't like leaving them alone long."

Catching sight of Gloria pointing the gun at John and Alicia, he stopped short.

"Go get Alicia, dear. I want her to spend some time with her children."

"Casey, please," John said appealing to his friend's conscience. "Gloria told us what happened, but it doesn't sound like you wanted anyone harmed. I don't want to have to fight you."

Gloria grinned. Casey was about the same height as John, but nearly twice his width. "That's a joke, and you forget I have a gun."

Casey hesitated. Alicia saw his indecision.

"What are you waiting for, sweetheart? I asked you to get Alicia. I'll deal with John."

Gloria kept the gun aimed at John's chest.

Then it happened in a flash. Alicia hardly had time to realize that Casey had grabbed Gloria from behind. He managed to force the gun from her hand, but not before it went off. She heard John let out a cry and fall. She rushed to his side, but Casey was giving her instructions.

"Quick, Alicia. Grab the gun and go in the house and call the police. I have her."

Gloria struggled in his grasp.

"You two-timer," she screamed.

"Stop squirming. I'll choke you if I have to." Casey wrapped one hand around her throat. "To think, I felt sorry for you, married to a man like Walter, but you're no better than he was. I thought I loved you. I would've done almost anything for you, but not murder."

He looked down at John whose eyes were closed, blood pooling around him as Alicia cried out his name. "Alicia, I'm so sorry. I had to disarm her. Get the gun. Call 911. Hurry. I hope he's alive."

Casey's words finally got through to her. She picked up the gun and rushed in the house to call the police.

Chapter Twenty-Six

It seemed Alicia was spending a lot of time in hospitals these days. After the police came and arrested Gloria, who they had to handcuff, and Casey who went willingly, John was taken by ambulance to Clarksville Memorial. Ramsay went down to the basement with Alicia and released the twins from the playpen Casey had set up. Alicia sobbed when she saw them and couldn't stop kissing her children as tears rolled down her cheeks. As she'd done after they were born, she counted all their fingers and toes to make sure they were unharmed and all in one piece. She didn't want to let them go, but she needed to be at John's side. It was then that Andy and Kim came down the stairs hand in hand.

"Detective Ramsay tells us you may need some babysitting help, Mrs. McKinney," Kim said. "We'd be happy to assist."

Alicia later learned that Andy's testimony to the police helped them figure out Gloria had killed Walter. When Alicia placed her urgent call, Ramsay and Stryder's team were already on their way.

***

Ramsay drove Alicia to the hospital in his police car. Kim and Andy had taken the twins back to Alicia's house to watch them together.

As Alicia rode with Ramsay, she remembered driving with him two years ago and how different she felt sitting beside him now. She'd doubted he could really make such a complete turnaround, but now she knew it was true. She was glad he would be taking over as Cobble Cove sheriff.

"Your husband was lucky," he said. "The bullet missed his heart. I hear they're giving him a room with his sister, so you can visit both of them. Her blood pressure is back to normal and holding steady, so they should be releasing her soon. John probably won't be kept long either."

"Thank God." Alicia sighed in relief.

***

Mac and Betty were already at the hospital when Alicia arrived. "Oh, my dear," Betty said. "I'm so sorry to hear what happened. Detective Stryder called and told us they were bringing John here. I hope he's okay."

"Sheriff Ramsay tells me he will be. He's in Pamela's room."

Mac grinned. "He's tough like me. They both are."

***

When Alicia went in to see John, he and Pamela were in the middle of a game of I Spy. As soon as Alicia walked through the door, John, who was closest to it, said, "I spy a beautiful lady who happens to be my wife."

Alicia was so relieved to see him sitting up, the left side of his chest wrapped in a white bandage. She ran to his side. "Oh, John. You had me so worried."

"I'm fine except for a bullet that ricocheted an inch from my heart. Remind me to thank Gilly next time I see her."

"Gilly?" Alicia was puzzled.

"I was wearing her pen in my breast pocket. The docs say the bullet was deflected by it. Unfortunately, the pen was destroyed."

"A writer saved by his pen, great story," Pamela said from the next bed. "You should write it, John."

"I think I will. Maybe I'll work it into that plot Alicia and I began in New York. I told you what a great time we had at Park Lane."

"Too bad your second honeymoon was cut short. I'll just have to send you to Europe next time."

Pamela wore a matching bandage around her head. Wisps of her ash blonde hair peeked from around the edges.

"You two look like war casualties." Alicia couldn't help but smile.

"How are Carol and Johnny?"

"They're fine, John. Casey took good care of them. I don't understand how he got involved in all this. He really didn't want to hurt anyone."

"I can get him a good lawyer," Pamela offered. "Sometimes love blinds us, but he woke up when he realized his friends were being jeopardized by that awful woman. I can't believe I took her for a man, but she's so tall and I was still groggy from sleep. She had on a black outfit and a ski mask. In the dark . . .." She trailed off, still uncomfortable picturing the scene.

"I still don't know the story about Andy," Alicia said. "He and Kim are back together, and he's watching the babies with her at our house."

"I never doubted Andy. I guess we'll know everything when the press gets ahold of the story." John grinned.

"What about the Christmas Fair? Do you think you'll be up to playing Santa next week?"

"I wouldn't miss it for the world, Ali."

"I should be released tomorrow," Pamela said, "and John's invited me to stay and join you at the festivities, although I think I'll take a room at Dora's Inn for the rest of my time in Cobble Cove."

Alicia thought about the inn's change of ownership. "Did you know Dora is selling the inn?"

"Yes. I heard that, and I know just the person who should buy it. Your friend Gilly."

"There goes my sister again with her wild ideas." John smiled and then winced as his shoulder contracted. Alicia moved closer to him.

"Still a little pain, but I didn't want to take anything that would put me to sleep until after I saw my beautiful woman."

"Oh, go ahead and kiss already. I won't look." Pamela laughed. "And my idea is not wild at all. I think Gilly will make a wonderful innkeeper."

"Do you really think she could run the inn and work at the library?" Alicia wasn't discounting the thought.

"Why not? Those funny cousins, Edith and Rose, will still be there to help, and Gilly's boys will love it. From what you've told me, they're getting old enough to lend a hand, as well."

Alicia began to imagine it. Gilly's house was always in a bit of chaos, but her friend was a natural hostess. She made the best breakfasts and decorated with just the right touches.

"I have another idea, Alicia, and I don't think you'll find this wild at all."

"Don't tell me. You want to move to Cobble Cove and open a hospital there."

"Not a bad guess, but I don't think I'm quite the small town type, and I get woozy at the sight of blood. Actually, I was thinking about Angelina Millburn. I know she's a patient here. John filled me in about her, and I told him there's no reason we should cancel that withdrawal when there's someone who can put that money to good use."

Alicia looked at her husband. She recalled their argument about using Pamela's money to help the Millburn's afford a bone marrow transplant for their daughter.

"Ali, I know there's no way this town could raise enough money to help Angie. Pamela wants to give it as a Christmas gift to the family, and I won't stand in her way. Dad always says things happen for a reason."

Suddenly, John started to squeeze his lips together, and Alicia thought he was in pain again. "Is it your chest, John? Do you want me to get the doctor?"

"No. I'm just waiting for my kiss."

Alicia went to the bed and leaned her mouth toward him. His response showed her he was stronger than he looked.

"That's my boy." Mac was standing in the doorway; Betty behind him. "I know they don't like many visitors in here at once, but I just wanted to drop by and say hi to both my children. I also smuggled in PB& J sandwiches. I made two in case Pamela wants to try our family recipe."

He reached under his coat and revealed an aluminum-foil wrapped package. "I'm sure it'll beat the hospital food they serve you."

Alicia pulled away from John, slightly embarrassed; but Betty said, "If a man can kiss like that, he's definitely not on his death bed."

***

The story hit the papers the next day. Alicia was back in the hospital. Pamela had already been released, and John was scheduled to leave the next day. Mac and Betty were now watching the twins at their house while Kim went to school. Andy worked on the office he promised he'd have done for Alicia before the opening of the Christmas Fair.

As she sat in the chair next to John's bed, he passed her the copy of the *Cobble Cove Courier* that Andy had produced on his own. The story said Gloria was facing lifetime in prison for charges of murder, kidnapping, and attempted murder. Casey's name wasn't included, possibly because of his prominence in town, but the article mentioned that an accomplice would be tried along with her. The robbery charge wasn't listed because Gloria hadn't been the person who'd stolen the jewels from Irene's store. A smaller article at the bottom of the page caught Alicia's eye. The headline read, "Gift Shop Burglar Apprehended." It featured a shot of the man Alicia recognized as the cigarette smoker, still posed wearing his long gray coat.

"Have you read this, John?" Alicia asked pointing to the article. "That was the guy I saw outside Irene's store, near her house, and who we saw together by Cove Point. I knew there was something menacing about him. How did they figure out he was the burglar?"

"They owe all that to my ace reporter."

"Andy? What do you mean?"

"Read it and see."

Alicia glanced back at the article and recited it out loud:

While Sheriff-elect Ron Ramsay arrested the kidnappers of the McKinney twins, Detective Stephen Stryder responded to information provided by Andy Phillips and Kevin Tucker regarding the whereabouts of the jewels stolen from the Cobble Corner Gift Shop on December 4th. After verifying this information, Stryder arrested Eric Palmer, the ex-husband of Maggie Palmer, daughter of gift shop owner, Irene Mallory. Palmer, a rock musician with previous arrests for muggings in the New Paltz area, had hocked the jewels for drug money. When police entered his home with a warrant, they confiscated a stash of cocaine. Both Palmer and his wife, who may also have been involved in the heist, are being held without bail at the jail in New Paltz.

"So Maggie's ex was the one who stole the jewels," Alicia said laying down the paper.

"Yep. That's why Andy was spending time with Kevin," John explained, "who, by the way, is not involved in drugs anymore. But he still had contacts who were willing to provide some information. When Andy told him about the gift shop robbery and even showed him the earrings that he was giving Kim, Kevin began to make some discreet inquiries among some of his old "colleagues." He discovered that Eric Palmer hocked the jewels and was using the money to support his drug habit. Andy also believed Palmer planned some muggings here in Cobble Cove, which explains who followed you that night from the library and why you kept seeing him hanging around town. The hard part was that Andy wanted to be sure that Kevin would be protected from any suspicion by the police for being involved and also from the drug dealers and Eric."

"And I assume he was ignoring Kim because he was protecting her, too?"

"Exactly. I think he did an excellent job cracking both cases and writing them up for the *Courier* while I was recovering. There just might be an extra cash bonus in his Christmas stocking this year."

Alicia smiled. "I guess you're practicing for your role as Santa Claus, John."

"Indeed, and just wait until I get out of here and give you your gift, Mrs. Claus."

Epilogue

It snowed lightly the first day of the Cobble Cove Christmas Fair. The paths around Cobble Corner were sprinkled with white powder, and a few flakes drifted around the square as Alicia wheeled Carol and Johnny, dressed in holiday outfits, up to the gazebo in their double stroller. Mac and Betty walked behind her. Mac held Fido's leash attached to a jingle bell collar as the dog gently pulled him, patting some snow on and off his paws. Pamela, by Alicia's side in her faux fur coat, joined her sister-in-law in the crowd of townspeople gathered around the large evergreen.

The smell of Italian food wafted through the chilly air as the Romanos manned a long buffet table with pizza, ziti, and other dishes from their restaurant. At another table, Claire offered cakes and pies, holiday-shaped cookies, and other sweets to the town's children and all those who enjoyed the bakery's delicacies. Duncan contributed subway heroes, cheese trays, and vegetable and fruit platters from the grocery. Gary and Duncan's wife, Wendy, helped set the food out on a table behind the gazebo while Patty stood in line with Angelina, who was wrapped in a warm red coat with white cuffs and collar. The girl's eyes were large and excited as she waited for the lighting of the tree and the arrival of Santa. Her parents had received the good news just the day before, that the infection that had caused her relapse was clear allowing her to leave the hospital while a search would be started for a donor.

Although the doctors warned that it was best Angelina avoid crowds due to a high chance of reinfection, they had okayed her attending the Fair for a few hours. Patty and Gary were overwhelmed with Pamela's gift and accepted it with tears and heartfelt gratitude.

Irene's store stood open inviting evening shoppers. Irene sat out front at a table giftwrapping holiday purchases. Her grandson, Toby, was inside with his mother, Maggie, who was arranging some displays of items that had recently been restocked. When Alicia walked by, Irene called to her.

"I have something for you, Alicia. Wait here." She went inside the shop and reappeared just a few minutes later holding a small package. "Don't open it until you get home. I hope you like it."

"Thanks, Irene." She wondered what the box, wrapped in paper featuring red and white Christmas bells, contained.

As Alicia glanced around the crowd, she recognized many of the new town residents as well as her old friends. All the library people, Ed the postmaster, and Phil the mailman were gathered together in front of the Post Office with its metal Eagle that would soon flap its wings to announce the hour. Donald and Roger in their long wool coats stood next to Vera, Bonnie, Laura, and her family. Laura held a cat carrier in which Sneaky's blue eyes peeked out, observing people in feline curiosity.

Sheila was talking to Jean and Jeremy. Jeremy was assigned to help in the tree lighting. When the director heard of Alicia and John's experience and what had happened to Walter, she was upset, but glad that things had turned out for the best. She already had an application in to the Board for a new full-time custodian.

Dora, Charlie, Edith, and Rose were on the other side of the gazebo. Alicia had not yet shared Pamela's suggestion with the innkeeper, but she planned to speak to Gilly about it after Christmas.

Dr. Donna, Leslie, the school nurse, the principal, and a few teachers from the school occupied a spot by Wilma's Beauty Salon. Wilma was there with them as was the minister and Chloe Gibbons wearing a multi-colored poncho from her clothing shop.

As the time approached for the tree lighting to begin, Kim, in a long red dress and Andy in a suit, both looking a bit old-fashioned and Dickens-like, took their places by the gazebo.

Sheriff-elect Ramsay walked to the front of the crowd and announced that, before the tree was lit, there would be some caroling entertainment for the audience. Laura and Lily joined Carter, Kim, and Andy, and the quintet sang a few holiday favorites.

When their performance was over, Ramsay invited the town's children to gather by the tree. Maggie, leaving the gift shop, brought Toby up while Alicia wheeled Carol and Johnny forward. Lily took her younger brother, Henry, by the hand and joined the line.

Jeremy and Angelina who were already by Ramsay's side were handed the control that would switch on the tree lights. Both of them pressed the button that Ramsay indicated, and the tree came to life with red, white and green lights. The crowd cheered. The sound of jingle bells rang across the square as John, dressed in his Santa outfit, strolled by ho ho hoing as he passed the waiting children. Taking a seat in the chair by the gazebo, he invited each child to sit on his lap and tell him what he or she wanted for Christmas.

Alicia allowed the other kids to take turns before the twins. After the last child sat on John's lap, she pushed Johnny and Carol up to the gazebo, both squealing with joy.

Betty and Mac stood watching from the side as Fido in his jingling collar woofed at the kids, who having had their time with Santa, came to pet him. Then Laura carried up

Sneaky, looking a bit uncomfortable in a cat-sized Santa cap. After she took him out of his cat carrier, she put him on her lap for the kids to pet. Alicia didn't know how the young woman did it, but she managed to keep the cat calm as the noisy children posed for photos with the pets. Their parents snapped away with digital cameras and phones that had already recorded their offspring's time on Santa's lap.

Alicia lifted Johnny and Carol out of their stroller and handed them to their dad. John's eyes twinkled under the white cottony brows he'd glued on.

"And what do you two want for Christmas?" he asked deepening his voice into what he probably imagined St. Nick would sound like. He turned first to Carol who was giggling. Alicia had a feeling her sharp daughter saw through John's disguise. Johnny on John's other arm reached out to tug on his father's fluffy Santa beard.

"Ouch, Johnny," John said in mock discomfort.

Alicia felt a tug at her heart.

"Hey, Mrs. Claus, why don't you come up here and join us?" John patted an open spot on his lap.

Alicia wasn't sure the whole family would fit, although Carol and Johnny seemed comfortable at their father's side. She attempted to comply with John's request being careful not to get too close to his chest because, although it was padded by the stuffing in his costume, his wound wasn't totally healed.

As she slid onto John's lap, Johnny turned his attention from John's beard and took a fistful of her hair.

"Now that really hurts."

Carol giggled.

"Stay right there." Pamela approached with a camera in her hand. "I want a family shot."

The camera clicked and captured one of the happiest moments of Alicia's life.

***

As people began to leave after the tree lighting, a figure emerged from behind the gazebo. John had abandoned his post and brought the kids over to play with Fido and Sneaky after the other children had gone. Alicia jumped at the sudden movement by the tree. She turned to see Casey standing in the spotlight cast by the Christmas lights. John noticed him too, and left the twins with his father. Betty, Pamela, and Sheila were among the last remaining people present as the fair wound down.

Casey faced Alicia and John. They had not seen him since the day he turned against Gloria to save his friends. The diner had remained closed the last two weeks.

"I wanted to visit you in the hospital, John, but I didn't know if that would upset you or whether they would allow me to do that. When this is over and the authorities decide my sentence, I'm planning to leave town. It's up to the folks here what they want to do with the diner. It might make a good spot for the high school." His voice was sad, and Alicia thought she saw tears in his eyes behind his thick glasses.

"Where will you go?" John asked.

"Probably to my parents in Florida when I'm done serving my time. I'll look for some work down there. I'm sure they can use someone at a McDonald's or another fast food restaurant. I always did cook a mean burger." He grinned, but the corners of his moustache quivered.

"I made a terrible mistake falling for that woman. I never had any luck with the ladies, but she seemed to really care for me. We started out as friends, late night chats after work, that type of thing. She told me how miserable she was with Walter, that he cheated on her with young women and beat her. She showed me the black and blues under her sweater. It made me sick." He paused.

"When she outlined her plan to kidnap the twins, I told her she was crazy. I didn't want a part of that. I tried to talk her out of it. I promised her that, even though I didn't have much money, I had a little saved from the diner. We could run away and live comfortably, but she said she was afraid Walter would follow us. She insisted that she needed a lot of money for a good divorce lawyer, that she deserved to make Walter pay for her suffering all the years of their marriage. I had no idea how much money she had in mind until she asked me to leave the ransom note in the crib. I should've gone to the police then, but she persuaded me it would be simple. We'd get the money and leave town. The kids would be fine." He swallowed.

"I felt like a Judas, but I was no match for Walter. I've never been a violent man. I would've done anything for her. I wasn't thinking clearly." Another tear formed behind his glasses.

"While I was at the town hall meeting before you left for the city, I knew she was going to your house to cut your Christmas lights because she wanted to make sure things would be easier for the kidnapping. She figured you would be too busy the next day to consider replacing them. I believe she even tested your door lock in case your babysitter used it. Gloria was great at planning and organizing. That was one of the reasons I hired her as a waitress. She helped me set all the menus and specials a week in advance." He sighed.

"When she shot Pamela, she told me she only meant to scare her, but the gun went off accidentally. I was in the nursery and had my back to the door when she pulled the trigger. I didn't even know she'd brought Walter's gun along. She fed the dog marijuana in a meatball to silence him. She said it was Walter's pot and would just keep Fido calm, but now I'm pretty sure the stash was hers." His voice hitched.

"When I got home that night, I put the babies downstairs. She left that all up to me and didn't want to go near them, which now I see was a good thing. When I was alone with them, I decided to call Kim in case Pamela was alive and could be helped. I guess I should've called 911 or fire rescue that might've been quicker, but I was afraid to take that chance. I changed my voice as much as I could, and I knew your babysitter wouldn't recognize it. I never told Gloria I did that. She just figured Kim showed up at your house for some reason. A lucky break, she called it. She wasn't worried about collecting the ransom money. She said John would have it whether or not his sister was alive. She went ahead and made the rest of the ransom calls to John's cell using a voice synthesizer app. She was proud of how it made her sound like a man, but she never let me hear the recordings. She showed me a bunch of cell phones that she said were untraceable. I think she dumped them after she made each call." Casey took a breath and blew out some frosted air, but he was determined to finish his story.

"Gloria killed Walter at home and told me he'd attacked her with his gun, after finding out we were involved. She said she managed to get the gun off him and shoot him. I was in too deep at that point to argue with her about helping her move his body. I told her we should just dump it in the cove, but she said we had to mislead the police or they would catch us before we had the money and could make our getaway."

The lens of his glasses were fogging both from the cold and the tears that threatened. "I made too many mistakes. I even disguised myself as a cop to check on Pamela in the hospital. I don't know if you guys recall I dressed up as a policeman for Halloween at the diner? The nurse kicked me out, but I was relieved to bring back the news that your sister was okay. Gloria didn't care. Then I finally came to my senses when she wanted me to take you hostage, Alicia, and I understand how you must feel about the worry I caused you and your family. I'm so sorry."

Glancing at John, Alicia said, "We're sorry too, Casey."

As he walked away, a few flakes clinging to his coat, John said to Alicia, his voice cracking slightly, "Even though I can't quite forgive him yet, I'm sorry to see him go. Does that make sense?"

"Of course it does," she said. "I hope things work out for him. He's a good man who made some bad decisions."

Alicia put her arm on John's, and they walked back to the others.

***

At home, they put the twins to bed. They were tired out from their adventure with Santa. John removed his costume in the bedroom as Alicia put on her nightgown. She'd chosen the red negligee that Gilly had given her as a gift. She had a feeling John was now up to lovemaking, and even though Casey's story had saddened her, she wanted to take advantage of the pleasant night's mood they'd shared among friends.

"Hmmm," John said stripping off his stuffed pants. "Maybe I should keep this suit on and give you that Christmas gift I promised earlier. By the way, I hope you like your new office. Andy did a great job finishing it while I was laid up recovering."

"I love it, and it'll be a perfect place to write. I heard you speaking with Mary Beth this morning. I guess you gave her the good news that we have the synopsis and first three chapters of our next book ready for her review." Alicia rolled down the covers and got in bed next to him.

John grinned. "I was so relieved to get that pain-in-the-you-know-what off my back."

"Are you up to some romance tonight, John?"

He lifted an eyebrow. "I think I can manage, but first Santa wants to give you another gift."

He got up from bed wearing only the top of his Santa costume and went to the bureau. He opened the top drawer where he kept his shirts. Reaching inside, he withdrew the wrapped box from Tinker's jewelry store.

"I know it's not Christmas yet, but I think this is a fitting gift to give you now."

He brought the box to the bed and lay it within her grasp.

"I might as well also open that gift Irene gave me tonight. I've been curious about it since she handed it to me." Alicia reached next to her and took the small box she'd left there after the Fair. Placing the two boxes next to one another, she realized they were about the same size.

"Open Irene's first," John said. "I want you to save mine for last."

Alicia ripped open the red and white paper adorned with Christmas bells and found a jewelry box inside. Lifting the lid, she saw a cameo broach nestled against a white velvet lining. Looking closer, she could make out that the pin featured a mother holding two babies. "Oh, gosh, John. I don't know if Irene has replaced all of the jewelry items that were stolen yet, but this is beautiful." She handed the piece to him.

"Interesting. Those might be twins. Irene probably chose it especially for you."

"How sweet of her. I'll treasure it."

John passed her back the pin that she replaced in its box. "Now open my gift, Ali."

John's eyes were intent as he handed Alicia the box containing the locket the old New York jeweler had told them so much about. When Alicia twisted open the tiny clasps that kept the silver locket closed, she found an oval space for a photo. The other side contained an inscription. It was the famous Serenity poem:

"God, grant me the serenity to accept the things I cannot change, the courage to change the things I can, and the wisdom to know the difference."

"See," John said after she read it aloud. "I think it fits you well. It fits both of us well."

Alicia held the locket in her hands and gazed down at it. "It does, John, and the photo Pamela took of our family will be perfect for the other side."

"Keep it near your heart, Ali."

"Oh, speaking of keeping something by your heart, I also have a gift for you."

She jumped up, the lacey fabric of the opaque nightie brushing against the bed, and retrieved a small, gift-wrapped box about the length of an index card from her bedside drawer. "I thought you would need a replacement for Gilly's gift."

John laughed as he unwrapped the present to find a gold Cross pen.

"It's not initialed yet, but you can have that done if you want. Don't forget to keep it in your shirt's breast pocket. It's a lifesaver."

"That it is, and so are you." John pulled her close and kissed her. "Merry Christmas, Ali. I wanted to save one last surprise for you, but now that we're sharing our gifts early, I think I'll tell you that I've decided not to go on the interview at Columbia this week. I'm staying right here with you and the babies where I belong. I'll find a job in Cobble Cove besides the paper. Andy and Kim seem to be managing well by themselves and I can devote more time writing our mystery series. Either way, I'll be able to keep an eye on my family."

"Oh, John. That's the best present you could've given me this year."

"Well, there is something else . . .."

He opened his arms, and Alicia fell into them, a very wide smile on her face.

About Debbie De Louise

Debbie De Louise is a reference librarian at a public library on Long Island and has been involved with books and writing for over thirty years. She received the Lawrence C. Lobaugh, jr. Memorial Award in Journalism for her work as Features Editor on the Long Island University/C. W. Post student newspaper, *The Pioneer*. More recently, Debbie received the Glamour Puss Award from Hartz Corporation for an article about cat grooming that appeared on Catster.com. She has published a short mystery in the Cat Crimes Through Time Anthology and two novels, *Cloudy Rainbow* and *A Stone's Throw*. She is currently working on a psychological thriller and lives on Long Island with her husband, daughter, and two cats.

Social Media Links:

Facebook:
https://www.facebook.com/debbie.delouise.author/

Twitter: https://twitter.com/Deblibrarian @Deblibrarian

Goodreads:
https://www.goodreads.com/author/show/2750133.Debbie_De_Louise

Amazon Author Page: Author.to/DebbieDeLouise

Website/Blog/Newsletter Sign-Up:
https://debbiedelouise.com

Author's Note

In response to some comments from readers, I want to clarify that Cobble Cove, New York and Carlsville, New York are fictional towns. However, other New York and Long Island locations mentioned in my Cobble Cove mysteries are real places, although the events that occur there are, of course, fictional.

In *Between a Rock and a Hard Place*, the Park Lane Hotel is also a real location, as are all the New York City sites mentioned including the Meow Parlour cat cafe. I have tried to depict these as authentically as possible through research because I have never visited Park Lane or Meow Parlour but hope to have the pleasure to do so one day.

My lovely niece, Elizabeth Banks, who recently became a mom, received a bone marrow transplant twelve years ago when she suffered leukemia. Although the young girl, Angelina, in *Between a Rock and a Hard Place* is not based on my niece, my sister-in-law, Dawn, provided some information about her experience to include for that part of the book.

I have an author's newsletter that I email twice a month that includes updates about my books, special offers, and a monthly contest. Last spring, I sponsored a recipe contest for Mac's infamous PB&J sandwiches. Even though Mac's recipe is a secret, one of my newsletter subscribers, Sunni Hancock, submitted a recipe that won the contest. I am featuring it below as part of Sunni's prize:

Grilled Peanut Butter and Jelly Sandwich

Ingredients:

2 teaspoons butter

2 slices white bread

1 teaspoon peanut butter

2 teaspoons any flavor fruit jelly

Add all ingredients to list

Directions

1. Heat griddle or skillet to 350 degrees F (175 degrees C).
2. Spread butter on each slice of bread. Spread peanut butter on unbuttered side of one slice of bread, and jelly on the other. Place one slice, butter side down, on the griddle. Top with other slice, so that peanut butter and jelly are in the middle. Cook four minutes on each side, or until golden brown, and heated through.

If any of you would like to subscribe to my newsletter, you can sign up on my website/blog at https://debbiedelouise.com.

Thank you for your interest in the Cobble Cove books.

Acknowledgements:

Writing the acknowledgements to my books seems to get harder as I continue to publish them. There are so many people to thank from those who provided research information to those who beta read my manuscript; edited and produced the book; helped promote me on their blogs and in their stores and libraries or by way of mouth; and those who simply supported and motivated me.

As always, I need to thank my family; my husband, Anthony, and daughter, Holly, for putting up with me while I worked on this book and spent less time with them.

I also need to thank my publisher, Solstice Publishing, and their staff especially Melissa Miller, K.C. Sprayberry, and my editor, Donna Patton. I also want to extend a special thank you to my beta readers and fellow authors, Judy Ratto, Elizabeth Roderick, and Kiarra Taylor for their helpful suggestions on fine-tuning my manuscript.

There were several people who also helped with research for this book. I need to thank fellow author and mother C.K. Brooke and Pediatrician Dr. Lauren Brunn for the information they gave me about the development and habits of six-month old babies. I want to thank author, Savannah DeZarn Blevins who is also a speech pathologist and Carolyn Lee who teaches anatomy and physiology for their assistance in helping me provide accurate details on bullet-shot wounds and outcomes. I also want to thank Dr. Mitchell Kornet, DVM at Mid-Island Animal Hospital, for his input regarding the effects of marijuana on dogs. Lastly, a special thanks to my sister-in-law, Dawn Banks, for sharing her and my niece Elizabeth's experience with bone marrow transplant donor searches and procedures.

I would additionally like to thank my followers on Twitter, Facebook, and Goodreads as well as those who follow my Ruff Drafts blog and subscribe to my newsletter. I also want to thank my library and the other local libraries as well as Christin Corwin at Barnes and Noble in Carle Place, New York, for stocking my books and allowing me to talk and sign them. A special thanks to my Jenny Craig counselor, Lauren, and the other wonderful folks at the Hicksville Center who keep my bookmarks and author information on display and all others who have spread the word about *A Stone's Throw*, the first book of my Cobble Cove novels.

Last but not least, I want to thank my readers and those who review my books You have no idea how happy it makes me feel when you say you couldn't stop reading or loved the twists.

If you enjoyed this story, check out these other Solstice Publishing books by Debbie De Louise:

Project 9 Vol 2

A reality pill… Canoples Investigations returns… Are we computers? plus many other stories in this science fiction anthology from Solstice Universe.

Ten authors with eleven tales to tell: Ray Chilensky, K.C. Sprayberry, Rob McLachlan, Debbie De Louise, Jim Cronin, Rick Ellrod, Natalie Silk, Arthur Butt, E.B. Sullivan, and S@yr bring you stories to delight and entertain.

http://bookgoodies.com/a/B01M0GARAL

Realms of Fantastic Stories Vol 1

Cats await a new arrival…

A queen in hiding…

Much more than an attic…

And other fantasy tales

Debbie De Louise, Margaret Egrot, KateMarie Collins, Rick Ellrod, Rocky Rochford, Stephen St. Clair, and K.C. Sprayberry will bring enjoyment to your day with these fantastic stories.

http://bookgoodies.com/a/B01LZH7XLP

The Path To Rainbow Bridge

A familiar poem for many pet lovers describes a place called Rainbow Bridge where pets go when they pass on and where their beloved human eventually joins them. If you have ever lost a special animal companion and wondered if Rainbow Bridge actually exists and what it's like, the answer is imagined in *The Path to Rainbow Bridge*.

This story, told from the cats' point of view, takes place during preparations for an incoming resident—a woman named Kate's elderly Siamese. The cats Kate has bonded with throughout her life also reside on Rainbow Bridge and are happy to welcome the new member of their fur family. However, a big surprise awaits one of them after the new cat arrives.

http://bookgoodies.com/a/B01LX0QRY0

Deadline

When college student Susan Shaffer wakes up on the wrong side of the bed in her dorm room, strange things begin to happen. Time seems to shift and draw her into an imaginary deadline that would rival those of the stories she writes for the student paper. Unable to face horrible news that she can't remember happening, she traces the events of the last few days. Discovering the awful truth of why these hours are a blank, she must meet a deadline that is truly deadly.

http://bookgoodies.com/a/B01M0LLST9

35981205R00177

Made in the USA
Middletown, DE
21 October 2016